The Thief and the Slave

The Divalian Chronicles

Prequel

S. T. Hobbs

Table of Contents

Prologue

THE THRONE ROOM OF KING Dival was as icy as the frost clinging to the windows. The vast hall held only two people that day - King Dival, seated upon his throne, and a haggard looking man standing before him, leaning heavily up on a cane.

"You failed me, Maurus."

Maurus, leaning most of his weight onto the cane, let out a bitter bark of laughter. "I failed you? Your Majesty, your plan failed. You refused my council. You ignored the facts. It was a disaster from start to finish. The only thing I failed at was bringing..." Maurus stopped, his face contorting in anguish.

"How dare you address me in that manner. It was your incompetence that led to this defeat. You've cost me my victory. Your son, Hamo, was one of many who paid the price for that. You deserve his death." Maurus' face went white, but King Dival wasn't finished. "Anyway, he's not even de..."

"Enough. Don't speak to me of my son," Maurus choked the words out through clenched teeth. "You took him from me. He died for your pride, your idiocy. And you will pay for his death."

King Dival was too stunned to speak at first. His face turned red with rage.

"Get out. Get out of my sight, Maurus. And if you utter such words again, they will be your last."

As the shutting doors echoed through the great emptiness of the throne room, King Dival held the piece of paper that had been crumpled in his hand up. The seal of Dorsten was just visible behind his hand. Staring at the words, his face turning red once more, he tore it into pieces and scattered them on the floor.

"You've made a mistake, Maurus," King Darien whispered into the emptiness. "A grave mistake. Your son is lost forever because of it."

Chapter 1

THE BITTER WINTER WIND BLEW wisps of loose snow across the ground, piling it in drifts against any obstruction in its path. The wind had a bite to it, and the small group of men that were making their way through it kept their heads down and their cloaks pulled tightly to their bodies. A single man rode behind them on a shaggy, brown horse.

"Glad we had those northerners doing most of the fighting this time around," one man spoke to no one in particular. Those near him did not even bother to look up - they stayed warmer if they did not.

"You shouldn't be too glad, Terrin, those men are the reason you're out here now," the rider called out. "If they'd have listened to one word Lord Bayner told them we wouldn't have to be here, fixing their mistakes."

"I don't see why Lord Bayner is so keen on making sure we take some of them alive. What's the use, Norman?"

"Money. He wants money."

"And how are a handful of survivors going to provide us with money?"

"He's hoping we'll pick up a few important ones, noblemen maybe, or a commander or two, someone their king would be willing to pay to have them back."

"Waste of time," Terrin muttered under his breath. They had been doing this for days, and he was tired of it.

"Waste of your breath if you keep complaining about it," Norman retorted, although his voice was lost beneath the thick scarf he had wrapped around his neck and over his chin.

A mighty gust of wind put an end to further conversation. The snow began falling from the sky again, reducing their visibility to only a few yards in front of them. Without realizing it, the group stumbled upon the latest sight of the northerners merciless attack. Bodies lay strewn about, some already half covered by the snow.

"Alright, spread out and look for survivors. We'll head back to camp after this, before this turns into a blizzard." Norman gave his orders without making any move to get down and join his men in the search.

The small group fanned out to cover the area. Some of the bodies they could tell at a glance were beyond any human help. Others they turned over, prodding and searching for signs of life. Twice they were rewarded. Norman, his face muffled against the cold and almost invisible, frowned. Two survivors were not worth the trouble they were going through.

"We're done. Bring them along and let's get out of here." He jerked sharply on the left rein of his horse, causing it to stumble over two bodies next to him as he made the turn. The sergeant would have thought nothing of this - his horse had trampled its fair share of the fallen in the past few weeks - had it not been for a low moan that came from one of the bodies.

"You," he pointed to Terrin who had avoided the burden of carrying one of the litters, "come check these out. You missed them earlier."

The man, grumbling, came and knelt beside the bodies. One lay mostly on top of the other. It was riddled with arrows and bore at least a dozen sword wounds. Not a chance of that one being alive, the man thought. Shoving the corpse aside, he examined the one underneath.

4

"This one's alive, barely. He won't make it back to camp," Terrin said, as he looked up and shook his head.

"Pick him up anyway. If he dies along the way, we can dump him then."

"Yes, sir."

Norman, satisfied that he had made sure none of his men were slacking, led the little band off toward their base camp.

The camp was not so far away, and it did not take long for the patrol to reach the roaring fires and dug in tents that made up their base. That was another benefit of hiring the northern mercenaries. They knew not only how to fight in this wretched weather but also how to survive in it, reasonably comfortable at that. They had taught the Dorstenian army how to use the snow to their advantage, insulating their tents by half burying them into the snowbanks.

A large tent in the middle of the encampment had been set up as an infirmary and this was where the patrol headed to deposit the survivors. Norman handed his mount off to a soldier and accompanied his litter bearers into the tent to finish his task. Lord Bayner wanted men of worth, men whose importance to Dival would make them likely candidates for a ransom. Sergeant Norman Turston was beginning to doubt that they would find any that fit.

The lanterns hung at short intervals from the wooden frame that held the canvas in place cast a flickering, uncertain light about the entire interior. Norman waited until his eyes adjusted to the lighting before he walked over to the first stretcher his men laid down. Already, the doctor was kneeling beside it, examining the man's wounds. Norman frowned as he took in the sight of the man's worn clothing. If he was someone important, he certainly did not look the part. He was not wearing the colors of a nobleman and bore no insignia that marked him as a commander.

"Not what we're after," he muttered to himself. He was surprised when the doctor answered him.

"It's a good thing, because he won't last the night."

Norman shrugged and moved on to the next. He had been in many battles, and the thought of another enemy soldier dying did not bother him at all.

The next man was no different. Shabbily clad in his uniform, with no officers' insignia. The sergeant shook his head and moved on. Lord Bayner would be disappointed once again.

He came over to the third and let out a low whistle between his teeth. This one was young, very young. Crouching down in the empty space between the litters, he put his hand on the boy's neck, feeling for a pulse, and was strangely relieved to find one. It was faint but there. The doctor joined him at that moment, his practiced eyes searching him for wounds. The most obvious were two arrows whose shafts still protruded from their entry points, one in his shoulder, another in his side just beneath his ribs.

"Have to get those out," the doctor said.

Norman nodded and rose to his feet, making room for the doctor to work. He watched as the man reached under the still body, checking to see if the arrows had gone clean through. The doctor shook his head as his hands felt nothing.

"Going to have to pull them straight out, too."

"That'll hurt." Norman winced at the thought of it. He'd suffered his fair share of wounds in his career in the army and knew the pain and damage caused by pulling an arrow straight out. He started to move away. It was not his job to take care of the wounded, his job was done. A wrenching scream brought him back again.

"Give me a hand holding him, would you, sergeant?" The doctor was working on pulling the first arrow out and the pain had awakened his patient.

6

"Calm down, now. We're trying to save your life," Norman said, his voice gruff but not without sympathy as he pinned the struggling body to the ground, allowing the doctor to finish. At the sound of his voice the boy's eyes opened. They were dark and wild with fear and pain.

"Where...am...," he was gasping in pain and unable to go on, but Norman guessed his question.

"You're safe."

"Home?" His face clouded with confusion.

"No," Norman smiled sadly. "No, you're a long way from home, son."

He watched as the confusion in the boy's face gave way to a twisted grimace as the doctor pulled the second arrow free. He did not scream this time, but let out a small, stifled cry.

"I think that'll do, sergeant. Thank you." The doctor was setting about washing and dressing the soldier's wounds.

The sergeant started to get up, but hesitated, watching the young man's face. He was looking about, his eyes frantic and lost, trying to piece together what had happened and where he was.

"Calm down. You're safe now," Norman repeated. "What's your name, son?"

"Hamo. It's Hamo," he answered, each word catching like a sob in his throat.

"Well, Hamo, the doctor is going to take care of you, and you're going to be fine." He met the boy's eyes and saw some of the fear recede.

Stepping out of the tent a moment later, Norman paused. War was an ugly thing, he thought.

Chapter 2

HAMO'S FACE TWISTED INVOLUNTARILY as a jolt from the wagon beneath him set off another wave of pain. He kept his eyes shut, trying to focus on not crying out with every motion, trying to push the pain away. It was a never-ending battle as needles of agony drove into his shoulder and head at every bump.

With each turn of the wagon wheel, Hamo's apprehension grew. Dorsten was drawing nearer by the hour, and it was the last place in the world he had ever expected to be. Lying in the hospital tent for those few days hadn't been so bad. In fact, the doctor treated him exactly the same as he treated his own men, alleviating the churning terror that came from falling into the hands of his enemies. While he was there, Hamo could almost forget that he was a prisoner, at the mercy of his foes.

Not anymore.

The wagon had been traveling steadily toward Dorsten for days now, stopping only for a few hours every night. Those hours were almost worse than the ones spent in jarring motion. Though everything possible was done to ensure the wounded's comfort, there was simply no escape from the bone chilling cold. What was meant to be restful turned out to be quite the opposite.

This morning the sky was free of its usual heavy blanket of gray clouds and the sun was shining, brightly reflected off the white of the snow. In the cold air, the glow of the sun felt almost warm. Hamo, his eyes still shut against the pain and the blinding glare of the sun against the snow, heard a shout from one of the drivers.

"There it is."

Twisting around in his seat, Hamo tried to turn in his seat to see what it was the man was pointing at. The movement caused fresh waves of pain to wash over him, and he gave it up, contenting himself with what other people saw and said.

Now that he was looking about, he noticed the man riding on horseback next to his wagon. With a start, Hamo recognized him as the same sergeant who had helped the doctor the day he was rescued, if that's what you could call being captured by your enemy. He had not seen him since that day. Without realizing it, Hamo stared at the man. It was something to distract him. And there was something familiar about the man, some similarity to someone Hamo knew.

"Need something?" The man noticed him staring and was looking at him now.

Hamo shook his head, and instantly regretted it as a throbbing sensation exploded inside it and black dots threatened to cover his eyes. His right hand went to his head as a soft moan escaped him.

"I just wanted to know what they saw," he finally managed to get out.

"Oh, that. We're at the border forest, that's all. A few more hours and we'll have reached the castle."

"Thank you." Hamo shut his eyes again.

Lost in his own thoughts, he missed the quick look of sympathy on the sergeant's face as the man watched him.

When the blue sky above his head was suddenly blotted out by a canopy of bare, dark branches mixed with a few evergreen boughs, Hamo opened his eyes again. This woods, he knew, was the border of Dorsten. He was officially in the land of his enemies, and so completely helpless that a slight tremor of fear ran through him.

"You're not going to be hurt, you know. We're not monsters over here." It was the sergeant again. Hamo met his reassuring smile hesitantly.

By nightfall, the deepening darkness and his own overwrought mind lulled Hamo into a troubled sleep and he was oblivious to the town taking shape in the near distance.

When he awoke, the first sensation to reach Hamo was warmth. He had not been warm since he'd started out with the army weeks ago. For several minutes, he lay still, savoring the comfortable heat without wondering where it came from.

Finally, his mind refused to ignore his surroundings anymore and Hamo opened his eyes and looked about him. Shifting to get his elbow beneath himself, he tried to sit up. Falling back on his bed with a moan, he gave it up.

He was in a room, not a tent, and that was different. The room had an earthy smell to it, mixed with the scent of pine wood smoke, and the ever-present odor of blood. As he lay there, looking about him, memory came flooding back. They were in the castle infirmary. They arrived late the night before, and he was only half awake when he had been pulled off the wagon and half carried, half dragged into this room. He had been given something warm and bitter tasting to drink and then he couldn't remember anymore.

Hamo wondered how long he had been asleep. It must have been a long time because the sun was well up in the sky, its light pouring through a window and forming a golden rectangle of light across the floor of the infirmary. Before he had a chance to puzzle over his fate now that he was in Dorsten, a commotion started just outside the door. Voices, indistinct but angry sounding, came from the other side of the thick wood. A moment later the door burst open, and three men came into the room.

"My lord, I must insist you wait," one of the men was addressing a young, well-dressed man in the group. "No one in here is ready to be moved. If you would just give it a few days..."

"Nonsense, doctor. They've been moved all the way to here, haven't they? Sergeant, show me what you've got."

With a start, Hamo recognized the sergeant. Following the movements of the three men with curious eyes as they moved around the room, stopping at a handful of beds to speak in low voices to their occupants, he had time to wonder what they were doing.

They were in conversation with one man for so long that Hamo started to doze off again. Sometimes it felt like all he did now was sleep, as if his body was trying to make up all the lost hours of the winter campaign.

A stinging slap on his face brought him back with a cry of surprise. He looked up to find the lord standing over him, pulling his hand away. He was saying something, but the slap set the black dots to swimming over Hamo's eyes again, and his ears were filled with a pulsing, ringing sound that blotted everything else out. The lord was raising his hand again, but to Hamo's relief, the doctor intervened. At last, Hamo could make out the words they were saying, although they were no longer talking to him.

"How are you so sure?"

"I asked some of the others. They all told me the same thing," the sergeant answered.

"Very well. Take him with the others," this the lord addressed to the doctor. He turned to go and caught Hamo's eye, realizing that he was aware again. "Well, well. I suppose you can talk now?"

"Yes," Hamo said cautiously.

"Good. Then perhaps you would be so kind as to reassure me that my sergeant has the right information about you," the lord spoke sharply, glancing back at the sergeant as he did so.

"I don't understand."

"Are you really the son of the King Dival's Captain?"

Hamo floundered, unsure. It could make trouble for him whichever way and he glanced at the sergeant standing just behind the very unpleasant lord. The man gave him an almost imperceptible nod.

"I am."

"I hope, for your sake, that your King really likes his Captain." The lord smiled but it was a thin, cold smile that did not reach his eyes. "Take him with the others, doctor.

Chapter 3

HAMO SAT, SHIVERING AND BORED, against the stone wall. With nothing else to occupy his time with, his thoughts strayed again and again in the one direction he wished they wouldn't - home, and how far away that was. The small shaft of pale yellow light that came in through the barred window high above his head did little to warm the damp cell. The spring weather that was turning the rest of the world green and warm and fresh, could not penetrate the thick stone walls of the castle tower.

Until recently, he had shared this room with three others, all minor noblemen from various regions of Dival who had taken part in the winter campaign and been captured like him. Yesterday, the last of them had been released in return for a ransom.

Hamo knew that they were hoping to ransom him as well. Lord Bayner, he had learned, was looking for any way he could to make up the money he owed the mercenaries responsible for Dival's winter defeat. The lord was hoping that King Dival would honor such a ransom in order to keep his Captain happy. Hamo doubted it. He had grown up under King Dival. King Dival was not only completely disinterested in keeping anyone under him happy, he was also incredibly tight fisted when it came to financial matters. Hamo did not know for certain, but he could imagine that the money that had come for the noblemen had been scraped together by their own families and estates.

Although there was nothing he could do about any of it, Hamo dreaded the moment when Lord Bayner found out the King's indifference. He was not sure what they would do with him after that, or what they had done with all the other prisoners that had been taken. Aside from the fact that he was sitting alone in a very cold, damp cell he had not been treated horribly. That would change the second he ceased to be valuable to them.

There was one good thing, Hamo thought, that would come out of all this. Even if the King refused to pay the ransom, he would have to tell Maurus that his son was still alive. Father and Mother would know that he had not died. The thought of Mother waiting at home for him was too much. His vision blurred and a single tear slid down his face. Fear and homesickness washed over him. The more he thought about it, the more frightened of it all he became. He remembered telling Father once that he was only scared of dying alone.

How wrong he was.

It was worse, far worse, to live alone, separated forever from those he loved. It was the one fate he had never imagined, never thought possible.

He could not have picked a worse moment. As he heard the key turning in the lock outside, Hamo hurried to brush away the lone tear, and to blink away the others that were forming. When the jailer entered, Hamo kept his face down, turned away so that the man could not see him. He had already been the brunt of a good many jokes because he was so young and small and, thanks to his wounds, weak. If the man saw that he was crying Hamo had no doubt that his life would be made even more miserable.

"Up," the jailer ordered gruffly.

Hamo started to his feet slowly. His head still filled with a nauseating pain every time he moved quickly, the result of an injury to the back of it, and he did everything he could to avoid that debilitating throbbing. The jailer was impatient, however. It seemed to Hamo that the man was always impatient when he came to fetch him.

Hamo, still keeping his face down, gritted his teeth as he felt the man's big hand clamp over his right arm and haul him to his feet, setting off a wave of pain through his shoulder. He was sure the man did it on purpose. He only ever grabbed him by the arm that had an arrow through it. The injury, like most of his others, had been mostly healed before he had been brought to this cell. Mostly. The jailer seemed determined to keep it fresh and painful.

"Let's go."

The jailer was not one to waste words, or time. Without relaxing his grip on Hamo's arm, he moved out of the cell and toward the stone staircase. Hamo, stumbling and gasping, his head swimming, did not have any choice but to try to keep up. He knew from painful experience that if he lost his footing, the man would simply keep dragging him.

Down, down, down they went. Hamo thought the staircase would never end. It wasn't until the jailer had deposited him unceremoniously on the floor of a room at the bottom of the tower that Hamo realized how hard he was biting down on the inside of his cheek, trying to keep from crying out. Beneath him, the floor seemed to have come to life, rocking and pitching.

"Here he is."

Hamo heard the jailer's voice as if it were coming from far away, and knew he was close to passing out. That was the last thing he needed. Hamo hated how weak he was. Hated how, even now, he could not stand fully on his own. Hated that these men could do whatever they liked with him, and he simply did not have the strength to fight it. Gripping the wall behind him, he managed to get to his feet.

"You know, Captain's son, I'm rather disappointed in your king's generosity, or should I say, lack thereof," Lord Bayner's voice carried across the room to him. The lord was sitting at a desk and was not even bothering to look at his young prisoner. "What sort of king refuses to ransom the son of his Captain - the man responsible for leading his army into war?"

He finally lifted his eyes and leaned back in his chair, arms crossed, studying Hamo's reaction. Hamo wasn't quick enough to hide the extent of his disappointment. Although the news was not unexpected, Hamo had hoped, with a wild, irrational hope, that Father could convince King Dival to act on his behalf. With that hope slipping away, home grew an insurmountable distance away.

"Of course, I'm sure your father could have put more pressure on him to pay for you. Perhaps he simply wasn't as interested in getting you back as I would have thought he'd be," Lord Bayner said, shrugging. A small, malicious smile graced his features as he watched the boy's body stiffen at the insult and his head snapped up to meet the lord's eyes.

"My Father would do everything he could to get me back," Hamo replied through gritted teeth.

"Of course, if you say so, I'm sure he did all he could to save you. There's no need for you to be angry with me. After all, I've done my part. I've been quite generous, I think, in even offering you for ransom." Lord Bayner leaned forward, folding his arms across his desk, and pursing his lips. "Still, it's a pity. For your sake, I mean. I really did not want to do this to you, but your father and king have left me with no choice." Lord Bayner studied his young prisoner with an indifferent eye. "You really haven't recovered very well, have you?"

"I'm fine." Hamo's anger was up, and he was not going to be patronized by this man. He did wonder what Lord Bayner did not want to do with him. He was sure it was nothing good. The man could not possibly be capable of anything good.

"You're not. But I don't care. Like I said, I've been generous, quite generous. I hope you'll forgive

16

me if I must now find something else to do with you. I didn't really want to do this to you." Lord Bayner turned to a man standing at the doorway. "He can go along with the rest of them."

Startled, Hamo stumbled as the guard took him by the arm. So, this was it, he thought as he allowed himself to be led outside. He would know now what they planned to do with him.

An hour later, Hamo found himself mounted on a horse without any idea of where he was going. A blindfold prevented him from taking any guesses and a length of rope securing his hands to the pommel of the saddle prevented any attempts at escaping. There were others in the group, other prisoners who had recovered from their injuries and were now fit to travel.

There was a tiny part of Hamo that was amused by the precautions the guards were taking to ensure no one escaped from the column. He himself could barely walk ten steps without falling over, and no one else in the group looked to be in much better shape. Still, they were thorough about it.

As the hours slid past, the full force of his disappointment and hopelessness settled over him. He wasn't going home. Not now, maybe never. He was a prisoner in a war that had not ended in years. The words of Lord Bayner rankled inside him, turning all his thoughts sour. If the day ever came for him to repay Lord Bayner's malice, Hamo knew he would gladly do it.

The horse beneath him had been steadily climbing for some time when it suddenly shifted and started to descend. This had happened several times in the last several hours and Hamo assumed they were riding through the mountains. He had seen the unmoving, silent masses that rose beyond the castle of Dorsten. They were bigger than anything he'd ever imagined.

At long last, bone weary and aching all over, the horses were stopped, and rough hands pulled him to the ground. Hamo let his legs fold underneath him, not even trying to stand. His head was spinning again, and he could feel another vice-like headache forming, blocking out everything going on around him. For the moment, he was glad that there was a cloth over his eyes. Darkness did not hurt as much as light. His gratitude was short-lived. Before he was ready to face the light the cloth was yanked off and he was left blinking and wincing in the bright sunlight. Hamo shut his eyes until the lightheadedness passed.

"They're all yours, Forbes," the leader of the column addressed a tall, lanky man who was standing nearby, before turning the horses around and heading back toward the mountain trail they had come down.

They were deep in the mountains. Hamo had never seen mountains before, and despite his circumstances, they were breathtaking in their enormity. As far as the eye could see around them, peak after peak rose up into the pale blue of the winter sky. The sight sent a sinking feeling of despair through him. They were so far from home. And why they were here, he could not even begin to imagine.

In the small valley they were in now, there were several crudely built wooden buildings. From one, thick billows of smoke rose from a stone chimney. Beyond the buildings a narrow, steep footpath ran up the side of the mountain to a point about halfway up. Here, a black, yawning hole opened into the very side of the mountain. Even from where he was sitting on the ground, Hamo could hear the racket and clatter of tools striking rock coming from the mouth in the mountain.

The man named Forbes stepped closer and Hamo got his first real look at the man. The only thing that was remarkable about him were his eyes. They were soulless. A chill went down Hamo's spine as Forbes' eyes rested briefly on him. Whoever this man was, and whatever his purpose was, Hamo wanted to be as far away from him as possible.

"Get up," Forbes addressed Hamo directly before turning to the entire group. "In case any of you were wondering, you're working for Lord Bayner now."

Hamo struggled to his feet, wobbling unsteadily for a few seconds. While Forbes continued to speak, he heard none of it. All he could think about was Forbes' first statement. He was working for Lord Bayner. Confused, Hamo turned the words over in his mind until at last, with a horrible clarity, he realized just what the man was saying.

They were slaves.

He was a slave.

Hamo's stomach turned at the thought as blood drained from his face. A sidelong glance at the other men in line showed a similar realization and reaction.

Forbes was making his way down the line, his face drawn up in disgust. When Lord Bayner offered him the task of overseeing his mining project in exchange for a commuted sentence, he'd jumped at the chance. Lord Bayner had promised to provide him with laborers, but the slaves the lord was providing him with were hardly up to the task. Mining iron ore out of the mountains was strenuous work. Most of this group looked on the verge of collapse, and the one at the end was too small to be of any use inside the mountain. His eyes continued to scan the group, until he came to a decision.

He pointed to a guard standing nearby. "Take these men up into the mine and turn them over to Bertram. All except that one," he indicated Hamo at the end of the line. "You come with me."

Hamo looked anxiously around at his fellow slaves, but no one seemed to take any notice of him. They were too caught up in their own misery to care about why he had been singled out. He was afraid to go with the man, afraid to leave the safety of the group.

"You, let's go. I haven't got all day."

Hamo was galvanized into movement by the stinging strike across his face. He saw, too late, that Forbes held a short leather whip in his hand. With one hand covering the stinging welt now on his face, he stumbled after the man toward the building with the stone chimney. When they reached the opening, Forbes grabbed his arm, his injured arm unfortunately, and shoved him through first. It was so unexpected that Hamo was unable to stifle the involuntary cry that came with the shooting pain. He found himself standing, swaying once more as the world spun around him, in a hot, smoky, and rather dark room.

"Drogo!" Forbes called out.

Out from behind a roaring furnace stepped the biggest man Hamo had ever seen, not that he could see him very well at the moment. The room was dark aside from the enormous fire in the center that cast uncertain shadows about the room. Hamo lowered his face, staring at the ground again, not wanting to be seen by this man. He was owned by these people, by Lord Bayner. Humiliated and frightened, he couldn't work up the nerve to meet this new man's eyes.

"What is it, Forbes?" the man said, his voice surprisingly soft and slow.

"This one's for you." The sergeant pushed Hamo towards the giant of a man.

"I cannot use that."

Hamo did not need to see the man's face to know how he felt about him as a slave. I'm not even a person to them, Hamo could not help but think as he shifted from one foot to the other.

"I really don't care. You said you needed help and he'll be worthless in the mines."

"That's not help," the disgust in Drogo's voice was clear. He stepped closer to Hamo, and Hamo leaned away as he ran a massive appraising hand over

Hamo's arm. "What do you expect me to do with him?"

"Feed him to your fire, then we won't have to waste any food on him." Forbes' laughter was as soulless as his eyes. Hamo's heart skipped a beat as he wondered if Forbes meant what he said or if it was merely a sick joke at his expense. A surreptitious glance in Drogo's direction showed him that the man did not appear to share the humor of Forbes words. "Honestly, I could care less what use you find for him. Just take him. I'll bring the others when they are done working."

"Alright," Drogo nodded slowly, as though it took him a minute to process what Forbes was saying.

"You," Forbes turned to Hamo now, "do as he tells you. Maybe you'll listen to him a little better than you did me."

Then he was gone, leaving Hamo to his new master who was still silently appraising him.

As the silence grew long and awkward, Hamo was unsure if he was supposed to be doing something. He knew, without looking up, that Drogo was still standing several feet in front of him. A heavy sigh from the man signaled the end to the silence.

"Fought in the war?" Drogo asked.

"Yes," Hamo's answer was barely a whisper.

"Eh? What was that, boy?" Drogo stepped closer to him, leaning one ear toward him.

"Yes, I did," he managed a little louder.

Drogo came closer still, grabbing his chin with a calloused thumb and forefinger and forcing Hamo to look up at him while placing his other hand firmly on Hamo's shoulder preventing him from retreating.

"Run into trouble with one of the masters?" he asked as he took in the welt already showing across Hamo's face. "Not off to a great start, then. Forbes doesn't forget things."

"Yes," his voice wobbled threateningly and Hamo tried to pull away from the man's hand. The last thing he wanted was to come apart in front of his new master who already thought so little of him.

Drogo maintained his grip a moment longer, studying the boy's face, then he took his hands away and stepped back, nodding to himself.

"Stay clear of Forbes. He's fond of the whip. So's Bertram. Though you won't see him. Not as long as you're in here," Drogo spoke in low, clipped sentences. "Come with me. I have to find a job you can do."

There were only two or three hours left of the working day by the time Hamo was turned over to Drogo, but for those hours he was kept busy.

"Furnace has to be kept going. That's what you'll do. There's wood there," Drogo pointed to a stack of neatly cut pine wood. "That'll run out. Tell me when it gets close. The bellows are there. You'll need to use them to keep the fire hot enough."

Hamo nodded his understanding. He did not trust himself to speak at the moment. As much as he hated to admit it, being thrown straight into work was probably the best thing Drogo could have done for him. It prevented him from languishing over his fate.

The task of feeding the fire sounded uncomplicated and easy but turned out to be quite daunting. It not only had to be kept going, but it also had to be kept at a stable temperature. There was a chute that fed the fire, but even putting wood into that brought him unbearably close to the heat of the flames. And the bellows were difficult to work. They had been made for someone taller and bigger than he was, most likely for Drogo himself. And his shoulder was hardly up to the task of working them.

After only a few minutes, Hamo sank down with his back to the cool exterior wall, letting his eyes close briefly. Just for a minute, he told himself, he just needed to rest for a minute and then he would get back up.

"It is not break time," Drogo's voice came from directly in front of him. "Fire is getting too cold."

Hamo noticed with worry that Drogo carried the same short whip tucked into his belt as Forbes. With a mumbled apology, he stood and went back to his task. The fire this time felt even hotter than before and was making it hard for him to think. Sweat poured freely down his face, stinging the newly opened cut. When he tried to wipe it away, he realized that his sleeve was just as soaked.

The next hour and half passed in a blur. Hamo grew clumsier with fatigue and heat by the minute. The heat, like the cold of the previous winter, was all-consuming. He couldn't get away from it, or its effects. His skin was on fire, and his stomach was nauseated by it, and his lungs were burning from the acid smell of smoke. And his head! His head was throbbing, squeezed by an invisible vice. It made all his movements sluggish, and more than once Drogo chastised him for working too slowly. It was only a matter of time before he collapsed.

When it did happen, Hamo was not expecting it. He was nearing the end of the pile of wood. He knew Drogo had told him to do something when that happened, but he could not think of what it was. The truth was he could not think at all, not with the nausea and the headache. Grabbing anything he could cling to, he made his way around to the front of the furnace to find Drogo. He opened his mouth to speak, but instead found himself doubled over heaving and retching. It had been many hours since he had last eaten anything so there was nothing in his stomach but bitter tasting acid. His knees buckled, but before he hit the ground, he felt hands on his shoulders lifting him up and moving him.

"Get out," Drogo's voice cut through Hamo's misery.

"No. I'm fine, please," he managed to gasp. He couldn't fail, not on his first day, not when Forbes' words were still ringing in his ears. What if it wasn't a joke? What if they could just decide he was useless and kill him?

Drogo ignored him, pulling him to the door and out into the fresh air beyond. Drogo's hands let go as soon as they were clear of the smelter, and Hamo found himself lying on the coolest, most pleasant grass he had ever felt in his life. Hot and sticky with perspiration, he wanted nothing more than to just lie there forever, unmoving. Hamo was not entirely sure how long he lay there, soaking up the cool, moist feeling of the grass. He sensed Drogo standing behind him.

He must think I'm a pathetic excuse for a slave, Hamo thought wearily, then realized he really did not care what this man thought of him. When the thought of moving stopped making him feel physically ill, he rolled over and managed to sit up. He was right, Drogo was standing directly behind him.

"It's the heat. You get used to it after a while," the big man spoke softly.

Hamo nodded, not sure what to say.

"Drink." Drogo thrust a cup into his hands.

The relief of the cool grass paled in comparison to what the water did for him. He drank it in gulps, realizing just how parched he had been. He had not drunk anything since very early that morning. The water was refreshing, reviving, and he was disappointed when he drained the last drop from the cup. Drogo must have noticed, and now he jerked his head toward a barrel that stood near the entrance of the smelter.

"Get more."

Then he reached down and grabbed Hamo's arm to pull him up. Hamo winced, as he always did, when someone chose that arm to manhandle him by. Drogo moved and spoke in an unhurried manner, but his eyes were quick, and he saw the momentary grimace. He raised his eyebrows but said nothing as

Hamo staggered to the water barrel and refilled his cup.

"We're done for today. Start bringing in wood for tomorrow. Then I will show you where you stay."

Hamo walked to the enormous woodpile outside the smelter. Glancing at the black hole in the side of the mountain that his fellow captives had disappeared inside of a few hours earlier, he saw a line of men making their way down the little footpath. Gathering up an armload of wood, he made the first of many trips back inside. It was going to take him a while.

Several trips later, Hamo despaired of ever finishing. A yell coming from inside the smelter startled him and he almost lost his hold on another load of wood. Walking around the side, he saw a cluster of men, the men he'd been brought here with, gathered under guard. Lowering his head, he hurried toward the door, aware of a smell that hadn't been there before. Something was being burnt. Something other than pine wood and metal.

Hamo was almost knocked back by two men, a guard and a slave, coming out of the door. He stumbled out of the way, losing several pieces of firewood. The same guard followed him in with another man in tow. Hamo moved out of their way and deposited his load before another shout tore through the air.

He hesitated in the shadows, watching as that man was led out and yet another brought in. Forbes was standing close to Drogo, his back to Hamo, almost blocking Hamo's view of the proceedings. Almost, but not quite. Hamo saw the next captive brought over to the bench, his right arm laid across it and his sleeve pushed back. He saw the tool in Drogo's hand, red hot at its tip. His mind didn't register what it was until Drogo had pressed it to the inside of the man's forearm.

A branding iron.

Hamo gasped and swallowed hard.

One after another, the men were brought in and branded. Hamo kept working, kept his head down, and tried to ignore the various sounds of pain emitted by his fellow slaves. Perhaps it was only for the ones sent into the mines. Perhaps, since he was the only slave working in the smelter with Drogo, he would be spared that final, painful indignity.

"That's the last of them," Hamo heard Forbes say and breathed a sigh of relief.

"No, it's not," Drogo's voice cut his relief short. "There's him still."

Hamo froze as both men turned to look at him.

"Right. I forgot about him. Come." Forbes motioned him forward, toward the bench.

Remembering the result of his hesitation before, Hamo obeyed. He watched Drogo place the iron back in the fire. A pair of hands reached around from behind him and forced his right arm onto the top of the workbench and rolled his sleeve up.

Hamo gulped, his eyes following Drogo's measured movements. He tested the guard's grip on his arm and found it more than he could fight against. It tightened even as he tried to pull away from it.

Drogo pulled the branding iron out of the fire and came closer. Hamo turned his head away slightly but couldn't force himself to tear his eyes off of the glowing red circle that came closer and closer to his arm. The heat of it touched his skin before the actual metal did.

He flinched.

As the iron pressed into his arm, Hamo suppressed a scream. Tears stung his eyes. His arm spasmed in the grasp of the guard. Every second it burned deeper, but still Drogo did not pull it away. Even when the iron was gone, the burning didn't stop. The man released his hold on Hamo's arm and Hamo brought it up close to his body, nursing the pain in it and trying in vain to stay quiet.

"Go. Finish your work," Drogo's voice broke through the cloud of pain.

Hamo obeyed.

It took even longer than before to complete his task as Hamo tried to cater to his burnt arm. Drogo eventually came out and helped him finish as the sun was going down. When it was done, Drogo motioned for Hamo to follow him down toward the slave quarters.

"You're in there." Drogo pointed to one of the wooden huts.

Hamo started to move toward the building when he felt Drogo's heavy hand clapped on his shoulder. He was conscious of the fact that it was not his wounded shoulder, and that was a relief. He turned, looking up at the big man with a question in his dark eyes.

"Don't run. And remember," the words were spoken so quietly that Hamo strained to catch them, "stay away from Forbes."

Chapter 4

WITHIN A WEEK, HAMO COULD imagine he'd spent his entire life in this valley. The routine was unrelenting. Up when the sun's first rays curled over the jagged eastern horizon. Joining the line of other slaves to get the small portion of food that was given them each morning.

From that point, his day diverged from every other slave's. While the others made their way into the mountain to mine out the iron ore lodged with the heart of the rock, he walked up the gentle slope that led to the iron smelter. Each morning, the smelter belched out its thick, odious smoke, promising a suffocating heat on the inside.

The long hours of each day stretched out before Hamo, lengthened by the heat and the inevitable ache that accompanied his tasks. His arm and shoulder throbbed with each pump of the bellows. His head pounded with the heat and smoke and stuffiness.

To Hamo's relief, though, Drogo's prediction proved correct by the end of the first week. As miserable as the heat was, his body slowly adjusted to it. It wasn't enough to keep him from dreading the start of every day, but it was an improvement. As his entire life shrunk into this valley and the eternal cycle of work, any improvement was welcome.

When evening came, he shuffled back toward the slave huts, joining the line of slaves waiting for their supper. The portions were meager, the flavor bland and yet his mouth watered for it. The constant gnawing pangs of hunger craved even the most distasteful sustenance and he wasted no time in devouring it. The men around him did likewise, and for the first few minutes of their time in the long, low hut the only sound that could be heard was that of everyone eating.

Tonight was no different. Hamo took his food in the farthest corner of the hut, the spot that had fallen to him on the very first night. Most of the time, his fellow slaves ignored him. The fact that he'd been singled out and separated from them in work made him an outsider to their shared misery. When Hamo saw the condition they returned in every evening, he couldn't complain.

So far, although Drogo carried a whip, he hadn't used it. The same could not be said for the unfortunate men working the mines. The difference created a rift that Hamo was both too shy and too weary to attempt crossing.

The scuffing sound of footsteps coming nearer made Hamo look up. He watched as three of the other men approached his spot and sat down, too close for comfort. The man sitting just opposite him reached his hand out and snatched the half-eaten bowl out of Hamo's hands.

"That's mine!" Hamo cried out.

"I want it," the man shrugged and took a bite. "You don't need it, anyway, seeing as you don't have to work like the rest of us."

"I still have to work," Hamo muttered under his breath.

"'Course, they wouldn't put you with the rest of us, would they?"

"I don't understand what you're talking about."

"Don't you? You're the Captain's boy, aren't you? Kept nice and safe while the rest of us did all the fighting and dying. Bet you miss having him around to protect you all the time."

"Shut up." Hamo turned away from the man. There was nothing he could say in argument. The man was right. Father made sure Hamo's unit was never the one left behind to be decimated by the enemy while everyone else got away. Hamo was never expendable to him. Although no one had mentioned it at the time, it was obvious that the memory still festered in the minds of those who were now trapped here with him. "Just leave me alone."

"Still think you're better than the rest of us? Well, you're not. Not here. Here you're nobody, just like the rest of us. And you don't get to tell me what to do. Your father's not here to look out for you anymore. Since he's the reason we're all here, don't you think it's fair you make that up to us and share your food?"

"Don't talk about my father like that. It's not his fault this happened..."

Hamo looked up just in time to see the man's hand coming toward him. Pain exploded across his face, and he recoiled with a cry. After the initial shock of pain wore off, anger took its place.

"What did you do that for?"

"Because I wanted to. See? Now you're the same as the rest of us."

Hamo glared at him, one hand covering the sore spot on his face, unable to think of any retort.

"Leave him alone, Warin, before you bring Forbes in here," another slave called across the room.

Warin didn't answer him. Instead, he ate the last of Hamo's food with deliberate slowness, watching Hamo as he took each bite. When he was finished, he tossed the empty bowl back to him and moved to his own spot on the other side of the room without a word.

Hamo watched him retreat, still nursing the side of his face where Warin had struck him. It wasn't fair, he thought. It wasn't fair that he was already consigned to long, silent days separated from anyone he might be familiar with and forced instead to toil with a man who spoke only when absolutely necessary. The men who worked the mines at least had the benefit of camaraderie.

As he sat in his corner, trying to ignore everyone else in the room, the fingers of his left hand wandered over the brand that was finally healing on his right arm. Absently, he traced the indelible symbol that gave these men ownership over him.

It took him longer than usual to fall asleep that night and when he awoke the next morning, the discomfort and tension of the night before lingered. Where Warin hit him was tender and bruised. When he received his portion of food, he ate it without waiting to get back inside and sit down. He couldn't afford to lose another meal.

Hamo slipped away from the group and made his way up to the smelter earlier than he was required to. At least in there, he didn't have to worry about the wrath and abuse of his own countrymen.

Entering the hot building, Hamo saw Drogo already there, already at work.

"You're early," Drogo said, looking up from where he was preparing the day's work.

"I know."

Drogo stopped what he was doing and studied Hamo.

"I told you to stay clear of Forbes." He gestured toward the bruise on Hamo's face. "You should have listened."

"It wasn't Forbes," Hamo said, still seething. It was one thing for his enemy to treat him like that, but his own fellow slaves? That was cruel. Without another word, he went to work.

Drogo did not say anything, but his eyebrows went up in surprise and he nodded his head slowly. Throughout the rest of that day, and the next several days, he quietly ignored the frequent breaks Hamo had to take, and when he found him sitting against the wall gripping his head between his hands, moaning softly, he had told him to lay down in a corner of the hot room and rest.

As summer hastened on, the only bright spot in Hamo's life was the fact that he was getting better at his work. Before, Drogo had spent much of the day correcting his efforts or telling him what needed done. Now, as the long hot days of summer neared their end, Hamo knew what was expected of him in the smelter and did it well. It was poor comfort, but comfort, nonetheless.

It was unfortunate timing one day that brought Hamo out of the smelter just as two horsemen rode into the slave camp. It was near midday and already they needed more wood. As Hamo bent to get an armful of it, his gaze idly followed the two riders as they neared. With a start, he recognized the foremost one to be Lord Bayner himself. He started toward the door with his burden, but Drogo was standing there now, watching the approach of the two men as well.

"Wonder what that's about," Drogo spoke to no one in particular. "He never shows up here."

Seeing Drogo standing outside the smelter, Lord Bayner altered his horse's course in his direction. Hamo, realizing they were riding straight toward him, lowered his face and ducked behind Drogo. The last thing he wanted at the moment was a conversation with Lord Bayner. Those always ended leaving him angry and humiliated.

"Drogo! I see you're still hard at work up here. What would I do without you?" The lord seemed in an exceptionally good mood.

"You'd find someone else." Drogo was as short with him as anyone else, and Hamo got the sense that this huge man was not intimidated by the lord.

"Of course, I would. But you're better at it than anyone I know. Have you seen Forbes around here? I rode all this way to discuss some business with him and I don't seem to see him anywhere."

"Most likely up there." Drogo jerked his chin toward the mine.

Lord Bayner started to turn his horse, then stopped, a wicked smile growing on his face.

"Who is that hiding behind you, Drogo? Someone who doesn't want to speak with me."

Drogo turned, realizing for the first time that Hamo had slipped in behind him. He raised an eyebrow at the boy's demeanor, and the way he stared steadfastly at the ground, not allowing anyone to see his face. Hamo had done the same thing with Drogo on his first day.

"He is my slave. Forbes gave him to me to help in the smelter," he replied as he stepped away from Hamo.

"Well, well, if it isn't the captain's son," Lord Bayner said. "Enjoying our hospitality?"

Hamo remained silent.

"Still blaming me, I see. I really did try to help you. It's your king's fault. I'm quite sorry that things have worked out this way for you."

Hamo lifted his head up enough to meet Lord Bayner's eyes but didn't dare answer him.

"You know I just spoke with your father. Maurus, isn't it?" Lord Bayner continued as Hamo stiffened and his curiosity was piqued at the mention of his father. "Such a useful man. He delivered something very valuable to us in exchange for some money. A great artifact from your country. It seems he and your king had a falling out of sorts. I admit, I was a little surprised that he did not ask for you in the bargain. In fact, he didn't even mention you. You know, I would have given you to him if he had only asked, since you're really not worth much as a slave. I guess he needed the money more."

Lord Bayner smiled at the slight figure in front of him. Outwardly, there had been no reaction, but the lord knew his words had their intended effect. Satisfied, he turned his horse toward the footpath leading up to the mine entrance.

Drogo stood watching the back of the departing lord, waiting for him to ride beyond earshot.

"Go inside," he said quietly when he was sure Lord Bayner could no longer hear.

Hamo stood as if frozen in place, although Drogo could see his chest rising and falling rapidly as he fought for control.

"I said, get inside," he repeated, pushing him back toward the door.

Hamo was unresisting. He fell back into the room then pulled away from Drogo. His face was in his hands, and an animal-like sound, halfway between a yell and a moan came from him. He staggered drunkenly toward the darkest corner of the room before dropping to his knees.

All the anger, and loneliness, and fear, and pain, and humiliation that he had bottled up since his capture unleashed themselves now. Another scream was torn from him, as his fingers yanked at a fistful of hair. Then his fists found the solid ground beneath him, pounding it until he could no longer feel them. And all the while, great, horrible sobs forced their way out of his chest. He was powerless to stop himself.

Over and over again his mouth formed the words, "I hate you. I hate you."

He was never sure afterward if he actually said the words aloud nor could he be sure who the words were meant for. That frightened him a little. He didn't want to hate Father. He wanted to hate Lord Bayner. But how could Father do such a thing? He wouldn't, would he?

It was some time before his grief and rage were spent. He crouched still on the floor, knees drawn up to his chest and shaking uncontrollably, unable to find the will to get up. He had time to wonder why Drogo had not come after him to get him back to work. Now that he was quiet, he could hear the fire roaring as strongly as it ever did. Casting a surreptitious glance toward the furnace, he could make out Drogo's head above the glowing flames, bent over his work. Apparently, he was going to simply ignore his slave's outburst. Hamo was grateful for that.

Drogo, however much he pretended to ignore the boy's outburst, was keenly aware of when his young slave had stopped crying and was starting to be in control of himself again. He waited until he was reasonably sure that it was over before leaving his work and approaching him.

"Get back to work," he said. As gruff as the command seemed, his voice was gentle, even sympathetic.

Slowly, Hamo got up. He kept his face lowered, Drogo noted, but he was doing what he was told. That was good, Drogo thought, a job would help distract him. But as the day went on it became more than obvious that he was distracted from his job and not the other way around. Hamo didn't look up once the rest of the day. Not even when Drogo told him to go back to his quarters without bringing in a fresh stack of wood for the next day.

Chapter 5

L OOK AT ALL THOSE PEOPLE!" Sabina was staring, with a wide-open mouth, at the crowds that were assembling. "I've never seen so many people all at once."

"I bet it's a million." Aldrid's face was smashed up against the window with Sabina's.

"Did they all come just for the king's coronation?" Sabina turned around to where Mother was sitting near the fireplace.

"Yes. Aldrid, be careful or you'll fall." Alina watched nervously as her son balanced precariously on the edge of a wooden footstool so that he could see the street outside. He was going to be short and slight, just like Maurus and Hamo.

"Aren't we going to go, too?" Al was asking.

"I don't think so," Alina answered. There was no one who would want them to show up. They were, after all, the family of the now notorious Maurus, thief of the king's sword and traitor.

"Please! I want to see the new king." Sabina turned her blue eyes pleadingly toward her mother, biting down on her bottom lip in excitement.

"No. I'd rather not," Alina replied rather shortly. Children did not understand about reputations and the burden of being constantly looked down upon.

At that moment, the stool Aldrid was balancing on slipped out from under him. Alina jumped up as he landed on the floor.

"Oh Al, I told you to be careful. You're going to hurt yourself." She picked him up, brushing invisible dirt off his knees.

Al grinned slyly up at her, the burn scar on the side of his face making it crooked. "Please, Mother. Can we please go?"

Alina looked at the boy. His little face already bore a strong resemblance to Maurus' and Hamo's. The same dark brown eyes. The same tousled brown hair. The only big difference was the scar on his left cheek and chin. She brushed a gentle finger across the scar, remembering the horror of the day when it was made. Little Aldrid's scream still haunted her. His crippled left arm still pained her. His grin widened when he noticed her staring.

"Oh, alright," she gave in with a sigh.

"That's not fair. You only said yes because Al asked you." Sabina spun around from the window, a pout on her lips.

"Sabina, how could you say something like that?" Alina asked, shocked.

Sabina suddenly found her feet very interesting and refused to meet Mother's eyes. She bit her lip, wishing she had not spoken up. Mother had finally agreed to take them, and she was going to ruin it with her big mouth.

"I don't know," she finally mumbled.

"Well, if we're going, you two are going to need to get cleaned up. Al, there's dirt all over your face. What were you doing?" She hurried away with him still in her arms.

Sabina was not the sort of child to let anything spoil her fun, and by the time they left the tiny shack they called home behind them, she was skipping back and forth trying to hurry the others along. The streets were unusually crowded on this coronation day. People had traveled a long way to see Prince Darien crowned king. King Dival had never been as popular among the people as his son had been. His passing had been met more with a national sigh of relief than national sorrow.

"Come on! We'll be late!" Sabina called back to Mother and Al.

"No, we won't. It's a long ceremony and you'll probably be bored to tears before it's over."

Sabina slowed down, waiting for them to catch up and slid her hand into Mother's.

"Do you think the new queen will be wearing a crown? If I was a queen, I would always wear a crown. And I would have lots of servants to do all my work for me so that I could play all day long," Sabina nodded confidently as she spoke.

"I wouldn't want to wear a crown all day. It would be boring," Al spoke up, not wanting to be left out of the conversation.

"Why would it be boring?" Alina asked him.

"Cause then you couldn't play. I like to play."

"But if you had a crown everyone would have to listen to you and do whatever you tell them to. That would be better than playing," Sabina argued.

"No, it wouldn't."

"Yes, it would."

"Sabina, stop arguing with your brother," Alina interrupted them.

Sabina waited until Mother wasn't looking to stick her tongue out at Aldrid. Aldrid returned the insult.

By the time they neared the castle, the crowd had already outgrown the courtyard and was spilling out into the grassy slope before the castle. Most would not get to see the actual ceremony, but it was customary for the new king to come out and greet his new subjects. Alina was quite content to stay in the back of the crowd. People were less likely to notice her and her two children in the back, and she could slip away before the crowd broke up.

Sabina and Aldrid spent the intervening minutes playing in the grass a few feet behind the bulk of the crowd. Alina watched the two of them. It was amazing to her how little Aldrid seemed to be affected by his useless left hand. It was as if it had always been like that, when in truth it had not even been a full year. Alina's face clouded as she thought about the past Spring and early Summer. Maurus, her husband, had been gone now for several weeks, and she feared he would never return. And Hamo, poor, young Hamo was dead. Stolen by the monster of war before he had even reached manhood. She tried to block the image of his face from her mind now. It would just make her want to cry and she did that enough already. The last thing she needed was to remember his laughing, dark eyes, his quiet sense of humor and good-naturedness, and how much he hated having to do housework. She smiled a little sadly as she remembered him on the day Maurus had come home the previous fall.

"Do the rugs really need to be beaten? Mother, you're the only one who even sees dirt in them." He *looked almost pained at the thought of having to do it.*

"It's for your father, Hamo. I want the house to look nice when he gets here."

"Father doesn't care about the house. He just cares about you when he comes home." He laughed.

Later that evening when Father had walked through the door, swinging little Sabina up into the air, Hamo had whispered in her ear as he passed her,

"He hasn't looked at the rug yet!"

Her thoughts were interrupted by the loud cheering of the crowd in front of her. Sabina and Aldrid, hearing the commotion, stopped their play and ran to her side.

"Pick me up." Al held up his good arm and Alina scooped him up so that he could see above the heads of the crowd. Sabina jumped up and down, trying to get high enough to see the new king.

The cheering was heartfelt. The kingdom of Dival had been at war for several decades and there was not a household that had not felt its effects. Most hoped that under a new king the war would become a thing of the past, and nothing more than a bitter memory. Alina wondered if her life would change at all under the new king. She did not have anyone else to lose to the war at present, it had already taken all it could from her. Perhaps with a different king, though, people would begin to forget about Maurus' crime, and maybe, just maybe, she could hold her head up again when she went out.

Chapter 6

IT WAS EARLY AUTUMN, but the air in the mountains already held a slight chill. Hamo could not believe that it had been only a year ago that Father had come home, and everything had been normal and comfortable and good. He would be sixteen soon, but he felt years older now, aged by hardship and not time.

His thoughts wandered dangerously close to homesickness as he made his way up the gentle slope toward the smelter. Most days he managed to keep such thoughts in check, drowning them out by focusing on his work. Today, with the restlessness of autumn in the air, he wasn't as successful. Autumn was when Father usually came home from the summer campaigns. Hamo would spend hours with him, hunting, fishing, or just tagging along with whatever business he had to attend to. His loneliness morphed into a physical ache. He wanted home and time wasn't healing that wound.

The snorting of a horse drew him out of his melancholy and he looked up, puzzled to see three shaggy beasts standing at the entrance with Drogo. While the horses in the camp were regularly used to haul away the iron they smelted, he couldn't divine what purpose they would serve Drogo today.

"Winter is coming. I need more wood. It has to be cut before the snow sets in," Drogo's slow words answered Hamo's unasked question. "Load that on one of the horses." The big man jerked his head toward a pile of supplies. "Be quick. We have a long way to go today."

Hamo bundled the supplies up in the sheets of heavy canvas and secured it to the pack saddle of the nearest horse, while Drogo harnessed the other two to a large, flat sleigh. Hamo noticed as he watched the big man finish that Drogo was carrying a longbow and quiver of arrows.

"Come on." Drogo set off toward the slope of the mountain opposite the mine.

This mountain had a dense evergreen forest going about two thirds of the way up its sides. As they left the camp behind them, Hamo noticed a thick wooden post embedded in the open meadow between the camp and the woods. Even from a distance he could see the chains on it and the dark stains on the wood. He glanced curiously at Drogo.

"It's for floggings. Keeps slaves in line. Don't ever end up there. You will die."

That was an unnecessary warning, Hamo thought. No one would try to end up there, and if they did end up there, he was quite certain it would be against their will. He nodded anyway.

His eyes were drawn to it again and again as they continued to the woods. It held a sort of fascinating horror, and he found himself imagining what it would be like to be chained there, having the flesh ripped from his back by a whip. He had experienced Forbes' once already, but that time the man had only been looking to get his attention, not to punish him for a crime. He shuddered with the thought of it.

Once inside the woods, Hamo was a little surprised to find there was a fair path to follow. The horses were apparently used to this and did not require any guidance as they trudged up the slope. The sleigh, without any weight on it, slid easily across the packed earth.

Even though the climb was tiring, Hamo admitted to himself that being out in the fresh mountain air was far more pleasant than being in that hot, smoky smelter. And when he got too tired, something that happened quickly due to his malnourishment, he could let most of his weight hang off the horse's harness.

Up here, he could almost forget, surrounded by the tall, stately evergreens, that he was a slave. If he closed his eyes and just listened to the sounds of the woods, the songbirds, the gentle, rustling of wind through the branches, the scurrying of squirrels and chipmunks, he could almost imagine himself at home. Father had taken him out hunting with him a few times when he was home from the war, and the woods reminded Hamo of those happier times.

They had been climbing steadily until late afternoon before Drogo pulled the team of horses off the path into a small clearing. The ground here leveled out a bit and a small mountain brook gurgled nearby.

"We'll make camp here."

"Oh," Hamo made no effort to hide his surprise. He had assumed they would be going up and back in a single day.

"You have a problem with that?" Drogo was looking at him now and Hamo was quick to shake his head. He was still very much aware of the fact that Drogo carried a whip tucked into his belt and he did not want to anger the man. "Good. Unload him. Set up a camp. Use the canvas there." He indicated the pack horse Hamo had been leading.

Drogo settled back against a tree and watched while Hamo slid the packs off the horse and unrolled the canvas and ropes. Hamo, for his part, was not entirely sure what to do. What exactly Drogo had meant when he said set up camp, he did not know. He assumed he wanted a tent but setting up a tent alone proved awkward. When he was finished, he cast a worried look at Drogo, uncertain as to whether he had done the right thing.

"Tether the horses. Get some water. Start a fire," Drogo simply moved on to the next set of commands.

Hamo moved to obey. The horses were docile beasts, used to their work and they stood patiently while Hamo undid their harness. Hamo had seen the way the cavalry men and knights had strung a high line between two trees and then tied the individual lead ropes of the horses to that line. He tried to imitate that now. The horses, free of their bridles, lowered their heads and began to placidly munch on the grass. Hamo paused long enough to scratch the ears of the little pack horse he had led before moving on to finish his tasks.

Dusk was settling in on them when the small pot of stew that Drogo had fixed over the fire was done. Hamo's mouth watered as the scent of the food hovered in the evening air and he tried not to look too hungry when Drogo spooned the thick substance into two wooden bowls. After a year of very meager rations, just the smell of food was torturous.

Drogo, his face normally so impassive, raised an eyebrow at the ravenous way his slave attacked his food. He did not even bother to wait for a spoon but scooped it straight into his mouth with his fingers.

Hamo thought briefly of how appalled Mother would be if she saw him eating like this, but the thought was quickly taken over by the fact that Mother would be appalled to see him like this at all - filthy, dressed in rags, and emaciated with hunger. With an effort, Hamo pushed thoughts of Mother and home out of his mind. It was no good to think about them. It just made him miserable. And it invariably led to thoughts of Father, and those were terrible and painful and dark.

Hamo's eyes widened in surprise when, after he had scraped the inside of his bowl clean, Drogo took it from him and refilled it. Two helpings of food had been nothing more than a daydream for months.

"Thank you!" he managed as Drogo pushed the refilled bowl back into his hands, this time with a spoon in it. He took the hint and managed to eat his seconds in a more civilized manner.

Drogo waited until he had emptied his bowl a second time before speaking again. "Woods are full of wild animals. We don't both sleep at the same time. Build the fire up. We'll take turns keeping it going tonight."

Hamo added wood to the fire until it was large enough to light up the entire little clearing. Then he returned to the makeshift tent, which was little more than the canvas stretched out and tied between three tree trunks. He was somewhat dismayed when Drogo motioned him toward one of the tree trunks and he saw a heavy chain secured around it. The other end Drogo fastened to his wrist.

"You're not running away on me," Drogo said dryly as Hamo stared at the shackle on his arm in disgust. "You watch the fire first. Wake me up in four hours. If it starts to die, you can reach the wood pile and put more on. Let it die, and we'll have wolves and mountain lions on us." Then Drogo wrapped himself in a sheepskin blanket and lay down at the other end of the tent to sleep.

Hamo sat for some time, seething at the indignity of being tethered to a tree just like an animal. He could not figure Drogo out. On one hand, he could be kind. He had given him extra food, and he had deliberately ignored the many breaks Hamo had taken when he first started working, and although he carried a whip he had never so much as threatened to use it on Hamo. But then he did things like this and reminded Hamo that he was not even a human to these people, but a piece of property that had to be chained up at night just like the horses.

Already the weight of the iron band felt as if it were dragging his arm down, chafing against his skin and he couldn't move without hearing the clank of the chain. He reached out with his free hand and twisted the iron band around, testing its tightness around his wrist. He didn't plan on running away, but he wanted to be rid of the cuff.

The action drew his eyes to the brand on his forearm. Now that it was healed, he forgot about it most of the time. Coupled with the shackle, its humiliation increased tenfold. He traced the symbol with his finger. Lord Bayner's symbol. He was the property of Lord Bayner. The thought was as sickening now as it had been that first day.

"If the horses get restless, wake me up," Drogo's voice drifted over from the other side of the tent and interrupted Hamo's musings.

"Yes, Drogo," he answered, but Drogo was already asleep.

It was amazing how quickly the forest could turn from refreshing and liberating into a ghoulish and eerie nightmare. Drogo had not been asleep long before the night sounds began to work their way into Hamo's consciousness and imagination. The hooting of an owl, the distant howl of wolves, even the snuffling, munching sound of the horses grazing near the tent were frightening when heard alone in the darkness.

He had been sitting with his back to the tree he was chained to but, almost without thought or decision, he inched nearer and nearer the blazing fire. Fire was their best defense against the wild animals. It's orange and blue flames enough to scare away the bravest of animals.

Already it seemed as if the flames were growing smaller. Worried, he moved to the stack of wood he had collected earlier, the chain he was fastened to clanking loudly with the motion, and threw more of it on. Once again, the fire leaped up, sparks shooting into the darkness above him. He sat close to the fire, both for its warmth and its protection. His eyes darted about the clearing, searching the blackness beyond for signs of something moving.

The hours dragged by, and despite his fear, Hamo's eyelids grew heavy and more than once he started to nod off only to jerk awake again. Once, he must have dozed for several minutes, because, when he started awake, the fire had died down considerably. His own carelessness scared him, and he got up and paced back and forth a few times to try

46

to wake himself up. It was when he lowered himself back to the ground that he first noticed it.

The horses were stirring. One of them was pawing at the ground restlessly, and snorting. There was an extra stirring in the nearby branches as well. Hamo could feel the hair on the back of his neck stand up as he moved backwards to where Drogo lay.

"Drogo," he called softly, not sure of how the man would wake up. As one of the horses let out another loud snort, he lost his reticence about waking the man. "Drogo, it's the horses. Somethings out there."

Instantly Drogo was on his feet, his hand reaching for the bow and arrows he had brought with him. He moved in the direction of the horses, scanning the night about him.

"Get me a light," he said, his voice was as slow and calm as ever.

Hamo selected a branch from the pile and set the tip of it in the flames until it had caught. He held it out to Drogo, but the man waved it away.

"You hold it. I might need both hands." Hamo noticed now that he had an arrow nocked to his bowstring. Hamo wondered if an arrow would be enough to stop an animal as big as a mountain lion.

"You woke me up for this?" Drogo stopped in his tracks, staring hard at the horses.

With the light of the makeshift torch close to them, Hamo could see now that the horse in the middle was the one causing the racket. The reason for this became clear a moment later as his eyes took in the sagging line he had tied between the trees. The horse had tangled one of its front legs in the rope and was now pawing the ground trying to get free.

Now that he could see it, Hamo felt ashamed of being so afraid that he had to wake his master. Drogo, it seemed, felt the same. With a grunt of disgust, he lifted the horse's leg out of the rope. Then he turned on Hamo.

Hamo was too stunned to move when he saw the whip in Drogo's hand, coming towards him rapidly.

The force of the blow sent him reeling backwards to the ground and wrung a cry of shock and pain from his lips. He looked up, terrified and confused by the unexpected outburst, at the big man standing over him now. He felt a rush of warm blood down the side of his face.

For a moment, Hamo worried that his master was going to strike him again, but Drogo lowered his arm, shook his head and muttered something under his breath.

While Hamo watched, white-faced and frightened, the man disappeared from out of the tent. When he returned to where Hamo was sitting, Drogo had a bucket of water in his hand. He sat down in front of Hamo. With one hand he reached forward and grabbed Hamo's face by the chin. Hamo flinched involuntarily at his touch and attempted to pull away.

"Stop," was all Drogo said.

His other hand reached into the bucket of water and pulled out a cloth. Turning Hamo's face to the side, he began to wash away the blood that was running freely. When he was satisfied that the gash was clean, Drogo pulled a small tin out of the pocket of his coat and from that he applied a cooling ointment to the wound. In all that time, neither said a word. Now, as Drogo finished, he motioned Hamo toward the tree he was chained to.

"Go to sleep. It's my turn to watch."

Hamo nodded, still afraid. He crawled back to the tree and curled up on the ground next to it, careful to lay on the side without injury.

He was more confused than ever by his master's behavior. Drogo appeared to almost feel bad about hitting his slave. But he had hit Hamo, and he had hit him hard. The entire right side of his face was throbbing despite the salve, and now that he was a distance from the fire Hamo was cold, and his wrist hurt from the weight of the chain on it. He lay shivering and feeling very sorry for himself for some time before he managed to drift off to sleep.

"Get up."

The quiet voice penetrated the fog of Hamo's sleep, forcing his eyes open. With a groan, he sat up. His free hand went to the side of his face and brushed against the swollen laceration, and he remembered last night. Drogo was crouching next to him waiting for him to wake up fully.

"Sun's up. We have work to do. Hold still," he ordered as he went to put more salve on Hamo's face.

Hamo lowered his eyes and bit down on his lip as he tried to keep from wincing. It was then that he noticed the soft sheepskin blanket that was covering him. He knew he had not had that on when he lay down the night before. Drogo must have put it on him.

"Thank you. For the blanket," Hamo ventured tentatively. After last night, he was less sure of his master.

"Brought you up here to work, not die of cold," Drogo said simply. "Snow will be here in a couple days. We need to get to work. Give me your arm."

Hamo held out his arm and allowed Drogo to unlock the iron band that had held him to the tree all night.

"I'm sorry about last night, Drogo. I didn't mean to wake you up for nothing." Hamo watched the shackle fallaway, not daring to look at Drogo's face.

"Forget about it. And don't do it again."

Nodding, Hamo got to his feet and followed Drogo out of the tent. The sun, barely visible through the dense trees, was just coming up against a pink and golden horizon. After a hasty breakfast of bread and dried meat, washed down with deliciously hot tea, the two set off into the woods.

Tree after tree fell to Drogo's ax through the day and Hamo was kept busy, stripping the branches off the fallen trees with his own ax. At midday, they stopped to eat. This was almost enough to make up for the blow Drogo had given Hamo. Three meals in one day were a luxury Hamo had come to believe was impossible.

In the afternoon they worked together on a two handled saw, cutting the great trunks into smaller pieces, and stacking them neatly in piles near the clearing. Drogo was as quiet out here in the woods as he was in the smelter, and not a word of conversation passed between the two except for the occasional command from master to slave.

For a week the pattern continued. It snowed on the third day of their being in the mountain, but Drogo was not satisfied with the amount they had cut yet. The work was harder in the snow, but, aside from the cut on his face, Hamo still preferred this to feeding the furnace in the smelter. Just one week of eating better and being in the fresh air was doing wonders for him and he felt better than he had in a long time.

Nights were the worst part. When it was completely dark out and the fire was stoked into a large blaze, Drogo would lock the shackle over Hamo's wrist. It grated against Hamo, unreasonably. After all, nothing about his situation changed when it was removed. He was still a slave. It was the fact that it was the starkest reminder of what he was, that he was no longer a person but a thing that bothered him.

By the end of the week there was a sore spot on his wrist from where it chafed. It was always Hamo's turn to watch first. No matter how many times he heard the night sounds of the forest, he could not quite shake his fear of them. The thought of being torn apart by wild animals was horrifying. Each night he was relieved when Drogo woke up to take his place. And each night, Drogo gave him the warm sheepskin blanket to sleep with.

When the week was over, and the wood was stacked high on the sleigh, Drogo harnessed two of the horses up while Hamo loaded the third down with what was left of their gear.

"What about the rest of it?" Hamo looked about at the neat piles of cut wood that still lined the clearing.

"We'll come back for it. It will take a few trips. Careful going down. Don't let him get ahead of you," Drogo motioned to the patient little pack horse. "Path shouldn't be too bad yet."

The going was slower due to the snow. It was after dark by the time they had reached the mining camp. Drogo hailed one of the sentries as they approached and the man let them into the camp. Hamo was exhausted and had been letting the sturdy little horse pull him along for the last couple hours. Now, he assumed, he would have to unload the pack horse and unharness the other two and take care of them before he could stumble wearily to his hut to sleep. Drogo, however, stopped him before he got started.

"Go."

Without waiting for Drogo to change his mind, Hamo slipped away to the crudely built shed that was his home. The guard at the door had seen him come in with Drogo so there was no need to explain why he was out so late.

Inside, he felt the eyes of his fellow slaves studying him as he made his way to his corner. He had been gone for a week and he had no doubt that they thought it was because he was being favored.

"Run into a little trouble there, boy?" Warin asked as he caught sight of Hamo's face. Although he had not hit Hamo again, he'd done everything else in his power to make Hamo's life miserable. "That ironsmith finally decided to give you a taste of his whip, huh? You know, I've heard he's the worst of the lot, once he's decided to be. I heard he beat his last slave to death."

Hamo ignored him, like he always did, and slumped to the floor in his corner. It was then that he noticed it missing. His blanket. The only protection he had against the coming cold of winter. A quick glance across the room showed him that Warin was the culprit. With a sigh, he lay down without it. It was no use trying to take it back from Warin.

He already missed the peace and quiet of the forest, and the sheepskin blanket, he thought wryly. Especially the sheepskin blanket.

Chapter 7

ALINA WATCHED THE FIRST FEW snowflakes drift lazily to the ground. She had tried to put off thoughts of winter for some time now, but winter was upon them now and she was at a loss. The little shack that they were able to afford would be bitterly cold in the long winter months, and she had neither the time nor strength to cut enough firewood to keep even a semblance of warmth in the main room.

If Maurus or Hamo were here they could do it, she thought. Then again, if Maurus or Hamo were here, they wouldn't be forced to live in this drafty hovel, eking out a miserable existence. Hamo had no choice about going, so she could never work up any anger towards him for his absence. Maurus, however, did choose. He had abandoned them on the pretense of seeking help for Aldrid. She could be very angry with him. Not that fuming over his decision did her any good. There was still the matter of getting her and her two children through the winter without freezing to death.

She chewed on her lower lip as she watched the snowfall thicken. There had to be something, some way. If there was some other job she could work that would bring in more money, that would help, but nothing came to mind. The snow grew heavier and stuck to the ground, slowly transforming the world to its winter wardrobe of white. When winter came down from the north, over the distant mountains of Dorsten, it came suddenly. Alina knew that in the next few hours the ground would be completely covered and would remain so for several months.

"Mother, can Al and I go out and play in the snow?" Sabina was sitting on the floor where she was supposed to be mending a shirt. Although she was only seven, Alina relied on her to do a good many of the household chores. For the moment, though, the sewing sat neglected in her lap, while she cast wistful glances out the window where some of their neighbor children were already out.

Aldrid, playing nearby, looked up when his sister asked, "I want to. Can we?"

"I...," Alina paused as a knock shook their front door. Who would be coming here? They never had visitors, not now. Distracted, she answered Sabina, "Bundle up warmly, and," she called over her shoulder as she went to open the door, "stay close to the house."

The man outside her door was dressed in the clothes of a King's Courier. Alina took a small step back in surprise.

"Can I help you?" she queried, although she had already seen the folded and sealed envelope in the man's hand.

"His Majesty, King Darien, sent this for you." The man extended his hand to her with the envelope.

Alina took it, and since the man was clearly waiting for her to, opened and read it. It took two or three times before she fully comprehended the request.

"The King wants an audience with me?" She looked up at the Courier in some bewilderment.

"Is the time acceptable with you?" It was apparently the Courier's responsibility to make sure such an appointment was understood and confirmed before he left.

"Yes. Yes, I'll be there. Nine o'clock tomorrow morning." Alina stared at the slip of paper again as the man walked away.

She returned to her spot at the window, this time watching Sabina and Al playing in the snow. Al was finding it difficult to make a snowball with only one hand and Alina smiled a little as she watched Sabina stop and help him.

Then her face clouded as she thought about the King's summons. It must have something to do with Maurus and the sword, she thought. Perhaps the new King was not as friendly as he had seemed, and maybe he was seeking vengeance for his father's stolen treasure. Alina had always been a little afraid of this under King Dival, but she thought it would change with Darien. Apparently not. Whatever it was, she had to go. It would be foolish to ignore a summons from the King.

The next morning, Alina stood inside the King's throne room, the place where he conducted all official business. She had left Al in Sabina's care earlier that morning and had made her way through the snowy streets to the castle that had once been so familiar to her. The throne room was one part of the castle she had not seen a lot of in the years that her and Maurus called it home.

Now, as she stood waiting for the King's arrival, she noticed the tapestries hanging on the walls like curtains to keep out the cold winter air. They were interesting pictures, she thought. They all seemed dedicated to telling a part of the story of Dival's rise to power and the subsequent conflict.

King Dival looked more majestic, more noble in his pictures. She smiled as she remembered the appearance of the late King. Fat would have been a better word to describe him. The makers of these tapestries were no doubt motivated by some means or another to show their King in a slightly better light.

Then there were the pictures depicting the great battles and victories of the Divalian army. It was funny how different the pictures were from the stories Maurus had told her. The pictures were a far cleaner version of the war, the artists had apparently forgotten all the blood that was spilled in battle. And they certainly seemed ignorant of the fact that Divalian soldiers had fallen in those battles as well as Dorstenian ones. Altogether, they painted a much tidier, braver side of the conflict.

Alina was so caught up in her study of the pictures that she was startled to hear someone clear their throat softly behind her. She spun around to find not only the King, but also the Queen, standing only a few feet away.

"Forgive me, Your Majesties. I had not realized you had entered." She dropped into a low, practiced curtsy. They must have entered unannounced, something Dival never would have done.

"They are very interesting pictures, aren't they?" King Darien spoke first. "Not exactly honest, but very interesting."

"Yes, they are," Alina agreed.

"Perhaps you would join us at the table. There are a few things we would like to discuss." The King led the way to one of the long tables that were set up before his throne.

Alina was surprised at the manners of the royal couple. They were so - unroyal. She sat down opposite them and waited. It was the Queen who spoke first.

"Mrs. Serbon, I'm so sorry for all that you have gone through. My husband and I are aware of the losses you have suffered through this war." Queen Freya was a beautiful young woman, the daughter of an outlying nobleman. But prettier than her face was her ability to empathize with those beneath her. As the mother of two young boys herself, she could sympathize with any woman who had lost a son in the war.

"I know my father never bothered to settle the matter of a pension with your husband. I would like to correct that."

"My husband...," Alina started.

"Stole the sword, I know. But the pension was as much for his family as it was for him. And we do owe him years of faithful service. We are offering you not only a monthly sum, but a house just outside town."

"Really?"

"Really. My Father made some grave mistakes as King, and I would like to fix as many of them as I can. My steward will arrange the details for you, most likely within the next week."

Alina was speechless. Such an offer put an end to all her worries about making it through the winter. The generosity of the new monarch was overwhelming, and when she left the castle walls, tears flowed freely down her face.

Chapter 8

WINTER IN THE MINING CAMP was brutal. Snow fell for days at a time, making any movement difficult. The cold, bitter and biting, was worse than it had been in the Void the previous winter. And the slaves were poorly dressed for it. Most were still clad in the threadbare remnants that they had been captured in.

Hamo had thought working in the smelter would be a benefit in the winter but was quickly disillusioned. While he was in there and working, he was warm. In fact, he was hot and by the end of day drenched in sweat from the heat of the fire. And that was what made it so terrible. The second he stepped outside of the smelter, he began to shiver as the cold wind whipped through his damp clothes and into his skin. He did not stop shivering until the next morning when he was close to the furnace. He missed his blanket, even though it was so thin it would not have done him much good. It was more than a little annoying to watch the other man use it along with his own every night while Hamo had nothing.

It was not long before the winter took its toll on the slaves. Most became sick and lethargic, deadened by the constant numbness of cold. The only bright side to it all was that their workday was considerably shorter. The sun went down early, and Forbes did not want slaves out after dark, no matter what. It made for too good of an opportunity for escape attempts. Work ended an hour before sunset.

It was on one unusually bright day when Forbes decided to have the slaves load the smelted iron onto sleighs to take through the pass to the town where it could be used to make armor and weapons for the army. This was normally done once a week and was the only day when the slaves did not work in the mines. In the winter months it was a little trickier because they had to pick a day when the weather was fairly mild, and no snowstorms were forming on the horizon.

Hamo's day was no different because of the loading. Forbes did not even bother to use him. He could not pick up the iron blocks by himself. He was of more use if he just kept the fire going.

Forbes was in a particularly sour mood as the loading went on. It was taking far too long. Already the sun was casting long shadows on the snow. The sergeant moved between the slaves, using his whip freely to speed them up.

There was one man among those working who was clumsier than the rest, Hamo noticed the first time he went outside to retrieve more wood, one who struggled repeatedly to pick up the heavy blocks of iron. Cringing at the brutality of it, Hamo watched as Forbes singled him out for an excessive number of blows.

It was a late in the afternoon and Hamo was out to get more wood at the same time that the clumsy slave was trying to pull another block off the stack next to the smelter. He tried several times to lift it but failed with each attempt.

Hamo, without thinking, bent to help the man get it up. Together, they managed to get it off the stack. The man muttered his thanks, and Hamo looked up at his face for the first time. With a shock that almost caused him to drop his side of the iron block, Hamo recognized him. He knew him, despite his gaunt, hollow, gray face.

Warin.

Hamo could not forget the face of the man who had bullied and goaded him at every opportunity. Before he had a chance to think any more about it, a shout distracted him.

"How dare you help that man! I said no one helps him." Hamo whipped his head around to see Forbes coming toward them, his face red with anger. "Let go of that now."

Hamo hesitated, his eyes meeting Warin's desperate ones. As much as he wanted to, Hamo couldn't ignore the pleading in them. The man was little more than a shell of his former self, wrecked by the hard work and bitter cold of winter. Hamo knew the block would drop as soon as he let go.

The hesitation was all that Forbes needed. His eyes held a dangerous light.

"You're disobeying me? You," he pointed to Warin, "put it down. Your little friend here thinks he wants to carry it instead."

"No...," Hamo started to say, suddenly very afraid of the cold malice he read in the man's eyes. Soulless, he remembered thinking when he first saw them.

"No? No, you don't want to help your friend?"

"No, I can't carry it. Not by myself." Hamo lowered his head, hiding his fear from this man.

"Drogo's spoiled you."

Forbes glanced around him and noticed that the other slaves were watching as well as the guards. A savage smile spread across his face. He would give them something to watch, and something to fear.

"Take him to the post. And get everyone else down there. I think it's time I showed our little friend here who is really in charge." He jerked his head in the direction of the two nearest guards.

Hamo felt the blood drain away from his face, felt everything but the thudding of his own heart receding into the murky distance. Numb, he was unresisting as one of the guards grabbed his arm and started to pull him away. He looked up in time to see

Drogo standing in the doorway, watching. His lips formed the man's name, his eyes begging him to intervene. There must be something he could do, Hamo thought. Drogo just shook his head slightly and turned back into the dark doorway, leaving Hamo to his fate.

The walk to the post out in the middle of the now snow-covered meadow was a blur, his legs moving without his control. Hamo let himself be dragged along; his eyes fixed on the post he had seen with Drogo when they had gone up the mountain to cut wood.

Memory of the dark stains on the wood and Drogo's word of warning crashed through his numbness, bringing about a terror so strong he almost crumpled. He found that he was shaking uncontrollably. His mouth was dry, and he ran his tongue nervously over his lips again and again.

Suddenly he was standing in front of it and the men who had brought him here were ripping his shirt off. They weren't at all careful to keep it in one piece, which confirmed Hamo's worst fear.

He wasn't leaving this post alive.

Then he was shoved onto his knees against it and his arms were pulled around to the opposite side and fastened in place by the chains he had seen earlier, making it difficult for him to draw a full breath. His back was to the dark woods, and he could see the other slaves gathered in front of him, but he couldn't make out any of their faces. His own face was pressed tightly to one side against the rough wood, and this prevented him from turning to see Forbes coming up on his other side.

Hamo was unaware of the slave master's presence until he heard the whistling of the whip and felt it tearing into his back, causing him to suck in a sharp breath and jerk violently against the chains holding him in place. This was not the short one that Forbes normally carried, but a long one with a knotted tip on it that grabbed his flesh and pulled it away.

He did not want to scream. He tried not to scream. He wanted to face his death bravely, the way Father would have been proud of him for. But the pain, the pain was awful. And it kept coming.

Up the gentle slope and safely behind walls, Drogo sat at a small table in his room built off the back of the smelter. His face remained the same stoic mask it always did, but his hands, balled into fists and resting on the table before him, were white knuckled. The cold mountain air carried sounds remarkably well, and this was the reason for the clenched fists.

Drogo had seen the entire affair, having followed his slave out the door to get a drink of water. He had known the second he had laid eyes on Forbes' face that there would be trouble. There was nothing he could do about it, he told himself. It was out of his control, and the boy clearly disobeyed. Discipline among the slaves rested squarely on Forbes' shoulders. He had not made an example of a slave for several months, and Drogo knew there would be no stopping him now that his mind was made up.

Drogo had witnessed his need for punishment many times and had never been particularly bothered by it. He wasn't now either. He couldn't be. A slave wasn't worth bothering about.

Still, there was a nagging guilt, a feeling of disappointment in himself. He shut his eyes, but that made it worse. In his mind's eye he could see the boy's face, blanched with fear. He could see the way his lips silently formed Drogo's name. And his dark eyes, begging, pleading for help. It was his eyes that bothered Drogo the worst. He had turned his back on those eyes. He had walked away without another look back.

He remembered the way the boy had looked up at him, terrified, when he had struck him in the mountain. He had regretted the action immediately. He had been disgusted with how easily he hurt someone so much weaker and smaller than himself. He did not want to be like Forbes.

As a deafening silence filled the room, it occurred to Drogo that though the boy had been his slave for almost a year, he had no idea what his name was even. It was information he'd never bothered to find out. It was not important. Now it seemed tragic that the boy should die and that no one even knew or cared what his name was. He should have asked him when he had the chance.

A new sound reached his ears and caused him to intake sharply. Distant, but distinct, it was a cry of agony that drowned out the rhythmic snap of the whip against bare flesh. Drogo's hands tightened further, and his jaw clenched as the sound echoed off the mountainsides. The screaming continued and Drogo knew, from having seen it happen before, that the boy had reached the semi-conscious point of being aware of one thing and one thing only - the pain. The flogging would be over soon.

Drogo stood up so quickly that his chair fell over behind him. He did not bother to pick it up again. He began to pace the small room. He knew what the boy did not. He knew that the worst part of the punishment would not be the flogging. The worst part had yet to begin. The worst part would start when night fell and no one else was around. The more Drogo thought about it, the worse he felt. Slave or not, the boy did not deserve the end Forbes was going to put him through.

Chapter 9

HAMO WAS NO LONGER AWARE of anything around him save the savage pain exploding across his back and sides. His body jerked and spasmed with each blow. The long whip wrapped itself all the way around his stomach several times, and when Forbes pulled it back, Hamo could feel his skin being shredded by the rawhide knot.

At last, the whip stopped falling on him. He was sobbing convulsively, he knew, but he could not stop and did not care.

For a moment, he wondered if Forbes changed his mind and was going to let him live because two of the soldiers moved toward the post to undo his chains.

"Leave him."

Forbes' voice was distant and satisfied. Hamo fought to bring his own ragged breathing under control. He felt the butt of the whip shoved under his chin, pushing his face up along the splintering wood. He could not make out the face only inches away from his own through the blur of tears, but Forbes' quiet, cold voice cut through the sound of his own sobbing gasps.

"It's been a hard winter. And the wolves get awfully hungry this time of year. I'm leaving you here to help them out. Don't worry, though, I'll make sure my men come back tomorrow morning and collect whatever is left of you. There might be enough pieces left to bury."

As the words sank through the fog in Hamo's brain, and the full import of their meaning dawned on him, he felt sick.

"Please... no... please... don't leave me," his voice was thick, and he was gasping. Any resolve to face death bravely was gone now, shattered by pain and fear. "Please. I'll do... anything."

Forbes did not bother to answer the pleading slave at his feet. He stood upright, studying the faces of the other slaves who were gathered to watch. He saw the new fear in their eyes and knew he had succeeded. It would be some time before any one of them dared to disobey him again.

"Everyone back to your quarters. No one," this he addressed to the guards, afraid that they might be tempted to help the slave at the post, "is to go near him for the rest of the night."

Leaning close to Hamo once more, he whispered, "Let's see if you can last the night out here."

Satisfied, he walked away, as the crowd dispersed.

Hamo was left alone, sobbing, sagging weakly against the post. The cold proved to be a mercy, for it did not take long before the pain began to dull with numbness and his blood froze. His own cries lessened as the pain did and, as the sun set, he finally grew quiet. Adrenaline forced him to stay awake, forced him to catch every sound that carried across the air.

The darkness grew deeper, but even in the darkness he could make out the dark red spots of blood that were splattered in the snow around him.

His blood.

Those blood spots would be like a beacon fire to every predator within miles, drawing them to him. He knew now why the post had been placed so far from the rest of the camp. Wild animals would not hesitate to come out of the woods to devour any victim left here. The thought was sickening. Every sound became a wolf or mountain lion in his mind, preparing to pounce. It was this mental anguish, as much as the physical pain, that made it so horrible.

The worst part was that his back was to the woods and his face was pressed, unmovable, to one side. He would not be able to see what approached him, he could only hear it and wait for the savage teeth to tear him apart.

Hamo shifted, testing the strength of the chains against his own, and whimpered as the fiery pain returned.

He had no idea how much time had passed when he first heard the soft crunch of snow beneath the feet of an animal creeping up behind him and to his blind side. His breath came in short, harsh gasps as he realized that it was not just an overactive imagination but a real, living thing that was creeping up on him. Terror, heightened by his own helplessness, coursed through him. He could not even try to fight off the attack of this wild animal.

It was such an awful way to die, such a lonely, painful, gruesome way to die. So far from home. So far from anyone who cared.

He could hear the creature's heavy breathing close to his ear and a primal scream rose in his throat as his body instinctively, uselessly, pulled against the restraining chains once more, sending spasms of renewed pain through him. The pain didn't matter. All that mattered was escaping this monstrous end.

A huge, calloused hand clamped over his mouth before the scream had a chance to escape him. Hamo stiffened, drawing in a ragged breath against the warm hand. And he heard a voice in his ear.

"Stay quiet," it whispered.

Hamo could see nothing of the person beside him but at the sound of the voice he stopped trying to pull against the chains and the hand lifted away. He felt the chains holding his wrists on the opposite side of the post lift up, pulling his arms painfully tight along the sides of the post.

There was a strong jerk on them that jarred his entire body and made him moan, but then his arms went slack and fell to his sides and the cramped, stiff muscles ached in protest.

He slid forward, down the rough wood of the post until he felt strong arms lifting him. Then a wave of blackness overcame him, and he knew nothing more.

Hamo woke up with a strangled cry. He was sitting backward in a chair, his bare chest leaning forward against the hard, wooden back of it. A pillow was tucked between the top of the chair back and his head, making it slightly more comfortable than it would otherwise have been. His hands, resting on the chair between his legs, were still in irons, the heavy chains carefully set so that they would not pull on his wrists.

There was a fireplace only a few feet from him, and the fire in it had been recently built up and was burning brightly, the flames flickering and dancing with the shadows.

With alarm, Hamo realized he had no idea where he was. He was not alone anymore. Someone else shared the room with him. He could hear their breathing and sense their presence behind his back, but when he tried to lift his head, he almost passed out again with the pain.

Whoever it was behind him moved close, and Hamo writhed, shrieking, in his chair as a cool, wet cloth brushed across one of the stripes on his back. The warmth of the fire had driven off the numbness caused by the cold, and the more awake Hamo became the worse the pain got.

"Stop. Please, stop," he cried out to the invisible person, his voice thick and feeble.

He tried to pull away from the hand that was causing him such agony, but the movement just made it worse, and he nearly fell out of the chair. Strong hands caught him and held him in place. He bit down so hard on his lip that he tasted blood in his mouth, but even so a whimper of agony escaped him.

He was supposed to be dying. Why couldn't they at least leave him alone to do that? Why did they have to draw out and prolong his agony? It must be Forbes, Hamo thought. Forbes was the only one who would do such a thing.

When Drogo's face came into his limited line of vision, Hamo's fear fell away into confusion. The big man was holding something in his hands and bringing it towards Hamo's face. It was a cup, Hamo saw.

Drogo slid one hand under Hamo's cheek and lifted his face up enough so that he could drink its contents. That movement alone brought more stinging tears to Hamo's eyes. As the bitter, burning liquid touched Hamo's tongue, he spluttered and coughed it out. The action sent shards of pain down his back, and he cried out again.

"Swallow it. It will help," Drogo spoke softly, in a tone Hamo had never heard him use before.

Hamo tried again, this time managing to get the liquid down. It felt warm all the down as he swallowed it and in a few moments the pain began to recede and melt away from his consciousness. It was still there, but not like it had been, not in the debilitating, tormenting way it had been.

Drogo waited until he saw the boy's face relax a little before he again brought the cold washcloth up against his shredded back. This time there was only a slight whimper from the boy, but he did not fight or pull away. Carefully, painstakingly, Drogo washed each laceration. He shook his head in disgust as he noticed how they wrapped all the way around the boy's stomach and chest, and even his arms. Forbes had been thorough. He always was.

The sound of the smelter door opening grabbed Drogo's attention. The boy did not appear to hear it, his eyes still half shut. He did, however, hear when an all too familiar voice called Drogo's name a moment later. His dark eyes, now wide open, flitted around the room in fright before coming to rest on Drogo.

"Please... please... don't let... him take me. Drogo?" He was starting to cry. Drogo could see the tears welling up in his eyes and his lip quivering. "Don't let him hurt me anymore."

"Forbes will not touch you," he said quietly, then walked out the door.

Hamo only heard the first part of the conversation.

"Where's the slave, Drogo?" Forbes' voice carried through the thin walls.

"With me," Drogo spoke as low and soft as ever.

"You're interfering with my job, Drogo. I have to maintain discipline over these slaves, and I have to punish them to do that."

"You did punish him."

"I wasn't done. I need to make an example out of him, show the others what they can expect if they disobey."

"He is my slave. You do not get to kill my slave."

Hamo would have cringed at the idea of belonging to anyone at any other time, but at that moment belonging seemed like a wonderful thing. Drogo moved away from his quarters and closer to Forbes so Hamo could not catch the rest of their words no matter how he tried.

"And what do you think will happen with the other slaves when they see that you interfered?" Forbes' face was red with fury, his lips pressed together in a thin line, tight line.

"The other slaves will be just fine. They already listen to you."

"You went against my orders. I'll be sure to inform Lord Bayner of your actions."

"You can tell him why he has to find someone else to do my job."

Forbes said nothing. Drogo was the best man in the country when it came to iron working, he knew, and Lord Bayner would not hesitate to give him the life of an insignificant slave to keep him happy and useful. Still, Forbes pressed on.

"He disobeyed me. And everyone saw it."

"He did nothing to deserve that death."

"You're going soft, Drogo." Forbes let out a short bark of laughter, shaking his head. "I've killed slaves like this before and it's never bothered you."

"It did this time."

"Why now? Does it remind you too much of home?" Forbes narrowed his eyes, watching for the slightest change in Drogo's face but he was disappointed to find none.

"That is no concern of yours."

"Fine. But he doesn't get out of work for this. It's his fault I had to punish him. I want him back to work first thing tomorrow. I'll be sure to come by and..."

Forbes got no further as an incredibly massive and powerful hand gripped the front of his shirt and twisted it around his throat. Drogo's face was only centimeters from his own and the giant of a man did not need to raise his voice at all.

"He is my slave, working in my smelter. I decide when he goes back to work, not you. If you lay another hand on him, Lord Bayner will have to find another murderer to put in your place."

Forbes pulled away from Drogo's hand and took a moment to recover his breath and his dignity. Straightening his clothes, he studied Drogo before deciding that continuing the argument was pointless.

"I'll take this up with him," he called over his shoulder as he left the smelter.

Hamo, unable to move from his chair in the other room, had strained his ears to catch some part of their final conversation but had been unable to. There was nothing very brave about the way he was feeling at the moment. He had a horrible fear that when the door opened again it would be Forbes, not

Drogo, and that he would be dragged back out to the post and his fear and torment would start all over again. He was aware that he was trembling again, and he was a little ashamed of himself, but the terror and pain he had experienced out there was like nothing he had ever known before.

He nearly wept in relief when Drogo reentered the room alone, his face as placid as ever. He said nothing to Hamo but went back to cleaning his wounds.

After several minutes of silence, Drogo sat back to inspect his work. The boy's back was as clean as he could get it and the blood was already beginning to congeal. He would have to put something on it and clean it often for the next few days to keep it from getting infected. It would be many days before he was fit to go back to work. Drogo sighed. It would be many days before he was able even to return to the slaves' quarters. The only thing Drogo could do was keep him up here in his own room.

He stood up and pulled the blankets down on his own bed. Turning again towards his young slave, Drogo remembered something he had thought of earlier.

"What's your name, boy?"

"What?" Hamo tried to twist around to see his face and grimaced.

"I said, what's your name? I want to know your name."

"Oh." He suddenly sounded so tired, so weak. "It's Hamo."

"Hamo," Drogo repeated it quietly, committing it to his memory. "Well, Hamo, you are safe here tonight."

Hamo had never realized just how nice it was to be spoken to by name. It was one of the most comforting things he had ever heard.

Much later, Drogo sat in a chair near his own bed, watching the sleeping figure on it. He had laid Hamo on the bed more than an hour ago, after making him drink more of the pain numbing liquid. Despite the drink, Hamo was sleeping fitfully, crying out often in his sleep and trying to toss and turn. The drink might numb his body, but there was nothing Drogo could give him to take away the tormenting fear of a few hours ago. It was clearly still vivid in the boy's mind, making his sleep restless.

Hamo had not even been aware of being moved to the bed by Drogo. He sat as quietly as he could while Drogo put the same ointment he used on him earlier in the woods, and then wrapped thick, soft bandages around his entire torso.

By the time the big man finished his work, Hamo was close to fading into oblivion. He swallowed the contents of the cup Drogo put to his lips, and then didn't remember anything else.

He was bewildered when he awoke later and found himself lying on his stomach on an actual bed. There was a blanket over him as well, and with the help of the fire, he was comfortably warm, a feeling he hadn't experienced in weeks. He tried to push himself up on his elbow, but the movement awakened a monstrous pain, and a big, calloused hand gently held him still. He looked up to see Drogo bending over him, another cup in his hand.

"Drogo? Where am I?" Hamo managed to speak.

His dreams, or rather, nightmares disoriented him, and he could not sort out what had really happened and what belonged to his imagination.

"You are in my quarters. You're staying here for now," Drogo answered.

"Oh. You're real then? You really saved me?" His dark eyes searched Drogo's questioningly.

"Yes. I saved you. Drink this and go back to sleep."

Hamo obeyed, swallowing with a grimace, and started to drift away again. Suddenly his eyes snapped open again, and his breathing quickened as he looked about the room.

"Is he coming to take me? Is he going to hurt me again?" he asked, frightened once more.

"No. Forbes isn't going to hurt you anymore. Go to sleep, Hamo."

Throughout the long hours of the night, Drogo kept watch over his young slave. He lost count of the number of times the boy woke up gasping or sobbing from some horror in his dreams. He ignored his pleas when he woke in such pain that he begged Drogo to just let him die.

Forbes had been right when he had said it never bothered Drogo before when he had punished a slave, and Drogo had seen him punish many slaves.

He detested men like Forbes and Lord Bayner, he always had. They hurt for the pleasure of watching pain. They hurt because it was the only way they could control people. Drogo had thought he kept himself above that.

Until that night in the mountain.

Until his own whip had cut a deep gash on Hamo's startled face. He had struck him for no other reason than that he was annoyed at being awoken. And that was exactly the sort of thing Forbes would have done.

Drogo had spent his entire life simply going along with where others led, content to live and let live. Tonight, however, he was ashamed of himself. Ashamed that he had sat by and watched and done nothing. Ashamed that the boy in front of him had become nothing but a piece of property to him, worth nothing but the work he had been able to produce.

Chapter 10

FOR FOUR DAYS, HAMO DID not leave Drogo's bed. If he had been fully conscious at any point, he would have felt bad that Drogo no longer had his bed to sleep in. But for those four days Drogo never let him wake up fully. When he started to, Drogo would make him drink more of the bitter tasting beverage, and he would go quietly back to sleep. He was not even aware of how much time had passed until he asked Drogo.

It was on the fifth day since his flogging, that Drogo helped him sit up, propped up backwards in a chair again. Hamo leaned weakly against the wooden back, unable to hold himself upright. This was the first chance Hamo had to really look around the home that had become his refuge.

It was a single, large room with bed, table, chairs, and stove all fitted into the space. Living alone, Drogo didn't need to bother with having separate rooms for anything. It was neat, and tidy, and mostly bare. No decoration of any sort was visible, no clue into the life of this strange master who had saved Hamo's own.

Hamo studied Drogo for a while as the man stood, with his back to him, searching for something. Drogo's size was magnified by the confined space, and his head very nearly brushed the low ceiling.

Hamo was still terribly confused by his actions. Drogo had simply walked away from Hamo, shaking his head, when they were preparing to drag him away for the flogging. Hamo had been sure then that that was the last he would ever see of the man. He had hoped, briefly, that he would intervene, but instead Drogo ignored him. Hamo knew that, although every other man, guard and slave alike, had gathered to witness his punishment, Drogo had not. He had apparently stayed up here in the smelter.

Now, here he was, alive and thanks entirely to this strange man. He had only fleeting memories of the previous four days, but through all of them Drogo had been something of a rock in a sea of fear and pain. In the bits and pieces of the previous four days that he did remember he knew Drogo had always been right next to him, calming him, comforting him. He wondered if he had left his side at all. He couldn't remember waking up one time to find him gone.

Drogo came over to the table with a tool in his hand. Reaching out he took one of Hamo's arms and carefully set it on the table, causing a brief grimace to flash across Hamo's face.

The chains that held him to the post were still locked about his wrists, and Hamo realized for the first time since his rescue that Drogo must have pulled them completely out of the wood.

Now, the iron smith set to work filing away the iron band. Hamo watched him, watched as the file bit into the metal making a funny rasping sound. The room was quiet, aside from the sound of metal grating against metal.

"Drogo?" Hamo started tentatively, glancing up at his master. In the months he had worked for Drogo, the man never spoke except when necessary, and Hamo never tried to start a conversation. He hesitated now, not sure if he should go on. Drogo grunted noncommittally in reply but did not look up. "Why did you do it?"

"Do what?"

"Why did you save me? Why didn't you just leave me to die like Forbes wanted?"

"You didn't deserve to die that way."

"Oh." Hamo looked down again, watching the file as it bit into the metal band, confusion written all over his still pale face. Drogo's answer wasn't much of an answer.

"I should never have helped him," Hamo gave up on getting anything more out of Drogo and spoke the words under his breath to himself.

"Should never have helped who?" Drogo had surprisingly keen ears.

Hamo looked up, anger replacing the confusion of a moment before on his face. "I should never have helped that man with the iron. All he's ever done for me is make my life miserable and if I hadn't tried to help him none of this would have happened."

"Hmm." Drogo nodded slowly. He thought he understood the boy. He remembered him coming in with a red bruise on his face one day and when Drogo chastised him for running afoul with Forbes, the boy told him it wasn't Forbes that gave it to him. Drogo guessed that the culprit was none other than the man Hamo had very nearly died for. "Then why did you help him?"

"I don't know. I just...I didn't realize it was him, at first. I just saw that he couldn't lift it, and it made sense to help him. I shouldn't have done it." Hamo was staring at the table again, reliving the horrifying moment when Forbes condemned him. "I wasn't even strong enough to help him, anyway."

"Hamo, don't ever say that again." Hamo was startled by the amount of conviction in Drogo's soft voice, but the man was not done speaking. "What you did for that man was the strongest thing anyone could have done. It was the right thing to do. I wasn't strong enough to do that. I let Forbes try to kill you and I wasn't strong enough to stop him."

"You saved me. I'd be dead right now if you hadn't come for me," Hamo started to say, confused.

"After I sat up here, listening to him tear your back apart." Hamo shuddered as Drogo spoke. The pain was still very, very present and the memory of being chained, helpless, to that post while Forbes had done his worst was fresh. "I should never have let him do that, but I was too weak to stop him. So don't you ever sell yourself short and tell yourself that you're not strong enough. I have never seen someone else strong enough to do what you did."

It was the most Hamo had ever heard Drogo say at one time, and the words were not at all what he had expected to hear. He sat in stunned silence for several seconds.

"You sound like my father," he said at last. Even as he said it, a cloud fell over his face. Father, who had promised to find him no matter what. Father, who had chosen to take money over his own son. Father, who had betrayed him.

Drogo saw the change in his countenance and guessed it had something to do with what Lord Bayner had told the boy earlier.

"The lord lies a lot, you know. What he told you about your father probably isn't true."

Hamo did not answer him, but instead lowered his head again to stare at the table. He did not want to talk about it, or anything else about home. It would only make him miserable. He did not need any help being miserable.

The sound of the file became the sole noise in the room again for another hour or so. Hamo tried to sit patiently, grateful that the irons would no longer be dragging on his arms, but he was still weak and holding himself upright for so long was excruciating. Even with the table supporting his arms, the damaged muscles in his back and shoulders throbbed. He wondered if they would ever work properly again.

At last, with a clatter, the last one came free. Drogo rose to his feet and came around to where Hamo was sitting.

"You've been up long enough. I need to get back to work."

As he said the words Hamo realized just how tired he was again. He allowed Drogo to help him back to the bed and was asleep almost as soon as his head lay on the pillow.

When Drogo came into the room on the tenth day after Hamo's beating, he carried a small bundle in his hands.

"Hamo, you're going back to the slaves' quarters tonight."

Hamo, who had been walking slowly back and forth trying to rebuild his strength as Drogo had suggested, turned in surprise at the abruptness of Drogo's statement. Drogo sensing it, held up his hand to forestall any questions.

"Forbes is gone for a few days. King Dorsten is dead. He didn't leave an heir. They are appointing Lord Bayner as protectorate of the throne. Forbes has gone to take part in the ceremony. He is one of the lord's most loyal followers. It's the best time for you to go back. He won't be here to take notice of you and Bertram doesn't care. When Forbes comes back, everything will be back to normal."

Hamo nodded his understanding. It made sense. He knew he could not just stay here forever, and although he dreaded the idea of going back to the slave quarters for more than one reason, it was only logical that he should slip quietly back into his old place while Forbes was away.

The truth was, though, that he was afraid of going back to the slaves' quarters. Here, in Drogo's quarters he had not had to endure the verbal abuse of his fellow slaves, nor had he shivered constantly from the cold, and best of all, no one - not Forbes, not Bertram, not any other guard - came into Drogo's room to threaten him or hit him.

Then there was the matter of his nightmares. He knew they started the night of his beating, and he assumed they were a result of the awful terror he had felt that night. He could not sleep without them coming, stealing into his subconsciousness. Drogo said nothing about them, mostly ignoring the times when his slave woke in a cold sweat, gasping and often crying out. Sometimes, when the nightmares were so bad that Hamo could not sleep, he would sit next to him, talking to him until he could relax again and sleep.

His fellow slaves would not be so generous. It would be another black mark, another thing they could make fun of him for. Just a few more days of refuge would be so nice.

"I don't have a shirt." It was the only thing he could think of that was safe for him to say. "They ripped mine up when they flogged me, and I don't know where it is."

Drogo actually smiled. It occurred to Hamo that he had never seen the man smile before. He wasn't sure what there was to smile about. It was still very much winter, and he couldn't go around in the snow only half dressed.

"I know. Take this." Drogo held out the bundle he'd been holding.

Hamo thought at first it was one of his, which would make it ridiculously big for him. He changed his mind as he pulled it on, and realized that, although it was too large for him, it was nowhere near big enough for Drogo.

"Where did you get this?"

"Never mind. The others are just getting back. Now go." Drogo waved him toward the door.

Hamo started toward the door, moving carefully. His back was still sore, and even though Drogo made him get up and move around, walking was both difficult and painful. As he reached the door, he stopped and turned around.

"Thank you, Drogo. For the shirt, and for taking care of me, and for saving my life, and... well, just, thank you," he studied the floor at his feet while he spoke, but when he looked up, he saw Drogo was smiling again.

S. T. Hobbs

The other slaves were already inside when Hamo came through the door. With practiced control, he kept his head down, his face hidden, from them. He could guess their train of the thought. Any minute now, one of them would make some taunt about how nice it was for him to be someone's favorite, to have someone who could save him.

Still keeping his head down, Hamo realized with some confusion, and a great deal of concern, that the room had gone completely quiet at his entrance, and as he made his way back to his corner the silence continued.

Then he saw it.

Neatly folded in his old spot, was his blanket. He stared, dumbfounded, at it, not quite understanding.

Someone cleared their throat directly behind him, and Hamo turned gingerly around to see the man who had stolen his blanket, who had gone out of his way to torment him, the man he had taken a beating for, standing there.

Now that he was looking up, Hamo could see every eye in the room was on him and this man. And it wasn't animosity in their faces that he saw, it was something different, something new, something he had never seen before. It was - respect.

"I'm glad you made it. We all are." Warin held out his hand and Hamo took it, wincing and not quite stifling a cry as the man pumped it up and down almost fiercely. The man noticed the pained expression on his face and immediately looked worried. "I'm sorry, I didn't mean to hurt you. Are you alright?"

"Yes, I'm alright. It just hurts a bit still."

Hamo was embarrassed by how bad the man clearly felt, and by the fact that everyone was still staring at him. He would have been more comfortable if they had started taunting him again, he thought to himself. Or if they would just start talking among themselves, or anything other than just stare at him.

80

"I," Warin hesitated, obviously struggling with his words, "I just wanted to thank you for what you did, for...you know. If I can do anything for you, ever, you just have to ask."

"Right now, I just want to sit down. It hurts standing up," Hamo's voice sounded small in his own ears. He wasn't sure what else to do.

"Of course." The man helped him lower himself to the ground. It was more difficult than Hamo had thought it would be, and he ruefully thought about how much he was going to miss Drogo's bed, although he felt bad about kicking the man out of it and leaving him no real place to sleep.

Once he was seated, the tension in the room dispelled and everyone was talking at once. Hamo leaned his head to the side against the wall and shut his eyes. He still had such a long way to go to get his strength back. He was as bad off as when he had first arrived as a slave. Idly, he wondered how much work Drogo was going to ask of him tomorrow. His thoughts were interrupted by a voice next to him.

"You should have heard how angry Forbes was when that giant took you." Warin was laughing as he remembered how thwarted their overseer had been. Hamo wished he could smile about it too, but the memory of Forbes' wrath and how close he'd come to taking Hamo back down to the post was too fresh. "He was storming about, yelling at all the guards, asking what had happened to you. Nobody saw the iron smith get you. You were just gone."

"Did he come into the smelter looking for you?" another man asked.

"Yes, he did. But I don't really remember it." In truth, Hamo remembered it in a way he would never forget, but he did not feel like talking about it. "I just know that Drogo wouldn't let him near me."

Later, as conversation died away, and the men lay down to sleep, Hamo was thankful. The quiet of Drogo's quarters had allowed him to rest whenever he wanted, which was often. He lay face down now in the dark, mostly quiet, room trying to sort through the sudden turn of events. He allowed himself a small smile as he thought about his new friend. For the first time since his beating, Hamo didn't regret his actions. Drogo had been right. The pain would eventually go away, the friendship and camaraderie would not.

Hamo was well aware of when Forbes returned to the mining camp a few days later. He watched him ride in from a distance. Drogo, it appeared, had been right, though.

For the first several days, Forbes did not seek Hamo out, and the only time Hamo saw him was when he was with the other slaves, overseeing them. Even at a distance, Hamo's reaction to the man was fear, and he hated himself for it.

Drogo promised him he was safe, that Forbes would not lay a hand on him again. Hamo wanted to believe, did believe him - at least he thought he did. Then he would hear Forbes' voice in the distance or see him lash out at one of the other slaves, and Hamo would find himself shaking uncontrollably again, a sick feeling in the pit of his stomach. It did not help that his nightmares still came, and that Forbes' face and voice featured heavily in those.

It happened when Hamo had stepped outside the smelter for a drink of water from the water barrel. Drogo still would not let him do any hard work, such as bringing in stacks of wood for the fire, and Hamo was glad of that. Even two and a half weeks after his flogging, some of the deeper lacerations were not fully healed.

He heard the footsteps behind him as he turned to go back inside, and felt a heavy hand clamp on his shoulder, where one of the worst wounds was. He moaned softly as the hand squeezed down on it and twisted it, forcing him to turn around. For one second, Hamo could have sworn he was in one of his nightmares, for there, only inches from his own face, was the malicious sneer of Forbes.

"I'm so glad to see you up and about, boy. I was really worried you weren't going to make it." His voice left little doubt that the opposite was true.

Forbes looked him up and down, noticed the slight trembling that Hamo couldn't stop, and saw the way his face had blanched. Then Forbes noticed something else, a dark shadow just inside the doorway, and his hand left the spot where it had been digging into Hamo's shoulder. Hamo let out a breath he had not realized he was holding as he saw Forbes turn to go.

"Oh, by the way, Lord Bayner wanted me to offer you his condolences," he said it as if it were an afterthought. "It seems your father was found dead some time ago, attacked by bandits it seems. Such a pity, he could have been so much more useful to us."

Hamo let out an involuntary gasp and stepped back away from the man, shaking his head in disbelief. "No. No. That's not true. It can't be. He's not."

"Of course, Lord Bayner also told me he didn't want you back anyway. Said he needed the money more, or something like that." Forbes cast one more look at the dark shadow in the doorway and decided he had taken enough revenge for the day. He could see the effect his words were having on the boy, and that was almost better than listening to him being torn apart by wild animals. It was made even more so when he heard the small voice behind him as he walked away.

"I hate you," Hamo whispered.

Forbes smiled to himself.

Drogo was back at work when Hamo went inside, so Hamo had no idea that the man's presence was what made Forbes stop. Nor did he know that Drogo had heard what Forbes told him about his father.

"Go get some rest, Hamo," Drogo spoke without looking up. There was nothing he could say that would help Hamo right now, and the best he could offer him was the solitude to grieve in.

Chapter 11

SPRING BROUGHT WITH IT a kaleidoscope of colors in the mountains. Before the snow was even fully melted, spring flowers were pushing their way up through the soil and showing their colors off to the whole world. Songbirds resumed their choruses, and the mountains came alive with warmth and sunlight. Spring marked the end of a full year that Hamo had spent here in this place.

It was still dark out, but Hamo was wide awake. Another nightmare had dragged him from his sleep, gasping and sweating and with his heart pounding. Most days he would have tried to go back to sleep since rest was such a precious commodity. This morning though, he had pulled himself up so that he was sitting, back against the wall, lost in his own thoughts.

Drogo had told him that they were going back up the mountain today. The winter supply of wood they had cut and hauled down was all but gone. There was so little cause for happiness as a slave that just the thought of being away from the main camp for a few days was remarkably pleasant. It broke up the drudgery of routine that filled each day.

Hamo rubbed the old injury in his shoulder unconsciously. It had become such a habit, especially after his flogging. He couldn't be quite sure, but he thought Forbes must have known about the injury because that was where he had used his whip the most. Hamo let out a rather heavy sigh as he thought about it and was startled to hear a voice whisper across to him.

"You alright?" It was Warin, the man who had once been his worst enemy in this room. Warin got up from where he was laying and sat down next to Hamo. "Heard you wake up."

"Sorry. I thought I was quiet."

Hamo was glad that the man no longer bullied him, but he did wish that the man did not feel so incredibly responsible for him now. From the day he had moved back into the slave quarters, the man had gone out of his way to help him. At first, Hamo was grateful for it. Warin had brought his food to him, and anything else he needed so that he would not have to get up and down. Now that he was fully recovered, the help just embarrassed him.

"You know, Hamo, you're the only one who has ever left this camp. The rest of us, we go up to the mine and we come back here," Warin whispered so quietly that Hamo was having a hard time understanding him. "You're going out again, aren't you?"

Hamo nodded. "We're leaving today."

Had it been a few months ago, he would have expected some verbal stab about how he was treated better than everyone else, but now? He was not sure where Warin was going with it.

"What do you think the chances are that someone could make it out of here? Run away, and actually get back home."

"I don't know," Hamo spoke doubtfully, knowing that Warin was hanging on his every word. "Not alone, I don't think, or without weapons. The mountains really are full of wild animals. You'd need to keep a fire going at night, but that would sort of give you away. And we don't even know where we are, remember? They made sure of that when they brought us here."

"Yes, they did. But has it ever occurred to you that the wagons leave with the iron every few days, and they always go the same direction? Now, my guess is, they take that metal straight to Dorsten. It must be what they use for their army. If someone were to, say, run away, all they would have to do is follow that direction generally and eventually it would lead out of the mountains, and I'm thinking it would lead out on the Dorstenian side. Making it home from there should be fairly easy."

"I guess so. But what about if you got caught? I'm sure Forbes has an exceptionally gruesome punishment for runaway slaves." Hamo shuddered as the memory of his own punishment filled his mind. "He seems to enjoy that sort of thing."

"Guess whoever ran away would just have to not get caught," Warin spoke absently, and Hamo guessed he was processing what he had said, trying to think of a plan.

"Warin, don't do it. They'll catch you, and if they don't, the animals will. It's not worth it."

"And this is? We're nothing to these people. You know what I've heard? I've heard Forbes is a murderer. He was supposed to hang, but Lord Bayner gave him a chance to serve him. That's who we're working for. And I don't want to spend the rest of my life here, slaving away for men who could care less whether I lived or died. I have a wife I want to get back to. It's not going to happen if I don't make it happen."

"What if the war ends? What if they finally sign a truce and we're released?"

"Hamo, how old are you?"

"Sixteen. What does that have to do with it?"

"In your sixteen years, has there ever been peace?"

"Well, no. I guess not." A wave of hopelessness came over Hamo as he took in Warin's point. He was right. There was no end to this war, and so there would be no end to their slavery. "I don't know, Warin, I just don't have a good feeling about it. I don't think you'd make it."

Warin opened his mouth to answer but stopped when he realized that others in the room were stirring. He held his finger to his lips briefly and Hamo acknowledged him with a small nod. He could not stop Warin from trying to escape, but he could keep quiet about it and give him the best chance possible.

Hamo, all thoughts of Warin and his plan gone now, was leading the pack horse up the mountain again, following Drogo and the team pulling a dray this time. Despite his situation, Hamo was enjoying himself. The wooded side of the mountain was bursting with new life and even the placid pack horse kept its head up and its ears perked, enjoying the beauty and freshness of the day. Having grown up near the seaside, Hamo had never seen the wildflowers and trees that made their home here.

He was glad the pack horse had no mind of its own and was more than content to follow the other two, because it freed him from having to guide it and he could instead pay attention to the very interesting forest around him. It also allowed him to let his mind wander.

Hamo didn't realize how much he was daydreaming, until he heard a quiet cough coming from the left of him. His head snapped around to find Drogo standing, arms folded across his chest, eyebrows raised, watching him. He had missed something. In consternation, he tried to recall what had just happened. When he failed, he gave Drogo a little disheartened shrug.

"I said, we're going to stop here for now." Apparently, Drogo had spoken to him, but he had not heard it.

"Sorry. I wasn't paying attention."

He scuffed the ground with a foot. He had not meant to ignore Drogo. He was not afraid of him, not since Drogo had saved him and nursed him back to life. It was impossible to be afraid of the man he owed his life to. Which was why he felt bad now. He was disappointing Drogo, and he really did not want to.

"Clearly." Drogo maintained his stern gaze for another second before turning to walk away toward a small level clearing. As soon as his back was turned to Hamo, a small smile played at the corners of his mouth, and he called back over his shoulder. "It's alright, Hamo, you can relax." His smile grew wider when he heard Hamo let out a sigh of relief.

Hamo went straight to work setting up camp, in order to make up for his moment of negligence. This time when he went to fasten the high line for the horses, Drogo stopped him.

"I'll do it. You're too small to pull it tight enough." Drogo had not forgotten the incident with the horses, either.

By the time the sun was setting, a roaring fire was going and Hamo was just finishing cleaning their dishes from supper out in the nearby creek. Nighttime brought the one truly bad memory he had of Drogo to mind. It had been on their first night in the woods last fall that Drogo had hit him for the first and only time. He had also kept him chained to a tree.

Hamo was as confident as he could be that Drogo would not hit him again, but it only seemed reasonable that Drogo would keep him chained up still. He was, after all, still a slave. His assumption was confirmed when he came back up to their tent and saw the chain secured around the tree, and the other end in Drogo's hand.

Resigned, he held out his arm, his head lowered so that Drogo could not see the humiliated flush that rose to his cheeks. He waited for several seconds but did not feel the familiar clamp of the iron around his wrist. Slowly, he raised his eyes while keeping his head down and saw Drogo watching him, a strange expression on his face.

"Are you going to run away?" Drogo finally spoke.

"No," Hamo shook his head.

"Good. You take the first watch." Drogo dropped the shackle to the ground and moved to his side of the tent. "Keep the fire big. And Hamo?"

"Yes?"

"Do not wake me up for anything foolish."

"Yes sir," Hamo acknowledged. "Thank you, Drogo."

The week passed far quicker than Hamo wanted it to. The weather was pleasant, the work different from his normal day to day labors, and alone with Drogo the fear that stalked him disappeared - in the daylight, at least. Nights were as bad as ever.

On the last night, Hamo was screaming, thrashing about, trying to fend off the wolves that were tearing at him. He could hear their howls, which sounded strangely like Forbes' laugh. In the distance, Father was standing by watching, watching, and all the while Hamo was yelling for him to help. He held his hand up to push one large, snarling mouth away, but it wouldn't go away. It hung onto his arm, shaking it back and forth. And the snarling growls morphed into human words.

"Wake up, Hamo, wake up. It's just a dream."

His eyes flew open at the sound of the voice, and he sat upright. He was panting heavily and felt a cold clammy sweat on the palms of his clenched hands. His eyes frantically searched for some sign of the wolves he was so sure had just been there, but the only thing he could see was Drogo sitting in front of him, his massive hand still holding Hamo's arm.

"Still having nightmares?" Drogo's deep voice helped bring him back to reality. Hamo, his mouth dry, just nodded. Drogo knew better than anyone else how terrible his dreams could be.

"There's nothing out there. Nothing's going to hurt you." Drogo, sure that Hamo was fully awake now, went back to his spot by the fire to keep watch. He looked over in mild surprise when Hamo moved over to join him.

"I can't go back to sleep just yet. Do you want to get some more rest before morning?"

Instead of going back into their tent to sleep, Drogo just leaned back against the thick tree trunk behind him and closed his eyes.

"Let me know when you're ready to go back to sleep."

Hamo nodded, staring intently into the glowing flames of the fire. His racing heart started to slow, and his breath evened out, but he was still unable to even consider going back to sleep.

After a minute or two he picked up a long stick and stabbed at the embers, sending a shower of sparks flying upwards into the darkness. Why did he have to have that dream tonight? It was one of the few good nights he had to look forward to, out in the fresh air, away from the smelter and from Forbes. Why did he have to dream about Father like that? He knew he cried out in his sleep, and he suspected he had called out Father's name.

Ever since Forbes had told him that Father was dead Hamo had been at a loss. Drogo told him not to believe everything he was told by those men, but what if it were true? What if Father really had decided that he had failed, that somehow, he wasn't good enough, and that money would be more useful? The thought was unbearable, unlivable.

But there were times when he convinced himself that it must be true. And when he believed it, Hamo was very, very angry with Father. He wanted to hate Father for that, but he missed him so much. And the thought that he was dead, that Hamo would never again see him even if he managed to get free of this dreadful place was devastating.

Father had been everything to him. He had looked up to him his entire life. Father, who always did the right thing, no matter how difficult it was. It was what had made him a good leader, it was what made people trust him. Hamo had wanted to be like that and had spent most of his life trying to live up to his father's reputation. Hamo could not imagine life without Father.

Lost in his own miserable thoughts, Hamo jabbed the stick into the glowing embers of the fire harder and harder, a little crease in his forehead as he thought about it. He hoped Forbes was lying, he needed Forbes to be lying. Of course, Forbes was lying. He just wanted to hurt Hamo. That was all. Hamo hated that man so much. Hated him for what he had done. Hated him more than he hated Lord Bayner. And that hatred, so dark and wild, was terrifying.

"If you keep poking that much harder, you might just push the whole fire over." Hamo jumped at the sound of Drogo's voice. He had almost forgotten that someone else was there. "Is there a reason you're doing that?"

"No. Not really. I was just - thinking."

Drogo might treat him more like a person than he used to, but Hamo was pretty sure slaves were not supposed to discuss personal matters with their masters.

"Hamo, I'm sorry about your father."

Hamo cringed inwardly. So, he had called for Father out loud.

"It's not your fault. I don't even know if Forbes or Lord Bayner were telling the truth."

"Hmmm." Drogo moved next to Hamo, and reaching over, took the stick out of his hand. "Your father, he was a good man?"

"Yes," Hamo answered emphatically, pulling his knees up to his chest and wrapping his arms around them. "Of course, he is...was. I wanted to be just like him."

"Then why would you believe what Lord Bayner said about him?"

"I don't, usually. It's just, sometimes in my nightmares, I see him there. And I ask him for help, and he just stands there."

Drogo said nothing and Hamo continued, the burden of his loneliness forcing the words out.

"He made me a promise, you know. When we were fighting. I had to kill someone," Hamo spoke the words softly, almost afraid to acknowledge the memory, "I didn't want to, but it all happened so fast. And he was laying there dying in front of me and aside from us, who were his enemies, he was all alone. And I told Father that was the only thing I was scared of. Dying alone, you know. And he made me a promise. He told me I wouldn't have to die alone. He told me he would come find me wherever I was. Then he was wounded, and they took him back to try to save him. And that was the last time I saw him. And I miss him so much. I miss when he used to come home, and when he would take me hunting with him and all the things we used to do together. He always knew what to do. I just wish I could have had the chance to say goodbye."

Hamo's hands found another stick and he resumed his vicious, mindless stabbing of the fire as the words tumbled out. He stopped speaking now, afraid that he said far too much, afraid that if he said any more, he would lose control of his very carefully checked emotions. Drogo did not want to hear about how homesick and lonely his slave was.

"Can you stop doing that?" Drogo reached over and pulled the second stick from Hamo's hand. "You're spooking the horses."

"Sorry," Hamo mumbled.

"Hamo, I don't know if what those men told you about your father is true or not. I do know they both lie a lot. And for whatever reason, they both seem to hate you more than the other slaves we have," Drogo's voice was slow, measured, as if he were carefully weighing each word before he said it.

"It's because my father is the Captain of the Royal Guard. I was supposed to be ransomed, but King Dival didn't want to pay for me," Hamo interrupted.

"That explains why they brought you here."

"What?"

"Did it ever occur to you that you are the only one your age here, that you're the smallest, weakest slave at the mining camp." Drogo did not say the words unkindly.

"All the time. Every time Forbes walks by."

"It's not because others weren't captured. Lord Bayner made a deal with the mercenaries that he hired. He had to turn over half of our prisoners as slaves to them. Being Lord Bayner, he made sure it was the ones of least value to anyone."

"It should have been me?" Understanding dawned in Hamo's dark eyes. "I would have been sent north with the others."

"Yes. You would be dead by now if you had been. Most of their slaves are. Dead or sold off to who knows where in their slave markets."

Before Hamo could say another word, a faint sound reached his ears. He rose to his knees, trying to peer out into the blackness beyond the fire. It sounded like - a scream.

It had come from far away, carried by the night air, but Hamo was sure he had heard it. He looked at Drogo, his dark eyes searching for an answer. Drogo shrugged. He had heard it too but had no better idea than Hamo did as to its source. Another sound reached them a moment later, howling.

"Wolves," Drogo said.

"But the first sound, that was a person. Wasn't it?"

"Yes. It was." Drogo had a better sense of direction then Hamo and was pretty sure now where that sound had come from now. "Hamo, start getting our things together."

Hamo got up, realizing as he did so, that dawn was not far off. Already the blackness was less heavy and more like a gray. He glanced back at Drogo, still sitting by the fire staring off into the distance. Drogo knew something, he was sure of it. Hamo hurried to tie everything in bundles. The dray they had loaded the night before in preparation of their return trip today. All that remained for them to do was load the pack horse and harness the team up.

"Drogo, it's all ready." He came up about half an hour later. In all that time Drogo had not moved from his spot by the fire.

"Good. Let's go. And Hamo?"

"Yes?"

"Never mind." Drogo shook his head as though to shake the thought away.

They were well on their way by the time the sun was well and truly up, Drogo leading the way and Hamo following with the pack horse. The closer they got to the valley with the camp, the gloomier the sky got. Gray thunderclouds piled over the tips of the distant mountains.

"Best hurry if we're to get down before that hits. You do not want to be stuck in the mountains when a spring storm hits," Drogo said as he urged the horses on a little faster.

As the trees thinned out near the foot of the mountain, Hamo could hear the first roll of thunder and felt the first few drops of rain fall. By the time they were crossing the open field to the mining camp, the rain was a deluge. It came down in walls, so that Hamo could only see a few feet in front of him.

Head bent down against the rain and wind that was picking up, he followed Drogo to the stable where the teams of horses were kept. Normally, he would not have been allowed anywhere near the horses, presumably to prevent him trying to use one to escape on, but today Drogo told him to come in with the pack horse.

"What's he doing in here?" The voice made Hamo look up from where he was undoing the pack saddle on the little horse and made his fingers tremble as they worked the leather straps.

"Helping me." Drogo did not bother to look up. He already knew who the speaker was.

"He's not supposed to be in here, Drogo, and you know that. Besides, I need him for the rest of the day." Forbes stepped between Drogo and Hamo.

"He's done working for the day," Drogo's voice became very guarded.

"No. See, we've had something come up while you were gone. One of the slaves decided he could run away. Naturally, he was caught and punished." Forbes was watching Hamo's face closely as he spoke and was rewarded by the pained look of horror that crossed it. "He was from your building. A friend, perhaps?" Then he turned back to Drogo, "Anyway, as always, everyone here had to witness his punishment. Everyone that is, except your slave. I think it's only fitting he should have some part in it. Besides, I can't spare anyone from the mines."

Drogo studied the man for a moment before he spoke. "What do you need him to do?"

"What's left of the runaway needs buried. He's going to do that." He pointed at Hamo as he spoke.

Drogo started to speak, started to protest, when Hamo interrupted him. "I'll do it." The anger in his voice was barely controlled, pushed down to just beneath the surface. His friend, for he was sure it was Warin, was dead because of this monster in front of him. The least he could do was give him a decent burial, a final resting place away from the devouring mouths of predators.

"Of course, you'll do it. You don't get a choice, remember? You do what you're told."

Forbes took a step toward him, but for the first time since he had met the man, Hamo did not shrink back away from him. He met his eyes, his cold, cruel eyes and this time it was Forbes who looked away as Hamo reached out to snatch the shovel he had carried in here to give him.

The clearing with the post was barely visible from the camp due to the rain, but Hamo could see a little mound next to the post as he approached. The guard who had accompanied him down here to make sure he didn't run away was in a foul mood for having received such an assignment in the rain and Hamo was conscious of the way the man kept fingering his short whip. At the moment, Hamo did not care. His anger was so barely controlled that he thought if the man struck him, there was a very good chance he would try to hit back.

"There. You can dig right there." The guard pointed to a spot some distance from the lifeless remains of Warin. Hamo pushed the shovel into the first bit of soft earth and began. He would be here a long time, he knew.

At first it was not too hard. The rain had softened the first few inches of earth, making it easy to shovel to the side. The deeper he went the harder his task became. The first few minutes also had the benefit of his initial wave of anger, and he pushed every ounce of strength he had into his task.

Unfortunately, such an outburst could not be sustained for long. And within a few minutes, Hamo began tiring. Despite his improved relationship with Drogo, he was still severely underfed and, having spent the entire day already working, exhausted. The guard noticed that his digging slowed and tried to hurry him along with his whip. Hamo barely felt it.

The rain also worked to make it harder. He lost his footing several times in the slippery mud. The wet wooden handle of the shovel chafed against the palms of his hands, and he knew that before long, they would be blistered up. Still, he kept digging, digging, digging. He lost track of how long he had been out here. It was dark out now, but the rain was still falling.

After a while the muddy brown earth began to swim in front of his eyes, and he knew he was pushing himself too hard, demanding too much of his body, but he couldn't stop. Not just because of the guard behind him, but for his friend. He could not leave him out here another night. His hands hurt, and if there had been any light, he would have seen a dark red stain spreading across the wooden handle. Still, he kept going. Every shovel full brought him closer to laying his friend to rest.

He was startled to find himself suddenly shoved to the ground, and three stinging blows of the whip laid on him. Then the guard was standing over him, grabbing the front of his shirt, shaking him, yelling in his face.

"I said that's enough. Bury him in it," the man shouted at him, and Hamo had the foggy impression that he must have said the same thing several times, but he had somehow missed it.

Hamo started to shake his head. It wasn't deep enough; animals would just dig it open. But the guard had had enough of standing out in the rain in the middle of the night. He pulled Hamo off the ground and drug him to where the body lay, already wrapped in a canvas.

"Put him in, now." He accompanied his words with another blow, this one across Hamo's face.

Hamo stood in front of the canvas, knowing that inside were the remains of Warin, and knowing he would have to touch it, would have to drag it across the ground to where he had opened a grave. The thought was suddenly repulsive. Even through the canvas he could tell there was very little left of his friend. His hands, bloody themselves, closed around the corners of the bloodied cloth and he began to drag it backwards.

The guard, satisfied that he was finally being obeyed, backed away to let him finish. Hamo let the bundle fall with a sickening thud into the hole. Then a horrible, uncontrollable heaving took over, and he was on his hands and knees, retching. It was worse than his first day in the smelter, when Drogo had dragged him out into the cool air. This time there would be no such relief. He felt the guard coming toward him, and tried to brace himself for a beating, but it didn't come. The man was staring down at him with something akin to pity.

"Get up. We're done."

"No... I... have... to... fin... finish. Have to... bury him," he spoke between heaving breaths.

With enormous effort his hands gripped the handle of the shovel and he braced himself against it to get up. His stomach was still churning, but he managed to scoop up the first shovelful and toss it in. Then the next, and the next, and the next. Slowly the hole filled back up, the thick mud covering all that remained of Warin.

The guard had stepped away again, after muttering just loud enough for Hamo to catch his words, "Forbes is right about you, you just don't listen."

Hamo let the shovel slip through his hands and fall to the ground. He sank to his knees, seeing nothing but the brown mound in front of him.

It was finished.

Warin was buried.

Hamo no longer had any control over himself. He was shaking, he was heaving, his head was throbbing, and his mouth could not form words, but he was finished. Warin was laid to rest.

Hamo was aware that the guard was pulling him up the slope toward the slave quarters. He tried to move his feet to keep up, but the awful shaking prevented him.

There were voices above his head, but his ears would not discern their words. Then he was shoved into his own dark quarters, out of the rain for the first time since it had started hours ago.

That was when he noticed how thoroughly drenched he was. That must be why he was shaking so hard, he thought. He felt the door close behind him, and simply sank down where he was with his back against it, letting the convulsions that racked his body take over completely.

Chapter 12

ALINA LOOKED UP FROM WHERE she was kneeling in the dirt, planting potatoes. Aldrid was running about their small yard, chasing a butterfly. Sabina was kneeling next to her, her hands covered in dirt as she helped Mother.

Having this little cottage on the outskirts of town was such a relief for Alina. It had enough yard around it that they could grow some of their own food, and it gave Aldrid a safe place to play. King Darien was certainly very different from his father. Alina no longer had to take in laundry for work.

"Are we almost done yet?" Sabina spoke up next to her. She brought a dirty hand up to her face and brushed a strand of hair away, leaving a brown streak across her cheek.

Alina smiled wearily. "Let's finish this row, and then you can go play with Al."

"Can we go play with the others?" Sabina missed having her friends from the castle to play with and had taken to playing with the neighbors' children any time Alina would allow her to.

"I suppose so. Just be careful with Al. He likes to try to do things he's not able to."

Sabina finished her row with renewed energy, spurred on by the prospect of fun. Alina watched as she jumped to her feet and wiped her hands on her clothes.

"Come on, Al. Let's go play," she called over her shoulder as she went to the gate. Aldrid hurried over, his short, little legs moving as fast as he could pump them.

Alina stared after them for a minute before going back to her work. The monthly pension she received was enough to help take care of them, but winters would be easier if they could grow and put up some of their own food, and Alina was determined to try.

Having spent most of her life in the castle, first because of her father, then because of her husband, Alina did not know much about gardening and preserving. She had everything she needed, whenever she needed it from the castle. She had not needed to give a thought as to where their food or clothes would come from. All that had changed now, though.

She finished up and went into the house to wash up before she heard a wail coming from the street. Hurrying to the still open door, Alina met Al there with Sabina racing up behind him. His little face was streaked with tears and the wailing sound was coming from him. Without a word, he flung himself into Alina's arms, his tears unabated.

"Oh Al, what's wrong with you? Are you hurt?" Alina stooped and pulled him away enough to inspect his face.

"They called me a name," Al howled.

"What did they call you?"

"They called me a... a... a," Aldrid stopped, his little face puckered up as he tried to remember the name some of the children had called him. "I forget."

"They called him a cripple," Sabina supplied.

"Oh, Al, I'm so sorry." Alina wrapped her arms around her little son. "Maybe you shouldn't play with them anymore. You either, Sabine."

"They also said something about Father." Al wanted to make sure Mother knew the full extent of the injustice done to him by the other children.

"What did they say?"

"I don't remember," he confessed. He had been too upset when they had called him a cripple and laughed at him to pay too much attention to their words afterwards.

Alina pulled him close again, her hand rubbing soothing circles on his back until his sobs quieted.

"Can I go back and play?" Sabina cut into the conversation.

"Not with those children. I don't want you playing with them anymore. That was a very mean thing for them to say to your brother."

"Oh." Sabina was disappointed. "But I was having fun. I'm sure they didn't mean anything."

"Sabina."

Sabina's head hung as she heard the warning note in Mother's voice. Without a word she shuffled into the house, pausing only long enough to stick her tongue out at Aldrid when Mother could no longer see her.

Aldrid, feeling better now that Mother had heard his complaints, was already moving on to something else. He was a busy child, even with his handicap, and never could stand to do nothing.

Chapter 13

HAMO MUST HAVE FALLEN asleep huddled against their hut's door. And someone must have gotten up and covered him with his blanket, because he knew he did not get it himself.

It was the stirring of his fellow slaves that woke him. He was still shivering, and his clothes still clung damply to him. There must not have been much night left by the time he got back. That was why the guard had been so frustrated with him. He realized that everyone in the room was looking at him, waiting for him to move, and it occurred to him that they could not leave the room until he got up.

He groaned softly as he got to his feet and moved away from the door. Every muscle in his body ached, and the chills were worse than ever. He stumbled across the room to his corner, only vaguely conscious of the way the others were looking at him. One or two of them were openly staring at him. Hamo couldn't shake the fog from his brain enough to even wonder why.

Clumsily he folded his blanket and put it on the floor in his spot, trying carefully to avoid looking at the empty space that had belonged to Warin. His head swam as he turned to leave the room, and he reached out for the wall to steady himself. He wished this infernal shaking would just stop.

The others were all gone by the time Hamo staggered out the door and made his way to the smelter. He'd missed breakfast but his stomach was too ill for food anyone.

He kept his head down, avoiding the gaze of any of the guards that might be milling around. He could not quite remember why, but he thought there was a reason that he wanted to avoid Forbes, more than usual, that is. He breathed a sigh of relief when he stepped inside the hot, semi dark smelter without running into his archenemy.

Drogo was already busy when he came in, but the big man put down his work and stared at Hamo. Hamo sagged against the wall, confused by the way Drogo was looking at him.

"What's wrong? You're staring at me like I'm a ghost."

"You look like one, Hamo." Drogo came around to where Hamo was standing, still trying to process the words he had said. "Why did you do that? I was not going to let him make you do it."

"I had to. For Warin." He wished Drogo would stop talking. It was making his head hurt. Actually, all of him hurt. He was aching all over, and shivering. He wished it would stop.

Drogo nodded slowly. He understood, but the boy looked awful. He was completely covered in mud, and his clothes were soaked, his face was ghastly white except for two very red, flushed spots on his cheeks. And he was shaking uncontrollably.

"When did you finish?"

"I don't know. Late, I think."

"You can't work."

"Please, Drogo. I have to. Forbes will..."

"Not do anything. You're sick. And," Drogo noticed Hamo's hands for the first time. He grabbed one and held it up before Hamo's eyes, "Your hands are useless."

Hamo stared stupidly at his hands, finally connecting the pain he had felt in them earlier with the fact that the skin on his palms was completely shredded. He looked from one to the other and then back up at Drogo.

"Please, Drogo," he repeated. "I want something to do."

The thought of just lying still for hours like he had to do when he was recovering from his flogging was terrifying. He did not want that much time to think, especially since the only clear thought he had been able to put together was how much he wanted to kill Forbes, and that was disturbing to him. He had never thought anything like that before.

"No. That's final."

"Drogo?" Hamo tried one more time.

Then his knees buckled, and he was on the floor, shivering again. Maybe Drogo was right, maybe he was sick. He remembered being sick like this once when he was little. He had a high fever and chills, and everything ached then, too. Only then Mother had been there to take care of him, and he did not have to worry about the dark thoughts that had filled his mind since last night. He missed Mother. He wanted her now, wanted to be taken care of by her. He could have told her about everything, and she would have listened.

"Absolutely not." Drogo lifted him up off the floor and started to help him toward his own room.

Hamo wanted to walk, tried to walk, but his legs didn't work. They were like jelly under him, and he had no command over them. He was surprised when Drogo just scooped him up in his big arms and carried him to bed.

It was warm, so warm, in bed, covered by thick, soft blankets and near the fire. Hamo did not even notice when Drogo left the room. He was asleep. For the rest of the day, he slept. When evening came, Drogo came back in from work. He went about fixing supper and built the fire back up, and all the while, Hamo slept. Drogo finally woke him up to get him to eat.

Hamo still ached all over, but his head was clearer, and the world wasn't pitching about him like the deck of a ship. And, more importantly, that awful shaking had finally stopped.

"Here. Eat." Drogo held out a bowl of soup for him. "When you're done, you can go back. Maybe tomorrow you can work again."

Hamo nodded as he held out his hands to take the bowl, noticing only then that they had bandages wrapped about them. He owed this man again, he knew. And he had no way of repaying him.

Chapter 14

MOTHER, AL'S FIGHTING AGAIN." Sabina called through the doorway.

A moment later, Aldrid stormed in, blood running down from his nose. At eight years old, he had already developed a quick temper, and had shown a great predilection for fighting.

"What started it this time?" Alina turned to face him, hands on her hips, her lips pressed together tightly.

"He hit me."

"Al hit him first," Sabina corrected.

"Sabina, stay out of it. Al, what started it?" Alina repeated. "Did you hit him first?"

"Yes. Maybe," Aldrid mumbled, holding one hand under his nose to catch the blood. "But he shouldn't have said what he did. He said I was a thief just like Father."

"Did you steal something?" This was something else that Aldrid had shown a great inclination for.

Aldrid shrugged, his sullen eyes turning to the ground.

"Al! You can't take things that don't belong to you. How many times have we been over this?" She put a hand over her eyes. Hamo had been so much easier at this age. Of course, Hamo also had his father at that age, which made a big difference. "What did you take?"

"Just this. And I was going to give it back." He held up a medallion. "It was on the ground, and no one was picking it up."

Alina might have believed him - if this was the first time. As it was, he had made a habit out of it, and he'd become quite a proficient liar. She turned to Sabina, eyebrows raised in question. Sabina just shook her head.

"I didn't see that part. I just saw when he hit the other boy, and the fight started."

"Are you telling me the truth?" She turned to Al, who was now mopping up the blood on his face with the sleeve of his shirt. "Stop doing that, I'll never get that out."

"Of course, I'm telling the truth." Al looked indignant at the thought of Mother doubting him. "I wasn't really stealing it. And he shouldn't have said that about me."

"Oh, Al." It was an expression Aldrid had heard many, many times in his short life. "What am I going to do with you? Why can't you just be more like your brother was?"

Aldrid scowled, the scar on his face growing more prominent, the way he always did when Mother brought up his dead brother. He did not even remember him, so how could she expect him to be more like him? Besides, being good hadn't helped his older brother any, had it? He died. Everyone was always telling him how brave his brother had been to try to help someone else and to die doing it. To Aldrid that didn't seem very brave, just dangerous and ultimately, useless.

He lived up to the one other name that was frequently thrown in his face much better. Father. All the neighboring children called his father a thief. So did the adults, but they usually did it while shaking their heads sadly. Yes, that was a reputation he could manage, and manage quite well. Mother was still watching him, waiting for some response.

"I'm sorry, alright," he muttered.

"I need you to be more than sorry, Al. I need you to stop taking things that don't belong to you. Now, let me see your nose." She pulled his face close to get a better look.

"I'm fine, Mother. It's just a little bit bloody."

"Look at your shirt and tell me if that's just a little bit of blood?" She looked at him, her eyes serious.

With a sigh, he gave in.

Chapter 15

HAMO WAS WALKING UP TO the smelter when he realized something was missing. He stopped a moment, studying the familiar wooden building, a puzzled look on his face.

It was the smoke.

There was no smoke.

In the three and a half years he had been a slave in this mining camp, the chimney had always been belching out its thick smoke long before he arrived for work in the morning. It had amazed him that Drogo could work as many hours as he did.

Of course, Drogo was not half starved and never had to worry about being hit with a taskmaster's whip and that had to make it easier to work, Hamo thought a little bitterly. He regretted the thought immediately. The only reason he was still alive was thanks to Drogo. Master or not, the strange giant had done everything in his power to protect Hamo.

A little unsettled by the lack of smoke, Hamo finished his short walk to the entrance and pushed the door open. Aside from the few coals still glowing from where he had banked the fire up the night before, the room was completely dark and there was no sign of Drogo.

Hamo tried to shrug off the growing feeling of alarm. Something must have come up, he told himself. He went about starting the fire in the furnace again, half expecting to see Drogo come in at any second.

When the fire was hot enough, and after three and half years Hamo was a good judge of when that was, he heard the door of Drogo's quarters creak open. In the uncertain light, Drogo moved toward the furnace.

"Hamo? Are you here already?"

"Yes. I've been here. Drogo, is everything alright?"

"It's fine. I'm fine. Just a little more tired than usual. You started the fire?"

"Yes." Hamo was watching Drogo carefully from where he was crouched on the floor, reaching for another log.

It occurred to him that Drogo was not a young man. In fact, he was aging a lot, his black hair peppered with gray, his face creased with wrinkles. A nagging seed of worry filled Hamo as he watched him slowly prepare his work for the day.

It was only the fact that Drogo was the best iron worker in the country that had allowed him to intervene on Hamo's behalf more than once. If he was not able to keep up with the work, Hamo had no doubt that he would be replaced by Lord Bayner. The lord was an efficient person, and it made sense to only have the best working for him. And Hamo did not want Drogo replaced. He did not want a different master. Another master could be cruel.

He also realized that he did not want to lose him because in the three and a half years they had worked together, Hamo had come to think of him as a friend of sorts. He had told him things he would never have dreamed of telling anyone else, except maybe Father.

Hamo made sure the fire was still good before making his way over to where Drogo was working. He stood next to him for several minutes, watching the way he added the huge chunks of iron ore into the smelt, and waited for it to slowly separate from the useless rock. Then Drogo poured off the melted iron into the casts.

"Drogo?"

"Hmm?"

"Teach me how to do that."

"What?"

"Teach me how to do that, what you're doing. Then I could help you, and you wouldn't have to work as much. I've figured out how to keep the fire going, I could do this too."

"You're asking me to give you more work?" Drogo's eyebrows went up.

"I guess so." Put that way, Hamo admitted it was an odd request for a slave.

Drogo looked down at Hamo. He was older now, but not much bigger than when he first came, thanks to the meager fare the slaves enjoyed. The idea of him doing Drogo's job caused a slight smile to tug at the corner of the big man's lips. But he was serious, Drogo could see that, he had the little crease in his forehead that showed how hard he was thinking about this. And in the three years he had known the boy, he had learned there was a lot of strength to him that didn't meet the eye.

"Alright." Drogo nodded his head. "I'll teach you. This is not the hard part though. The hard part is when I make things with the iron."

"You make things? I thought you just melted it down and separated it so that it could be sent down the mountains."

"Most of it. Lord Bayner also has me make things with it, too. Like swords for him and his closest men. Anything that he doesn't trust others to make."

"Oh. I don't know if I could do that. But I can help you with this part," Hamo said confidently.

Drogo studied him for another moment, remembering when Forbes had first brought him in and handed him over to Drogo. He wished there was some way he could get Hamo out of this place, and back to his home. If he had any money to speak of, he would have paid Lord Bayner what he wanted for the boy and set him free. He'd been forced to grow up away from everything he had ever known, and there was no future for him as a slave. Drogo had never fought in the war, but he knew it must be a terrible thing to bring a half-grown boy to this place.

In the weeks to come, Drogo taught Hamo how to smelt iron, and pour it into the casts that would be taken down through the mountain pass. He had to admit, when Hamo was competent enough to do the job without him watching over his shoulder, that it was nice not having to do quite so much work. As Hamo had noted earlier, he was not getting any younger.

Chapter 16

6 Years Later

A L! AL! WAIT UP FOR me!" Sabina ran down the street, narrowly avoiding upsetting a man pushing a hand cart on her way. Ahead of her, a small, cloaked figure walked resolutely onward, seemingly deaf to the call behind him. Sabina was out of breath when she finally reached him. "Didn't you hear me?"

"No," Aldrid lied.

"Al, why do you have your hood on? It's the middle of summer."

"I like to wear it."

Aldrid had reached that awkward age of boyhood where he was completely mortified by the scar on his face. It had bothered him at random times throughout his life, those times generally coinciding with times when other children called him names such as "Scarface".

Mother always reassured him at those times that it did not matter what a person looked like, it mattered what they were made of. At thirteen and a half, though, Aldrid reached the conclusion that it very much mattered what he looked like. And he was determined not to let anyone see his face. Hence the cloak and hood in the middle of summer.

The cloak served another purpose as well. Hiding the other sore spot of Aldrid's ego - his arm. He twisted a part of the left side of the cloak up and tucked it into his belt so that his entire left arm was hidden beneath the folds of fabric.

"Where are you going?" Sabina tried to change the subject in the hopes of getting her brother in a better mood.

"Home," Aldrid answered shortly.

"Well, where have you been?"

"Out."

"My goodness, Al. What is wrong with you? How can you be so gloomy on such a beautiful day?" Sabina threw her arms out wide and spun a slow circle, taking in the warm sunny day.

"Wasn't paying attention to the weather," Al muttered. He eyed a stranger passing close by them, noting the purse of money that hung from his belt. If Sabina weren't there, he could have snatched it easily and no one would have been the wiser. The missed opportunity worsened his mood.

"Oh. So, what were you doing out?" Sabina was not ready to give up yet.

"Mother wanted something from market." He held up a small bag he had been carrying in his right hand and shook it with annoyance.

"I see." Sabina paused and waved at someone across the street. "It's Stephan! I wonder what he's doing in town."

Stephan used to be a regular visitor to their family, back when Father was home. And even after Maurus' disappearance, he had come around from time to time to check in on them. He had felt responsible for Hamo's death and the effect it had on Maurus.

It wasn't until a few years ago that the small family had stopped seeing him regularly. That was when he retired from his position as sergeant-at-arms and moved out of town onto a small farm where he bred and trained war horses for the and cavalrymen and kept remounts for the king's couriers.

Stephan crossed the street to where the two young people were standing. Aldrid grimaced and lowered his head, avoiding Stephan's eyes. Stephan never failed to make at least one joke at Aldrid's expense.

"Look who it is? My, you've grown Sabina! And who is that under the hood? It can't be young Al, is it?" Stephan looked at the small, hooded figure in front of him. "Don't you think it's a little warm out for all of that, Al?"

"I want to wear it." Aldrid wondered why everyone thought it their business to comment on his wardrobe choices.

"I see." Stephan caught Sabina's eye and saw the small shake of her head as she lowered it to hide a smile. His own face split into a grin. "Well, I hope you're very comfortable in your cloak. Are you two on your way home, then?"

"Yes. Do you want to come with us?" Sabina always loved when Stephan came over. He had been like an uncle to her.

"Maybe later. I have some business to take care of up at the castle."

Sabina waved to him again as he walked away.

"Why'd you have to make him notice us?" Al asked crossly. Stephan had made fun of him, and it was an unforgiveable offense to Aldrid.

"He's a friend, Al. You know some of us actually have those." Sabina looked at her younger brother in disappointment.

"Not me."

"Only because you're rude and cross with everybody you meet."

"I am not. It's just that nobody likes me."

"Really?" Sabina sounded like Mother as she said the word, making Aldrid defensive. "I wonder why that is ?"

"It's different with you. People like you. They think you turned out well. People don't like me."

"Has it ever occurred to you that people like me because I don't walk around looking like this?" Sabina did her best to mimic the smoldering scowl on Aldrid's face as she crossed her arms on her chest.

She held the expression for a second before bursting out laughing. "There, you're doing it now!" She pointed at his face.

"I am not."

Sabina's face turned red from her effort to not laugh as Aldrid's face fell into the exact expression she had just imitated. "Oh, forget it, Al. Let's just get home."

Chapter 17

ALDRID WAS OUT IN TOWN again, wandering up and down streets, searching for something interesting. Beneath the privacy of his cloak, he had already collected two such interesting items – namely, the full money purses of two unsuspected townspeople who happened to walk too close to him.

The market square of Bren was always busy, and it was a favorite place of Aldrid's to visit. He slipped away as often as he could, which was pretty much every day.

Sliding his right hand inside his cloak, Aldrid thought about the success of his afternoon. Although Mother was always commenting on how much she wished he would behave more like Hamo, Aldrid was following quite closely in his father's footsteps. Today was no different.

Aldrid had heard the words, "He's a thief, just like his father," so many times that it was almost a matter of pride for him now. He could pick pockets quite skillfully, and the unwitting owners never knew until they reached for their purse and found it had disappeared.

Mother, of course, had known of his habit since he was little. More than one neighbor had brought him home to her, having caught him at it. That was when he was little and had lacked the skill he had now. It had been months since anyone had caught him at it. Mother hated that he did it, but Aldrid no longer paid much attention to her scolding. Anytime she spoke to him about it, he lied.

What Mother did not know was what he did with all the money he stole. She never saw a coin of it. It was Aldrid's best kept secret. Stashed in a secret hiding spot in his room, he added to his collection frequently. In his childish imagination, he dreamed of using the money one day to go and reclaim the sword his father had stolen, and by doing so remove the black mark against him and his family. The fact that he was using stolen money never bothered him. After all, people expected him to be a thief.

On this particular day, he was in a darker mood than usual. Not only had Stephan come over for dinner the night before, but just a few moments ago several of the older boys in town had chased him away, calling him all sorts of ugly names. It was unfair of them, Aldrid thought crossly as he wove his way in and out of the groups of people filling the market square.

His attention was diverted from his own wounded pride when he saw a man in front of him, with a leather money purse tucked into his belt. It was the man's action of adding coins to that purse that had caught Aldrid's attention. Aldrid smiled, a smile made crooked by the scar on the left side of his cheek and chin. Watching the man from under the hood of his cloak, Aldrid decided that he could easily slide the purse out of the man's belt without anyone noticing.

With practiced skill, he moved a little faster, closing the gap between him and the man. Head down, but eyes intent on the man's broad back, Aldrid waited for the perfect moment. When the man walked past a large group of people gathered beside a fruit cart, Aldrid made his move.

It worked every time, and he had done it many times before. He used the presence of so many people to mask his own subtle movements as his right hand slid carefully around the purse. With only the barest amount of pressure, he began to lift it free. The man never even turned in his direction.

Aldrid let out a little yelp of surprise as an iron grip closed over his wrist. He tried to let go of the purse, but the grip crushed the little bones in his wrist together, preventing him from moving his fingers. Only when a tiny whimper of pain and fear slipped out did his intended victim turn around. Aldrid wasn't looking up at first, but when he did, his heart dropped.

"Trying to rob me, boy?" It was none other than Stephan, who after a moment recognized his captive and gave a low whistle. "Al? Really?"

The crowd around them had stepped to the side, and were to a person, watching the little drama unfold.

"It was just a joke...," Aldrid started to protest.

"It's a good thing you caught him, Sir. He's a quick one, and sly. Gets away with it almost every time," said the farmer who owned the fruit cart speaking now.

Aldrid stole a quick glance at his face. With a grimace he recognized him as the man he had just stolen a sum of money from only the week before. The farmer had chased him quite a way before giving up the pursuit. Of course, the memory was still fresh on the man's mind.

Aldrid began to squirm, trying to loosen Stephan's hold on his hand but the farmer wasn't the only one speaking now. There were several people who accused him and with each accusation, Aldrid's heart sank. These people were really very unfair, he thought as he stared down at the ground. He had not done them that much wrong for them all to be jumping all over him accusing him of this and that.

He tried once more to free his wrist from Stephan's iron grasp and when it wouldn't come loose, he looked up at the big man.

"What are you going to do with me, Stephan?"

"What ought to be done with you, thief," the farmer spoke up again. "Even if he doesn't want to take you in, I am. A time or two in front of the Magistrate might set you straight."

Aldrid felt his face whiten. All the other times neighbors had caught him, they had taken him back home to Mother. No one had ever threatened to take him to the Magistrate.

"Stephan?" Aldrid did not try to conceal his fear.

Stephan didn't answer him. He just stared down at Aldrid, a mixture of disappointment and disapproval on his face.

A pair of hands pulled Aldrid's cloak away from him and the two purses that he'd stashed in his belt were removed by the farmer.

"Looks like you've been at it again today, too. What do you say, sir?" The farmer turned to Stephan. "A thief's got no business being out on the streets with everyone else. I'll be taking him if you don't want to."

To Aldrid's horror and dismay, Stephan relinquished his hold of Aldrid's wrist into the farmer's hand. Aldrid found himself being propelled down the street. Twisting around, he saw Stephan still standing there, looking after him.

The Magistrate's office was a small stone room built off the side of the castle. It could be entered without setting foot inside the gate and only a few feet away from it, Bren's prison lay – a long, low stone building with iron bars in its windows.

Aldrid swallowed hard as they stood in front of the Magistrate's desk. He listened without a word as the farmer laid out his complaint and produced the money purses he'd just taken off of Aldrid.

"We'll keep him tonight. Come back in the morning to settle your claim with him." The Magistrate pushed his chair away from the desk, motioning for a prison guard to take Aldrid out.

"Just a minute." A familiar voice reached Aldrid's ears, and he turned to find Stephan standing in the room. Hope fluttered in his heart briefly. "I have a claim against him as well, Magistrate. It was me he was trying to rob when I caught him."

The hope was extinguished as quickly as it came. Aldrid couldn't believe his ears. Stephan was supposed to be a friend. He was their family's friend, one of the few they still had after Father's betrayal. He stared now at him, but Stephan refused to meet his gaze.

"Very well. Like I told this gentleman, I'm done for the day, but I'll have him locked up and you come in the morning, and we'll settle this then," the Magistrate said, turning to the guard. "Put him by himself for tonight."

Aldrid's arm was limp in the guard's grasp, and he followed unresisting as the man led him out the door and the few steps to the prison.

As the cell door clanged shut behind him and Aldrid heard the bolt slide into its place, he sank down on the cot.

"This isn't happening. This can't be happening," he whispered into the silence. The silence gave him no reassurance. This was happening and he couldn't stop it. Tomorrow morning, he'd be hauled in front of the Magistrate and sentenced.

The Magistrate was known to be hard on criminals, and the usual punishment for a thief was indentured servitude. Aldrid had seen some of the indentured servants around the castle and town. They were always given the hardest, most unpleasant jobs, the jobs no one else wanted to do. Aldrid's own laziness balked at the idea of being made to work for anyone. This was due in part to the fact that Alina did not expect much work from him with his crippled hand.

His only hope lay in the fact that Stephan was an old family friend. Maybe he was just threatening? Maybe he was somehow going to show up tomorrow and make everything better. Surely, he would not actually want to put Mother through the humiliation of having her son appear before the Magistrate, not if he were a real friend.

The thought of Mother undid him. Mother would be sitting at home, waiting for him to come and he wouldn't. It was Stephan's fault. Stephan and that nameless farmer. If they'd just let him alone, Mother wouldn't be put through this.

Pressing his knuckles into his eyes to keep the tears that threatened him in check, Aldrid sat back against the wall. There was nothing to do now but wait and he hated waiting.

Stephan, meanwhile, waited until Aldrid was safely locked away before making his way to Alina's. She would find out one way or another and finding out from a friend would soften the blow as much as it was possible to.

With a heavy heart, he lifted his hand up and rapped on the door. Alina smiled when she opened it and saw him, but her smile faded when she read his face.

"What is it? What's wrong?"

"It's Al," Stephan said, stepping inside. Guiding her to a seat, he explained. Alina's face fell as she listened.

Burying her face in her hands, she cried softly. "I don't know what to do with him, Stephan. He's done it since he was little because it's what his father did. But this, this won't make him any better. He'll be marked for the rest of his life."

"There might be a way around that."

"How?"

"When the Magistrate sentences him tomorrow, I can claim him. He won't have to go on one of the work gangs. And maybe, just maybe, I can get the Magistrate to keep the band off him. He's awfully young for it."

"Will he let you do that?"

"Yes. If I claim him, the Magistrate has to."

"And what would you do with him?" Alina looked up at him, mingled hope and worry on her face.

"Alina, something has to change with him. If he keeps this up, no one will be able to help him. If I claim him, I will make him work. He probably won't like it all that much."

"He'd have to leave. I wouldn't see him. Stephan, I can't do that. I've already lost Hamo. I can't lose him too. And I can't put him through that. Think of everything he's gone through. The boy doesn't have a father."

"You won't be losing him. He would have to come with me, but if he gets put on a work gang, you're not seeing him either. I'll bring him around when I can."

"Oh, Stephan." Alina's face went back into her hands.

"Alina, you've had more than enough to worry about these last few years. Let me worry about this. He'll be alright. And, with a bit of help, he'll turn out alright."

Chapter 18

ALDRID'S KNUCKLES, GRIPPING the edge of the narrow cot, were white. The sunlight pouring in through the window above his head told him that it was morning. Morning meant his doom. His fate was to be decided. He shifted on the hard cot, trying to get comfortable but it was hopeless.

The cell he was in was not nearly as horrible as he had first envisioned it when he heard the Magistrate's plan. His imagination concocted a cramped room in the darkest corner of the dungeon, filled with rats and spiders, and stagnant puddles of water, and maybe some green slime growing up the walls. It was none of those things. In fact, aside from the fact that he could not leave, it was quite comfortable.

That was not what was bothering Aldrid though. Most of the night was spent in sleepless anxiety, dreading this morning. He wasn't sure if Mother knew what had happened to him. And if she did know, would she show up this morning for his sentencing? He couldn't decide if that would make it better or worse. The longer he thought about it the more convinced he was that it would just make things worse. He couldn't bear the thought of her sad, disappointed face.

Through the long, dark, sleepless hours of the night, Aldrid tried to imagine just what his sentencing would be like. By morning, he decided that he was probably going to be condemned to spend the rest of his life as an indentured servant, working himself to death. It was a horrifying thought. But perhaps more horrifying than that was the thought of standing up in front of the Magistrate with people watching him, being made a spectacle for them.

It was all Stephan's fault, he reminded himself. Stephan could have just let him go right away instead of giving everyone else the chance to accuse him as well. It wasn't fair that Stephan was among those accusing him today. He hadn't actually taken anything from the man.

When a rather amused looking guard came to collect him in the morning, Aldrid was all but convinced that he was on his way to the gallows, if they did not decide to torture him for a while first. If Stephan had anything to do with it, they would definitely go with the torture.

The Magistrate's office was not a large room. A huge desk in the very center of it made it seem even smaller than it was. The Magistrate himself was an elderly man who had held the office for as long as anyone could remember. He was known for his ill humor, and quick judgments. No one had to wait long for his decisions.

Before yesterday, Aldrid had never actually seen the man. Now, he was hoping this would be the last time. He was a little surprised at how very ordinary he appeared. He'd always had it in his head that the Magistrate would look ogrish and gross. He was neither of those things. He was a little on the plump side, with thinning gray hair and an equally gray mustache and eyes that squinted because he could not see clearly more than a few feet in front of him.

As Aldrid took his place in front of the desk, heart in his throat, he caught sight of Stephan leaning with his back against the wall, arms crossed on his chest and looking quite serious. The farmer was there too, looking altogether too pleased with Aldrid's demeanor. Aldrid fought down an urge to make a face at the man.

"What's your name, boy?" The Magistrate was speaking to him.

"Aldrid Serbon," Aldrid said, hating how small and squeaky his own voice sounded in his ears. The Magistrate glared at him, and Aldrid quickly added, "Sir."

"Aldrid Serbon? You're the son of the sword thief, then, aren't you?" The Magistrate's squinting blue eyes stared piercingly at him.

Aldrid opened his mouth to speak but was interrupted by Stephan's voice from across the room. "I don't think that has anything to do with the charges that were brought against the boy, sir."

"No, no, of course not. Still, it's interesting how the son's turned out. A bit of 'like father, like son', isn't it?"

Aldrid felt his face going red. He hated when it did that, it made the scar more prominent. If Stephan said something in agreement with the Magistrate just then, Aldrid would never forgive him, he was sure of that. Stephan did not comment further.

"So, Aldrid Serbon, this man here, Stephan," the Magistrate squinted down at a paper on his desk, "Ah, yes, uh, Stephan Turston accuses you of attempted robbery. And this man," he gestured toward the farmer, "Calvin Horsett, accuses you of another robbery. How do you answer those charges? I should warn you before you answer, that should you claim innocence, there are witnesses who will be summoned." Again, his piercing blue eyes were fastened on Aldrid's face.

"I did it," Aldrid had his head down and mumbled the words so quietly that the Magistrate could barely hear him.

"Good. I always like it when criminals own up to their crimes. It makes my life so much easier. Now, as to your sentence, it is the first time you've been in my office, although I've heard from a good number of people that it's not your first offense." He looked meaningfully up at Aldrid who was holding his breath waiting for his next words. "I sentence you to three years of service as an indentured servant. You will be given a work assignment..."

"Your honor," Stephan interrupted once again. Aldrid turned to face him, eyes glowering. What else was this man going to do to him? He was already stealing three years of his life, and Aldrid didn't actually take anything from him. "I believe there is a provision in the law for a thief to work off their debt in service to the person they robbed."

"That is correct. Although almost no one does that. It's more trouble than it's worth, generally."

"I, however, do wish to claim my right to his service for the next three years, in return for his attempted theft."

Aldrid stared openly at Stephan, not quite believing or understanding what was going on.

"You're sure? Mr. Horsett has an equal claim to his service. Is that something you're interested in, Mr. Horsett?"

"Absolutely not. What would I want with a thief? I'd be looking over my shoulder all the time trying to make sure he doesn't rob me blind."

"Very well. You do understand that you will become solely responsible for him? Although he will still have to wear the band of indenture as required, of course."

"I do. I want it waived."

"That would be most irregular, sir. That band is what identifies them as criminals serving a sentence. It's part of the punishment."

Aldrid knew what they were talking about. He had seen it on the criminals working outside the castle. They each wore a thick iron cuff around their wrist. The cuff never came off. It was a permanent mark against anyone who transgressed the law.

Nervously, he wondered if it hurt when they put that cuff on. He imagined it did since it had to be fitted on when the iron was hot.

"It can be waived though, I think." Stephan moved across the room so that he was standing directly in front of the desk next to Aldrid, facing the Magistrate. "I'll make you a deal, Magistrate. You leave the cuff off for now, and the first bit of trouble he gives me, or the first time he tries to take off, I'll bring him down here and hold him still myself so you can put it on."

The Magistrate considered both Stephan's words and his determination. Leaning back in his chair and folding his arms across his chest, he nodded slowly.

"I suppose that's fair. Considering his age and all."

"Excellent. Now, Aldrid, you heard the deal, right? You behave yourself for three years and don't cause me any grief, and you'll be free to do as you please after that. You slip up one time, though, and I am quite serious about bringing you back here. And I don't think you'll like that very much. Understood?"

"Yes, Stephan." Again, his voice sounded so small and meek.

"Good. Wait over there while the Magistrate and I sign these papers."

Aldrid sat on a hard wooden bench at the far end of the room, watching as the Magistrate and Stephan signed away an enormous chunk of his life. At least, it felt enormous. Why in three years he'd be sixteen and practically grown. It wasn't fair, he thought.

When he noticed the farmer leaving the room, he glared after him. At least, he wasn't going with him, Aldrid conceded to himself. Stephan was bad enough. Mr. Horsett would have been an endless nightmare.

Finally, Stephan got up and started for the door. "Let's go home."

Aldrid wasn't sure which home Stephan was talking about, but he was hoping that he meant to take him to his home at least long enough to say goodbye to Mother. Stephan had a firm hold of his wrist again as they left the Magistrate's office amidst the stares of everyone.

Aldrid would have happily turned into a rock to get people to stop looking at him. He could read the disdain and judgment in their faces, and for once he could not hide beneath his hood. When he started to pull it over his head on their way out of the office, Stephan snatched it off and took hold of his arm, preventing him from pulling it up again.

With relief, he realized that their hurried steps brought him to his own front door. Stephan nudged him toward it.

"Go on then. Say goodbye and then we have to leave. I'm already late leaving because of this. And don't try slipping out the back," he called after him as an afterthought.

Aldrid pushed the door open and almost wished he hadn't come home. The look on Mother's face was every bit as awful as he'd imagined it, so hurt and disappointed, and he had a moment to be relieved that she hadn't been there in the Magistrate's office with him. He did not mean to hurt her. He just could not help himself. She rushed forward and pulled him against her, barely hiding the fact that she had been crying.

"Oh Al, why?"

Aldrid didn't pull away from her embrace the way he normally did, not yet at least. Everything was happening way too fast, and he clung to Mother. He didn't bother trying to her answer, either. Now that his life was flipped upside down, there wasn't a good answer as to why he'd done it.

"Promise me you'll be good for him?" Mother took no heed of his silence and kept talking. "He won't hurt you, or be cruel, I know he won't. He will help you. He's a very good friend of ours."

"I'll be fine, Mother," Aldrid finally pulled himself together enough to say. "I'll see you in three years. It's not really that long."

His own arms tightened around her as he realized with a pang that three years was equal to an eternity at the moment.

"Goodbye then, Al. I love you." She planted a kiss on his forehead.

"Where's Sabina?" Aldrid pulled away and glanced around, looking for her.

"Al, she had to work. This was all so sudden; she couldn't come home. I'm sorry." Mother had tears in her eyes, and Al was suddenly very suspicious of a blur forming in his own.

"Tell her I said goodbye and tell her I'll miss her." He fled out the door before he broke down and cried in front of Mother, pulling his hood on as he went.

Stephan was waiting for him, leaning back against the front of the house. This time, he did not pull the hood off his head, nor did he seem to notice the quick movement of Aldrid's arm across his eyes.

Stephan led Aldrid by the arm to where a wagon, piled high with supplies, stood.

"Get in," he ordered him.

Aldrid climbed up into the seat at the front and waited while Stephan untied the horses from their hitching post. It occurred to him that he had absolutely no idea where they were going. He knew that Stephan moved away from town when he retired from the military and settled down on a farm somewhere.

Now, as Stephan climbed up next to him and slapped the reins to get the horses moving, Aldrid thought about how much he actually liked the town, and the people there, and his home. His eyes were blurry again, and something stuck in his throat, making it hard for him to swallow. He tried to ignore the fact that there was something wet sliding down his cheek. For a few minutes, no words passed between them, and Aldrid was very glad. If Stephan had made him talk, he could not hide the fact that he was crying.

Stephan, though he pretended not to, saw the way Aldrid kept reaching up and wiping a tear away. He was quite aware of the little hiccupping breaths that Al was trying so hard to hide. And for a moment, Stephan felt truly sorry for him. Alina was right, the boy had been through a lot in his young life. But there was no help for it now. If Stephan backed out of his part of it, Aldrid would simply be turned over to the work gangs. He kept the horses' heads moving toward home.

"Cheer up, Al." He reached over and clapped the boy on the shoulder, saying, "It won't be so terrible. Just think, in three years you'll be free to go wherever you please, and you'll know everything you need to know about raising good war horses."

"I don't want to know about raising war horses." Aldrid couldn't keep the tears out of his miserable voice. "I just want to go home."

"I'm sure you do. But you made a choice, Aldrid, and choices have consequences."

"I did not choose this," Al's sullen voice came from beneath his hood.

"No. You did not choose this consequence. You definitely choose to try to steal from me," Stephan said soberly. "Don't worry, though, three years isn't very long at all." Actually, three years was a very long sentence for a first-time offender, especially one as young as Aldrid. Stephan suspected it had something to do with the Magistrate's opinion about the boy's father. "You'll get to see your mother from time to time, and it will go by faster than you think."

"I will?" Aldrid looked at him for the first time, his eyes suspiciously red.

"Any time I go to town. I have to take you with me wherever I go. That's part of the deal. You didn't honestly think I wasn't going to let you visit your mother, did you?"

"Yes. I did." Aldrid realized that he had only assumed he would be allowed no contact with his family, he had never known for sure that that was true.

Stephan started to laugh, then realized that Aldrid was completely serious.

"I'm not that mean, Al. I couldn't do that to your mother."

"Oh." Aldrid was a little put out that Stephan's only reason was about how hard it would be on Mother, and nothing to do with how hard it would be on him. The man really was very unfair, Aldrid thought. To accompany the thought, he slid to the very edge of his seat, as far from the unfair man as he could get and pulled his hood even lower over his head. Stephan, catching the action out of the corner of his eye, shook his head in amusement but said nothing.

For several hours the only sounds were the soft thudding of the horses' hooves in the dirt and the creaking of the wagon wheels beneath them. From time to time, Stephan would whistle a tune to himself, but otherwise the two occupants of the wagon were quiet. Aldrid spent the time reiterating to himself all the reasons why he should not be here. He was exhausted from having slept so little the night before, which did little to improve his mood. When Stephan pulled the wagon off to the side of the road beneath a copse of trees, he was thoroughly cross.

"Off you go, Al. We'll rest the horses a bit and have something to eat." Stephan ignored the scowl on his face. Aldrid climbed down without a word of acknowledgement. "Get together some sticks for a fire," Stephan told him.

Al scrunched his face up in a grimace. Mother never made him do much of anything. He was going to miss that.

With a heavy sigh, given solely for the benefit of his travelling companion, Aldrid wandered about the little grove in search of sticks. He picked up the smaller ones that he found, leaving several bigger, heavier branches on the ground. When he deposited his puny load next to where Stephan was crouched, unrolling a bundle, he sank down to the ground.

"That's the best you can do?" Stephan did not even look up from what he was doing.

"What? It's enough to start a fire," Aldrid answered defensively.

"It's mostly twigs. They'll burn in a few seconds. Weren't there any bigger branches or logs lying around?"

Aldrid shrugged.

Stephan spun on him with surprising speed. "I asked you a question, boy. Now answer me."

"I didn't see any," Aldrid lied.

Stephan's eyes narrowed as he looked at the little figure sitting beside him. He couldn't see most of Al's face with the hood on, but he did not need to see his face to know that he was lying.

"Get up."

"What? I did it, alright. I did what you told me to." Aldrid's voice took on a little whine.

"Yes, you did. And now I'm going with you and you're going to do it again. And we'll see if this time you can manage to see a bit more." Stephan waited until Aldrid got to his feet, then set off.

"Look. There's a bigger branch. Did you see that one earlier?" Stephan pulled Al's hood down again before he let him answer.

"Yes." Somehow lying wasn't quite as easy when your face was visible and a great big, terrifying man was glaring down at you, Al thought.

"Pick it up."

"But it's heavy."

"Pick it up anyway."

For several minutes Aldrid followed Stephan around as they found more wood. Each big branch they came across, Stephan was careful to ask if he had seen it. Aldrid had managed to keep hold of all the wood with just his right hand, which was fortunate since Stephan seemed to have forgotten that his left one was damaged. At last, Stephan was satisfied, and they returned to the wagon.

"Don't lie to me again to try to get out of work, is that clear?" Stephan said as he started a fire.

Aldrid started to just nod his head, but then remembered that Stephan wanted an actual answer. "Yes, Stephan."

"Good. Now why don't you get that bucket off the back of the wagon and fill it up with water." Stephan was not the sort of person to linger on a problem after it had been resolved.

Aldrid, who had been fully expecting a long lecture on the evils of laziness and lying, was surprised by the abrupt shift. He fetched the bucket that was secured to the wagon, but then hesitated. Stephan had said to fill it up with water, but he had no idea where this water was to come from.

"Um, Stephan...," he had never initiated any kind of conversation with Stephan, or with just about anyone else for that matter.

"Hmm?"

"You said to get water, but where am I supposed to get it from?"

"There's a creek, just beyond the trees. It's been running close to the road for the last several miles. Did you not notice it?" Stephan looked a little puzzled and Aldrid realized with dismay that the creek he was talking about was visible and had been the whole time.

"I guess not," he answered a little shamefacedly.

Stephan watched him walk toward it, shaking his head in wonder. The boy wasn't stupid, Stephan knew, he just did not pay attention to or think about anything aside from himself. It was going to be a long three years.

Chapter 19

THE ROAD SLIPPING AWAY beneath him was hypnotizing, Aldrid thought. They were moving again and had been for the last hour. Aldrid was sitting, once more, as far away from Stephan as he could get. His chin was cradled in his right hand, while his elbow rested on his knee. The bouncing, swaying movement of the wagon under him, as well as the endless monotony of brown dirt flying beneath the wagon were making it very hard for him to keep his eyes open. Without realizing it, Aldrid's head became heavier in his hand, and his eyelids drooped half shut. It was the pressure on his shoulder that made him start awake again.

"Lay down in the back for a bit." Stephan jerked his chin toward the back of the wagon.

"How long is it going to take?" Aldrid was awake enough now to ask the question that had been bugging him all day.

"A few more hours. Normally I'd be almost home at this point, but I left a lot later than usual this morning." Stephan was generous enough to not remind Aldrid why he left so late. "Now go back and get some sleep. I'll bet you didn't get much last night, did you?"

Aldrid shook his head as he climbed over the seat and settled himself in amongst the sacks of feed and various other supplies that filled Stephan's wagon. He had never slept anywhere but home in his own bed, and for a second the thought of home was almost too much to bear. Then his eyes shut and Aldrid was fast asleep.

Stephan glanced back at him once or twice as the horses continued their homeward plodding. Laying there like that, Aldrid looked just like Hamo had at that age, Stephan thought. Actually, the brothers had both taken heavily after their father, only Hamo had scowled a lot less, Stephan thought with a small smile. The smile was gone a moment later as a fleeting image passed before his mind's eye.

The last time he had seen Hamo.

He had been alone, surrounded by a ruthless, merciless enemy and Stephan could not reach him. He had tried, oh, how he had tried. The worst part of the memory was that he had caught Hamo's eye in that last moment and had seen his fear and shock before he had fallen, before a single, sickening stroke from an enemy's sword had slammed into the back of his head ending his life. Stephan wished more than anything in the world that he could go back and change that. If he had saved Hamo, he would have saved Maurus. And if he had saved Maurus, he would not have to help Aldrid now.

As the sun sank behind the western horizon, Stephan slapped the reins down across the horses, urging them forward faster. The scent of home in their nostrils, the horses moved off with a good bit more energy than they had the rest of the day. Stephan no longer needed to guide them; they knew where they were going. They were rewarded after about half an hour of trotting as the wagon came up over a small rise and Stephan's comfortable little farm lay before them. Stephan waited until the horses were stopped in front of the barn before turning to wake Aldrid.

"Al, we're here," he said, shaking his shoulder.

The boy sat up, his dark eyes blinking in confusion, a tousled shock of brown hair sticking up all over the place on the top of his head. For several minutes he sat unmoving, trying to reorient himself. Then he remembered where he was, and why he was there.

"Help me get this stuff in the barn and then you can go to bed." Stephan was urging him down from his perch in the wagon bed.

Groggily, he obeyed, swinging his legs over the back and lowering himself to the ground. After so many hours on the moving wagon, his legs wobbled a little beneath him and Stephan reached out a hand to steady him.

"Come on. The sooner we finish up, the sooner you can go back to sleep."

"Do I have to help?" Aldrid looked up at Stephan piteously.

"That does happen to be the reason I drug you all the way out here, remember?"

"But I'm tired." It would have worked for Mother. She would have let him just go to bed.

"So am I. Now let's get this done." Before Aldrid could raise another argument, Stephan shoved a parcel into his hands. "Take this into the house and set it on the table. Then come back."

Aldrid finally accepted that he would get no sympathy from Stephan and with another heavy sigh he carried the parcel inside.

Once inside, he took a moment to look around what would be his home for the next three years. It was very clean and organized, the result of Stephan spending so many years as a sergeant. But it lacked any kind of decor, aside from a few military trappings.

If Aldrid hadn't been so tired, and in such a bad mood, he would have realized that it was quite a comfortable place. All he could think of now though was about his own home, now far, far away. A little ache sprang up inside him as he looked around the unfamiliar house and compared it to his own lost home. The distance between what he saw as little more than his prison and his home was as big as an ocean.

When at last the wagon was unloaded and the horses rubbed down and fed and watered for the night, Stephan led the way back into the house.

"I wasn't exactly planning on bringing someone back with me, so there isn't a bed for you." Stephan opened the door to a side room and ushered Aldrid inside. He had a bundle in his hands and an armful of blankets that he dropped on the floor. "You can sleep on the floor with these for now and we'll build a bed one of these days. Here," Stephan held the bundle out, "Your Mother packed some of your stuff for you."

Aldrid took the bundle. He had been too overwhelmed by the speed at which his life was falling apart that morning to even think about packing any of his belongings. Now here he was holding a little piece of home in his hands, and all thanks to Mother.

A wave of homesickness, quite physical in its intensity, washed over him, and he turned away from Stephan. He hated Stephan at the moment, and he was not going to let him see him cry over his mother.

"Goodnight, Al. Best try to get some sleep tonight, we've an early morning tomorrow." Stephan for once did not demand an answer. He knew Aldrid was probably going to cry himself to sleep that night. And he felt bad for him. He had, in one twenty-four-hour period, lost everything he held dear. It would get better, though, Stephan was sure of that.

Aldrid felt as if his eyes had barely shut when Stephan was bending over him, shaking him awake again. When he went to open his eyes, he found they were swollen and puffy, the result of crying himself to sleep. He hadn't meant to. He turned away when Stephan gave him the bundle from home and pulled himself together quite nicely.

That is, until he opened the bundle and found a small letter Mother had hurriedly written to stick in.

That was too much, and he buried his face in his pillow, crying until he wore himself out and went to sleep. Even now, as Stephan urged him to get up, he realized that the little piece of paper was all crumpled up in his right hand. Apparently, he did not put it up when he fell asleep.

"Come on, Aldrid. The sun'll be up soon, and we have a lot to get done today," Stephan was talking again.

Aldrid sat up, rubbing his eyes sleepily. The window above his head was still dark.

"But it's nighttime still," he complained.

"No. It just means we beat the sun up," Stephan replied cheerfully.

Aldrid thought that cheerful people in the early morning had to be the worst kind of people he had ever been around. How could you be cheerful when your whole body felt heavy and sluggish, and your eyes refused to stay open? He started to lay back down and pull the blanket over his head.

"No, you don't, Al. It's time to get up, and if you lay there another minute, I'll make sure you're up. I don't think you'll like it." Stephan still sounded cheerful, but there was an undertone of seriousness.

Aldrid would have been wise to heed that undertone. Stephan had spent years training men much harder than Al, and he was truly a master of motivation, although those motivated rarely enjoyed it.

Aldrid decided to play like he had already fallen back asleep. Once again, it was a trick that worked on Mother. But Stephan was wise to it. He left the room and came back a moment later with a bucket in his hand. He paused a moment, taking in the crumpled paper now lying next to Aldrid, and decided to pick it up out of the way.

Aldrid had in fact started to doze back off, when the most horrifying, dreadful thing happened to him. His face was drenched in icy cold water. Not just a little bit either, an entire gallon of it.

Spluttering, yelling, coughing, and gasping all at once, Aldrid came up from his now wet blankets.

"What did you do that for?" he yelled when he finally got enough breath to do so.

"I told you to get up, you didn't listen," Stephan answered calmly. "Now, normally I would tell you to get up and come to breakfast, but since you decided to be like this, it's a little different. You get up, then clean this mess up, and hang those blankets outside to dry, and then you can come have breakfast."

"But I didn't make this mess," Aldrid protested. This was too unfair.

"Sure, you did. I warned you, and you decided not to listen. Now you can stand there pouting about it all morning and not have anything to eat, or you can get to work. What's it going to be?"

Aldrid thought hard. If it was anyone else, he could have whined or moped his way out of it, but Stephan was never moved by either of those tactics. No, Stephan meant what he said. Which, although Aldrid could not have put his finger on it, was a relief.

"I'll clean it up," he said, admitting defeat.

"Wise choice. Breakfast will be waiting for you whenever you finish up. And I would try to make that not very long if I were you. My food is edible if it's hot, not so much so when it's cold. Oh, by the way, here's this back." Stephan held out Mother's letter that he had moved out of the way. Aldrid snatched it from his hand.

"You took this from me?" He was offended, mostly because he never wanted anyone to know the contents of that letter.

"No, I saved it from becoming as soaked as you are right now. Don't worry, I wouldn't read it. That's between you and your mother. Now you'd better get moving."

When Stephan left the room, Aldrid stood staring at the large puddle of water on the floor in dismay. He had no idea how he was supposed to clean it up.

140

His dismay grew when he realized that the clothes in the bundle had fallen victim to the deluge of water Stephan had poured on him as well. Now he had nothing dry to put on. How could Stephan do that to him? How could anyone be so cruel and still call themselves human?

Finally, he decided that the only course of action was to mop up the rest of the water with the already soaked blankets. As he stalked out of his room, trailing an armload of soggy bedclothes, Stephan called out to him.

"There's a line right next to the barn you can hang those on."

Aldrid did not bother to answer but drug his load out the door and into the yard. He was not even a little careful to keep the wet blankets from dragging on the ground. Stephan, watching him from the doorway, started to say something about it, then changed his mind with a shrug. He'd figure it out soon enough, Stephan thought.

Stephan was right, Aldrid thought, as he tried to swallow the cold, thick remains of a porridge. It would have been better hot. Either way, he did not have much time to dwell on it. He barely finished half of it before Stephan told him it was time to go.

"If you want more time to eat, I'd suggest you get up when you're told. There are chores you need to get done, and those aren't going to wait until you feel like it," Stephan said as he hurried him out the door.

Aldrid shivered as the cold morning air hit him. It was summer and the days were hot, but nights were starting to cool off as the season reached its end, and his wet clothes made it worse. The horizon was just starting to turn gray with the dawn as Aldrid followed Stephan toward a small outbuilding. Stephan carried a lantern with him to light up the interior.

As Aldrid stepped inside his nostrils wrinkled as the pungent odor of animals struck them. Aldrid never had much to do with animals. They did not have so much as a dog at home, and the only animals he was ever around were the horses that people used in town. He didn't remember them smelling so strongly. Aldrid decided then and there that he did not like farming. If only Stephan was not so set on seeing him punished, he would not have to be here in this smelly barn listening to this big man who pretended to be his friend tell him what to do.

"This is the cowshed. Every morning and every evening you're going to come in here and you're going to milk the cow. After you're done milking in the morning you are going to take her, and the calf out to pasture. Every evening, you're going to bring them in. Understood?"

"That's a lot of work!" Aldrid was horrified.

"Not really. It's only part of what you're going to do, anyway."

"But I don't even know how to milk a cow!" Aldrid's voice took on a whining note.

"Aldrid, how old are you?" Stephan asked abruptly.

"Thirteen." Aldrid was confused, and for a second, hopeful. Maybe Stephan hadn't realized how young he was, and he would change his mind about how much work he could do. His hopes were dashed as quickly as they were raised.

"Stop whining then. That is too old for you to ever talk to me like that. Is that clear?"

"Yes, Stephan."

"Good. Now as I was saying..."

Aldrid had one more card to play and interrupted Stephan now to remind him of it. "My hand. How am I supposed to milk a cow with only one hand? You need two to do it." He was careful this time about his tone.

"You're not doing it this morning. I'm going to show you how." Stephan paused to think for a moment. "We'll see about it later today. For now, just watch and pay attention."

Aldrid breathed an internal sigh of relief. Stephan couldn't make him do it, not with his crippled hand. With that thought in mind, he did not bother putting his mind to the task of watching and learning. When Stephan sat down on the low stool next to the docile cow and sent steady streams of milk into the bucket, Aldrid found himself daydreaming about all the things he would rather be doing. He was surprised when Stephan was already finished.

"Did you pay attention?" Stephan was standing up now, carrying the bucket of fresh milk to the door.

"Of course." Aldrid wasn't going to ever have to prove that he was paying attention, so the lie was never going to be discovered.

Stephan barely hid a knowing smile as he walked out the door.

For the rest of the morning and most of the afternoon, Aldrid shadowed Stephan. He was shown how to feed the horses, how to brush them until their coats were glossy and sleek, he was shown how to oil and rub the leather saddles and harness pieces.

Finally, by late afternoon, he had a pretty clear idea not only of what he would be spending the next three years doing, but also how little free time he was about to have. His feet dragged dejectedly through the dust as he followed Stephan back to the house to fix dinner, his shoulders slumped forward with the weight of this new knowledge.

"Think you can remember everything I showed you today?" Stephan asked as he went about cooking their supper.

"Umm...I think so." Aldrid stood a little uncertainly, wondering what he was supposed to do with himself. "Stephan?"

"Yes?"

"What if I can't get it all done? What if you gave me too much work to do?"

"You think I gave you too much?" Stephan looked up from cutting a piece of meat.

"Sort of. I mean, that's a lot. I won't have any time to do anything else."

"That's the idea. This is supposed to be a punishment, remember? What do you think it would be like if you were on one of the castle work gangs? Think they'd be worried about making sure you have free time?" Stephan replied. "Besides, it'll make the time go by quicker if you are busy. You should be thanking me for making sure you have plenty to do to distract you from being homesick."

"I'm not homesick!" Aldrid said indignantly.

Stephan did not answer, he merely lifted his eyebrows up and the corners of his mouth went up.

"Well, maybe a little," Aldrid admitted. He hated when Stephan looked at him like that, it always made him tell the truth.

"Come here, Al." Stephan motioned him to come closer and sit down.

Aldrid sat, perched on the very edge of the chair. He watched Stephan with bewilderment. The man pulled up a chair just in front of him and sat down as well.

"Give me your hand."

Aldrid held out his right hand, the confusion on his face deepening.

"No, the other one. The one you've been hiding all day." This was true. Aldrid had tucked his cloak up into his belt just like he was used to doing at home so that his crippled arm was invisible to everyone else.

Slowly, hesitantly, Aldrid untucked the corner of his cloak and pulled it away. He held out his crippled arm toward Stephan and waited for the usual look of revulsion. It was the reaction everyone had when they saw it, even people who tried to be polite usually took a moment to hide their initial disgust. Stephan had been a soldier for a long time, though, and had seen far more hideous wounds. He didn't even blink when he took Aldrid's hand in his own big, calloused ones.

"So, this is the one you can't use, huh?"

"Yes. Mother said I burnt it when I was three and the doctor couldn't help me."

"I remember that." He could never forget it. It was the same winter Hamo had died, the same winter Maurus had been wounded and crippled. It had been a hard winter for the little family. "So why can't you use it?"

"What?" Aldrid had never been asked such a question.

"You heard me. Why can't you use it? What won't it do?"

"The doctor said I can't. And Mother told me I can't. It's because the skin has tightened, and I can't feel anything in some parts." It was such a strange question for Stephan to ask. Couldn't he see the way the skin was contracted, pulling his fingers into each other and curling them up so that he could not fully open that hand?

"Have you ever tried to use it for anything?" Stephan was running his own fingers over the hand, poking and prodding, carefully watching Aldrid's face to see if he reacted.

"Ouch!" Aldrid tried to pull his hand away as Stephan pulled one of his fingers away from the others. "Why did you do that?"

"You didn't answer me. Have you ever tried to use it?"

"No. Why would I? It hurts and Mother says I can't."

"Hmmm. I see." Stephan let Aldrid pull his hand away. He leaned back against his chair, chewing his lip, deep in thought.

Aldrid started to squirm in his chair as he watched Stephan. He had a feeling he knew the direction the man was going in and he did not like it. Maybe now would be a good time to reiterate how certain the doctor had been that he could not use that hand. Aldrid pushed the thought away quickly.

Stephan may not even be thinking along those lines, and he did not want to put the thought in his head.

"Al, give me your hand again."

Aldrid held it out, more gingerly before. He suspected Stephan had something in mind. He was right. Stephan put his own hand against the palm af Aldrid's.

"Try to grab my hand."

Aldrid hesitated, looking doubtfully down at his warped hand.

"Do it."

Aldrid's forehead creased with a little frown as he concentrated on commanding muscles he hadn't used in years. Stephan smiled a little as he saw the expression. Hamo used to look like that when he was trying hard to do something, or when he was thinking of something unpleasant. Aldrid's face almost mirrored that of the brother he no longer remembered. Aldrid was more than a little surprised when his fingers did, in fact, curl obediently about Stephan's hand. It hurt, and he had no force in the grasp, but he did it. He looked up at Stephan in astonishment.

"Thought as much," Stephan said, leaning back in his chair again. "You've been told your whole life you can't use it, so you've never tried. Looks like the doctor was a tad bit off, though. You can't use it as well as your other hand maybe, but it's hardly useless."

"But it hurt."

"I imagine it did. It's done nothing but sit, tucked away inside that cloak of yours for years. You need to work it a bit, build up some muscle in that arm. And it just so happens that I have just the perfect thing for that." Stephan let a wide grin split his face.

"You do?" Aldrid was almost excited at the prospect of getting the use of his hand back.

"Yes, I do. Let's go milk that cow."

"What?" Aldrid cried. "How's that supposed to help?"

"It's perfect for it. You don't have to open your hand all the way up, which is the one thing it can't do. And it will work the muscles in your hand and arm that haven't been used for years. All you have to do is squeeze, just like you did with my hand just now."

Just when he was beginning to think that Stephan cared about him and was helping him, it turned out that all he wanted was to convince Aldrid that he really could milk the cow. Aldrid's face went from excited to angry in a second.

"That's not fair. You did all this just so you could make me milk your silly cow!" he accused.

"Of course, I did." Stephan still had that ridiculous grin on his face. "Now, let's see how well you remembered my lesson this morning, shall we?"

Aldrid knew he was in trouble the minute he settled himself on the stool. He tried to envision what Stephan had done that morning, but his brain could not replicate what it had not really seen, and Aldrid knew he was about to pay the price of his daydreaming.

"Well, go on. You can't just sit there staring at her and expect the job to get done." Stephan had known all along that Aldrid had not paid any attention that morning. He had almost called him out on it and told him to stop daydreaming but had thought better of it. It was one of those little lessons that Aldrid was better off teaching himself, he thought.

Aldrid ran his tongue over his lips nervously. Now that he was sitting here, the cow looked a lot bigger, and, quite frankly, a lot less patient, than she had that morning when it had been Stephan on the stool. With trepidation he tried to mimic Stephan's earlier actions, but without success. He squeezed the teats, but no stream of milk came out.

"What am I doing wrong?"

"Everything. You didn't watch me this morning, did you?"

"Yes, I..."

"Stop right there, Al. What did I say about lying?" Stephan glared at him and Aldrid dropped his eyes and looked at the floor. "Look at me Aldrid." He waited until Aldrid lifted guilty eyes up to him. "You did wrong. You didn't listen to me. Now own up to it and make it better. Don't try to lie or bluff your way out of your mistakes, it just makes it worse, and people will never trust you."

"People already don't trust me."

"Because you lie and steal. You've never given anyone any reason to trust you. Now, let's start over. You did not pay attention when I tried to show you how to do this, did you?"

"No, I didn't." Aldrid had never met anyone so stuck on telling the truth. What did it hurt if he lied a little? It wasn't a very big, important lie, really.

"Now, get up and I will show you one more time. Maybe this time you can make yourself focus?" Stephan shooed him off the stool.

Suitably chastised, Aldrid watched carefully, his eyes glued to Stephan's every move, and when Stephan motioned for him to come and try, he managed, with some difficulty, to produce a satisfying stream of milk. He looked up at Stephan with triumph in his eyes. Stephan did not seem duly impressed.

"Keep going. Finish up."

A few moments later, and Aldrid's left hand was aching and stiff. It protested it's sudden and unexpected use.

"My hand hurts," Aldrid complained.

"Good. That means you didn't lose all the feeling in it. Keep going."

"But it hurts to keep going." Aldrid tried again.

"You'll be alright. It's making the muscles stronger, that's why it hurts."

Aldrid realized, once again, that he wasn't going to win this one. With a heavy sigh, he started milking again. By the time he finished both hands were sore and aching. But he was glad to hear

Stephan say that they were done for the night. After a supper of beef stew, Aldrid was more than ready for bed. Tonight, he was too tired to even think about crying himself to sleep. His eyes were shut before his head hit his pillow, and when Stephan looked in on him only a few moments later, his breathing already had the deep, even rhythm of sleep.

Chapter 20

FOR THE NEXT WEEK, ALDRID was busier than he had ever been in his short life. The list of chores had no end, it seemed. If, by chance, he had a minute to sit down and rest, it was inevitably the minute that Stephan came to check on him and give him something else to do.

Stephan had been right about one thing. With his time and energy completely eaten up by work, he had thought very little about how much he missed Mother and Sabina and home. Nights were the only time he might have had the luxury of that thought, but, completely unused to the amount of work now being demanded of him, it was all he could do to keep his eyes open through the end of dinner.

There were several times throughout that first week when he honestly questioned Stephan's friendship with his family. Mother and Father must not have known what kind of man he really was, Aldrid thought grouchily one rainy day, as he was sitting on a pile of straw in the barn, cleaning an already clean saddle that Stephan had told him to. If they had known, they would never have been friends with him. He was like a taskmaster, always looking over Aldrid's shoulder, making sure he wasn't taking any shortcuts or cutting any corners in his work.

That was what Aldrid despised most about the man. With anyone else he could get away with slacking, but not with Stephan. It was one of the qualities he had developed as a sergeant, to spot laziness and weed it out.

By the end of the week, Aldrid was sure the three years would never end. Stephan, it appeared, was determined to work him to death.

Still, there was a tiny spark of satisfaction that he felt when he lay his head on his pillow and felt true exhaustion for the first time in his life. And stranger still, was the way that spark of satisfaction would show up when he had completed a task without Stephan's intervention or prompting. The first time he had been able to milk the cow by himself had been a moment of exultation he had never had before. Now that moment was being repeated in a dozen different ways.

His hand was growing stronger too. It still ached quite a bit, but in a good way, in a useful way. By the end of the week, Aldrid wondered how he had ever gotten along without it. How had he never even tried to use it? Everyone had said he could not use it, so he did not bother to prove them wrong.

It was on the morning of the seventh day since he had come to Stephan's farm, that Aldrid gave voice to a question that had been puzzling him. He knew all the things he did around the farm, but aside from showing up to boss him around frequently, he had no idea what Stephan did with his time. Probably sits around thinking of more things for me to do, Aldrid imagined. This morning he decided to try to find out. He was clearing the table from breakfast, another job that Stephan decided was good for him.

"Stephan?" he asked.

"What?" Stephan was pulling on his leather boots to go outside but stopped to see what Aldrid wanted.

"What do you do all day?" Aldrid decided the moment the words left his mouth that he probably should not have asked. Stephan was probably going to tell him it was none of his business and that if he had time to think about it, then he must have time to do more work. To his surprise Stephan straightened up and thought for a moment.

"Why don't you come with me and see?" he said.

"Seriously? But what about..." Aldrid stopped himself. Why in the world would he want to remind the man that he was supposed to be working?

"Your chores?" Stephan guessed his thoughts and grinned as he finished it for him. "You'll have time to get what needs done, done. Get the milking finished up and turn the cows out, then come meet me at the stable."

For the first time since he had arrived, Aldrid dashed outside, eager to do the milking. He wasn't sure what Stephan would show him, but anything was better than slaving away all day.

Stephan chuckled to himself as he watched the boy's small figure disappear into the cow shed. Aldrid was adjusting to his new life. Stephan had noticed the way he sat from time to time, moving the fingers on his left hand, his brows furrowed in concentration as he figured out how to make them work. It seemed incredible to Stephan that no one had ever even bothered to try. They had just taken the doctor's word for it.

Except Maurus, Stephan frowned a little as he had the thought. Maurus had never accepted that his son was a complete cripple. It was why he had been so desperate for money. He had wanted to take him to another doctor, one who might be more willing to try something different for the boy.

When Aldrid came running into the stable a half hour later, Stephan was waiting for him.

"Carry this and come with me." He pointed to a saddle and bridle hanging up.

Aldrid frowned a little. He should have known the offer to just watch was too good to be true. Stephan just wanted to make him work more. Nevertheless, he went to grab the saddle and bridle. He knew better than to argue.

It was the only time Stephan ever reminded him of why he was here. He made sure to point out, whenever Aldrid complained that it was too much or that he shouldn't have to do it, that he was here through his own choice. Otherwise, no word was ever said about how he had tried to rob Stephan or of how he had robbed other people. Aldrid could not have put it in words, but he felt the difference and unconsciously appreciated it.

Stephan led one of the horses out of its stall and took him out the back of the stable, Aldrid trailing behind with the tack. Aldrid had to feed and water and brush these horses every day, but otherwise he had nothing to do with them. They were just another smelly animal that took up his time and energy. He had known, of course, that Stephan trained these horses for war. But what it meant to train a war horse, Aldrid had not the slightest idea.

There was a paddock behind the stable and this was where Stephan led the animal. Now that they were out of the darkened barn, Aldrid could see that this horse was a dark, glossy brown, almost black. Its legs looked almost funny with its four perfectly matched white socks rising from the hooves up to the horse's knees. Another white marking started between its ears and extended to its velvety nose. Out in the paddock the horse's head was up and its ears forward, alert to every sound and movement.

Aldrid thought it looked frightfully big, and the way it pranced a circle around Stephan was equally terrifying.

"He's pretty, isn't he?" Stephan was asking him.

"He's big," Aldrid said cautiously. Maybe he didn't want to know what Stephan did all day. Stephan might get it into his head to put Aldrid up on one of those monstrous animals.

"You know, I'm not going to tell you to get on him." Once again, Stephan had the uncanny ability of reading Aldrid's thoughts. "He's not ready for anyone to ride him yet. Today he just gets to figure out what the saddle is and how it feels to wear it."

"Oh." Aldrid tried to keep the relief out of his voice. He was surprised to find that he was, at the same time, disappointed. Frightened as he was of the powerful animal, there was a part of him that wanted to learn how to ride a horse.

Fascinated, Aldrid watched as Stephan brought the saddle close to the horse and the horse shied away from it. This was repeated again and again until, at last, the horse became bored with it and stood still next to the strange object.

"Why don't you just put it straight on him?" he asked.

"That would be a waste of time and energy. See, if I do it this way, he convinces himself that it won't hurt him, and I save myself the trouble of having to do that."

"I see," Aldrid said, though he wasn't sure at all if he did. "So, when you put it on him, he'll be ready to ride?"

"Oh no! It takes a lot of time to train a horse, especially if you want that horse to be good enough to ride into battle. Time and patience."

"What do you have to teach him to be able to go into battle?"

"He has to be steady. He can't spook at loud noises or sudden movements. He can't be skittish about going into strange places. He has to obey the slightest command. If his rider needs him to move over even just one step, he has to do it instantly. It could mean the difference between his rider's life or death."

"That's a lot." Aldrid thought training war horses was definitely not for him. Patience was not something he had in great quantities.

"Want to try your hand at one of them?" Stephan asked him suddenly.

"Try what? Riding him?" Aldrid asked in alarm.

"No, not him. One that's already trained."

"Can I? I mean, with my hand. You don't think it would be too dangerous?" Aldrid wanted to, but he was nervous of how big the horses were.

"You might fall off, but you can learn not to." Stephan shrugged. "Want to?"

"Yes. I think so."

The horse Stephan pointed out to Aldrid in the stable was a bit smaller than the one he had been training. Aldrid couldn't really tell what he looked like in the shadows of the barn, but when he led him out into the bright mid-morning sunlight, he decided that this one was prettier than the one Stephan had earlier. He was an almost dusty brownish gray color with a black mane and tail, and instead of white socks like the other one had, his were black and they extended a little way above his knees and hocks. His face was all the same color except that it shaded into black on his nose.

"You'll saddle him up. You should never get on a horse that you don't know how to saddle," Stephan said, as he showed Aldrid where to put the blanket on the horse's back, and how to put the saddle on over that. Aldrid was small for his age and had a hard time getting the heavy saddle up over the back of the horse, but the horse was a patient one and waited calmly while he tried several times before succeeding.

"Good. Now when you tighten his girth make sure you pull it good and hard. This one will hold his breath and wait until you get on him before he lets it out again."

"They can do that?" Aldrid asked in disbelief.

"Believe me, they can. You'll think you have the saddle on as tight as it can go and the next thing you'll know, you're hanging upside down under the horse because he let his breath out and the whole thing slid."

Aldrid stuck his tongue out of the side of his mouth and furrowed his brow as he pulled as hard as he could on the girth strap. When he could not pull it any further, Stephan showed him how to tie it so the knot wouldn't slip. Then Stephan tugged on the girth and pulled another few inches up.

"See what I mean? He was holding out on you. Always check twice."

Aldrid nodded his acknowledgement. This was turning into a much better day than he had thought he could ever have here. Now that he was going to ride, he could barely contain his excitement. He bounced from one foot to the other in anticipation and impatience. Stephan noticed and smiled.

"Think you're ready?"

"Yes!"

Stephan stepped to the side and passed the reins to Aldrid. Since Aldrid had only ever seen people ride, and had never done it himself, it took several clumsy, awkward attempts before he could pull himself up into the saddle. It didn't help that he could only get a good grip with his right hand.

Once up, Aldrid almost regretted his haste in wanting to ride. He was a very long way up, and his head spun a little when he looked down.

"He's really big!" he mentioned to Stephan.

"He's smaller than the other one. Actually, he's the smallest one I have."

"Really? Why?"

"Small horses don't generally work well for armored men. They need horses that are heavier and stronger. I only kept him because he's a good one to lead the young ones on. He's slow, and steady. He's also blind in one eye. He had a little accident when he was a colt."

"Oh." Aldrid hadn't noticed that before. "Does that mean you have to do anything different for him?"

"No. He's figured it all out pretty well on his own. I try not to come up on his blind side, but honestly, his hearing is so good it doesn't really matter. No, I can use him like any of the others."

"Does he have a name?" Aldrid asked.

"I call him Casper."

"Casper? That's not a horse name!" Aldrid had never given much thought to naming an animal, but that certainly was not a name he would have picked.

"I don't think he cares. Now are you going to just sit up there talking or are you actually going to go somewhere on him?"

"How do I make him move?" Aldrid looked a little nervously down at the ground as he spoke.

"Tap him with your heels, but don't do it too hard. He'll take off then."

Aldrid gingerly brushed his heels against the horse's sides. The horse did nothing.

"What am I doing wrong?"

"You didn't touch him hard enough for him to think a fly landed on him. Now do it like you mean for him to go."

Aldrid tried again, and this time the horse took one lazy step forward, then another. The movement caught Aldrid unprepared, and he clutched the horse's black mane with his hand. The feeling of something moving beneath, moving him, was entirely foreign to him. Without realizing it, he leaned forward, closer to the horse's neck. It felt like a much safer position.

Unfortunately, it was just about the worst position for him to be in when the horse spotted a clump of grass and decided to stop for a snack. Without warning, he came to a standstill and dropped his big head to the ground. Also without warning, Aldrid kept moving. Over the horse's lowered neck, and straight onto the ground in front of him.

"Ouch!" Aldrid landed, sitting down with a jarring PLOP. "What happened?" He looked accusingly over at Stephan. "You said this one was safe!"

Stephan could not answer for several seconds. He was doubled over, bellowing in laughter. By the time he got himself back under control, he was wiping tears from his eyes.

"He is. He's a great little horse, but you, Aldrid, are a terrible rider! He thought he could get away with it."

"He did," Aldrid pointed out. He could feel his face going red. He hated being laughed at.

"Only if you let him." Stephan finally grew serious. "Stand up and get back on."

"I don't want to now. That hurt." Aldrid got up, rubbing the spot he had landed on.

"No, you have to. If you fall off, you always get back on. Go ahead." Stephan motioned him back toward the animal who was still calmly munching his clump of grass.

Aldrid approached him cautiously, warily. He looked docile, and even half asleep as he ate at the moment, but Aldrid suspected the horse had done it on purpose and was now just waiting for another chance to do it again. Stephan shouldn't make him get back on. The horse hated him and was going to just throw him off again, he was sure of it. But Stephan would never agree with him and arguing wouldn't get him anywhere. So, he reached out a tentative hand and grasped the loose rein. The horse obediently followed him back to the center of the paddock and stood patiently while Aldrid scrambled up on top of him.

This time, though, when Aldrid put his heels to the horse's flanks, the horse would not budge. Aldrid kicked harder, then harder still, before finally looking over at Stephan, his hands raised in a question.

"Look at that. You and that horse have something in common after all," Stephan said, laughing.

"What are you talking about?" Aldrid turned confused eyes toward the man. "What do we have in common?"

"You're both lazy and stubborn and would rather not work. But then, he is blind in that one eye, so maybe we should just give him the day off." Stephan was grinning again, a mischievous twinkle in his eye.

"So how do I make him move?" Aldrid's face grew red with frustration at the way this man was making a joke of him.

"You know what, Aldrid, I'm going to let you figure that one out. You sit there until you can think of a way to make him go. And by that, I mean, he goes when and where you want him to, not just him wandering around because he is bored and looking for food." And Stephan turned to walk away. "I'll come check on you in a bit to see how you're doing." He called over his shoulder as he disappeared into the stable.

"That's not fair!" Aldrid called after him but got no response. Apparently "fair" was not a word in Stephan's vocabulary.

Aldrid had never met such a stubborn, pig-headed animal as Casper. He actually never met many animals at all, but if he had, he was sure Casper would still take the prize as the most stubborn, pig headed one.

He sat atop the unmoving beast, wishing he had never thought it was a good idea to learn how to ride. Stephan knew this would happen; he was certain. In fact, he bet Stephan anxiously awaited the day when Aldrid would ask him about his work just so he could set him up like this. The more Aldrid thought about it, and he had plenty of time to think about it, the angrier he became.

In the meantime, Casper became bored just as Stephan said he would. He spotted another mouthful of grass on the other side of the paddock and shuffled his way towards it. Aldrid was not expecting even that slow movement and came very close to falling off again. It was only by sheer willpower that he regained his seat and held on.

For a moment he considered getting off and telling Stephan that he made the horse move. But the thought was gone as soon as he remembered Stephan's uncanny ability to drag the truth from him no matter how much he wanted to hide it. No, he would have to stay here until he figured this horrid horse out. Aldrid decided then and there that he hated horses.

For nearly an hour, Aldrid sat on the dusty brownish gray horse as it wandered back and forth between bites of grass. The second Aldrid tried to kick him to go, or pulled on a rein to turn him, he stopped. There was no saying how long he would have been there if he did not remember something Stephan said. Stephan said the horse was lazy and stubborn like him. He was still a little peeved over being compared to a horse, but now a new thought came to him.

It occurred to him that on the days he complained the most or tried to cheat on his work were the days when Stephan magically found more work for him to do and would hang over his shoulder nagging him until he got it done. Maybe, there was some way he could do that to the horse. His forehead creased in a little frown as he thought hard about what he could do to nag the horse into moving. His face brightened as he had a thought. So far, his effort amounted to kicking the horse one or two times, and then giving up and sitting there.

This time, he gathered the reins in his hand so that he was ready. Rather than kicking him only once or twice, he kept at it, clapping his heels against the horse's sides as hard as he could while still maintaining his balance. For a moment nothing different happened, then Casper decided he'd had enough and was not going to get away with anymore. He started forward.

Aldrid almost shouted his triumph but stopped himself in time as he thought that might startle the horse. Casper was moving, not because Casper wanted to, but because he was doing what Aldrid was telling him to. Experimentally, Aldrid pulled on the right rein, and Casper, now content to obey, turned his feet in that direction. Around and around Aldrid went, turning left, then right, then left again, stopping and starting until he was sure of himself. When Stephan came back to check on him, he would find that Aldrid had succeeded.

Unbeknownst to Aldrid, Stephan watched the entire affair from just inside the shadow of the stable doorway. His smile grew wider than ever when he watched Aldrid's face wrinkle up in thought and then clear as an idea came to him.

Now, as Aldrid moved Casper around the pen, he sauntered out as if he just happened to come by at that moment. Stephan had never seen so much as a hint of a genuine smile on Aldrid's young face. He was always looking either completely indifferent, or he was scowling. As Stephan rested a foot on the bottom rail of the wooden fence though, and his eyes met Aldrid's he noticed the grin on the boy's face and the way his eyes lit up with triumph and excitement.

"I see you figured out how to make him move?" Stephan motioned for him to bring the horse over to him. "Come on down and see if you can still walk now."

Aldrid was a little confused by the last part. Why wouldn't he be able to walk? But as he slid awkwardly down the side of the horse, he realized with horror that he could not really feel or control his legs. They simply folded up under him and he found himself for the second time that day sitting in the dust.

"What's wrong with them?" he asked, alarmed.

"Nothing. It happens usually when you ride for the first time. Especially since you spent over an hour on him. How did it feel?" Stephan nodded toward the horse.

"You mean making him listen? It felt great!" The smile returned to Aldrid's face briefly, and then a look of suspicion came into his dark eyes. "You knew he was going to do that?"

"I thought he might. Like I said, he's a good little horse, but if he thinks he can get away with being lazy...well, you know what he'll do. He's a bit like someone else I know." Stephan looked pointedly at him for a moment. "You remind me of your Father."

Aldrid dropped his eyes. He wished Stephan had not said that just then. All he ever heard from people was that he was just like his father, and usually they followed up by saying he stole just like Father did.

"But I wasn't stealing anything just now?" He was confused why this moment in particular made Stephan think he was like Father.

"I didn't say you did." Stephan searched Al's face. "Why would you think that's what I meant?"

"It's what everyone means when they say I'm like Father." Aldrid ran his fingers through the dust, scrawling a senseless pattern in it as he tried to ignore Stephan's gaze.

"I'm sorry to hear that."

"What did you mean, then?"

"I meant that you're a thinker, like you Father was. A planner. If you put yourself to it, you can see a problem and find a solution to it. That's what you did with that horse. I didn't tell you how to make him move. You figured it out on your own. Your Father was like that. That's how he became Captain. He was good at forming strategies, of overcoming logistical problems, of thinking through how to make things work."

Aldrid wasn't looking at the dirt anymore. He was staring, with wonder in his eyes, at Stephan as he spoke. No one, not even Mother, ever talked about Father this way.

"What else was he good at?" Aldrid's voice was quiet and small.

"He was good at riding a horse," Stephan said with a smile. "He was good at leading people. Men were willing to follow him into battle. If King Dival had tried to lead them, they never would have gone. But they would follow your father. He was good at caring for those under him. He was a good Father and husband."

"Until he decided not to be," Aldrid added bitterly.

Stephan lowered himself to the ground next to Aldrid. "Aldrid, I can't make any excuse for what your father did in the end, but I think there is something you should know. The winter you burned yourself was a terrible one. It was the same winter the King had ordered us on a winter campaign, and your father was badly wounded. He almost didn't make it. When he did heal up, he couldn't walk properly. And just about the same time, I showed up to tell him his oldest son had died in battle. That broke him, Aldrid. That and the fact that he came home to find you scarred and crippled from your accident. He was devastated. He didn't know what to do. The King stripped away his position as Captain because of the failure of the campaign. He felt like the only thing he had left worth trying for was you. He never believed that you were as crippled as the king's doctor said you were. He thought if he could just find a doctor who would try to treat you differently, then maybe he would not have failed. But he needed money to do that. That's why he stole the sword. He stole it to try to help you. I know that doesn't make what he did right. But he wasn't trying to be a bad Father. He was trying to help you."

Aldrid looked away, into the distance, a thoughtful expression on his young face. There were two things Mother never talked about. His Father and his brother. The only times they were mentioned was when she was frustrated with him. Then she would compare him to Father and tell him she wished he was more like Hamo.

But she never talked about them, about what they had been like, what they had enjoyed, what they hated. It was as if she had shut out any memory of either of them. All the things Aldrid had ever wanted to know about his father and brother crowded into his mind, but he couldn't put the thoughts together enough to ask Stephan any questions.

"He would have helped me more if he had stayed," Aldrid said at last.

"You're right. But at the time, he couldn't see that. Grief has a way of blinding people, and so does anger." Stephan got up and brushed himself off. "Let's get Casper put up and finish up chores for the day."

Chapter 21

ALDRID REMAINED UNUSUALLY thoughtful for the next few days as he went about his work. Every opportunity he had, he'd follow Stephan and ask him anything he could think of about Father and Hamo. If Stephan minded, he didn't show it. And for a while, things went smoothly.

It was almost two weeks after Aldrid's riding lesson when Aldrid thoughtfulness disappeared. Stephan woke him as usual well before the sun was up and Aldrid drug himself through his morning chores. Dark, heavy rain clouds chased the dry, sunny weather away and turned the day gloomy.

Aldrid studied the sky as he carried the milk back into the house. It would rain soon, and when it did it would rain heavily. In the distance, thunder rumbled. Sighing, he stepped into the house.

"Do I have to put the cows out today?" Aldrid asked Stephan at breakfast, as he looked out the window and saw the steady drizzle outside.

"Why wouldn't you? Cows don't mind the rain and it's not that cold out." Stephan did not bother to look up, so he missed seeing the face Aldrid made. "Hurry up, though. You're dragging this morning."

"But it's cold and rainy. I don't feel like it." It was a sorry excuse and the minute he said it, Aldrid regretted it.

"It's not about whether you feel like it or not. It's what you're supposed to do," Stephan replied.

Aldrid went through the motions of cleaning up breakfast and washing up the handful of dishes they'd used. He took far longer than usual, hoping against hope that Stephan would change his mind. Surely when he went outside and saw how downright nasty the weather was, he would rethink the importance of putting the cows out. He watched anxiously as Stephan went outside and waited for him to come back in and tell him to forget it.

When several minutes went by, Aldrid resigned himself to a long, wet walk out to the pasture. Stephan meant for him to take the cows all the way out to their pasture even in this inclement weather. Scowling, Aldrid pulled on his own boots and his cloak before heading out into the rain.

Stalking out to the cowshed, Aldrid pondered once again about the disadvantages of being a farmer. Farmers had to go out in all kinds of weather, and he hated it.

Of course, Stephan would find something to do inside the barn or house all day. He would leave all the outdoor jobs for Aldrid to do. That's why he insisted on making Aldrid work for him, so that he could have a nice comfortable life while someone else did all the unpleasant things. It really was not fair or kind of Aldrid to think so little of the man after he had taken the time to tell him about his Father, but Aldrid was not in the mood to be kind.

As the day went on Aldrid's mood grew darker and darker. All the good, encouraging thoughts that filled his mind after his conversation with Stephan about Father were gone, chased away by his own gloominess. There was a part of Aldrid that wanted to get them back, but the greater part of him was enjoying his self-pity. He hadn't felt this sorry for himself in weeks, and there was a certain enjoyment to making himself miserable.

Because of the gray clouds, the evening was darker than usual, and by the time Aldrid finished his other chores and was getting ready to bring the cows in he happened upon a truly terrible thought. He waited until he saw Stephan go into the house, and then kept out of sight for a while longer in the cowshed. Stephan could not see the shed, or the pasture beyond it from the house. If Aldrid did nothing to arouse his suspicions, there would be no reason for Stephan to think that he had not completed his chores. He had been so good about it for the last couple weeks.

A crooked little smirk crossed Aldrid's face as he thought his plan out. If the cows were alright out there during the day, there was no reason to think that they weren't alright out there at night. He would pretend to bring them in and to do the milking. Since he was the one who strained the milk, Stephan would have no reason to check on it. He would wait until the morning, by which time he hoped the weather would have cleared, to bring them in.

When he came in a while later, carrying the empty milk bucket, Stephan was busy over the fire.

"Finish up?" Stephan wasn't looking at him.

"Yes, I just did." Aldrid thought he did a good job keeping his voice normal. He went about, pretending to take care of the milk that was not there.

"Good. Supper's ready." Stephan did not appear to suspect a thing. Aldrid was inwardly congratulating himself. He would not have to get all wet and cold tonight after all. Of course, he would have to be very careful to make sure Stephan did not notice in the morning, but he thought he could manage.

Aldrid's appetite deserted him and rather than eating, he just stared at his food. The food seemed to stick in his throat, and his stomach felt almost queasy. He glanced at Stephan, half expecting him to guess what he'd done but Stephan wasn't even looking at him.

It was nonsense, he told himself, he did things like this all the time back home. The way the thought of home suddenly intruded into his brain startled him a little. He should be home, not here. If Stephan was not so mean, he would be home. Well, tonight he was going to get the best of Stephan. For some reason the thought did not make him as happy as he thought it would.

"Are you feeling alright?" Stephan was watching him closely from across the table.

"I'm fine. I'm just tired, that's all." Aldrid's heart skipped a beat at the thought that Stephan had guessed his secret.

"Hmm. Well, let's get this cleaned up and you can go to bed," Stephan said, and Aldrid let out an internal sigh of relief.

When he crawled beneath his blankets a half hour later, he found he could not just fall asleep. For a while he tossed and turned, restlessly. He knew Stephan was still up, out in the main room and more than once he almost got up and told him the truth. But each time he made up his mind to do so, he thought about how angry Stephan would be and finally decided that he would just take care of it in the morning. With that thought in mind, he gradually drifted off to sleep.

Stephan, sitting in the room just outside Aldrid's door, was well aware of the boy's restlessness. He had suspected something was amiss over supper. Aldrid's appetite was typical of a growing boy - ravenous and insatiable - but tonight he had barely touched his food. He waited until no more sound came from the bedroom before getting up and heading outside.

"Get up, Aldrid." The voice broke into Aldrid's sleep, dragging him back to wakefulness.

For a second, he lay still, wondering if it was just part of a dream. When a hand roughly shook his shoulder, he decided it was not a dream and his eyes flew open to find Stephan bending over him.

"Get up right now," Stephan was saying.

Aldrid's look of confusion turned quickly to one of guilt as he remembered. Stephan must have found out that he left the cows out and that he had not milked them in the evening. He wondered what time it was. It felt like the middle of the night. He did not have long to lay there thinking about anything. Stephan was pulling him up by the arm.

"When were you going to tell me that you didn't actually finish up? Or were you just planning on hiding that forever?" Stephan's voice was sterner than Aldrid had ever heard it before. "Get your clothes on."

"What? It's the middle of the night," Aldrid protested.

"So? You could have done it when it was supposed to be done, but you decided not to. Now get dressed, you have work to finish."

Miserably, Aldrid pulled his clothes on and followed Stephan out into the other room.

"Get your boots on," Stephan ordered.

Aldrid sat to put them on, sincerely wishing that he had never thought of trying to deceive Stephan. He never met anyone who was able to see through all his tricks and lies the way Stephan could.

"Now, you are going to go out there and bring the cows in and then you are going to do the milking and take care of the milk and then, and only then, can you go back to bed, is that clear?"

"It's dark... I mean, yes, Stephan." Aldrid hung his head. "Am I going out there by myself?"

"Of course. I'm not the one who decided to not do my work and then lie about it so there's no reason I should be the one who walks all the way out to the pasture and sits up for the next hour doing what should have been done earlier."

Aldrid did not see any chance of escape. He put his cloak on, pulling the hood up over his head to protect against the rain. As the door shut behind him, he realized just how very dark it was. Aldrid had never been particularly afraid of the dark, but then, he never had to walk all the way out into a big open pasture and hunt down two big cows either. The task was daunting. And now that he was fully awake, he was mad that Stephan was being such a stickler for him doing it now. The cows had already been out half the night, it wasn't going to hurt them to finish out the night outside. Stephan was cruel for dragging him out of his sleep and making him go out here all alone. It could have waited for morning.

The walk to the pasture was the longest he had ever taken. The ground that he could cross easily in the day seemed to have become an evil being committed to tripping him up and slowing him down. Each time he fell, his clothes got wetter and muddier. Fortunately, the cows, perturbed at the disruption to their schedule, were waiting by the gate. He jerked on the lead rope of the mother cow to get her to walk, but she was ahead of him. Impatiently she moved forward, throwing him off balance so that he landed, sitting down in the mud.

"You stupid old cow!" he yelled at her as she and the calf made their own way to their shed. He had no choice but to try to catch up with them.

By the time he let them into the cow shed, Aldrid was thoroughly drenched and covered in slimy mud from head to toe. He angrily kicked at a sack of feed that was sitting against the wall, then hopped back on one foot as he realized it was a lot more solid than he had thought.

It was not until he was sitting on the three-legged stool, his head resting against the cow's side that another idea came to him. It was a wild one, one he wouldn't have dared plan in the light of day. If it were not for the fact that it was the middle of the night and he was completely muddled both by his anger and his tiredness, he would have dismissed the idea immediately. As it was, the longer he thought about it, the better the idea seemed. There was really only one way out of this mess that he found himself in. If he stayed Stephan would be harder on him than ever. But Stephan had unwittingly given him the means he needed to leave. He had shown him how to ride.

His overactive, but tired, imagination decided, with its usual flare of drama, that the only hope he had of a normal life was to leave everything behind. He could slip away tonight and make it back home long enough to get his stash of money, and then he could get onto a ship and sail far, far away. It was a far-fetched and completely unreasonable plan, but Aldrid was in a very unreasonable mood and so it appealed to him.

The windows in the house were completely dark when he emerged from the cowshed, and he assumed Stephan had gone to bed. Of course, he had. Stephan did not care if his indentured servant - more like a slave, Aldrid thought - was cold and wet and tired and miserable. All he cared about was the work being done. He really was despicable. He would pretend to be nice like on the day he had shown Aldrid how to ride. But on the inside Stephan was horrid, just waiting for a chance to abuse him.

Instead of carrying the full bucket of milk into the house, Aldrid made his way into the barn. He groped his way over to where Stephan kept the saddles and then counted off the stalls until he knew he reached the one Casper was in. He lifted the latch and slipped inside.

It would be hard to saddle Casper in the dark, but he would just have to manage. He tried to remember how Stephan had shown him to do it, but he was very cold, and his fingers were clumsy. He forgot that he was supposed to check the girth more than once, and having pulled it tight once, was satisfied that all was ready.

He led Casper outside to mount him and then turned him toward the lane that led away from Stephan's house and to the road. It was nothing more than wagon ruts in the ground and in the dark it was hard to see, but he thought he was on the right path. This was confirmed when he reached the road. Here, though, he was in a quandary. He had been asleep when Stephan had brought him here, so he had no idea which direction to take. It ended up being Casper who chose. The little horse pulled his head to the left and started down that road and Aldrid, with nothing better to go on, let him. The rain let up and the clouds were breaking up so that every now and then he caught a glimpse of the moon and stars high overhead.

As Casper plodded onward, Aldrid wondered if he should risk telling Mother about his plan or if he should just slip quietly into the house in the middle of the night and leave without telling her goodbye. That did not seem right, but he was sure she would try to talk him out of his plan if she saw him. Goodness, she might even turn him back over to Stephan since she had no idea how mean he really was. No, it would be better for him to cut all ties with home and make his own way in the world, he was sure of it. It was a big, grand thought, and it suited his mood perfectly. The details of making his own way were not important at the moment.

Aldrid was confused when he found himself riding into a forest. He did not remember passing through one on his way here. It must have been while he was asleep, he decided. He was more confused when he realized, in the light of the unveiled moon, that he was not actually on a road anymore. Casper was shambling rather aimlessly through the trees, stopping here and there to snatch a bite off the bushes growing up all around him.

Aldrid felt more and more alarmed as he went along, and he began to think that perhaps he had made a terrible mistake. He did not have too long to consider his terrible mistake. Having never ridden through a wood before he was unaware of how quickly and suddenly a low hanging branch could knock him off the horse. He was looking down at the ground when an awful THWACK resounded through his head, and he felt himself tumbling backwards off of Casper. Casper chose that moment to turn and head for home and by the time Aldrid sat up, holding a hand to a rapidly swelling lump on his forehead, the horse had disappeared from sight.

Aldrid almost cried, he was so miserable. His wet clothes made him cold. He was tired. And now that he was sitting here, alone in the dark forest, he was scared. Maybe he had been too hasty in thinking he could run away. Stephan did not seem nearly so bad when compared to the terrifying noises that came from the forest.

Without any idea where he was going to go, Aldrid started walking. If he just kept going, surely he would come across something or somewhere. The forest could not go on endlessly. His head was aching from where the tree limb had struck it and he was a little dizzy, but he thought he was going forward in a fairly straight path.

He was rewarded much sooner than he expected. The sky was just turning its predawn gray when he noticed a solid black shape in the distance. It was a building of some sort. By this time, Aldrid's eyes were heavy and his footsteps slow and shuffling. He could hardly get one foot in front of the other. As he neared the building, he recognized it as a long, low barn. He reached the door and slipped inside, not even caring if someone was in there or not.

He found a pile of clean straw in the farthest corner and decided that he could not go another step unless he slept a bit. The straw looked so inviting and comfortable and before he knew it, he was asleep.

Chapter 22

WHAT ARE YOU DOING HERE?" The voice was high pitched and piercing.

"Wh... wha... what?" Aldrid sat up, bewildered. He looked about him, trying to remember where he was and how he had gotten there.

In front of him stood a girl, maybe a year or two older than him, with her hands on her hips, glaring at him.

"I said, what are you doing in our barn?" she asked again.

"I... uh... um... I was... uh." Aldrid couldn't collect his thoughts enough to come up with a good answer. He did not want to say that he was running away, because that would lead to all kinds of unpleasant questions and answers. But he could not think of another good reason to be in someone else's barn, sleeping in someone else's straw.

"Who are you?" the girl demanded and then looked more closely at him. "And what happened to your face?" Her own wrinkled up in disgust as she spoke.

"That's really rude." Aldrid could finally think of something to say, and he bristled defensively at the insult in her voice.

"You're sleeping in my barn without asking permission. I don't have to be polite to you," she retorted.

Aldrid felt he was losing this conversation and tried to steer it to safer waters. "I'm just getting ready to leave."

"Wait a minute!" Realization dawned on her face. "Aren't you that boy Stephan has with him? The thief?"

Aldrid started to answer no when another voice interrupted, one he had not expected at all to hear, one that made his heart sink to his feet.

"That's right, Emilia."

Aldrid spun around, dismay written all over his face. There was Stephan standing in the doorway and looking not at all amused.

"If you would be so kind as to give us a few minutes alone, Emilia. I've already spoken to your father about this little matter. Aldrid was right, we'll be leaving just as soon as we can."

Emilia, as the girl was called, nodded and left the barn, glancing curiously back at Aldrid as she went. Everyone in the neighborhood had heard about the thief Stephan had working for him.

Aldrid stood in front of Stephan, looking at the ground, shifting from one foot to the other nervously. His plan last night certainly did not include this possibility.

"Did you honestly think you could get away with that little stunt?"

Aldrid nodded glumly.

"Well, let's do a bit of math, shall we? Let's see, you owe me a little less than three years of service for trying to rob me in town. Now you stole my horse, that's another ten years automatically. You also stole my saddle and bridle, that would be another five years. You left an entire bucket of milk sitting out to spoil and cost me half a night and this morning hunting you down, so we'll say that's another year. Congratulations, boy! You must really love working for me because you just earned another sixteen years of it."

"That's not fair!" Aldrid looked at him in horror.

"Fair! You really want to talk about fair, Aldrid? I'm the one who is out a horse. I'm the one who is out a valuable saddle and bridle. Tell me, is that fair?" Stephan's voice was controlled but there was real anger in it, the first Aldrid had ever heard.

Aldrid shook his head. "Please, Stephan? You'll get your horse and stuff back. I'll find it."

"And what if I hadn't caught up with you? What if you had made it away? Did you have some plan to get them back to me then, or were you just going to keep them?"

"I hadn't thought that far..."

"You're right. You didn't think. Not about anything or anyone but yourself, as usual. You got in trouble last night because you didn't do your work and then you got mad and decided to take off. You can't just run every time you mess up, Aldrid. Your life would be easier if you would own up to your problems and fix them. Where were you even planning on going?"

"Home."

"Your home?" For the first time since he had arrived Stephan's face softened a little, and, although Aldrid was too ashamed to look at him, the corners of his mouth turned up ever so slightly.

"Yes."

"And you thought this was going to get you home?"

"Yes," Aldrid repeated, annoyance creeping into his voice at how hard it was for Stephan to grasp his destination.

"You know, if I were you, and trying to get to your home, I would have gone the other direction. It would have made more sense considering that is the direction your home is in."

Now Aldrid understood, and his head hung even lower. Stephan was making fun of him. And Aldrid's own ignorance gave him the perfect tool to do it. Of course, with his luck, he had picked the opposite direction. His gross misfortune seemed to put Stephan in a slightly better mood, which Aldrid thought was unfair. He corrected himself mentally as he thought of that word, remembering what

Stephan had to say about it. Stephan was right about one thing, this was entirely Aldrid's own fault. He did not say those words out loud, but Aldrid was quite sure he had never admitted that anything was his fault in his entire life.

"Where's Casper?" Stephan was still speaking to him.

"I lost him. Last night. I fell off and he ran away."

"Ran home most likely. Guess you're walking." Stephan turned sharply and walked out of the barn, and Aldrid knew he had no choice but to follow him.

Stephan did not let Aldrid out of his sight the rest of the day. He accompanied him around the farm as he did his work, and when night came, he announced that Aldrid was going to have to sleep on the floor in his own room so that he could be sure he was not going to take off again. Aldrid was already wretched by the time Stephan told him that they were going to town the next day.

Aldrid remembered then what he had forgotten. The threat Stephan made that day in front of the Magistrate. He was taking Aldrid to town to have an iron cuff put on his wrist, the cuff that would bind him forever to a life of difficulty and distrust.

Aldrid regretted bitterly that he ever thought of running away. Stephan needed only to tell the Magistrate and those sixteen extra years were sure to be added to his sentence, and coupled with the cuff, Aldrid would never have the chance to become anything other than a criminal. Stephan was angry with him for running away and that was the best punishment he could give Aldrid.

Worse than the looming punishment, though, was Stephan's wrath. Stephan truly angry with him. Aldrid hadn't thought he cared, but it hurt. He wondered when the man's opinion came to matter so much to him. Stephan was the first person in Aldrid's short life to see him as something more than a cripple, more than the son of a thief, more than a thief himself. And now, through his own folly and impulsiveness, he just lost the only person who believed in him. Stephan would forever look at him the way everyone else did.

His sleep that night was fitful, and when Stephan woke him up very early the next morning he got up as quickly as he could. It did not make sense to put Stephan in a worse temper by dawdling. After a quick breakfast, he climbed onto the wagon seat next to Stephan. He kept his head down and turned away from Stephan.

They had been on the road for some time before Aldrid worked up the nerve to speak.

"Does it hurt?"

"Does what hurt?" Stephan glanced over and noticed the boy's white face and understanding dawned on his face.

"When they put it on. The cuff, you know." Aldrid couldn't quite bring himself to meet Stephan's eyes, though he could tell Stephan was looking at him.

"Yes. It does."

"Oh," Aldrid gulped. "Like burning?"

This was Aldrid's phobia. Mother said it had to do with his accident when he was little, but he was absolutely terrified of being too close to fires or anything else that could create that horrible burning sensation that he vividly remembered. The accident had faded from memory, but the pain never had. He even had bad dreams sometimes where he was being burned and he would wake up to the awful sensation, usually in the crippled hand.

"Yes. I imagine that's what it feels like. It has to be hot when they put it on."

"Oh," he said again and then fell silent.

It was a testament to how much Aldrid had changed in the last few weeks that he did not beg and plead for Stephan to turn back and not take him to town. He had spent most of his life talking and cajoling his way out of trouble. This was the very first time that he seemed resigned to accept it. Stephan watched him for a minute before turning his attention back to the road. Aldrid did not see the subtle look of approval in the man's eyes. All he could think about was how frightened he was of having it put on. It was more than just the pain that scared him.

It was early evening when the towers of the castle rose up in the distance. Aldrid stiffened and squirmed in his seat at the sight of them. He glanced over at Stephan, hoping he had not noticed, but he was staring straight ahead.

Aldrid had assumed they were going straight to the Magistrate's office again, so he was both surprised and confused when the wagon stopped in front of his own home. He looked at Stephan in bewilderment, but now it appeared as if Stephan was not willing to meet his eyes.

"Go ahead." Stephan waved him toward the door that was already opening.

The sight of Mother standing there broke the spell of confusion and Aldrid was jumping off the wagon seat and running into her arms. He had never been so happy and so miserable to see anyone in his whole life.

"Oh, Al, I had no idea you were coming." She stopped and held him at arm's length from her. "Al, what's wrong? What happened to your head?"

Aldrid all but forgot about the lump on his forehead from the branch. It was the least of his worries in the last twenty-four hours.

"Oh that. I hit my head on a branch. It's alright." He hoped Mother wouldn't ask any other questions. He knew if he started talking, he would end up crying, and he did not want to do that.

"Stephan, you didn't tell me you were coming?" Thankfully, she turned her attention to Stephan as he came up behind Aldrid.

"Well, Al and I have a little business to take care of here in town, and I thought he might like to stop in and say hello."

Aldrid dropped his eyes and felt the color drain from his face a little as Stephan spoke. He did not want to think about why they were in town, not while he was with Mother. Poor Mother! She would be so ashamed of him from now on. Fortunately, Mother was so happy to see him, that she wasn't in the mood to ask too many questions about why they were here.

"You'll stay for dinner, won't you?" She looked anxiously at Stephan. Since he now had complete authority over her son's life, he was the one who had to agree.

"Of course. I think Aldrid prefers your cooking to mine," he answered with a smile. Aldrid glanced over at him again, but Stephan was still not making eye contact.

"Good. Sabina should be home soon, and I know she'll be happy to see you. Al, are you sure you're alright?" She looked at her youngest in some concern. He was pale, and he kept running his tongue nervously over his lips. She knew something was bothering him.

"I'm fine." He looked away quickly. It would almost have been easier to just go and get it over with right away, he thought. Stephan was dragging this out and it was making him miserable.

The evening disappeared far too quickly for Aldrid's liking. Try as he might, and he did try very hard, he could not concentrate on anything. Not the food in front of him, or the conversation around him. He realized with dismay that his eyes kept shutting. He had had so little sleep in the last two nights that he could barely keep himself awake now. Stephan and Mother were both talking about something from the past when Sabina slid her chair quietly next to Aldrid's at the table.

"Al, how are you really getting on?" Sabina had always bounced back and forth between feeling annoyed and jealous of her little brother and feeling sorry for him. Since she had not seen him in weeks, and he was clearly bothered by something, she was in the mood to feel sorry for him and sympathize with him about his troubles.

"I'm getting on fine." Aldrid forced his eyes open and tried to think of something to say that would keep Sabina from asking any more probing questions. "I can use my hand a little now."

"Really? How?" Sabina's smile was genuine.

"Stephan showed me how. He made me try to grab his hand, and I could. So now I can use it a little."

"Well, that's wonderful!" Sabina was beaming at him, and somehow her smile made him hurt worse. Sabina was generally very kind to him and always tried to cheer him up. She would be so devastated to find out why they were really in town.

Sabina turned to watch Stephan and Mother's conversation, and by the time her attention was brought back to Aldrid, his head was pillowed in his arms on the table, and he was fast asleep. Mother noticed too.

"Sabina, can Stephan and I have a few minutes alone?"

Sabina was a little surprised at the request, but Mother's eyes were begging her not to question her and to just go quietly.

"Of course. I'm tired anyway, so I'll just head to bed. You're staying in town for a few days, though, aren't you, Stephan?"

"Only tomorrow, we have to leave the day after that, but we'll drop in when we get the chance."

"Good." Sabina slipped quietly to her room.

With her daughter gone, Alina turned toward Stephan.

"What's really going on with him? And don't try to tell me something isn't. I know my son and he's absolutely miserable right now." Her eyes searched Stephan's face for some clue as to the trouble.

Stephan smiled a little. "He thinks we're here so I can make good on a threat."

"A threat? Stephan, what kind of a threat?"

"When the Magistrate sentenced him, he was going to insist on putting the band of indenture on him right then and there. I made him a deal to keep it off and I told Aldrid that if he gave me any trouble, I'd bring him right back here and have them put it on."

"He gave you trouble?" Alina was as horrified as Stephan knew she would be.

"He ran away from me. Night before last. He got mad because I made him get up and finish a chore he had told me was already done."

"But Stephan, that cuff, it never comes off."

"I know."

"How can you do that to him? You told me you were trying to help him. How is that helping him? He'll never live it down! Oh, Stephan, surely there's something else you could do to punish him, something less permanent. I can't let..." Alina had a lot more to say about it, but Stephan held up his hand and interrupted her.

"I never said I was going to. I said that's what he thinks is going to happen. Alina, you can't honestly believe that I would do that to the boy. I know it's permanent. I don't want him having to live his entire life judged by one mistake, one failure. I want him to try to make something better of himself."

"And is it working? Is working with you actually helping him?" Alina recalled the conversation they had had the night Aldrid was taken to the Magistrate's office.

This time, a very big smile filled his face. "Oh, it's working alright. Maurus was right, you know, about his hand. It's not completely useless. He's learned how to make it work, and he's starting to own up to his own faults. When we were coming here, he didn't beg me once to change my mind, just accepted that it was the way it had to be."

"And you're really not going to put him through that?" Alina needed to hear him say it again, she needed to be sure that her young son was not destined for a life of misery.

"I'm not going to put him through that. But I'm not telling him that, and you'd better not either. It doesn't do him any harm to be scared about it. It's the meekest I've ever seen him. Might make him think twice before he does something foolish like that again."

Chapter 23

STEPHAN ROUSED ALDRID FROM his spot at the table and told him it was time to leave. Forlornly, Aldrid said goodbye to Mother, knowing that the next time he saw her she would be so ashamed of him that he did not think he would be able to bear it. Maybe he could ask Stephan to take him straight back to the farm when they were finished, that way he did not have to see the pain in Mother's eyes and did not have to see the way he broke her heart. He was not sure at all that Stephan would agree to that. He would probably tell him something about how it was all his own fault and that he deserved to see how much he hurt his mother. Yes, that sounded like something Stephan would say.

Stephan took him to an inn in town and they shared the small room for the night, Aldrid, of course, getting the floor. Tired as he was, his dreams were very troubled and mostly included the horrible burning pain he could not forget. Several times he woke up through the night, certain that his arm was on fire again. Stephan appeared to sleep through all his restlessness.

As was usual with Stephan, appearances had little to do with reality. He was fully aware of how poorly Aldrid was sleeping, and by the way he kept waking up, he figured he was having nightmares. But, like he had told Alina earlier, he thought it was a good idea for Aldrid to be scared at the moment.

When morning finally arrived Aldrid was both thankful and dismayed. The night had been awful, and he wanted it to end. But now that morning was here, he was so much closer to his punishment that he thought maybe he would like to go back to the night.

Rather than go through the trouble of harnessing the horses, Stephan decided that they could walk up to the castle. With one hand firmly clamped around Aldrid's right arm, he set off. Aldrid had the chance to pull his hood over his head, but not the chance to tuck his cloak up over his left arm. He could feel the eyes of everyone they passed on him, boring into him accusingly. It was as if he already had the band on.

Aldrid looked up in consternation when he realized that they were passing under the great stone gateway of the castle. He gulped and tried desperately to still the racing in his heart. He could feel it, hear it, pounding in his ears. He was sure Stephan must be able to hear it too, and all the other people milling about the courtyard. Why did there have to be so many people? He would like to just get this over and done with as quickly and quietly as possible. He hoped he would not cry out or scream, but he was not sure he would be able to stop himself.

"Stephan?" His voice was barely a whisper, but Stephan caught the word and stopped, turning to look at him. "Are you going to be there?"

"Where, Aldrid?"

"When they..." He hesitated, biting his lip. He did not want to actually say what they were going to do, but he could not think of another way to say it. "When they put it on, you know. You will be there, right?"

As much as Aldrid did not want to admit it, he preferred the idea of Stephan being there with him. It would help, he was sure.

Stephan looked down at the boy's pale, frightened face, and almost told him. He had told Alina the night before that it would do him some good to be afraid about it for a while. Now, seeing the despair in his face, he wasn't sure. In fact, he opened his mouth to tell him, but got no further.

"Al! Stephan!" The bright voice came from across the courtyard, by the gate. Aldrid turned in horror. He had forgotten that Sabina worked in the castle kitchen. Now she would know even sooner. He shut his eyes with a tiny groan.

"Al, you look ill. Are you alright?" He wished they would stop asking him that.

"I'm fine," he mumbled. He was glad when Stephan started speaking and prevented Sabina from asking anymore questions. He did not listen to a word either of them said. Sabina was right when she said he looked ill. Now he felt sick too. This waiting was nauseating.

At last Sabina was giving him a quick hug, saying something about how she must get to work. He was relieved when her footsteps receded into the distance, leaving him alone with Stephan again.

Stephan seemed to have forgotten about their interrupted conversation and Aldrid's unanswered question. He took Aldrid's arm again and led him into the castle interior. Aldrid did not remember anything about living in the castle. He was too young when they had left it. If he was not so terrified of what he was sure was to come, he would have found their walk up and down the castle corridors, winding their way to some unknown destination, fascinating. As it was, he could not have told anyone afterward what he had seen in the place. He was simply too scared to notice.

They were outside a set of ornately decorated doors when Stephan let go of his arm and motioned him to sit on a nearby bench.

"I have some business to take care of in there, and I'm afraid they won't allow you to be in there with me. Wait here a bit and I'll come and get you when I'm done."

Aldrid nodded and sat down to wait. He could not decide if he was relieved or upset about his fate being postponed. He was tired, he realized, as the minutes ticked by and there was no sign of Stephan's return. There was a window in the wall opposite him, high above his head. And the sun streaming in from that window was very warm and comfortable. He leaned his head back against the wall and shut his eyes, letting the heat from the sun make him drowsy. Before he knew it, he was dozing.

He woke up with a start and realized that the sun was no longer there. At first this puzzled him. Then he realized he must have been asleep a long time. Most of the day, it seemed. Still, there was no sign of Stephan. What was taking him so long? If he listened carefully, he could hear the murmur of voices coming from the other side of the double doors, although he could not make out any of their words. Stephan must be in there still, he thought. The bench he was sitting on hadn't been too bad earlier, but now it was hard and uncomfortable. He shifted and squirmed this way and that, trying to find a better position, before finally deciding there wasn't one. Just then he heard one of the doors opening.

Stephan was laughing at something someone else had said and turned to call out a reply as he stepped out into the hallway. He glanced down at where Aldrid was still sitting.

"Well, Al, are you ready to go?" His voice was cheerful.

"I guess so," Aldrid answered, not at all sure that he was now.

"We'd best hurry then. Your Mother's expecting us and I'm sure she has a wonderful meal ready."

"Mother? Is that where we're going?" As much as Aldrid did not want to have that cuff put on, he was beginning to tire of this waiting, and the anxiety it was causing him. "Please, Stephan, can we just get it over with? I think I'd much rather."

"Aldrid, there's nothing to get over with." Stephan was trying hard not to smile.

"What? But I thought..." Aldrid looked up at the man, bewildered and just the tiniest bit hopeful.

"I know. And I let you think that, because I wanted you to think about what it would be like to have such a permanent consequence." Stephan sat down on the bench next to Aldrid. "Al, I could never let them put something like that on you. In fact, I wish they wouldn't be so quick to put it on most of the other men who wear it."

"So, you're not going to punish me?" Aldrid could have wept with relief.

"I didn't say that. But I think punishment should lead to the chance to do better. In your case, clapping an iron band on your wrist to tell everyone what a terrible criminal you have been isn't going to do you any good."

"Stephan, I'm sorry. I shouldn't have run away or stole your horse. I'm sorry, really I am."

His dark eyes were earnest as he met Stephan's smile. He had thought those words a lot of times in the last day, but had never been able to say them, not when Stephan could mistake them for an attempt to escape punishment. Now that they were out, though, Aldrid realized what a relief saying he was sorry could be.

"I know you are, Al, and I forgive you. Now, let's go see your mother. You wouldn't want all her good cooking going cold, would you?"

Chapter 24

ALDRID WAS ON HIS WAY TOWARD the house, his arms full of wood. Behind him, Stephan's axe rose and fell with a satisfying *THUD*. They had been at the task all day, and yet the pile of logs needing to be split and stacked had not seemed to diminish. Aldrid sighed a little as he thought of it. Fires were incredibly greedy, needing all that wood to keep them going. With winter now settling over the countryside, they needed more than ever.

At least it made for a different day, Aldrid thought as he neatly stacked this armload of wood on top of the others. Ever since they returned from town, Aldrid's days pretty much run together. There was little to distinguish one from the other.

That trip to town was just now starting to be far enough behind him that he could think about it without feeling absolutely wretched and embarrassed. Stephan meant what he said when he forgave him, and not one time did the man bring it back up. That was one nice thing about Stephan, Aldrid thought. Everyone else in his life made a point of reminding him of the bad things he had done. Stephan just moved on.

"Al, I think we'll be done for today." Unheard by Aldrid, Stephan had come up behind him. "Go ahead and get the cows in and then check the horses' water, it's cold enough to freeze."

"Alright." He moved toward the stable when Stephan called after him.

"And Al, remember to be careful with that latch
on the paddock. Make sure you get it all the way
shut."

Aldrid nodded his acknowledgement as he moved
away. He noticed the breaking latch on the gate
several days ago. When he pointed it out to Stephan,
the man decided it would be a good thing to teach
Aldrid to fix, but they had not yet had time to get to
it.

Away from the house and yard, the wind was
more biting, and Aldrid pulled his thick woolen cloak
close around him. The ground was already white
with the season's first snow fall, and the water
trough in the horse's paddock had frozen over again.
Aldrid went into the stable to fetch the small hatchet
Stephan kept there to break up the ice in the water.

Back outside, he could see the cluster of horses
standing, backs to the winter wind, waiting for a
chance to drink. In the growing dusk, they all looked
the same color, but he could pick Casper out of the
group. He stood at least two hands shorter than any
of the other horses. Casper was the only one Aldrid
really liked. The rest still fell into the category of
smelly animals that required far too much work on
his part. But Casper was the one he knew he could
ride, and so he had a soft spot for him. His least
favorite was the dark brown one he had watched
Stephan work with. Even Stephan agreed with him
when he said the horse was mean. Stephan had told
him he would never make a good war horse. He was
jumpy, flighty, and picked too many fights. Aldrid
tried to stay as clear of him as he could.

He had broken up the ice on their water enough
times now to be quick at it now. He brought the
hatchet down in a few quick strokes, and watched
the water bubble up between the cracks in the ice.
Casper was always the first to drink, since he was the
oldest, and one of only ones who permanently
resided at the farm. Aldrid hung out long enough to
scratch the thick, shaggy winter coat. His fingers

were just reaching that spot on Casper's neck that the horse loved so much when he noticed how dark it was getting. At first, he thought he had taken too long, but a glance at the western sky showed a thin dark line of clouds forming over where the sun should be. Another snowstorm, Aldrid thought.

By the time he had returned the hatchet to its hook on the stable wall, the clouds had gotten bigger, nearer. Aldrid had seen winter storms blow in quickly before and knew he only had a little time left to get the cows in before it hit. He certainly did not want to be stuck out in the cow pasture in the middle of a blizzard.

The further out he got, the worse the weather became. The wind, which had been biting before, was howling like a living being. It pulled at the edges of his cloak, lifting them away from him and letting in the cold. And the sky was darkening rapidly.

In the distance, Aldrid could make out a white haze, and he thought it must be snow falling already. He was glad to see both the cows waiting for him at the gate. They had no desire to be stuck out in this weather either. Grabbing the older one's short rope, he started the trek back toward the barn. This direction, he was moving away from the wind and that was a relief. By the time he had brought them to the cowshed, the last of the daylight had fled.

Firelight from the house poured out from the windows, and he knew Stephan would have supper ready whenever he finished up with the cows. It would be warm, and Aldrid hurried himself at the thought. It felt like it was getting colder by the minute.

Finally, the milking was done. Aldrid shuddered as a gust of wind hit the cowshed and set it to rattling. With his head bent down to avoid the mighty gusts of wind, he started for the house.

A strange sound stopped in his tracks. It was separate from the howling, beating wind. A creaking sound followed by a *BANG*. He heard it several

times before he could place where it was coming
from. The first snowflakes were whirling along with
the wind when he traced the noise to its source and
stood looking at the open paddock gate in horror.
He had closed it properly; he was sure of it. He
squeezed his eyes shut trying to replay his every
movement when he left the horse paddock. It was
too fuzzy. He had been in a hurry. Maybe he hadn't
been as careful as he should have been. Either way
it was open now.

He hurried toward it and swung it shut against its
post. This time, he carefully secured it, the way
Stephan had shown him. He started to walk away
when it occurred to him that he had no idea how long
it had been open. Wishing that it had not happened
tonight, of all nights, he turned back to the paddock.
He would just check and make sure all the horses
were in there. Surely none of them would have been
crazy enough to run off in this weather. They formed
a black mass, pressed tightly together against the
side of the barn, out of the wind.

Stephan would want them in this weather, Aldrid
thought. And the only real way for him to count
them was to bring them into the stable and put them
in their stalls. Then he would notice if one was
missing.

Quickly, he slipped inside the barn and stood for
a moment, relieved to be out of the wind. There was
a door that opened directly to the paddock, and
Aldrid had seen Stephan open the door and just let
them all come in. He had said they all knew where
their stalls were and did not need help finding them.
Aldrid hoped that was right as he lifted the bar and
swung the door out. The wind caught it from his
hands and slammed it against the side of the barn.
The horses were startled at first, but quickly
recovered and filed into the safety of the barn walls.
Aldrid watched anxiously.

There was one empty stall. Without even
thinking, Aldrid knew which horse it had belonged

to. It was that dark brown one that was so mean. If any horse was to disappear, that was the one Aldrid would have preferred.

Aldrid shut the barn door, blocking out the bitter wind, and looked around him. A few weeks ago, he would have gone to the house and just pretended like nothing happened, or he might have told Stephan in the hopes that he would do something. But he had been trying so hard since Stephan had brought him back here without making him get the iron band. And Stephan was always and forever telling him to own up to his own mistakes and failures and to make them right if he could. The only way he could make this right would be to go out and find that horse. Aldrid stood for several minutes, the conflict evident on his face had anyone been there to see it. He did not want to go out in that storm, but he did not want to face Stephan without at least trying to make his mistake right.

At last, he came to a decision. The horse, he imagined, could not have wandered far in this weather. The least he could do was try. If the weather got too bad, he could turn around and go back. Surely Stephan would be satisfied with the effort.

He grabbed the lantern that Stephan kept hanging up on a nail by the door of the barn and lit it. When he stepped outside, he almost turned back toward the house. The wind was awful, and the snowfall was getting heavier.

The tracks were clearly visible in the old snow at first, leading away from the gate, and out toward the open field. Holding the lantern up so that he could follow them, Aldrid had his back to the wind. That must have been why the horse went this direction, he thought, it was the easiest way to go. The tracks led further and further away, but as long as he could clearly make them out, Aldrid did not want to turn back. He turned to look behind him once and was a little frightened by the fact that he could no longer make out the barn or the house. The only reason he kept moving forward was that he knew he had the tracks to follow home as well.

Time lost any meaning to Aldrid as he put one foot in front of the other, following the hoof marks before him. He had no idea that they were growing fainter and fainter as new snow fell heavily. He also was not aware of how far away from Stephan's home he had wandered. His eyes had become fixated on finding the next set of tracks and the cold had worked its way into his brain, making every thought sluggish and foggy.

He was surprised when he was stopped cold by a solid, and painful, object directly in front of him. His body bounced off it and he staggered back, staring at it, trying to put together what it was. At last, he realized it was the trunk of a big tree. As the thought occurred to him, he paused to study the landscape around him and found to his discouragement, that he was in the middle of a woods. At least, he thought he was. Even with the light of his lantern, he could not actually see very far in front of him at all. But the wind was broken by the many trees.

He turned to find the tracks again, but by now they were almost invisible. Aldrid was too cold and tired to realize the danger of his own situation. He was shivering, despite his thick cloak, and his teeth were chattering so hard, he thought they might just break off altogether. He still had not seen the horse, and almost without thought, he placed one foot in front of the other in the direction he thought the horse had been traveling.

Aldrid had no idea how long he had been walking. The snow was piling up in great drifts, and he fell several times. Each time it was harder to get back up. Finally, he sank into one and knew he could not get up anymore, did not want to get up anymore. He let the snow close in around him, feeling strangely warmed by it.

Ironically, it was the horse who found Aldrid and not the other way around. He had been close behind the animal, without knowing it. As he sank into the deep snow, and just sat there, he became aware of a strange snuffling, woofing sound near him. Then there was a big, soft, wet face pushed into his own. Aldrid had actually forgotten why he was even out here in the snowstorm, and he opened his eyes in bewilderment. The horse's head loomed huge in front of his eyes.

"Oh, there you are," he said sleepily. He knew, subconsciously, that he should get up. There was something important about this horse, something he had to do with it. But it was too much trouble to remember it. The only thing he could come up with was that he should get back so that Stephan would not think he had run away. He knew that was important. Stephan had to know that he was not trying to escape. But it was easier to just close his eyes, easier to just sit still. He was so sleepy, so sleepy...

Chapter 25

STEPHAN WAS IN THE HOUSE, fixing supper for the two of them when he glanced out the window and noticed the black line of clouds on the horizon. They were blowing in from the northwest, which meant they were coming down from the mountains of Dorsten. Any winter storms coming from there were sure to be bad ones.

For a moment he thought about calling to Aldrid and telling him to hurry up and finish before the storm got here. It was likely to be a blizzard once it arrived, and blizzards were not the type of weather you wanted to be out in. He decided against it. He had told Aldrid to take care of the cows and check the horses' water. That should not take him very long.

The minutes passed, and the wind outside picked up. The windows rattled in their sashings, and a cold draft filled the room. Stephan was sitting at the table, drumming his fingers impatiently. Supper was ready, and Aldrid had not come in yet. He wondered what could be taking the boy so long. A particularly strong gust of wind struck the side of the house.

Finally, Stephan could stand it no longer. He rose from his seat, and pulling on a thick coat, and then a cloak over top of that, he opened the door. The force of the wind nearly pushed it back into his face. Already snowflakes were falling, although in the wind, falling was the wrong word to describe what they were doing. The wind was driving the flakes horizontally through the air and piling them up into drifts.

It was the cowshed that Stephan went to first. Everything inside appeared to be in order, except that there was no sign of Aldrid. That meant he had to be in the stable. Stephan made his way over, his head bent down against the wind. When he first stepped inside, everything seemed alright in there, too. He was turning to leave, thinking that Aldrid must have passed him and already gone into the house, when he noticed the single empty stall.

Stephan's skills as both a hunter and a soldier were very keen, and it did not take him long to find the two sets of prints that led away from the paddock and into the open country beyond. One was made by a horse's hooves. The other by a boy's feet. Stephan guessed what had happened and cursed. Even now the paddock gate was swinging open, the latch undone by the force of the wind.

Judging by the quickly dropping temperature, and the ever-increasing snowfall, Stephan knew he had only a short window of time before he lost any ability to follow Aldrid. Unlike Aldrid, however, he knew what it meant to be out in a storm like this and rather than setting straight off he went back to the house and gathered several blankets, along with a length of rope. He also added to his own clothing, pulling a hat, scarf, and gloves on. After rolling the blankets into a bundle and tying them up so that he could carry them on his back, he set off. It had only taken him a few minutes to prepare, but even so, the tracks from the paddock were harder to find.

"Aldrid, your mother is going to kill me," Stephan said to himself, shaking his head as he started after the tracks.

He knew a little bit more about where he was going, and he knew a bit more about tracking. As long as he kept the wind to his back, it was safe to say he was following the same direction as the horse and boy. Most things moved away from the wind. The woods did not come as a surprise to him either, as they had to Aldrid. He knew when he had reached the sheltering presence of the trees.

The snow was not coming down as heavily inside the forest. The number of evergreens that grew in between the other trees helped to slow its fall. Here, Stephan could make the tracks out more clearly. He could also see the many times Aldrid had apparently fallen down, and how he had started walking in a sort of zig zagged line, rather than straight forward. The boy had been tiring when he got this far, and the cold had been starting to affect him.

Stephan had no idea how close behind Aldrid he had been the whole time. His departure had been no more than thirty minutes after Al's. In the end, that was what saved Aldrid. Stephan followed his quickly disappearing tracks deep into the woods, his concern growing with each step. His lantern could only shed light on a very small circle around him, and had it not been for the large mound the horse's body made in the snow, he might have missed them altogether.

Snow had fallen on the animal after he had dropped to his knees, making it look almost like another drift, but when he heard and sensed Stephan's approach, the big head had turned, shaking from it the white powder.

"Easy, now."

Stephan reached for the horse's halter and when he did, the lantern in his other hand cast its light on another snow-covered mound. This one was much smaller, and bits of cloth were showing underneath the snow.

"Aldrid! Aldrid, wake up!" Stephan almost yelled at the boy, shaking him.

Aldrid was so tired. And warm. He had been very cold and the sudden switch to warmth was nice. So nice. He could just close his eyes here and rest a bit. Then he could remember why he was here. But there was something, just outside of his consciousness. A sound, trying to penetrate the deepening fog. There was something else too. A movement. He could not quite identify it. It felt like... like... shaking. Yes, he was shaking. But he was not doing it to himself. Someone else was shaking him. And someone else was yelling at him. That was what that sound was. He knew that now. He supposed they wanted him to do something. They didn't realize he had no command over his own body anymore. Besides, he could not understand the sounds. They had no meaning to him.

He wished whoever it was would just let him lie still and rest. That was all he really wanted to do. Suddenly, his face was stinging. He tried to open his eyes to see what had happened. At first, he was afraid he could not do it, but after a moment his eyelids opened and there was a blinding light in front of him. The sounds he heard began to take on substance and he found he was able to understand them.

"Come on, Al, wake up. You have to wake up." The voice was familiar, but it took another minute before Aldrid could place it.

It was Stephan. The thought snapped his brain awake. Stephan. What was he doing here? And why was he yelling at him? Aldrid hadn't done anything wrong. He knew that. He could not remember what he had done exactly, but he was sure it was the right thing.

"Did the right thing," he mumbled aloud without realizing it.

"Oh, thank goodness, boy! You're awake, you're alive." Stephan sounded so relieved that Aldrid felt bad.

"No. I was just sleeping. I'm so tired," he said the words wearily, as if it took everything in him to form them.

"You have to get up."

Everything inside him screamed in protest, but Stephan was pulling Aldrid up onto his feet. He had the funny sensation of standing on nothing. He could not feel anything from his knees down, it was like they had simply fallen off.

"My feet?" he mumbled.

"Can you feel them?"

Stephan was shaking him again. Why was Stephan shaking him? Why was he so angry with him? He hadn't even been this angry when he had run away. Maybe that was it, maybe Stephan thought he was running away again. He should tell him he wasn't it. But talking took so much effort.

"Aldrid, stay awake."

The shaking started again, and this time he was sure Stephan slapped him across the face too. He did not really feel it, but he saw the hand as it closed with his face. Never had Stephan hit him. He must be furious.

"Come on, Al. We're going to start walking. I need you to walk, alright?"

It was funny, because Stephan did not sound like he was mad, just worried. It's because I'm dying, Aldrid thought with sudden clarity. I'm dying, just like Hamo. He did the right thing and he died. Now I did the right thing, and I'm going to die. Aldrid wasn't quite as afraid of it as he thought he would be, but then, he could not really feel anything. Everything was so foggy, so distant. If only Stephan would let him lay down again, he really was more comfortable that way.

But Stephan was pulling him forward, dragging him along the ground. Aldrid thought he might be moving his legs, but he could not be sure. He still felt as if there was nothing under him. Stephan had both hands on his shoulders and was pushing him forward, through the snow. The action made Aldrid start shivering again, with such a violence that he thought he was going to fly to pieces.

"We have to keep moving, Al. Have to get you home." As Stephan said the words, Aldrid decided he was right. He did want to go home. He wanted to see Mother. Without realizing it, he had said her name out loud.

"Your Mother is going to kill me if I can't get you home," Stephan responded.

Aldrid thought it was funny that anyone would think such a thing.

There was something big and black moving alongside of him, and after a moment, Aldrid recognized it as the horse he had come after. That was good. He must have found it.

Aldrid had no idea of what his own body was doing, or of the time that was passing, or of the distance he was going. He was aware from time to time that Stephan was shaking or slapping him, usually after he had sunk to his knees - at least he thought they were his knees. And always Stephan was pushing him forward. He was conscious of the sharp force of the wind against his face as the woods were left behind, and he turned away from it and sank to the ground to get away from it. This time, though, Stephan did not immediately try to get him up. He had something big, and soft, and warm in his hands, and he was wrapping it around Aldrid, making sure it went over his head and covered much of his face. Then he was pulling him back up. With that thing wrapped about him, the wind was not quite so fierce.

The big, black shape of the stable loomed up in front of him as he sank once more to the ground. He was so incredibly tired. Rather than pulling him up, Stephan simply slid his arms under him and lifted him up, carrying him toward the house. He was so glad that Stephan finally understood how exhausted he was. He shouldn't have made him walk all that way.

The light inside the house hit his eyes painfully and he turned his face to bury it in Stephan's shoulder. Stephan was not yelling at him now, or shaking him, and he thought maybe Stephan was done being mad at him. That was nice. Stephan would let him sleep then. But it would be hard to sleep if his body would not stop this awful convulsing. It was making him ache.

Stephan set him down near the warm fireplace. Then he started taking Aldrid's clothes off. That was odd, Aldrid thought. Couldn't Stephan see how cold he was? Taking his clothes off would only make him colder. But he did it anyway, and when they were all off, he wrapped another thick blanket around Aldrid and moved him closer to the fire. The shivering was so painful now. He wished he could make it stop, but he seemed to have lost any control over his own body.

When Stephan tried to make him drink something, he was trembling so hard he could not get his mouth to it. Stephan helped and the most deliciously warm liquid filled his mouth. He had no idea what it was, but it was the best thing he had ever had. The best part of it was the way it felt warm all the way down. He wanted more of it. He tried to reach his hand out to take the cup from Stephan, then realized with a dull horror that he could not feel his hand either. He could see it, trembling violently in front of his face as he reached it out, but he could not feel it at all. Fortunately, Stephan knew what he was reaching for, and brought the rim of the cup to his mouth once more. Aldrid let out a little gasp of pleasure as the warm fluid filled his mouth again. It was so nice and hot.

Now he could lay down. There was a pile of blankets beneath and around him, and the fire was burning brightly near him, making the air pleasantly hot. Stephan was doing something with his feet, but he was too weary to bother finding out what. He just lay there, letting his eyes drop shut, the light of the fire glowing red against his eyelids. He could just sleep and sleep.

When Aldrid woke up again, he was crying in pain. It had been coming over him gradually in his sleep. It had started with a slight tingling sensation, but now it felt as if his feet were sitting in a fire. He tried to sit up, but his muscles did not work. Stephan was still doing something to his feet, and that was what was making them hurt so badly.

"They're burning!" Aldrid cried.

"You can feel them?" Stephan glanced at Al's face. Tears were streaming out of Aldrid's eyes as he nodded.

"Good."

"How is that good?" Now that Aldrid was fully awake, he was trying hard to not cry, but he couldn't quite keep a pathetic sniffle out of his voice.

Stephan smiled at him. "Because it means you'll be able to walk when this is all over and done with. If you still couldn't feel anything, your feet would be beyond saving and you'd never walk again."

"Oh." Aldrid was a little alarmed at the idea of losing his ability to walk. "But they will be alright, won't they? I mean, since they hurt now."

"Yes." Stephan got up from where he was sitting at Aldrid's feet and moved closer to his head. "Give me your hands now."

Stephan began vigorously rubbing Aldrid's numb hands now. Aldrid wanted so badly to go back to sleep, but his feet still felt like they were on fire and burning was something he was so afraid of. He had to look down at his feet more than once to convince himself that they really were fine. In a matter of minutes, his hands distracted him from the pain in his feet. As blood flow returned, so did that agonizing fire beneath his skin. He bit down on the inside of his cheek until he tasted blood. Stephan, finally satisfied that he had not permanently frozen his hands and feet off, sat back and studied Aldrid for a minute.

"What were you thinking, Al?" he finally said.

Aldrid was very tired. He was cold, and his hands and feet were burning, and every muscle and joint in his body was throbbing. He tried to summon enough energy to explain what had happened, but the effort was too enormous. Stephan saw it and shook his head.

"Never mind, Al. Get some rest now. You'll feel stronger in a bit." He got up and left Aldrid to sleep.

Sleep was such a happy state to be in. Hours flew by and Aldrid was not in the least bit aware of their passing.

When he woke up, he was alone, lying in front of the big fireplace. Stephan was nowhere to be seen and judging by the dim light coming in from the windows, the day was far gone. Aldrid was afraid that Stephan must have woken him up to do chores and he had fallen back asleep out here by the warm fire. He struggled out from under the blankets, wishing he didn't ache quite so much. The aching would make chores much slower. As he got to his feet, his legs wobbled threateningly beneath him, and he clutched the back of a nearby chair to keep himself up. His head was hurting, he noticed. And he was hot.

Pushing aside the thought, he tried to take a step toward the door. He made it exactly two before his legs gave out completely and he was left sitting in a little heap in the middle of the room. Funny, he thought, now he was cold, so cold that the terrible tremors were coming over him again.

Stephan chose that moment to walk in carrying an armful of wood for the fire with him.

"Al, what are you doing?" He looked curiously at the boy sitting in the middle of the floor.

"I have work..." Aldrid started, and realized his teeth were chattering again as well. What had happened to him? He had been so hot a minute ago, he thought.

"No. No, you don't. Not right now. You look awful. And I'm sure you feel at least as bad as you look."

"But you said it didn't matter how I felt, I just had to do it." Why was Stephan such a confusing man?

"I was talking about feeling lazy, not about when you are actually sick. Which is what you are right now. Look at you, you can't even walk across the room. How, exactly, were you planning on making it to the barn?" Stephan put down his armload of wood and went to help Aldrid back to bed.

"Are you angry with me?" Aldrid looked up at him, his dark brown eyes worried.

"No, I'm not angry with you. Why?" Stephan was laying the back of his calloused hand against Al's forehead, frowning.

"I just remember you yelling at me, and hitting me, and shaking me. I was afraid you were mad because you thought I had run away again. You did do those things, didn't you?" He sighed as he spoke as if just speaking the words were a great burden.

"Al, I was trying to save your life. You can't sleep when you're that cold, you'll just freeze to death. Your Mother would have had my head if I had to go back and tell her that you had died in the woods chasing down a runaway horse."

"You didn't think I was running away?" It was something that had bothered him since Stephan had found him, although he had been too cold, and his brain too muddled to remember it.

"No. You went after the horse, didn't you?"

"Yes. I was trying to make it right."

"Make what right?" Stephan was more than a little confused, and for a minute thought the boy was delirious.

"I forgot to latch the gate all the way. That's how he got out. I was trying to make it right." It was a great weight off Aldrid's mind to know that Stephan knew why he had gone off without telling him.

"I see." Stephan did not say anything else, but he felt a warm glow of pride for the boy. Aldrid had come a long way from the sullen little boy he'd first brought here months ago. "Get some sleep now, Al. You'll feel better when you do. And let me decide when you start chores again, alright?"

Aldrid nodded. Now that he knew Stephan was not angry, and that he was not shirking his work, sleep sounded wonderful. Curled up beneath a pile of blankets once more, he shut his eyes.

Chapter 26

A LDRID, HAVE YOU EVER been hunting?"
Stephan asked him over breakfast one
morning.

It had been several weeks since Aldrid had been
sick. He had tossed and turned in bed with a high
fever and a terrible cough for several days. But he
was young, and in good health, and the many hours
of working outside in the sun had made him
stronger, so that in the end his body won the fight
and he had recovered. Now, with the wonderful
resilience of youth, no one would have been able to
guess how sick he had been by looking at him.

Aldrid's mouth was full of food, but he shook his
head.

"I didn't think so. Your Father used to take Hamo
with him, but I guess you were really too young. Do
you want to go?"

"Yes! Now?" Aldrid was ready to leap out of his
seat and run out the door at that moment.

"Slow down. Not until next week. Sir Edwin
invited me to go with him, and I thought you might
like to come along."

"Who's Sir Edwin?" The name was vaguely
familiar, but Aldrid could not place it.

"This farm borders his estate. He's the King's
cavalry commander, and a very old friend of mine.
Your father and he were good friends as well - fought
together and shared command for many
campaigns."

"We're going to go then?" Aldrid squirmed in his
chair with excitement.

"I'm going for sure. I'll have to see if you can behave yourself and get all your work done for the next week, and then I might take you," Stephan said seriously but lowered his head to hide the smile at the corners of his mouth.

Aldrid looked up at him, his dark eyes hurt. "Oh, come on, please, Stephan. I haven't done anything bad in forever. And I've been getting all my chores done on time, and I haven't cheated on any of them in so long."

Stephan nodded his head thoughtfully. "That is true. But I don't know. I think it would be better if I wait to make sure this week. Of course, if I did take you, I'd have to find something you're able to shoot." He pursed his lips as if the thought had just occurred to him.

Aldrid looked instantly disappointed. He knew he could never shoot a longbow such as Stephan had. Even though he had some use of his left hand it was nowhere near enough to be able to draw and hold such a bow. Stephan was watching him, and the smile he had been trying to hide grew wider.

"When you're finished up with the cow, come back here. There's something I want to show you."

Aldrid hurried to finish his breakfast and clean up from it so that he could get to the cow. It was still very dark outside thanks to the short winter days, but as long as the weather remained so bitterly cold, Stephan had decided to keep them in the shed and feed them on the hay he had harvested the summer before, so all Aldrid had to do was milk and feed them. The calf had more than doubled its size since Aldrid had first come to Stephan's farm and had an almost insatiable appetite.

Thirty minutes later, Stephan was sitting at the table with an oddly shaped object, wrapped in a canvas, sitting in front of him. Aldrid came in breathless from running, his dark eyes taking in the package, and Stephan's face.

"Would you like to see it?" Stephan asked him.

"Yes, of course!" Aldrid was biting his lower lip in anticipation, as Stephan slid it across the table. He fingered it for a moment, wondering what in the world Stephan could be giving him and why. Then his impatience took over and he pulled the canvas off to reveal a crossbow. It was smaller than the ones he had seen some of the soldiers carrying, but it was the perfect size for him. His eyes wandered admiringly over it.

"It's for me? You're not just messing with me?" He looked nervously up at Stephan.

"It's really for you. I think it's the best choice for you, with your hand and all. And every man should have some weapon they know how to use."

"Does Mother know you're giving this to me?" Aldrid was not sure how Mother would feel about her fourteen-year-old son having his own weapon.

"She doesn't, no. But she won't mind. I mean, Hamo was taking sword lessons from the time he was ten at the castle, and he had his own bow he would take hunting when he went with your father. So, I don't see why you shouldn't have something like that bow."

"I'm different than Hamo though."

"What do you mean?" Stephan cocked his head, studying Aldrid. "Why would you say you're different then him?"

Aldrid shrugged. "I don't know. I guess I mean people trusted him. They don't trust me. He always did the right thing, and I didn't." He was careful to use a past tense when referring to himself. He had been trying so hard lately to do the right thing, and to live up to the impossibly high standard that everyone's opinion of Hamo had set for him.

"Your brother was definitely not always good. People tend to pick and choose what they remember of the dead. Since he died bravely, people choose to remember the good in him. They do the same thing with your father. They remember the one terrible thing he did and forget all of the other good things he did in his life. Hamo wasn't all good, and your father wasn't all bad. Now, I can't argue with the fact that people trusted Hamo. A lot of that had to do with the fact that at the time they also trusted your father. It also had to do with the fact that he had character. He did what he was supposed to do, even when he didn't like it. He wasn't a chronic liar or thief, and he treated other people well for the most part."

"So, what was he not good at?" Aldrid was curious about the brother he could not remember. Mother refused to talk about him. Aldrid had learned long ago to not even bother to ask. Sabina was willing to talk about him, but her memory was only slightly better than Aldrid's own.

"He let people push him around, didn't stand up for himself very well. And he hated housework. It used to drive your mother crazy how much he tried to get out of helping her with it while your father was gone. He was a bit lazy like you, too. If he didn't see the point in doing something, he'd rather not do it. And he liked performing experiments on injured animals he found, usually in your mother's kitchen." Stephan could see the way Aldrid was listening intently to his every word. "I remember coming home with your father once, and Hamo had picked up a half dead frog he had found who knows where. He'd decided it needed an operation, and that the best place to do it would be on your parents' bed. I'm not sure that I've ever seen your mother so distraught at the sight of frog blood all over one of her best quilts."

He laughed as he remembered the incident. He and Maurus had laughed for at least five minutes, Hamo had cried, mostly because the frog had died anyway, and a little because Mother was so mad at him, and Alina had yelled at everyone.

Growing serious again, Stephan continued, "And he was a horrible soldier."

"Really?"

"Really. He never wanted to be one and never saw the point in trying to be better. If he had, then maybe..." Stephan's words trailed off.

"Sometimes I wish he hadn't been so brave and good. Then I would actually have a brother. I miss not having him." Aldrid had never confessed before how much it bothered him that the war had stolen his chance to get to know his older brother. Father, he reasoned, had made his own choice. Hamo had not.

"You know, Al, sometimes I wish he hadn't been so brave either. Telling your parents was the hardest thing I have ever done in my life. But what he did was the right thing."

"It didn't really work out for him, though, did it? I mean, he did the right thing and he died. If he'd just kept running, he'd still be alive."

"But he might not have been able to live with himself. There's a big difference between those two. Doing right doesn't mean that everything turns out well, it just means you're at peace with yourself no matter what happens."

"Hmmm." Aldrid's forehead creased as he thought about Stephan's words.

"Enough of this, though. Let's go try this crossbow out and see how well you do with it." Stephan got up and started to bundle up against the cold.

Aldrid sat for another second, lost in thought, but then he, too, got up and ready to go outside. The sun was finally making its appearance for the day, and there were only a few thin, wispy clouds high in the sky. No snow today, Aldrid thought as they stepped outside.

Chapter 27

STEPHAN DID NOT HAVE TO wake Aldrid on the morning of the hunt. He was wide awake long before the sun rose. Bundling up against the cold, he raced through the morning's chores. When it was time for him to eat, he sat on the edge of his chair, gulping down the few mouthfuls of food that his excitement allowed him to.

"Ready already?" Stephan smiled as he watched Aldrid squirm impatiently in his chair.

"Yes. The cow is milked and fed and so are all the horses. We just have to leave." Aldrid wished Stephan would move a little faster this morning. Everything he did seemed agonizingly slow.

"Well, if you're so anxious to be on our way, why don't you go ahead and get a couple horses saddled up."

"Which ones?" Aldrid was hoping he could ride Casper since that was still the only horse he had ever been on, but he had no idea which one Stephan might want.

"You can ride Casper; I'll ride the black one."

Aldrid was out the door before Stephan had finished the sentence. By the time Stephan came out, Aldrid had both of them standing right at the front door saddled and ready to go.

"You don't think you might be a little too excited for this, do you? I mean you did have that fever a few weeks ago. I wouldn't want you getting worked up and making yourself sick again. What would I tell your mother?" Stephan looked sober.

"What? You don't mean that, do you? I'll calm down. I won't be too excited, I promise, Stephan." Aldrid's face was stricken.

Stephan started laughing at the way his face fell. "I'm just kidding, Al. Get up and let's go. We don't want to keep Sir Edwin waiting. He does love his hunts."

Aldrid let out a breath of relief as he pulled himself up onto Casper's back. "Does he do this often then?"

"Oh yes, very often. Especially in the winter, when there isn't too much excitement going on anywhere else. He says it's to keep himself and his men sharp. I think he just likes the fun of it."

"Will there be other men coming too, then?"

"Not this time. This time he just invited me."

"Does he know I'm coming too?" Aldrid was worried that Sir Edwin might not take kindly to the fact that Stephan had invited a third member to their party.

"Not yet. He won't mind though." Stephan sounded so confident that Aldrid was reassured. "Did you get any more practice in with that?" He nodded toward the crossbow Aldrid had slung behind his back.

"I practiced every day. But I still miss - a lot. It's hard to hold it still." Aldrid was less than pleased with how well he progressed with the crossbow in one week. He felt he should have picked it up faster.

"Well, if you weren't still missing a lot, I'd be surprised. It takes hours of practice to become good with any weapon. Keep working at it, you'll get it."

Aldrid was a little relieved to hear that he at least wasn't doing horrible with it. He secretly hoped that it was a hidden talent that would come naturally to him. Apparently, that's not how it worked.

Aldrid was curious as they rode through the woods beyond the open field that spread out behind Stephan's barn. This was where he had wandered in search of the horse. He shuddered a little as he remembered how very near he had come to dying that night. Stephan noticed the slight movement and guessed what he was thinking about.

"Looks a bit different in the sunlight, doesn't it?" He gestured toward the scenery.

"MMhmm. Stephan, what do you do on a hunt?"

Aldrid did not want to appear completely naive and lost on his very first time hunting. Especially since they would be with Sir Edwin. He had never met Sir Edwin, but he pictured a rather stuffy, self-important type of man. He did, after all, have a title and he was one of the most important military leaders in the kingdom. He probably would not even deign to acknowledge Aldrid's presence on the hunt.

"You will stay next to me. He has a few hounds he'll use to help flush out game, and we'll shoot at it. It's pretty simple really. Of course, there's always the chance that we'll ride around all day and not see a single thing to shoot at, but that's part of the fun."

As the woods opened up ahead of them, Aldrid got his first glance of what the knight's estate looked like. It was quite large, but it lacked the magnificence of the castle he had grown up beneath the shadow of. Instead of towering toward the sky, it sprawled across a slight rise in the ground, surrounded by several outbuildings.

"There you are, Stephan!" A middle-aged man came out the front door of the manor house as Stephan and Aldrid dismounted.

"Edwin, it's good to see you again." The two men grasped each other by the forearm. "It's been a long time since. I was beginning to think you'd forgotten me."

"Who's this with you?" Edwin noticed Aldrid standing self-consciously by Casper's shoulder. "You a friend of Stephan's?"

Aldrid nodded his head in quick, bobbing movements. This man was definitely not what he was expecting. There was nothing stuffy or overbearing or arrogant about him. In fact, Aldrid got the impression that the man was quite easy to get along with.

"That's Maurus' boy, Aldrid." Stephan was introducing him.

"Is he now?" Edwin turned to look at Aldrid with more interest, and Aldrid held his breath waiting for some word about how disappointing his father had turned out or what a terrible thing it was he had done or how he hoped the son had turned out better. Sir Edwin said none of those things though. He just stated, "Should have guessed. He looks just like Maurus."

"I told him you wouldn't mind if he came along with us today."

"Of course not. Are you ready to go?"

As Aldrid went to get back on Casper's back, Edwin leaned close to Stephan's ear and whispered, "There's something I need to talk to you about."

Stephan nodded, his face serious for a moment. He had thought Sir Edwin had something in mind when he had suggested a hunt with just the two of them.

Aldrid was content to ride behind the two men as they made their way through the heavy forest. Ostensibly, they were on the lookout for signs of deer or any other game. In reality, the two men were in deep discussion, and paying little attention to the ground before them.

"There's something up. Something big. We've heard rumors from here and there about the Dorstenians preparing for a campaign." Sir Edwin kept his voice low so that only Stephan could hear him. "Darien wants to avoid more fighting if he can, so he doesn't want to mobilize unless he's sure. He's afraid any action on our part will come across as threatening."

"That is sort of the idea." Stephan was a little perplexed.

"Well, yes. But Darien's a much different king than his father. He's not going to commit to a battle if one can be avoided. He's asked me to come to the castle. Officially it will be to serve a stint as garrison commander. In reality, he wants me in charge of collecting information and putting together a plan. He doesn't fully trust the new Captain. And he doesn't want to show our hand until he has all the facts."

"I see. What does that have to do with me? You know I retired. I've served more than the required years, and I'm not in any hurry to go back to it."

"I know that. We don't need you in that role anymore. But you have, from time to time, been very useful in another role."

"You want me to get into Dorsten? Find out what's really going on?" Understanding dawned on Stephan's face.

"You're the only one we can trust who actually grew up over there. You've been in and out more times than any of us can count. You know where to go, how to get around, how to avoid suspicion. You're the best choice."

"I suppose so."

It was all true. Stephan had been born and raised in the mountains that now belonged to Dorsten. He had been sixteen and desperate to go to sea when he had come to the town of Bren. Shortly afterward the old King had died, and the one kingdom was rent into two. Stephan had belonged to Dival since then.

"You've never run into any trouble the other times you've gone, have you?" Sir Edwin asked.

"Not once. I don't mind going this time, either. There's just one little problem."

"What's that? I can find someone to look after your place while you're gone." Sir Edwin was a little confused. Stephan was not one to raise objections in a matter of patriotic duty.

"It's the boy. I can't leave him."

"Why not? I can have someone look after him as well, or he can come with me to the castle until you return."

"It's not that easy. He's indentured to me. He owes me service for trying to steal from me. The agreement is that he doesn't leave my property without me, for any reason. If he does the Magistrate can take him and put him on one of the castle work gangs for the rest of his sentence. I can't let that happen to him." Stephan glanced behind to make sure Aldrid was still unaware of their conversation. "It'll destroy him."

Sir Edwin nodded thoughtfully, his fingers unconsciously drumming a rhythm on his leg. "You could take him with you," he said at last.

"Are you serious? What would his mother say?"

"Well, technically, if he's bound to you for the next two years, there's nothing for her to say." Sir Edwin was more sympathetic than his words sounded. He had been close friends with Maurus himself and knew how devastating the loss of Hamo had been to the entire family. But he had reason to believe that the enemy was planning something big, and if that were the case, he needed to know all he could and the only way for that to happen was if Stephan went and gathered the information for him. "Like you just said, you've never run into any trouble on their side. They take you for one of their own. Chances are you'd both be just fine."

"I don't know if that's a chance I want to face Alina with," Stephan said with a shake of his head. "She's lost one son already."

"If you don't, our army could be decimated, and that's an awful lot of mothers who lose," Sir Edwin pointed out.

"I know, I know." Stephan rubbed the bridge of his nose, trying to weigh their chances against what they could gain. "Alright. But if we get in a spot where I feel like he's in too much danger, I'm coming home, with or without your information. That's the best I can promise you."

"I'll take it." Sir Edwin smiled. "By the way, we think their next move will be involving northern

mercenaries again. That's what we're really after. If
it's just the Dorstenian army, I'm sure we can
manage. The northerners, though, that's another
matter altogether. They made mincemeat of our
armies last time we went up against them."

"I'll keep my eyes open for them," Stephan said
grimly. He had little respect for the way the
mercenaries fought, for the way they singled out the
weakest, the ones who were alone, and cut them to
pieces. There was nothing fair or honorable about
the way they fought, and if they were coming back,
the Divalian soldiers deserved to know.

"Not much of a hunt, is it?" Sir Edwin called back
to Aldrid abruptly and Stephan knew their
conversation was at an end.

"I don't really know, sir. I've never been on a hunt
before." Aldrid moved Casper up a little closer.

"Well, we've shown you a rather poor sample of
one then so far. Why don't you join us up here and
see if you can spot any tracks?"

Aldrid pushed Casper up alongside Stephan's
horse, all the while scanning the ground for the
telltale signs of a passing animal. He glanced over at
Stephan and was taken aback by the seriousness of
his face. He looked troubled about something, and
Aldrid wondered uneasily what it was that he and Sir
Edwin had been so deep in conversation about. He
thought about asking but decided against it. They
had been very careful to keep their voices low, out of
his hearing. He shrugged a little and went back to
searching the white ground. He couldn't quite get
his thoughts back to that task, though. A little worm
of worry burrowed into his concentration. He was
worried because Stephan was worried.

The morning after the hunt, Aldrid was halfway
through his chores when Stephan called him back to
the house. Aldrid had spent the rest of the day and
all of this morning puzzling over Stephan's mood,
and what had passed between Sir Edwin and him.
He could not come up with anything. As he made his

way back to the house, Aldrid hoped that this had something to do with the mystery.

"You wanted me?" he asked when he had stood for several seconds, waiting for Stephan to notice him. He had never seen Stephan so preoccupied.

"Yes, I did." Stephan looked up from where he had been staring into the fire. "Al, we're going to go somewhere."

"Really? Are we going to town?" Aldrid felt his excitement rising at the prospect of seeing Mother again. He had thought he would not get to see her until Spring came again. That was what Stephan had told him.

"No. Somewhere you've never been before. Somewhere that could be dangerous. I wish I didn't have to take you along, but I don't see a way around it. If I leave you here, I'm breaking my end of the bargain and they'll put you on one of the castle work gangs."

"Oh." Aldrid swallowed hard. He had tried to forget that those even existed. It's where he was supposed to be, where he would be, if it had not been for Stephan who insisted he work off his debt on his farm. "You're not thinking about leaving me, are you?"

"Not really. I just don't know what I'm going to tell your mother. She will kill me." This was the second time Aldrid had heard Stephan say something like that about Mother.

"Are you really that scared of her?" He could not help but grin at Stephan.

"Yes, yes I am. If I show up on her doorstep to tell her I've lost another one of her sons, there's no telling what she'd do. It doesn't matter anyway. I can't leave you behind and I have to go, so that's the end of that."

"Where is it you have to go and take me?" Aldrid could not think of any very dangerous places that they should go.

"Dorsten."

Aldrid took a step backward in shock. Of all the things he thought might come out of Stephan's mouth, that was the last. No, less than the last. He hadn't even thought that was a possibility.

"Dorsten? Like, our enemy, Dorsten?"

"Yes. I think that's the only Dorsten."

"Why would we want to go there?"

"Information, Al. The king thinks they're planning something big, something that involves the same mercenaries they hired during the winter campaign. If that's the case, we need to be ready for them. But someone has to go and find out what's true and what's just rumor."

"Why you? I thought you retired. They can't make you go, can they?"

"I retired from the military. I'll never retire from serving my country. And they pick me because I grew up there."

"What?" Aldrid was stunned for the second time that morning.

"You heard me. I used to live in Dorsten, only then it wasn't Dorsten. Both of our kingdoms were united under the old king, and we were free to travel anywhere within them. I had an idea that I wanted to go to sea, and so I came this way when I was sixteen. My timing was bad, though. I had only made one voyage on a trading vessel when the old king died, and the kingdom was split. I ended up on this side. And this is the side I've been on ever since."

"I see." Aldrid's eyebrows were still raised in surprise. "Didn't you have family on the other side?" Aldrid couldn't imagine just leaving your whole family behind and taking another side in a war.

"A brother, a few years younger than me. We were orphans, which was why I wanted to go to sea so badly. I thought it might help get me a start in the world."

"Where is your brother?"

"No idea. Haven't heard from him since I left. This isn't getting us where we need to go, though. We'll pack today and head out first thing tomorrow morning. And Al, I need you to promise me you'll do exactly as I say. I don't want you taking any foolish chances, trying to be a hero. You're only coming along because I'm not allowed to leave you behind."

"I promise I'll listen to you. Do you think we'll run into trouble?"

"Most likely, no. I haven't yet, and I've crossed the border many times. But there is always a chance."

Aldrid was not sure if he felt more excited or afraid. He had never had any great ambitions to become a hero, thanks to his crippled arm. The closest thing he had dreamed about was somehow reclaiming the sword Father had stolen. Even as he thought about it, a spark of wild hopefulness sprang up. If he were in Dorsten, maybe, just maybe, there would be a chance to get the sword back and to expunge all the wrong Father had done. He wondered if he should suggest such a thing to Stephan but decided against it. Such an attempt would increase their danger, and Stephan would not do that.

"What needs to be done?" Aldrid from a few months ago would have waited until Stephan told him that he had to do something.

Stephan smiled as he thought about how different Aldrid was, and how much he had grown up. Maurus would have been proud of him.

"Start by getting your clothes together. Then come see me."

Chapter 28

HAMO SAT HUDDLED IN THE back corner of the hut, his blanket wrapped as tightly around him as he could get it.

In the nine years he had been a slave up in the mountains, he had never known such a bitter winter. It left him with a deep, rasping, violent cough that he could not get rid of. It was a fit of coughing that had woken him up long before daylight. That, and the fact that the man he was lying next to was now a cold, stiff corpse, and no matter how many times Hamo saw one he simply could not bring himself to lay down and go back to sleep next to it. He was not even sure who it was that had died next to him. He no longer knew most of the men in his hut. And he didn't want to know them. It was easier to just sit, huddled in his corner alone, ignored and ignoring everyone around him. It made it less devastating, less depressing, when he had to see them die.

He was one of only two or three still alive from the original group. The others had died of various causes - exposure, exhaustion, starvation, accidents in the mines, and cruelty. Hamo had lost count of how many men he had seen Forbes kill. But there were always more to replace those that were lost. Until recently. Their numbers were so severely dwindled that they only filled one hut, albeit a bit crowded.

Forbes. There was not a name or word in Hamo's vocabulary that could conjure up as much hatred as that one. He dreamed of killing the man, of making him suffer the way he had done to so many other people. It was in fact, this hatred that helped keep Hamo going. He would not give the man the satisfaction of just dropping dead. If there was ever a chance to repay Forbes for all the evil he committed, Hamo wanted to be alive to take that chance. Forbes was the sort of person who not only enjoyed suffering in others, but who looked for ways to maximize their agony. He learned long ago that the only time Hamo was even a little bit happy was when Drogo took him on their wood cutting trips up in the mountains twice a year. Forbes turned them into a nightmare for Hamo. Starting with Warin, he had someone killed at the post every time they were away. Since noise reverberated well off the mountain slopes, Hamo could always hear the horrifying screams as the victims were torn to pieces. And he was always the one tasked with burying their remains.

The only bright spot in his life as a slave was Drogo. Drogo doggedly looked out for him and took care of him. Drogo had taken to giving Hamo some of his own food at lunch. He was careful not to give him so much that it was noticeable to Forbes, but the little bit helped. He also allowed Hamo to sleep for a few minutes in his own quarters, close to the fire, each day during their midday break.

But Drogo was growing old, Hamo could see it more and more with each day. Hamo first noticed it years before, and, afraid that he would be replaced by a crueler master, had done everything he could to help him at his work. The result was that Hamo was very good at something he had never dreamed of spending his life doing - iron work. Drogo taught him not only how to smelt it, but also how to form it into useful tools and objects.

Hamo noticed some of the others starting to stir. His few minutes of peace and quiet were coming to an end. As much as he tried not to, he resented the men around him. He hated when they tried to draw him into a conversation, as many of the newcomers did. Any desire he might have had in the past to talk about home and family was dead, destroyed by years of hopelessness. They were just distant memories now far beyond his reach.

In the dim light of dawn, he kept his head down, so that no one would make eye contact and try to address him. He could not wait until the guard opened the door to their little prison and he could escape to the quiet drudgery of the smelter. Drogo never tried to ask him questions about what he had left behind. Drogo only spoke when necessary, and Hamo learned to enjoy that. He never realized how like Drogo he had become, but he finished growing up under Drogo, and developed many of his habits.

"When did he die?" It was the man on the other side of the body that spoke, and after a second it dawned on Hamo that he was the one being addressed.

Hamo shrugged without even looking at the man. What did it matter what time he died? He was dead, just like they were all eventually going to be.

Finally, their door was unlocked, and Hamo could get his food and disappear up the slope into the smelter. No more questions, nothing but work in there. It was safe.

The wave of heat that still lingered from the smoldering fire was a welcomed relief from the endless cold. Within hours, though, his clothes would be dampened with sweat, and it would make going back to the slave hut that much more miserable.

It was late afternoon, and due to the short winter days, the sun was already sinking toward the western mountain peaks.

"I have to go speak with Bertram. Finish up what you are doing. Then you can go," Drogo said.

Hamo watched him go and turned back to his work. He was not in a particular hurry to finish up. The sooner he was done, the sooner he would be trapped in the close confines of the slave hut with the others. He preferred to be up here, alone.

Hamo was kneeling in front of an opening in the furnace, stoking the fire so that it would be easier to start the next day. He did not hear the footsteps coming up behind him, and the uncertain shadows cast by the fading winter sun and the fire prevented him from noticing someone standing behind him. His first clue was a stinging pain on his shoulder that threw him off balance.

"Do you ignore Drogo like this?" Forbes said from behind him. "Stand up when I talk to you."

Hamo got to his feet, biting down hard on his tongue. Forbes must have said something to him that he missed. And Forbes must have waited until he had seen Drogo leave. He would not dare to hit Hamo as long as Drogo was around.

"I asked you, where's Drogo?"

"In the mine. He said he had to talk to Bertram." Hamo kept his head down, cringing. He knew he did not have the self-control to keep the hatred he felt for this man off his face. And the expression would only serve to annoy Forbes further.

"You know, Captain's son." Hamo grimaced at the way Forbes addressed him. It reminded him too much of Lord Bayner. "I might have been wrong about you at the beginning. I didn't think you'd last a week here. Now almost all your friends are dead, and you're still here. Maybe I should move you over to the mines. They've lost a lot of slaves up there." He paused, waiting to see if Hamo would respond. He knew as well as Hamo that an assignment to the work in the mines would spell his certain and imminent death. "Not that it's going to matter where any of you are working in a week," he added as an afterthought.

Hamo didn't raise his head, but he lifted his eyes enough to see the man's face. He wondered briefly what he meant by the offhanded comment. Not that it mattered. It was sure to be nothing good. Hamo had long ago given up any hope of returning home.

Forbes waited another minute staring at Hamo. He had hated him from the moment he had been brought up here, because he was too small to do the kind of work that Forbes needed done. His hatred only increased since then, fueled mostly by the fact that Drogo had taken a liking to this slave and intervened on his behalf. It annoyed Forbes, and Forbes hated being annoyed.

"Get back to work." He raised his short whip, and Hamo braced himself, waiting for it to hit him, but it never did. A large shadow filled the doorway just then and a hand closed over Forbes' uplifted arm.

"I don't think so." Drogo's low voice made Hamo look up.

Forbes lowered his arm, his face twisted with anger, but he decided against a confrontation with the big man.

"Ah, Drogo, you're the one I was looking for. I need to speak with you, alone." He looked pointedly at Hamo.

"Go," Drogo ordered Hamo, nodding toward the doorway.

Hamo slipped out into the gathering twilight, glad to escape Forbes again, but dreading another night in the slave hut. He'd never been claustrophobic, until he had been repeatedly confined every night with twenty other men.

Chapter 29

ALDRID HAD NEVER BEEN SO far from home in his life. And he had never been so close to the enemy's homeland. Not that he was actually very close at the moment.

He and Stephan had set off early in the morning, two days ago, and had been riding steadily northwest since then. Aldrid had heard people talk about the no-man's-land between the two kingdoms, the barren fields that stretched mile upon mile farther than the eye could see, fields that had been turned into massive graveyards and desolate burial grounds. People called the place the Void. Where the name had started, he was not sure. But it was as fitting a name as ever he'd heard.

Stephan and he had reached it earlier that morning, and had been riding just inside its perimeter, toward a very dense, and nearly impassable forest that lay to the west of it. When he had first seen the Void, Aldrid had come very close to vomiting. The smell of it had reached him long before the sight of it had. It was, Aldrid thought, the drabbest, most dismal, forlorn, empty place he had ever seen or imagined. Void was right. There was nothing but the lingering smell of death and decay. Nothing grew in it, nothing lived.

"Was it always like this?" Aldrid asked Stephan after he had recovered himself enough to speak.

"No. Not at all. It used to be one of the prettiest stretches of scenery in the entire country. But the war sort of destroyed it. Now it's just a battleground and one giant grave. It's not much to look at now, is it?"

Aldrid shook his head forcefully. "Why do we always fight there?" It would make more sense to find a new place, one that the enemy might not suspect.

Stephan laughed a little at the question. "Tradition, mostly. And the fact that the sea lies to both the south and the east, and the old Sar Forest lies to the west. There is no other place for a large army to get through."

"But you said we're taking the forest."

"We're two people, not an entire army. The Sar is our safest route into Dorsten. There's an old trading road that hasn't been used in years. It's almost entirely overgrown, but there is enough of it left to follow. It's been almost completely forgotten by both sides, and so no one guards it. That's how we'll slip in and out."

"Hamo died out there, didn't he?" Aldrid's eyes were drawn again and again to the horrible spectacle.

"Yes," Stephan answered shortly.

"Was it close to here?" Aldrid did not pick up on Stephan's reluctance.

"Very close. We were within sight of our own border forts."

"It must have been awful to die, so close to being safe. I don't think I would have gone back to help anybody. I would have got away as fast as I could." Now that he had seen the Void, the war seemed much messier, and Aldrid was sure he could never be so brave.

"It was awful," Stephan agreed, then spurred his horse to a canter, tugging the pack horse along. He suddenly felt as if he might be sick himself if he stayed in this place much longer. "I want to make the woods before night." He called back over his shoulder as Aldrid tried to catch up.

The old Sar Forest was unlike the woods around Stephan's farm. There most of the trees were stripped of their leaves for the winter, with only a smattering of evergreens holding onto their colors. In the Sar, there were almost no other trees than the evergreens, making it a dark, and foreboding sort of place. The fact that most people avoided it just made it worse.

Aldrid would never have dared enter the place alone, but Stephan rode so confidently into it, that he thought it would be silly for him to hesitate.

"How long do we have to ride through here?" Aldrid was looking around, trying to take in his surroundings.

"A few days, maybe a week or so. Depends on how fast we go."

"Are there any bears in here?"

"Lots." Stephan was slightly ahead of Aldrid, so Al could not see that he was smiling. "There are wolves too. Lots of wolves. If you listen very carefully, you might be able to hear some now."

Aldrid's eyes darted about, peering into the dark shadows beyond the trees. He did hear something. Maybe it was a wolf. Or a bear. Aldrid kicked Casper up to the side of Stephan's horse.

"Stephan? What do we do if we run into a bear or wolves?" His dark eyes were bright with anxiety.

"Aldrid, we're nowhere near them." Stephan laughed and decided to enlighten him.

"How can you tell?"

"Look at Casper." Stephan nodded toward the dusty brown gray horse under Aldrid. The horse's head was down, his ears lowered to the sides, his single eye half shut. "If there was a bear or wolf within ten miles of these horses, they would be dancing around and making such a ruckus we could not ignore them."

"They would? You're sure?" Aldrid wanted to believe him, but wolves and bears were frightening.

"I'm sure. You know, this isn't the first time I've come this way."

"Oh, yes. I forgot. So, I just have to watch Casper?"

"Sure. You watch Casper, and I'll watch the trail." Stephan was grinning at him. "We're actually going to stop and make camp here soon, before we run out of daylight. We'll take turns keeping watch tonight."

After his first night in the Sar Forest, Aldrid began to enjoy himself a little more. He could not spend the entire time afraid of every little shadow. Stephan was in a hurry to get to Dorsten and back home again, but he took the time to let Aldrid practice with his crossbow, and they were rewarded one afternoon when he finally hit a deer with one of his quarrels. That night they feasted on the fresh meat, then Stephan took what they could not carry with them and put it far from their campsite to lure any wild predators away from them for the night.

Five days after leaving Stephan's farm, Aldrid had begun to feel like the entire world was this deep, dark, close forest. It seemed endless. But on the afternoon of the sixth day, Aldrid was pleasantly surprised to see the trees thinning out, and beyond them the most magnificent sight he had ever seen. Mountains. Rising majestically, soaring to meet the sky with their snowcapped peaks, they were the biggest thing Aldrid had seen, aside from the sea. As far as he could see, the mountains went on, growing smaller and smaller as they receded into the distance.

"Impressive, aren't they?" Stephan looked over at Al, staring open mouthed at the sight.

"They're huge!" Aldrid shook his head in wonder. "Is that where we're going?"

"Yes. We have a pretty clear idea that the Dorstenian army is on the move. What we need to know is if they've hired the northerners who live beyond the mountains to fight with them. If they have, we're in trouble. We have to cross the mountains far enough to find out if they are on their way."

"Can we do that? I mean, they look really big to climb."

"We're not climbing them, mostly. There's only one pass that's large enough to bring an army through and that connects the northerners to Dorsten. We're going to follow that pass and see what we find."

"I don't see any pass." Aldrid squinted his eyes, trying to see a break in the wall of mountains before him.

"You can't see it from here. You'll see it tonight. Let's stop here and rest for a bit. We'll do our next bit of the trip at night. Don't start a fire. No point in letting anyone see us here."

Stephan dismounted and looped his horse's reins around a low hanging branch and Aldrid copied him.

"So, what are we going to do if we find the northerners are fighting for them?" Aldrid was chewing on a piece of dried beef, his back against one of the tall, straight pines.

"Get back to the King as fast as we can. We'll need all the time we can get to be ready for them."

"The northerners are the ones who killed Hamo, aren't they?" Aldrid could not leave the subject alone.

"Yes." Stephan closed his eyes and lay back against a tree trunk. "You keep watch for a while. Let me know if anything comes close."

He didn't want to talk about Hamo's death or who had killed him. He was already second guessing his decision to bring Aldrid along on this trip. What would he tell Alina if something happened to him?

Chapter 30

G ET UP." THE SINGLE command was enough to pull Hamo from his fitful sleep. Framed in the doorway, one of the guards stood. "Everybody out."

Hamo noticed that it was still dark outside. That was odd. Forbes never allowed them outside their hut in the dark. Since he was at the back, he was one of the last ones to leave. He noticed that all the others were pausing just outside the door and wondered why as he waited.

When it was his turn to go through the door, he no longer had to wonder. His arms were grabbed and pulled together in front of him by one guard, while another locked iron shackles over his wrists. He had only been made to wear shackles twice in the last nine years. On his first wood cutting trip with Drogo and then again when he had been chained to the post to be flogged.

Instantly, his mind filled with visions of that awful moment, when he had been left chained up to die. They were not only degrading and humiliating, but they also reminded him of the worst experience of his life. They felt like lead weights on the ends of his arms, and he knew that after only a short time they would tear into his skin and make his arms ache.

Once they were locked in place, he was shoved toward the waiting group of slaves. Most were looking around in confusion. He glanced up and saw Forbes, mounted on a horse. He remembered something Forbes had said to him a few days before, something about it not mattering where anyone was assigned to work anymore. This must have something to do with whatever he was talking about.

Drogo knew about it, Hamo was sure. In the last few days, Drogo had been even quieter than usual. Several times, Hamo had looked up to find Drogo staring at him and was surprised to find his eyes full of unfathomable sadness. Hamo hadn't felt sadness in such a long time, just anger and hate and hopelessness. Once, Drogo had started to say something to him, something that wasn't a command. But he had stopped himself and walked away, leaving Hamo a little puzzled.

Hamo wasn't as puzzled now. Clearly, they were being moved, although he had no idea where to. Drogo was not coming with them, Hamo was sure. And for a moment, a feeling of sorrow, so long dormant inside him, sprang up. He would miss his quiet, kindhearted master.

Involuntarily, he glanced toward the black shadow of the smelter. It stood out against its dark gray surroundings. He wondered if Drogo were watching now, if he knew that his slave, that he had protected and taken care of for nine years, was about to be dragged off into the unknown. Hamo wished he had a chance to say goodbye, a chance to thank the man for being the only one who cared whether he lived or died.

His thoughts were rudely interrupted by a hand grabbing his irons and pulling him toward another man. A chain, only a couple of feet in length, connected him now to one of his fellow slaves. Idly, he searched the man's face, wondering who he was paired off with. He knew they had shared the same hut, but he had not ever bothered to speak to him. Now, he was tethered to him, and would probably remain so for the rest of their trip, however long that might be.

There was one thing that Hamo was very sure about as they were led off toward the same mountain pass he had been brought through nine years ago, and that was the fact that he was leaving Drogo's protection far behind him.

The path they followed was rugged and would have been difficult to traverse in the best of conditions. Half-starved, exhausted, cold, and under the constant threat of their masters' whips, progress was slow. The cough that Hamo had developed through the winter was made worse by exertion. Each time a violent coughing fit overcame him, he was unable to keep up. Inevitably, Forbes found this a fitting excuse to beat him. The first time he had felt the leather biting into his side and arm, he thought miserably of how much he missed Drogo.

Forbes, for his part, had been waiting with a sort of savage enthusiasm for this day when he could do what he liked to Hamo. Had Drogo not interfered so much, Forbes might have just forgotten about Hamo. But it had been a strong point of contention between the two men, and now that Drogo was no longer around to protect his slave, Forbes took full advantage of it.

Lord Bayner had given him express orders that, of the twenty-three slaves still left alive at the mine, all of them were to reach the northerners. He didn't care what condition they were in, just so long as they were alive, and he would be paid for them. There were no longer enough to keep his mine going, and it had become more of an expense than a production. So it was that Forbes, no matter how much he beat any of them, made sure that they were still alive, even if it meant their fellow slaves had to drag them along.

By the end of their first day of marching, Hamo could no longer stand or walk on his own. A dozen times he had lain helpless beneath the blows of Forbes' whip, wishing that he would just leave him to die. But every time, Forbes had ordered the man he was chained together with to get him up and bring him along. If Hamo had not been in such acute pain himself, he would have felt very sorry for the man he was fastened to. It had to be exhausting holding up someone else on this march.

As the sun sank lower in the sky above the mountains and a halt was called, Hamo's companion let him collapse to the rocky, snow-covered ground. Hamo lay where he fell, facedown, unable to move himself. His companion was, of necessity, only a foot or two away from him, half sitting, half-laying, trying to recover his breath from their exertion.

Hamo hated Forbes. He wanted to kill Forbes. And he wanted to die. Hamo knew they were heading north, and that could only mean one thing. By the time he reached the northerners, he would be far beyond use. Forbes chose that moment to address him.

"Missing Drogo, aren't you?" He used his booted foot to turn Hamo onto his side, eliciting a low groan from him. "I need one of you to get a fire going. You're good at that, aren't you? Find something around here to burn and get a fire going, Captain's son."

Hamo tried to lift himself off the ground but fell back again, letting out a cry of agony. He knew what was coming, and he hoped it would be the last, hoped that Forbes would finally finish him off and end his misery.

"Just kill me. Please," he whispered through gritted teeth.

The fury that Forbes unleashed on him was certain to be his end. He felt Forbes' booted foot hit his body again and again and then his whip took over. The pain could only be compared to the pain he had felt at the post so many years before. Rather than stopping though, it grew into a terrible crescendo that threatened his consciousness. Forbes was yelling, cursing him, or maybe it was his own voice raised in a never-ending scream, he couldn't tell, but the sound was fading and distant.

He was dying.

Just like he wanted to do. But dying hurt so much.

Then it was over.

Chapter 31

"STEPHAN, HOW LONG WILL IT take us to get through the pass?" Aldrid shifted in his saddle, turning to take in the heavily wooded, steep slopes that rose up on either side of them. They had entered the pass last night, and had been riding since then, breaking for only a few hours to rest.

"Until we find something. I'm not planning on riding all the way north. Winter's still on, and up there it's ten times worse."

Aldrid hoped they would find something quickly. As impressive and breathtaking as the mountains had been from the distance, here inside the pass they made him feel a little claustrophobic. The sides closed in on them, and around every bend was yet another mountain. It was the same feeling he had when riding through the Sar Forest. Trapped. That was the word for it.

Aldrid decided he did not like feeling trapped. And since Stephan had mentioned the presence of mountain lions living up here, the mountains had lost a lot of their original beauty in his eyes. Aldrid cast frequent looks down at Casper's head, checking to make sure the horse beneath him was still relaxed.

He was so caught up in his thoughts of mountain lions and being trapped forever between two mountains, that he failed to notice Stephan pull his horse to a halt in front of him. Casper, never the most motivated of animals, stopped himself and the pack pony that was tied to Casper's saddle pommel followed suit.

"What is it?" Aldrid started to ask, but Stephan held up a hand to silence him.

Stephan was peering into the trees that grew halfway up the mountain, a troubled expression on his face. For a moment, Aldrid could not guess what had grabbed his attention, then he heard it too. Voices, bouncing off the natural walls of the mountain sides, carried through the pass like a tunnel.

Stephan didn't say anything, but nudged his horse toward the tree line, away from the open road they had been on. Aldrid followed him, heart in his throat. This was the part of their trip that he had been both the most excited and the most nervous about. His boyishness looked forward to the danger in a way that only a young person could. But he was terrified of freezing up or doing something foolish if they were in a dangerous situation. That would be humiliating.

Stephan, rather than stopping and waiting inside the safety of the trees, kept riding toward the source of the sound. The sloping ground made it harder for the horses to keep their footing and after a few minutes, Stephan stopped and motioned for Aldrid to get down.

"Whoever it is, they aren't that far in front of us, just around that bend, I'd say. We'll walk and lead the horses a little closer," he whispered to Aldrid. "And Al, if I tell you to go, you get on that horse and ride for your life, do you understand?"

Aldrid swallowed hard as he nodded.

The voices grew louder as they made their way around the curve of the mountain, and when Stephan deemed it close enough, he looped the reins of his horse to a nearby tree, indicating that Aldrid should do the same. He secured Casper and pulled his crossbow out from behind his back. He wasn't sure if he would need it, but it felt like the right thing to do given the circumstances.

"We'll be quieter without the horses," Stephan explained in a whisper, his own bow ready in his hand.

The pines that covered these mountains served another good purpose beyond hiding Stephan and Aldrid. Over the years, dead needles had fallen from the trees, forming a soft and soundless carpet. It was easy to step lightly across them and not make a sound.

Aldrid could hear the voices distinctly now, although the words were lost to his ears. Someone was shouting. And there was a single cry, drawn out and pain filled. Aldrid shuddered as he heard it and met Stephan's concerned eye.

The trees opened up suddenly, revealing a small clearing near the road. Stephan and Aldrid dropped behind a fallen log, watching the scene unfold. Aldrid was confused. Of the nearly thirty men in the clearing, all but three or four were chained together.

"Who are they?" he whispered in Stephan's ear.

"Prisoners of some sort. Slaves, it looks like. But that doesn't make any sense. Slavery's been outlawed in both countries for over a hundred years. I wonder where they got them from."

Aldrid caught his breath as one of the men who appeared to be a guard began kicking the fallen body of one of the slaves. He clamped his hand over his mouth in horror as the guard raised his arm and he caught sight of the whip in his hand, snaking down through the air toward the prone figure. Again and again, he watched it fall, until he could not bear to watch it anymore.

Of their own volition, his hands were pulling back the string of his bow, settling a quarrel in the groove. Aldrid had been given to impulsive action his entire life, and now was no different. He had the crossbow up and sighted before Stephan knew what he was doing, and the quarrel was spinning away before he could stop him.

Aldrid shot in a hurry, and even when taking his time, he had not yet become very good with the crossbow, so it was no surprise that his quarrel missed its intended target, the heart of the man doing the beating. It did, however, bury itself in his leg, just above the knee, and the man dropped to the ground.

Stephan may not have known what Aldrid was doing in time to stop him, but his reflexes had been honed in through a hundred different battles. His own bow was up, arrow nocked and ready to fly.

The three other guards were turning around, looking about them, searching for some clue of what had happened. The fourth lay still on the ground, writhing and yelling. Aldrid, now that the moment was past, felt ill. He had just shot to kill someone, and he had done it without thought. He turned to Stephan, who was staring fixedly at the group in front of them.

"I did the right thing, didn't I?" he whispered. "He was going to kill that man if I didn't stop him." He desperately needed Stephan's reassurance.

"Load that bow again and shut up," was Stephan's terse response.

Aldrid took his words to mean he hadn't.

Stephan was calling out to the other guards now, telling them to put their weapons down. Aldrid's eyes were blurred with tears as he pulled the string back on his bow again. He failed Stephan, he disappointed him, after promising him that he wouldn't. And he nearly killed someone, had intended to kill someone.

The guards hesitated warily. They had not seen where the first shot had come from and had no clear idea as to how many people opposed them. The disadvantages lay entirely on their side though, and after that moment's hesitation, they each removed and put down their own weapons. It was not until Stephan had made them step away from the weapons, that he emerged from the trees. Aldrid wasn't sure what Stephan wanted of him. He knew he was upset about Aldrid's actions and was determined not to act without Stephan's direction again.

Stephan, although terse with Aldrid, was far from angry. The boy had acted only naturally, and Stephan could not fault him for trying to save someone else's life. But it did present an awkward dilemma now. He had four Dorstenian soldiers captive, and twenty-three slaves who looked to be in terrible condition. One less than twenty-three, he corrected himself grimly, as he took in the unmoving and bloody form of the slave that had been receiving the beating.

The three guards who he had now ordered to sit down together away from their weapons did not appear to be the sort to put up any kind of fight, so long as they thought they'd be killed for it. And the fourth was still rolling on the ground crying in pain near the still form of the slave he'd just killed. Stephan half wished that Aldrid's aim had been a little truer. The man deserved to die.

"Al, come here," Stephan called without taking his eyes off the three guards. Aldrid came up to him. "You watch those three. If they so much as try to get up, shoot them." Aldrid nodded, although his face was completely white.

Stephan went over to the man on the ground. As he had suspected, there was a ring of keys on the man's belt. He snatched them off and tossed them to the nearest slave.

"Get those off." He motioned to the irons the man wore. "Pass them around."

It took only a few minutes for the slaves to free themselves. Stephan picked up some of the shackles and took them over to where the three guards sat. Now that the slaves were free, he noticed the three men looked considerably more uncomfortable. They must not have ever thought the tables could turn, Stephan thought with a wry smile.

"Your turn. Put these on." He tossed the shackles to the nearest one. Glancing nervously at the men who had so recently been beneath him, the man did as he was told. Stephan waited until all three had them on, and then attached them to one single chain similar to the way they had secured their own slaves.

With them secured, he turned back to the wounded guard. Since he had been the man with the keys, Stephan assumed he was the leader. As he got close to him, the man tried to drag himself away. Stephan leaned down and grabbed him by the shoulder with one hand, while his other hand gripped the crossbow bolt still protruding from his leg. In one swift motion he jerked it free. When the man howled in pain, he shook his head in disgust.

"You deserved that," he said as he pulled the man toward his companions. "Al, are you alright?" He noticed for the first time since Aldrid had let loose his shot, that his young companion looked almost sick.

"Is he dead?" Aldrid had glanced frequently over at the still form on the ground, willing it to show some sign of life, but so far, he had seen nothing. It would be awful to think that he had watched someone be killed. Aldrid was appalled at the thought.

Stephan followed his gaze and shook his head uncertainly. "I don't know, Al." He looked around at the newly freed slaves and singled out one of the stronger looking ones. "You, watch these four. If they start to move, let me know and I'll put an arrow through them. Al, go back up and get our horses."

Aldrid was more than happy to leave the scene for a few minutes. The lifeless body and the sight of the man he had shot were too much for him.

With Aldrid gone, and the guards taken care of, Stephan approached the still body. He had little hope of finding any signs of life, which was why he had sent Aldrid off. He knelt down beside it and placed his fingers against the man's neck. It was sticky with already drying blood, but to Stephan's surprise he felt a faint, and faltering, pulse. He sighed. It wasn't that he didn't want the man to live. But he was in no condition to move, and Stephan felt as if they were going to need to move and move quickly very soon.

Gently, with practiced hands that had cared for many wounded, Stephan turned the man over a little to get a better look at him. With a gasp, he recoiled as if he had touched fire, and stared in disbelief.

"What is it? Is he dead?" Aldrid had just come up behind him.

"He's your brother. He's Hamo."

Chapter 32

HAMO HAD SLIPPED AWAY into darkness under the blows of Forbes' whip. He was dying, he knew, and in a way, he wanted to die. He'd wanted to die for a long time.

In spite of the darkness, he had the vague idea that Forbes was no longer flogging him.

Maybe he was already dead, or maybe Forbes was going to drag this out the way he had tried to so many years before. Hamo wished he would not. Could the man not at least kill him quickly? Hadn't nine years of loneliness and suffering been enough for him?

Different noises drifted through his consciousness, noises that had no connection to what he thought was happening. There were other voices.

For one moment, he thought a voice sounded familiar, stirring some deep memory. He must be very close to dying, Hamo thought, or already dead. He was hearing things.

Then there was nothing, no sound, no movement, nothing. It was dark. Hamo was grateful for the peace, for the stillness. This was better. This was how he wanted to die.

A hand was on him, gently resting against his neck. He tried to move and found that he had absolutely no control over his own body anymore. It was as if the muscles had simply frozen in place.

The hand moved and now it was turning him over, making the darkness recede, bringing him back to light and pain and agony and misery. Bringing him back to life.

Once again, the familiar voice was in his ears. Where had he heard it before? It was from a long time ago. From his childhood maybe.

He was being moved again. He wanted to scream in agony. He wanted to beg them to just let him lie still and die. He was going to anyway. It would be easier if they just let the darkness take him, like he wanted. His lips parted to say the words but all that came out was a pitifully weak cry.

Hamo tried to open his eyes. He wanted to see who it was who was keeping him from dying. It was not Forbes. Forbes would not have been so gentle in moving him.

Drogo perhaps?

Had Drogo come after his slave in the hopes of saving him?

With an effort that drained him of everything he felt he had left, he managed to open his eyes. Even that small movement hurt.

At first, even opened, his eyes wouldn't focus. The black spots he had been used to getting right after he was wounded so many years ago, danced in front of his vision once more, blotting out whatever was before him.

As they faded, a face became clear. A face he could not quite place, although he felt as if he should. It must belong to that familiar voice, Hamo thought.

The face was talking, it was saying something and Hamo tried to concentrate on the words, tried to sort the sounds through the ringing in his ears. He caught the last part of what the man was saying.

"...me, Stephan."

With a sigh, Hamo realized who it was. And then he passed out.

Chapter 33

HAMO? BUT HE'S DEAD. You said he was dead." Aldrid stared at Stephan as if he had gone crazy.

And for a moment, Stephan thought he might have. He'd seen Hamo die. He'd seen him fall. But then he looked back down at the bruised, bloodied face of the young man in front of him, and knew he was not. It was Hamo.

"It's him alright. What's left of him, anyway," Stephan added the last part under his breath. He turned Hamo over a bit more, and as he did so a soft, anguished cry came from his lips. "Get those keys and get these off of him." He indicated the iron bands around Hamo's wrists.

Aldrid hurried to obey, his face still shrouded in disbelief. All these years, he believed his brother to be dead. Everyone believed his brother to be dead. Yet here he was. Or at least, Stephan said he was. Aldrid could not actually remember enough about his brother to know what he would look like. He would have to take Stephan's word for it.

He brought the keys back and knelt down next to Stephan to unlock the shackles, noticing, as he did so, how badly injured his brother was, taking in the bloody cuts the whip had made all over his body. Aldrid's hands shook badly as he tried to undo the locks, and Stephan pushed his hands out of the way to finish the job.

"He's going to live, right?" Aldrid's dark eyes turned pleadingly toward Stephan. To get his brother back just to lose him again would be awful.

"I don't..." Stephan had started to answer him, but Hamo's eyes opened just then. It was clear he did not recognize either of them. He stared at Stephan, uncomprehending. "You're alright, Hamo, you're safe now. It's me, Stephan." Stephan saw the light of understanding in his dark eyes and then he was gone again, mercifully unconscious.

Stephan laid him gently back on the ground and stood up, one hand stroking his chin thoughtfully as he considered their position.

"Al, I'm afraid this is going to make our plans a little difficult," he said quietly so that the small crowd of recently freed slaves could not hear him. "He's in no shape to move at the moment, and probably won't be for a while. No, I'm not thinking of leaving him," he held his hand up to stop the protest already rising from Aldrid. "Fortunately, none of them got away." He jerked his head toward the four new captives. "As far as anyone else knows, these slaves are still on their way under guard to who knows where. That might buy us a little time, but I don't want to be here more than a day or two."

"What are you thinking of doing then?" Aldrid copied his whisper.

"We'll make camp here tonight. I'll do whatever I can for Hamo, and hopefully, he can recover enough in a day or two to start home."

"Are you angry with me, Stephan? For shooting that man and stopping him," Aldrid asked the question that had been bothering him.

"Angry with you? Al, you just saved your brother's life. I'm not angry about that. I just don't know how we're going to manage."

"He will live, won't he?" Aldrid looked down at the unconscious form of his brother.

He had not seen many injuries in his lifetime, but Hamo did not look as if he would survive. Blood had already soaked through what was left of his threadbare clothes, staining the snow around him a deep scarlet. And now he could hear the shallow, ragged breathing that came from years of exposure and illness.

"I hope so. We're going to do everything in our power to make sure he can. Go ahead and start setting up camp, and I'll take care of him."

Aldrid moved to do as he was told, noticing as he did so that most of the freed slaves were sitting about, looking a little uncertain as to what was happening. It dawned on him that they had no idea who he and Stephan were, or where they had come from. They watched him curiously as he collected wood for a fire and piled it in the middle of the clearing. And when he had lit the wood, and coaxed the first little flame to life, they moved closer to its warmth.

When it came to getting food ready, Aldrid hesitated. If it were just him and Stephan, he would have pulled out some of their dried meat, and bread and that would have been dinner. But he knew they didn't have enough to feed almost thirty people. He approached Stephan.

"What are we going to do for food? You and I didn't bring enough, and they're all starving."

Stephan stopped what he was doing and looked at the group of men sitting by the fire as if he had just remembered them. His gaze took in three pack horses that had been tethered to a nearby tree.

"See what they have on those. They had to have brought something along with them to eat. And I'm sure our friends over there are quite anxious to share." He motioned toward where the four guards were still sitting under the watchful eye of one of their former slaves.

Aldrid had to walk near the captives as he made his way to where the horses stood. He could hear the loud moans of the man he had shot, but any pity or uneasiness he had felt before was gone, obliterated by the sight of what that man had done to his brother. It served him right to suffer a little, Aldrid thought.

Stephan apparently shared the sentiment. When he had done all he could for Hamo, and had moved him, with the help of a couple of the stronger slaves, to a spot near the warm fire, he was not in any hurry to attend to the other wounded man. Instead, he sat down and ate a meager supper first. He wanted to know more about what was going on.

"Are all of you from Dival?" he asked, after the food had disappeared.

"Yes. Is that where you are from?" It was one of the men sitting near him that answered him.

"It is. How long have you been here?" He spoke directly to that man.

"Nine years, same as that one." The man pointed to Hamo. "We came at the same time, and we've been here the longest. The others they've brought in from time to time. I guess whenever they were fighting and had a chance to take prisoners."

"Where were they taking you now?" That was the question that was truly nagging at him. If there was someone expecting slaves at a certain time, they might get suspicious if they didn't turn up. He couldn't wait around for that to happen.

"Forbes never said." The man motioned toward the captive guards.

Stephan studied the four men for a moment. The wounded one was clearly the leader. If anyone knew what was going on, it would be him. Perhaps it was time to take care of his leg and ask him a few questions.

"Are you going to take us home?" It was a different man, seated on the opposite side of the fire who interrupted Stephan's thoughts.

"We'll do the best we can." Stephan got up from the fire and made his way to where the guards were sitting.

Forbes was not a brave man. He was a coward. And the speed at which he had found his own life flipped upside down had stunned him. In all the years he had spent as a merciless slave master, it had never occurred to him that he might one day be in the position of seeking mercy. Now, as he watched Stephan approach, he began to whimper and pull away as far as his short chain would allow him. Stephan had clearly singled him out as the leader. Worse still, he had overheard the exclamation that had left Stephan's lips when he had turned over the body of the half dead slave. He knew the slave Forbes had tried to kill, knew him by name.

"Please don't hurt me," he said as Stephan unlocked him from the others. "I didn't mean to do it. I wasn't going to kill him."

Stephan ignored him and pulled him to his feet. Had Forbes had some small measure of fight in him, Stephan might have hated him. As it was, he was simply disgusted by this sniveling coward who had so easily hurt those who were beneath him, and then tried to grovel for mercy from his new captors. Forbes, always so quick to inflict pain on others for his own amusement, somehow did not find his own pain very entertaining as Stephan made him walk towards the fire. He howled with pain and tried to drop to the ground, but Stephan's grip on his arm was firm and he soon found himself sitting in the circle of uncertain light caused by the fire, surrounded by the faces of men he had spent years abusing. Stephan was immediately less terrifying to him than his former victims.

He looked up to Stephan. "Please, don't let them hurt me, don't let them kill me."

"Shut up," Stephan responded. "I haven't decided what I'm going to do with you yet, although from what I've seen, killing you seems like a perfectly reasonable option."

"No!" Forbes screamed. "It's not my fault. I was just doing what I was told. I was just following his orders."

"Whose orders?" Stephan asked.

"Lord Bayner. He said to take them north. He said to sell them to the northerners. That's what I was doing. Just what I was told to do."

"I see." Stephan almost smiled to himself at how easily the man had given him everything he wanted to know. A thought came to him. "Al, was there a saddle horse with the pack horses?"

"Yes."

"Go see if there are any saddle bags on it and bring them here."

Aldrid hurried off in the growing darkness. He was glad to leave the fire for now. The scene there was sickening to him. He hated Forbes for what he had done to Hamo, and he was disgusted by him as well. But to see a grown man succumb to such utter terror was a little frightening for him to see.

The horse nickered softly at the sound of his approach, and Aldrid stroked its side as he fumbled with the ties on a leather pouch attached to the saddle. He wondered what it was Stephan was looking for as he carried it back to the light of the fire.

"Thank you, Al." Stephan took it from him and Aldrid retreated to a spot next to where Hamo was laying.

Since he had passed out earlier, Hamo had made no other move, no other sound. Aldrid had wondered from time to time whether he was still alive or not and had been sitting next to him to check periodically.

"You're not going to kill me, are you?" Forbes' voice was pleading.

"I said, I don't know what I'm going to do yet," Stephan started to say.

"I do. Tie him to a tree. Let the wolves have him." The voice was quiet, strained and gasping, and cold, very cold. It was a voice Aldrid had not heard before, but it came from right next to him. Hamo was awake.

"Hamo, that's a little brut...," Stephan began, but the reaction from the other slaves was overwhelming.

Before Stephan quite knew what was happening, several of the men had already grabbed the hapless Forbes and were dragging him, shrieking, from the protection of the fire and camp. Aldrid looked from his brother, to Stephan, to Forbes, and back to Stephan, his face a mask of horror.

"Stephan? You're not really going to...," the question trailed off as he saw Stephan shrug.

"I don't know that I could stop them, Al," he said quietly. It wasn't the scene with Forbes that he was watching, Aldrid noted, it was Hamo. Stephan's face did not mirror the horror that was in Aldrid's. But Aldrid thought it was the saddest he had ever seen the man look. And Aldrid understood. Hamo's wounds went so much deeper than the bloody stripes on his back.

"It's what Forbes did to him, you know." A voice from the other side of the fire was speaking. It was the man who had arrived at the slave camp with Hamo. "The first winter we were there. He made Forbes mad, disobeyed him or something. Forbes chained him to a post and beat him until there wasn't an inch of skin left on his back. Then he left him hanging there, waiting for the wild animals to devour him. He should have died that night."

"Why didn't he?" Stephan asked. Aldrid was too sick to speak.

The man laughed, a short, harsh bark of a laugh. "Why? Well, you know, when we first got there, Forbes didn't even bother putting him in the mine to work with the rest of us. He was too small and weak. He gave him to the iron smelter. That man must have really liked him, because he went down to the post after dark and pulled him free, chains and all. Just ripped them straight out of the wood. Took him up to his quarters and wouldn't let Forbes near him for days. It was the angriest any of us had ever seen

Forbes." The man was still obviously amused by the night his master had been thwarted.

Aldrid shifted his seat so that he could see Hamo's face. His brother's eyes were closed again, but Aldrid got the sense that he was still very much awake. He wished there was something to do, something he could say that would make everything better again, but his own eyes were filled with tears, and he didn't trust himself to speak. Tentatively, he slid his own hand into one of Hamo's thin, calloused ones.

The men returned to the fire, and Aldrid could hear Forbes' cries in the distance, he could hear him begging for mercy. It was a sound he wished he could block out entirely. He listened as the men joked among themselves about how fitting the slave master's end would be and about how much he would scream when the wolves showed up.

He glanced at the other three captives, who remained completely silent through the entire exchange. A new fear was evident in their eyes as they watched the cluster of men around the fire. Aldrid had the uncomfortable feeling that if Forbes was killed in this manner tonight, the others would suffer the same fate shortly. Judging by the looks on their faces, they had come to the same conclusion.

Aldrid sat still next to Hamo and watched as one by one the freed slaves fell asleep. The fate of their former master was not enough to keep them awake in their weakened and exhausted state.

As stillness fell on the campsite, Forbes' cries became even clearer and took on a new note of hysteria. Stephan was sitting nearby, his face drawn in a frown. Al knew neither of them were going to sleep any time soon.

Chapter 34

HAMO WAS AWAKENED BY Forbes' first pleas for mercy by the fire. He listened to Stephan's voice, questioning Forbes. He still could not quite convince himself that Stephan was real, or that he was rescued. He was in too much pain to feel any sort of elation at the thought, and he was in too much pain to try to rest.

A savage satisfaction came over him as he managed to speak the words that condemned Forbes to the same death that Forbes had condemned him to. He heard Stephan start to speak out against it, but the other slaves had suffered greatly at Forbes' hands as well, and now that the suggestion was made, they were determined to see it happen. After nine long years, Hamo could have his revenge.

Although he shut his eyes again because it was more than he could manage to keep them open, he heard one of the men explain how Forbes punished him in a similar fashion.

Maybe that would help Stephan and whoever it was with him, understand why Forbes deserved such a death. Hamo hoped that Stephan, if it was indeed Stephan, would understand.

He opened his eyes long enough to see the man's face, and the deep sadness on it. He didn't want Stephan to be sad because of something he did. But there was nothing for it.

For nine years, he dreamed of a chance to get back at all the suffering Forbes caused him. The memory of that night, although it happened nine years ago, was still ever present in Hamo's dreams. He would never get over the fear and agony he suffered then.

Now the campsite was quiet, and he guessed that the others were asleep. He wished he could sleep as well, but his body was wracked with pain. And he could still hear Forbes. As much as he dreamed of such a day, the sound of the man's voice stole whatever hope of rest Hamo had. He grew restless, wishing the man would just shut up and let him sleep.

It was no good.

Even as he lay there, reveling in his revenge, he remembered something. Something Drogo said to him mere days after he rescued Hamo from certain death. Something about the strength of doing the right thing. If Drogo were there at that moment, he would have looked at Hamo the same way Stephan looked at him - sad, disappointed. And Hamo could not bear the thought.

He was weak.

Weaker than he had ever been in his entire life. Weak, because he could not make himself do the right thing. It was no longer in his power to stop what was happening, he could not even sit up on his own.

"Stephan?" His voice was hoarse and strained as he tried to push himself up a little on his elbow. He was not even sure if the man was awake and could hear him, but he had to try. He had to live with himself.

There was the sound of someone moving, someone coming toward him. He felt Stephan kneel down next to him.

"Hamo?"

"Let him go. Can't kill him. Not like that. Not because of me."

It took everything inside of Hamo to form the words, and Stephan leaned close to his mouth to catch them. But it was worth it, for the great weight that was lifted from him. He felt Stephan squeeze his hand, and whisper to him.

"Welcome back, Hamo."

Then he was gone.

Aldrid, sitting next to his brother, was unable to catch the whispered exchange. But as he watched Stephan slip away into the darkness, he noticed that Hamo's restless stirring finally stilled. Whatever words they spoke, Hamo was peaceful now.

Forbes was no longer calling out when Stephan came up to the tree he was fastened to. He was facing away from the camp and so experienced the ghastly sensation of hearing something coming up behind him and being completely helpless to stop it. Stephan unlocked the chain that held him in place and Forbes slumped to the ground, trembling and crying unashamedly with relief as he realized it was not a wild animal. He lay there until Stephan yanked him to his feet. Stephan held him up so that his own face was only inches from the broken man's face.

"You should know that the only reason I let you loose is because that boy you just tried to beat to death asked me to do it. You owe him your life and after what I've heard about how you've treated him, you'd better be glad it wasn't up to me. Because I don't think I would have been as merciful as him."

Forbes did not even try to meet Stephan's gaze. He hung limp in his grasp, shaking convulsively still. Stephan glared at him for another moment before hauling him back to the camp and the relative safety of the firelight. No one but Aldrid was awake as he let Forbes drop to the ground in between him and the fire, and then sat down facing him.

"Can't I go back with the others?" Forbes glanced nervously at the former slaves sleeping all around him. He feared what they would do, should they wake up and find him still alive.

"No," Stephan said. "And you'd better not try slipping off or causing me any trouble, because I'm not feeling very compassionate at the moment."

Forbes sat huddled on the ground, whimpering a little over his injured leg, and trying to calm the tremors that had taken hold of him. His eyes, still bulging with fear, darted about the campsite and fell finally on the spot where Hamo lay, apparently asleep. He stared at the young man, confusion slowly taking the place of terror. Stephan plainly said that he was the one who asked for him to be set free, but after what Forbes did to him it simply made no sense. Even while he stared, he felt another set of eyes boring into him, and looked at the dark shadow sitting next to Hamo.

Aldrid had pulled the hood of his cloak up over his head in the cold night air and wrapped the sides of it well around him. He did not move during the exchange between Forbes and Stephan, but watched it all intently, and with some relief, from beneath the shadow of his hood. Now that he knew he would not have to listen to another's gruesome death, he could breathe a little easier.

"Stephan, what are you doing?" Aldrid broke the ensuing silence. He noticed that Stephan had retrieved the leather saddle bag Aldrid brought him earlier. It was forgotten in the heat of the moment.

"Seeing what our friend here -" he waved a hand toward Forbes " - is up to. I have a feeling selling slaves up north wasn't the only thing they had in mind. Was it?" The last part he addressed to Forbes, with a smile that did not reach his eyes. "I think our friend owes us a little information since we have so graciously spared his life. And here it is." Stephan held a sealed letter up in triumph. "Well, is there anything I should know before I open this?" He was looking at Forbes again.

"No. I don't know anything. No one ever told me anything." Forbes' voice took on the same whining tone he used earlier.

"You're unbelievable!" Stephan shook his head in disbelief. "I have half a mind to put you right back where I got you from."

"NO!" Forbes' voice rose in pitch.

"Whatever." Stephan broke the seal on the letter and perused the contents. "So, you had no idea that Lord Bayner is bringing the northerners in to fight? And you had no idea that while you sold your slaves off to them you were giving them battle orders? Amazing! I would not have thought Lord Bayner would have picked such an ignorant man for such a mission."

Forbes lowered his eyes and said nothing. Stephan considered questioning him for more details but decided against it. Whatever he said, Stephan would never be able to fully trust it. The letter, although Stephan did not show it, complicated their situation.

"Al, come over here." Stephan wanted him to read it as well.

Aldrid took the paper and read it carefully, not fully understanding its import. Stephan, meanwhile, decided Forbes had served his purpose, and took him over with the others. He did not want the man overhearing the conversation he and Aldrid would have to have.

"What does this mean?" Al held the paper up as Stephan returned.

"I'm afraid it means we're not going to be able to camp here for two or three days to give Hamo a chance to recover some. Those orders set the date for their attack in twenty days."

"But we made it here in ten?"

"You and I, both riding, made it in ten days. We've picked up twenty odd men who are in more or less bad shape, four captives, and him." He pointed to Hamo. "He won't be able to walk. All that together is going to make our trip home a bit slower, and we need to get this information back with enough time for the army to be ready."

"So, what are you planning?"

"The only thing I can. We break camp in the morning and start heading back. I'll have to make a

258

stretcher to carry him on. And we'll just have to move as quickly as we can."

"Will he make it?" Aldrid glanced with concern at Hamo.

"I hope so, Al. We don't really have another choice though. We'll slow down when we can and give him as much time to rest as we can. We'll make it work. But if we stay, if we're here when the northerners come through the pass, we'll all be dead."

Chapter 35

IT WAS A STRANGE CARAVAN that set off early the next morning. Stephan spent the night fixing a stretcher for Hamo, and Aldrid stayed up to help him, and to keep an eye on their captives.

As Aldrid climbed onto Casper's back, he realized how very tired he was. He had heard of people being able to fall asleep in the saddle, and he wondered if he would be able to do the same. He hoped so, because at the moment he was fighting to keep his eyes open.

He had not been sure last night how exactly Stephan intended to carry Hamo all the way back to Dival. In the morning, he no longer had to wonder. Stephan brought their four captives over to where Hamo was laid on the stretcher. He addressed Forbes.

"Since you owe him your life, I'm sure you'd love to make that up to him. And I have the perfect opportunity for you to do that."

Aldrid ducked his head down to hide a smile. Stephan was using the same condescending tone he used on him when Al first came to work for him.

Forbes started to protest, on account of his leg, but he noticed the vicious gleam in the eyes of his former slaves. They were disappointed to wake up and find that he was not devoured during the night, and by the way they were looking at him, he guessed they would not hesitate to tear him to pieces themselves if he gave them an excuse. He shut his mouth again without a word.

"Pick him up. And I'd better not catch any of you jostling him around. If he doesn't make it home alive, neither do you." He waited until he was sure all four understood his words. "Let's get going."

Stephan had their four captives lead the way with their burden down the pass, riding just behind them to ensure their cooperation. Aldrid brought up the rear and led the string of pack horses.

Even after half an hour, Aldrid realized what Stephan had been talking about. Their pace was agonizingly slow. And it was not likely to get any faster. Aldrid glanced behind him frequently, as though he expected to see an army breathing down their necks, but the defile behind them remained empty.

Throughout the day, Stephan called frequent halts. Each time they stopped, Aldrid hurried to his brother's side to check on him. Hamo woke up off and on throughout the day, sometimes moaning in pain, and asking for water, at other times quiet and looking around him. When Aldrid bent over him and helped him get a drink of water, Hamo looked at him in some bewilderment.

He accepted that Stephan was real, that he was the same man he had known years before, but he did not recognize the boy who was so frequently attending him. He wanted to ask, but the act of traveling was beyond draining. More than anything, he wanted to be allowed to lie still and rest, but that was apparently not an option. At one point he woke up to find Stephan sitting next to him.

"How are you doing, Hamo?" Stephan gave him a reassuring smile.

"It hurts. A lot," he said, his voice weak and hoarse. "Can we stop?"

"I wish we could. But I want to get you home."

"Home?" Hamo had given up all hope of ever seeing home again.

"Yes. Home. And we're going to try to get you there as quickly as we can."

Hamo nodded slightly, letting his eyes shut again. Home. It was such a lovely word. He could fall asleep again thinking about home.

Stephan watched him for a minute, his face falling into a frown. He laid his hand on Hamo's forehead and his frown deepened. Hamo was hot. And his breathing was worse, far worse, then before. Each breath was drawn slowly, laboriously, as if he was sucking for air. And every time a convulsive fit of coughing took over, some of his wounds would break open.

"Is he alright?" Aldrid was leaning over his shoulder. "Is it too much for him?"

"I don't know, Al. He's running a fever, and his cough's gotten worse. We'll have to keep a close eye on him. But we have to keep moving as well."

Stephan's concern grew over the next few days. At first Hamo woke up often throughout the day, and either Stephan or Aldrid could help him eat, or get a drink of water. By the end of the week, though, he was slipping into delirium more and more often, and had fewer lucid moments.

Each day as they rode through the dense Sar Forest, Aldrid rode in the back, looking out for anyone following them. Stephan was right, though, and the escape of twenty-three slaves went unnoticed. Still, Aldrid could not shake the feeling that they were in a race against time, a race they were losing.

On the evening of the twelfth day, Stephan pulled Aldrid aside. They were forced to stop and make camp early that afternoon because of Hamo. His wounds were broken open, again, and he was thrashing about so much on his stretcher that it was no longer safe to carry him.

"Al, we've got to stop. I'm afraid if we keep pushing this hard, we're going to kill him."

Aldrid had already thought the same thing and nodded his head in agreement. "What about that information, though? What's going to happen if our side doesn't get it?" His dark eyes were troubled.

"We can't work miracles, Al, though I wish we could right now. Without that news, there's a good chance our army will be destroyed. If we didn't have those four to worry about," he gestured toward their prisoners, "I'd just ride on ahead and then come back for you all. But I can't risk leaving you here with them. And I don't know that you know enough about taking care of someone in Hamo's state, either."

"I could do it."

"No Al, I'm not going to risk it. If those four think they…"

"No. I mean, I can ride ahead. We're not that far from the border, and once I'm over that I just have to follow the road we took to get here, right?"

"Al," Stephan ran a troubled hand over his face. "Al, I can't let you do that."

"Yes, you can. You need to." Aldrid wasn't sure what the problem was. There was no sign of the enemy, so he was at no great risk riding ahead.

"You don't understand. Your indenture. If I let you ride off by yourself, off my property, I'm breaking the bargain. It won't do me any harm. But it means they can restart your sentence, and you won't be with me. The Magistrate will put you on one of the work gangs, and he'll put a band on you."

"Even if I'm bringing them this news?" Aldrid had not known all that.

"They might take that into account. But they don't have to. And I don't mind saying that our current Magistrate is a stickler for procedures like this."

"And he already thinks badly of me," Aldrid added. He still remembered the Magistrate's comments about him and his father.

"Yes, I'm afraid he does. So, you see, I can't let you do that. You'll be throwing away any chance you have at a normal life. We'll just have to hope the army can hold them off." Stephan knew as he said it that there was no chance of such a thing. But he couldn't kill Hamo. He'd lost him once before, and he would never be able to live with himself if he did it again.

Aldrid, sensing that Stephan had nothing more to say, moved to a spot just outside the light of the fire. He pulled the hood of his cloak up, shrouding his troubled face in even deeper darkness.

And Aldrid thought.

Stephan thought no more about him and Aldrid's conversation. Having secured their prisoners to a tree for the night, he settled down near Hamo, and was trying to staunch the blood that was flowing once again from his shredded back. Hamo, in his delirium, was doing himself a lot of harm. Stephan was too preoccupied with the task to hear Aldrid creep up softly behind him.

"I'm going to do it," Aldrid whispered.

"Do what?" Stephan paused what he was doing and turned to meet Aldrid's earnest dark eyes.

"I'm going to ride ahead and take them the information," Aldrid spoke with a conviction that he had never felt before.

"Al, I already told you..."

"You told me what might happen. But if somebody doesn't warn them, a lot of our people are going to die, right?"

"Yes, probably. But Aldrid, think..."

"I did. I can work three more years. And I'll get used to wearing that cuff. But if those soldiers die, that's it. There's no bringing them back. It won't be dangerous. We're still ahead of the enemy." Aldrid had already decided that if Stephan did not agree to his plan, he would simply take off sometime during the night, but he desperately wanted Stephan's blessing.

"You're sure? What will your mother say?"

"I don't know. Maybe she'll be proud of me?" Aldrid smiled a little. "But it doesn't matter, does it? I mean, this is the right thing, isn't it?"

Stephan grabbed Aldrid and pulled him close, much to Aldrid's surprise. "Yes, yes, it is." And I never thought I'd hear you say something like that, Stephan thought to himself.

Aldrid pulled away from him. "You'll let me go then?"

"You do understand what you're risking?" Stephan could not quite make himself believe that this was the same boy he had caught robbing him.

"Yes, of course I do. You just explained it all to me." Aldrid looked confused now.

"Then, I'm not going to stop you. They do need to be warned. And if you're riding by yourself, you can make it to the border in a day, and to the castle in two more."

"Can I start now?"

"No. Get some sleep tonight and start in the morning. Casper will need to rest too, if you're going to be riding him hard for the next couple of days."

Aldrid slept fitfully that night, because although he had told Stephan that he wanted to go, he was scared. What if he got lost, or ran into trouble? He had never born the sole responsibility for such an important undertaking before, and he was having some misgivings. But he wouldn't go back on it, that he knew for sure.

At the first sign of dawn, he was up. Stephan was still sitting by Hamo, who had actually fallen into a deep sleep for once. Stephan had spent the night writing a note to whoever Aldrid was able to talk to. He hoped it would be Sir Edwin. Now he handed that, along with the saddle bag containing all of the orders and dates for the northerners' attack, to Aldrid.

"Stay in the woods, but not so deep that you lose sight of the Void. As long as you follow that, you'll make it back just fine. You should reach the border by dark, and just follow the main road back to the castle. Don't kill your horse, but hurry. The more time they have to get ready the better it will be."

Aldrid started to move to where he had Casper standing saddled and ready.

"And Al, if they don't lock you up or anything like that, get your mother. We'll keep moving as we're able to. Bring her to my house, and if we haven't reached there yet, take her to the nearest border fort and I'll meet you there. I think she's waited long enough to find out that Hamo's still alive."

Aldrid nodded.

"But Al, it might not be a good idea if you tell her why," Stephan lowered his voice. "I don't want to scare you, but there is a chance he might not make it. I don't want you getting your mother's hopes up for nothing, alright?"

"I understand. But, Stephan, try to keep him alive. Do whatever it takes."

"You know I will. Now get going. You're wasting daylight."

As Aldrid left the motley group behind him and rode off into the dark woods alone, a terrible loneliness settled over him. It would be a long couple of days. And when they were over, who knew what kind of reception he'd receive from the castle?

He pressed his heels into Casper's side and urged him into a canter for a bit. Whatever awaited him, there was no going back now.

Chapter 36

T HE SENTRY AT THE GATE was drowsy. It was the final hour of his watch and all he could think about was going to bed. He was nodding off, his chin sinking to his chest, when a clatter of hooves jerked him back to attention. He peered into the darkness beyond the torchlight, trying to see who was coming. It was a single rider, and they were moving quickly.

Snatching up the spear he had leaned in the corner, the sentry stepped in front of the gate, ready to bar the newcomer's entrance. Suddenly, the rider came into view. The horse, although moving at a canter, was clearly worn out, its head hanging low and its feet staying close to the ground.

"Halt!" The sentry called out, shifting his spear to confront the rider.

"I need to... I need... to speak... with Sir... Edwin" the rider said, breathless as he pulled his horse up in front of the guard.

"Who are you?" The sentry tried to get a better look at his face in the flickering light, but his hood was pulled up, hiding it in a shadow.

"Tell him... Aldrid Serbon... message from Stephan." Aldrid swayed wearily in his saddle. For two and half days he had been riding with only enough of a break here and there to rest Casper.

"Serbon? You're the sword thief's son?" Suspicion grew on the man's face.

"Yes, I am," Aldrid answered sharply. He had not ridden this whole way just to be turned away at the last moment because of who his Father was. "Please, I just need to get a message to Sir Edwin."

"You're not authorized to come into the castle after hours. You'll have to wait until the gates open in the morning."

"This can't wait," Aldrid cried. "You don't understand. Sir Edwin needs this message."

"What's going on down there?" A third voice called out from the wall above them. "Who is that asking to see me?"

"Sir, it's the sword thief's son. He says he has a message for you from a Stephan. I've already told him he can't come in now."

"Let him in this instant." The note of command was sharp and impatient.

"Of course, Sir. I just thought, being who he was and all..."

"Thought what? That he was coming here to sack the castle single handedly? Let him in."

"Right. Yes, sir." The sentry jerked his head toward the gate. "Go on in, then."

Relief flooded Aldrid as he nudged Casper through the gate and slid off, the flagstones sending little shards of pain through his feet and up his legs. Aldrid had not known it was possible to be this tired, or that he had so many muscles in his body that could all ache with equal intensity and agony. Without another thought, he let his legs fold up beneath him and sat on the cold stone.

He was only kept waiting a minute, which was a good thing. If he was left for much longer, they would have had to wake him up from a dead sleep.

"Aldrid, what is going on? Where is Stephan?" Sir Edwin was crouching down, eye level with him.

"In the bag, on my horse. Their battle plans. And a note from Stephan." Aldrid could barely keep his eyes open and trying to form a sensible thought was nearly impossible.

Sir Edwin was on his feet rummaging through Casper's saddlebags to find the papers. Aldrid meanwhile had given up entirely on trying to stay awake. He simply lay down on the stone courtyard and let sleep take him.

Sir Edwin glanced at the papers Stephan had taken off of Forbes enough to see their importance. Then he turned his attention to the note Stephan had scrawled out. It added to Forbes' information the fact that he was traveling through the Sar Forest with twenty-three former Divalian soldiers who had been serving as slaves in Dorsten. Sir Edwin frowned as he read it. He had not been aware that Dorsten practiced slavery. The note also contained a request regarding Aldrid. As he read it, Sir Edwin looked down to where the boy lay curled up, obviously too exhausted to care where he was.

"Aldrid, Aldrid." He shook him gently by the shoulder and was rewarded a moment later when Aldrid's dark eyes opened and looked sleepily up at him. "Come inside. Let's get you a bed to sleep in."

"No. I have to get Mother. Hamo's still alive. She needs to know."

Sir Edwin raised his eyebrows at his words. He remembered Hamo, remembered when he had fallen in battle many years before. Was it possible that he was among the twenty-three rescued?

"Not tonight. You need to sleep, or you'll be no good to tell anyone anything. Tomorrow morning is more than enough time to tell your mother." He slid his arm under the boy and pulled him to his feet.

Aldrid wobbled precariously for a moment and then allowed Sir Edwin to take him by the arm and lead him inside. He felt like he was in a dream as he shuffled along, his eyelids heavy with sleep. When Sir Edwin sat him down on a bed, he fell over onto the pillow and could not remember another thing.

It was many hours before he woke up, surprised to see late afternoon sunlight flooding through the high window in the room. Aldrid sat up quickly, then wished he hadn't. His sore muscles were not quite as refreshed as he had thought they would be. Once he was sitting up, it occurred to him that he had no recollection of where he was, or what had happened, beyond a foggy memory of talking to a man during the night. The room around him was quite unfamiliar. He wondered if he was allowed to be up and leave the room, or if he was supposed to stay here.

Curiosity got the better of him, and he tried the latch on the door. It was unlocked. Quietly he slipped out into the empty corridor, and tried to remember what way he had come in. He might have stood there wondering for quite some time had not Sir Edwin picked that moment to come check on him.

Sir Edwin had had little chance to sleep the rest of the night and so had put Aldrid in his own bed. Now he came down the hallway to find Aldrid standing outside the bedroom door, looking very perplexed.

"Finally awake, then, I see," Sir Edwin greeted him with a smile. "I thought you might just keep sleeping forever."

"Did I give you the message?" Aldrid was suddenly worried that his dim memory from the night before was a dream and not an actual memory.

"Yes, you did. And many thanks for it. Without that warning, there's no telling what might have happened."

"Good."

"You said something last night, though, about your brother. Something about him still being alive?"

"Yes. Can I go home now? Stephan wanted me to bring Mother to meet Hamo." Aldrid was glad it was Sir Edwin he was talking to and not the Magistrate. He had a feeling the Magistrate would not allow him to leave again.

"I don't see why not. I think, considering the circumstances, it's safe to say you weren't running away from Stephan," Sir Edwin said. "I'll show you out to the courtyard, then I have to get back to work."

Aldrid was halfway across the courtyard when a voice reached his ears.

"Aldrid Serbon?"

Aldrid froze in his tracks. He knew that voice, and he knew what it meant. Reluctantly he turned around. There, just coming out of his office, was the Magistrate. Aldrid had been hoping to saddle Casper up and get away from the castle as fast as he could.

"What are you doing here? Where's Stephan?" The man squinted suspiciously at him.

"He's not here. I was..." The Magistrate didn't give him a chance to finish before he called a guard over and gave orders for Aldrid to be locked up for the night.

"No. Wait. Sir Edwin said...," Aldrid tried to protest. Once again, the Magistrate did not let him finish his sentence.

"You're here away from your master, and that's against the law. We'll discuss what that means for you in the morning." The Magistrate left him in the hands of the guard.

I know exactly what that means for me, Aldrid thought as he watched the rigid old man walk away. If there was some way he could get a hold of Sir Edwin, surely, he would not let this happen to him. He was the one who had given his permission for Aldrid to leave again. But that hope seemed impossible as the guard hurried him across the courtyard and locked him in the very same cell he had been in once before. Aldrid smiled ruefully as he looked around the little room. Last time he was here because he had done something wrong. This time, it was because he had done something right. And this time there was no Stephan to save him.

Aldrid could only manage to doze most of the night and was not really sorry when he saw the sun coming up outside. Being alone was not something he enjoyed, although, he thought, he probably wasn't going to enjoy being around people much either today.

Inside the Magistrate's office for the second time in his life, Aldrid tried to ignore the awful pit in his stomach. The Magistrate looked him over with a rather satisfied air.

"I knew you'd be back here. Troublemakers like you always manage to find their way back to my office," he finally said. "If you thought your life with Stephan Turston was hard, I'm afraid you'll like our work gangs a lot less. Do you have anything to say for yourself?"

"I wasn't running away. Stephan knows I'm here, he agreed to let me come."

It was apparently the wrong thing to say. "All the more reason for me to remove you from his service and put you to work here."

With a sigh, Aldrid realized that there was nothing he could say that would change the Magistrate's mind. In fact, judging by the look on the man's face, he had not only already made up his mind, but was quite enjoying the ordeal it was for Aldrid. He was not surprised by the man's next words, although he would have done anything to get out of it.

"Take him to the blacksmith and have him banded," the Magistrate said to the guard at the door. "When he's done, put him to work cleaning the stables for now."

Aldrid found himself sitting on a hard wooden bench in an open sided smithy. He had told Stephan he could get used to it. But now his palms were sweating, and he felt sick to his stomach as he watched the blacksmith. He had to wait until the blacksmith finished what he was working on, and the waiting was agonizing.

"Alright, bring him over here." The blacksmith had a deep voice that carried over the sound of the roaring fire and the ringing of metal against metal.

Aldrid felt the guard sitting next to him take him by the elbow and make him stand up. He moved toward the blacksmith's workbench in a daze. He did not mind, he told himself. It was to save Hamo, and a lot of other soldiers. He'd learn to live with it. And the pain would eventually go away.

"The less you move, the faster it goes." The blacksmith did not even bother to look at him as he spoke. It was one of his more unpleasant tasks as castle blacksmith and he had done it many times before.

Aldrid nodded automatically as the blacksmith pushed his sleeve up and out of the way. The guard had a firm hold on him, preventing him from pulling away, and the blacksmith had one hand on his arm. He shut his eyes, turning his head away from the blacksmith, and the red-hot band he was preparing. He could not bring himself to watch.

As hard as he tried, Aldrid could not quite keep quiet or still. As he felt his throat constricting in a cry of pain, he bit down on the cloth of his cloak. That only succeeded in muffling his cry of agony. It was every bit as bad as he had imagined it would be, burning, searing pain that was straight from his nightmares. He was thankful, even in the moment, that Stephan had refused to let them do this to him at the beginning. He might have hated Stephan forever if they had, in the same way that he already hated the blacksmith, the guard, and the Magistrate for it.

As the blacksmith pushed his arm into a bucket of cold water, Aldrid gasped with relief. The blacksmith let him leave it there as long as he wanted, and Aldrid felt a little less hatred for the man. After all, it wasn't his own idea or rule he was enforcing.

"Alright, let's go," the guard's voice cut through Aldrid's momentary relief, and he had to pull his arm out of the cooling, soothing water.

Aldrid followed the man toward the castle stable. He was immediately conscious of the way people were looking at him, staring openly at his arm, and he had the same desire to hide it away like he did his crippled hand.

Chapter 37

ALDRID WAS MISERABLE. HERE he was mucking out horse stalls, and all the while Hamo was alive, and Mother had no idea. And his arm hurt. It hurt worse than anything he could have imagined. He wished the guard had let him leave it in the cool water longer. Then maybe it wouldn't hurt so bad now. Every movement of the pitchfork caused the band to rub painfully against the blistering skin, chafing it.

Of course, Stephan had said that this might happen, and he had accepted it at the time. But it did seem really unfair that Mother had to wait even longer to find out about Hamo. Aldrid would have smiled as he had the thought, except he was too miserable to. Stephan had told him more than once, and in very certain terms, of how he felt about Aldrid using the expression 'it's not fair'.

There was no one standing over his shoulder, making sure he was doing his job well, and Aldrid got the sense that this task was just to fill up the rest of his day. Tomorrow, he would be assigned to one of the actual work gangs. He would be little more than a slave for the next three years of his life. Like Hamo, the thought came abruptly, uninvited into his musings. No, better than Hamo had been. He was sure no one would beat him to death or leave him to be devoured by wild animals. And he had an end in sight. He just had to get through three years.

"Aldrid?" The voice was familiar, although Aldrid had to turn around and see who it was before he could place it.

"Sir Edwin." Aldrid tucked his hand behind his back quickly. He could not bear to have someone who had actually been quite kind to him see the band.

"What are you doing here? I thought you were on your way to get your mother."

"I was. I...," Aldrid hung his head. "The Magistrate stopped me."

Sir Edwin noticed then the way Aldrid was keeping his right arm behind his back and in one swift motion he reached out and pulled it forward into sight. Aldrid did not have time to resist, although he winced as the band shifted again.

"Aldrid, I'm sorry. I should have made sure you got out of here alright. Stephan won't be happy when he sees this."

"Well, if it makes him feel any better, I'm not very happy about it either." Aldrid managed a very small, shaky smile that looked closer to tears than anything else. Somehow Sir Edwin's pity just made him want to cry. "And I can't tell Mother about Hamo now either. He's not going to let me go."

Sir Edwin let Aldrid's arm drop back to his side and looked up thoughtfully.

"We'll see about that," he said at last. "Come with me, Aldrid. We're going to have a word with the Magistrate."

Aldrid hesitated before leaning his pitchfork against the wall and following the man out and toward the Magistrate's office. He was getting sick of seeing the place, he thought. Still, he hoped there was something Sir Edwin could do.

"Sir Edwin, what brings you here?" The Magistrate looked up at the sound of the opening door.

"He does. You're not going to punish him."

"It is the law, Sir Edwin. He ran away from the man he owed service to."

"Ran away? And ran straight to the castle? That doesn't even make sense."

"It's not my job to make sense of the criminal's motives. Why he came to the castle isn't my concern. What is my concern is that he is a criminal, just like his father, and he should be marked as such and punished as such."

"In light of the fact that he just delivered important information regarding our upcoming battle against the Dorstenians, I feel like you should take a more lenient view."

"The matter has already been settled." The Magistrate picked up a piece of paper and fluttered it in the air.

Sir Edwin snatched the paper out of his hands and tore it to pieces. "It's not anymore. And if you persist in making an issue about it, I will go to the king about it. I rather fancy Darien will be on my side in this."

The Magistrate looked from Sir Edwin to the shredded paper and then back to Sir Edwin. Sir Edwin was one of King Darien's favored advisors. He was not a good person to make angry.

"Perhaps I was too hasty," he said with a conciliatory smile. "I suppose, in light of what you've just told me, I could reinstate him with Stephan for the rest of his service."

"I suppose you could. Come on, Al. I think there's some news you've needed to tell your mother."

By the time Aldrid was lifting the latch to his own front door, it was late in the afternoon.

"Aldrid? Is that you? What're you doing here? Don't tell me you're running away again. Oh, Al, you can't..." Alina grabbed her son by the arms, searching his face. Aldrid was glad her eyes were on his face and had not yet noticed his arm. When she let go of him, he was careful to keep it behind him, tucked just out of sight.

"I'm not, Mother." Aldrid could not help but feel a slight twinge of disappointment at the way Mother assumed he must be running away. "Listen, please. Stephan and I found..." He stopped himself as he almost blurted out Hamo's name. "We found something. You have to come with me. Please?" He noticed the reserve on Mother's face.

"I don't know, Al. You mean right now?"

"Yes. I was supposed to come get you as soon as I delivered my message at the castle, but I was really tired, and I slept for a really long time, and then I ran into trouble with someone, so it took me a while to get here. So, please, can you come with me now? It's really important, honestly it is, Mother."

"And where are we running off to?" Alina was completely lost.

"To Stephan's."

"Al, that's a whole day's ride away! I can't just go running off like this. What about Sabina? She won't have any idea where we've gone. And when are we coming back?"

For a second, Aldrid wished Mother had just a tad bit more spontaneity. It would make this easier.

"We could maybe leave her a note?" he suggested. "I don't know how long we will be there. But you'll be glad you came, I promise." Though, as he said the words, Aldrid had a fleeting misgiving that he was speaking too soon. There was a chance Hamo had not made it. Stephan had been doubtful. "Trust me, Mother? You'll be angry with yourself if you don't come."

"Just what is it you and Stephan have found that I would be so anxious to come and see?" Alina could not think of a possible answer to her own question.

"Umm... uh... well, you see... Stephan said, that, uh, I'm not supposed to tell you." This was never going to work, Aldrid thought.

"I see. And I'm supposed to drop everything and abandon Sabina and come and see this mysterious thing you and Stephan have found without any idea how long I'm going to be there?"

Aldrid nodded.

"Please?"

Alina hesitated. She did not want to go, but Aldrid was so desperate, so insistent. And to be honest, this was the first time she had ever seen him care about anything beyond stealing and fighting. Maybe it was worth it to humor him. But it was such a long trip.

"Al, I don't know..."

"Mother, it's Hamo," Aldrid blurted out, abandoning secrecy. Mother wasn't going to just drop everything and ride an entire day away on the promise that Stephan and he had located something important. "We found him."

Mother's face went ashen as she shook her head. "Al, don't... don't make jokes about that. You know very well your brother's dead."

"But he's not. Please, Mother, just believe me. I wouldn't joke about this. We found him, and he's alive." Or was, Aldrid almost added.

Aldrid forgot about the band on his arm, forgot about everything else, as he grabbed Mother's arm and tugged her towards the door. She allowed him to. In fact, she appeared incapable of doing anything on her own.

"He's alive," she murmured, tears springing into her eyes. "He's alive. My son's alive."

"Yes." Aldrid couldn't keep the impatience out of his voice. "And we have to go to Stephan's. That's where he'll be."

At last, his words reached her, and Alina pulled away from him.

"I have to tell your sister. We must let Sabina know. Oh, Al, is he really alive?"

"He is. But...," Aldrid hesitated. The hope and longing in Mother's face was painful to witness. "But he's hurt and sick. We have to hurry."

In Aldrid's mind, hurrying meant walking out the door within the next two minutes. Alina, however, couldn't manage that. As she hurried through the house, writing a note for Sabina and collecting anything she could think of that Hamo might need or want, Aldrid watched with growing agitation. When at last she was ready to go, there was the matter of how they were going to get there. Aldrid had Casper, of course, but he wasn't big enough to carry both of them for that long. Mother was undeterred by that dilemma. With Aldrid tagging along behind her, she asked around until she found someone willing to take them.

With the town dropping into the distance behind him, Aldrid was finally able to breathe freely. He had done what he was supposed to, and thanks to Sir Edwin, there wasn't going to be any trouble for it. All he could hope for now was that Stephan had made it to his house, and that Hamo was still alive. The wagon they were riding in bounced along, making Aldrid sleepy.

"Al, how did you find him?" Mother asked after a very long time and waking him up from his doze.

Aldrid's face fell. He hadn't thought about her asking that. Something warned him that she wouldn't be happy to hear that Stephan had taken him into the country of their enemies.

"Al?" Mother asked again, worried by his silence. "You did really find him, didn't you?"

"We did. At least, Stephan says we did. I don't actually remember him, at all."

"Then tell me how, and where? It's been so many years. Where could he possibly have been for so long that we didn't know about?"

Aldrid shifted so that his face was concealed from the light of the lantern that hung on a short pole set up in the front of the wagon.

"We found him in Dorsten."

"What?" The shock and horror in Mother's voice made Aldrid wince. "What were you doing there? Why?"

"Stephan took me. He had to." Aldrid risked a glance in Mother's direction and regretted it. He hurried on. "It's a good thing he took me too. I had to ride ahead and warn Sir Edwin that the enemy is planning on attacking. And I got to tell you about Hamo, and I wouldn't have been able to do that if I hadn't gone."

"But you could have been killed or..."

"I wasn't," Aldrid offered, his voice small and coaxing. "Everything worked out."

The wagon rolled to a stop at last. Stephan must have heard them coming up the lane. He was waiting outside his front door when the two now weary travelers came to a stop. Aldrid searched his face anxiously, afraid of what he might find there. Stephan smiled at him briefly. Aldrid had never seen Stephan look so tired, but the smile was reassuring.

"Al, take care of the horses. I want to talk to your mother alone."

Aldrid led the horses toward the barn, casting one backward glance at Mother and Stephan. He had assumed Stephan's smile meant all was well. What if he was just trying to make him feel better instead?

He tried to keep his mind on rubbing down the tired, sweaty horses, but that proved difficult. More than once he slipped over to the door of the barn and watched the house, looking for some sign that would set his mind at ease.

As he led Casper to his stall, he heard the barn door open and spun around to see Stephan coming in.

"Is he...," Aldrid couldn't quite bring himself to say the word.

"No, he's alive. Not well, but alive."

"Oh, thank goodness. I was so worried. And then Mother wasn't going to come with me. I had to tell her. I'm sorry."

"It's alright. I'm sure she wasn't thrilled with the idea of running off in the middle of the night for something she wasn't sure about. I think it's safe to say, though, that she's glad she came now. Al, why are you hiding your arm?" Stephan shifted the conversation abruptly.

"The Magistrate saw me as I was leaving."

Aldrid held out his arm reluctantly for Stephan to see. He himself had tried not to look at it since it had been done. Now he could see the skin around it had turned an angry red and was blistered up painfully.

"Al, I'm sorry. I never meant for this to happen to you."

"I know."

Aldrid turned his face away because he had the awful urge to cry about it. Not just because it was a permanent mark against him, but because the look on Stephan's face was so devastated. He realized the truth in Stephan's words. Stephan had never intended for him to be hurt; he had done what he had to help him.

"I shouldn't have let you go. This wouldn't have happened if I hadn't."

"But then, you might have tried to go too quickly, and Hamo might have died. Or they wouldn't have had any warning about the attack."

"I know, I know. I just wish there had been a different way. Or that our Magistrate wasn't such a stickler for protocol. Speaking of which, if he caught you and had you banded, there's no way he just let you come back here." Stephan looked suddenly suspicious. "Don't tell me you ran away from one of the work gangs."

"I didn't. Sir Edwin happened to come in while I was cleaning stalls, and he talked to the Magistrate, and said something about how the King would agree with him and then the Magistrate said he had been too hasty and that I could finish out my service with you."

"I'm sure the Magistrate was happy about all that." Stephan smiled a little.

"Not really. But I think he was a little scared of Sir Edwin, especially when he talked about the King."

"Oh, I'm sure he was. Our Magistrate is a good one, but sometimes he misses the real idea of justice."

"How is Hamo?" Aldrid didn't want to talk about the Magistrate anymore.

"Not good. But I think he will get better, especially now that your mother is here. When we reached the border fort, a doctor had to burn the infection out of several of his wounds, and that helped bring the fever down and made it safe enough for me to bring him here. But he's half starved, and sick, and it's going to take him a long time to get over that."

Aldrid's face twisted in a grimace as he thought about it. Burning was such an awful pain, he thought, as he glanced down at his very red wrist.

"What about the guards we captured? What did you do with them?"

"Turned them over to the fort commander. I told him who they were and what they'd done, and quite frankly, I could care less what he decides to do with them. If he sends them back to the castle, they'll stand trial for what they did to our men."

"And the other slaves?"

"They all had families and homes they wanted to get back to. I assume that's where they went."

Aldrid leaned back against Casper's stall wall. Weariness overwhelmed him and he tried unsuccessfully to stifle a yawn.

"Oh, by the way, I put Hamo in your room. You can sleep in the other room."

"What about Mother?"

"I don't think she's going to be leaving Hamo's side anytime soon," Stephan replied. "Why don't you go get some sleep? You look like you're about to fall over standing there."

Aldrid started to the door, then turned back.

"Stephan? When Hamo gets better, can we not tell him why I'm here?" It was a thought that had been bothering him.

"You don't think that would actually matter to him, do you?"

"I don't know. I just think it would be nice if he didn't know. You know, since he's been so brave and good and all, I just don't want him to think of me as a thief. I'd rather keep it a secret."

"Wouldn't be very honest though."

"No, I guess not."

"I won't tell him, anyway. I think that would be up to you. And I wouldn't worry too much about it. I mean, if he could let Forbes go after what that man had done to him, I don't think he'll hold it against you."

"You're right, I suppose."

"Now get to bed." Stephan waved him away.

Chapter 38

HAMO WOKE, GASPING, FROM a horrifying nightmare. He had no idea where he was, or how he had gotten there, or who else was there. For days, he had tossed and turned, tormented by feverish nightmares and haunted by delirious memories. This time, as he lay trying to calm his rapid breathing, he knew something was different.

The fever was gone.

He was tired, but his mind was clear, or at least, as clear as it could be. There were events, both real and imagined, that needed to be sorted out. Hamo had no idea how long he had been out of it, how much time had slipped away while he was trapped in his fever. He had the fleeting notion that it must have been a while.

Slowly, he turned his head to the side, and searched the room he was in. It must be night, he thought as he noticed the single candle sitting on a small table near his bed. The candle was the only source of light and made it difficult to study his surroundings.

He sensed someone else was in the room with him, although he could not make them out. He could hear their even breathing, and assumed they were asleep. It made sense that someone was sitting in here. He had an idea that he had not been left alone much since his rescue. Stephan had been there, that he knew for sure. Stephan was the one who rescued him, who brought him back to life in the mountains. He wondered why Stephan happened to be in the mountains in the first place. Surely, he had not come in search of him after all those years.

Vaguely, he recalled that Mother had been there as well. But that was not as distinct as his knowledge of Stephan's presence. She had seemed like a dream, floating in and out of his consciousness, just beyond his reach. He wondered if she had ever really been there at all, or if his own desire to see her again had brought her to life in his dreams.

Whoever was sitting in the room with him woke up. Hamo could hear them getting up and moving towards him. An awful fear filled him, so unexpected that he did not have time to fight it down. It was a fear that he was not with Stephan or Mother, but Forbes who was just waiting to torture him further. He pulled instinctively away from the unseen person, realizing as he did so just how difficult it was for him to move.

"Hamo, are you alright?" The voice was Stephan's, and Hamo began to relax.

"Stephan? It's you?"

Stephan stepped closer, into the flickering light of the candle. Hamo caught sight of his face and sank back with relief. Stephan put the palm of his hand against Hamo's forehead.

"Your fever's broken, finally. Your mother will be glad to hear that."

"She's really here?"

"Yes, she is. She's here and worried sick about you."

"I thought she was just in a dream. Where am I?"

"My house. It's closer than home, and I wasn't sure you'd make it that far."

"How long have I been here?"

Stephan pursed his lips together, thinking. Truth be told, he had not been counting the days. They had been slipping away too quickly to note. "A couple of weeks, maybe. I don't know for sure. Long enough for us to be worried about you."

"You saved me." Hamo desperately wanted to make sense of all the bits and pieces that were floating around in his brain.

"Well, technically, your brother did that first."

"Brother? You mean, little Aldrid?" How could that be? Aldrid had been just a toddler when he had left.

"He's not so little anymore, and he was very much the one who shot Forbes and stopped him from killing you. Of course, we had no idea it was you at the time. We've thought you were dead for years. I have to admit, I've never been more surprised in my life when I turned you over and saw your face."

There was something nagging at the back of Hamo's mind as Stephan spoke. A memory from so long ago. Something Lord Bayner had said to him.

"He knew I was alive," Hamo said it bitterly.

"Who did, Hamo?"

"Father. He knew I was alive, and he didn't want me." That was what Lord Bayner had said, all those years ago. Hamo had tried to convince himself it was not true, that Father would never choose to abandon him like that, but years of abuse and suffering had worn down his resolve, and he had grown to believe Lord Bayner. "They tried to ransom me, in the beginning. But no one wanted me."

"Hamo, that's not true. I don't know anything about this ransom, but I know your father had no idea that you were alive. If he had, Hamo, he would have torn that country apart trying to find you. You know he would have."

"Is he really dead?" Hamo turned his face away toward the wall as he spoke. Stephan's response was what he had been expecting. But how could Father not have known? Had King Dival really not told his own Captain.

"Yes."

"So that part was true." Hamo had become so used to the idea that Father was dead, that he could not bring himself to feel anything now.

"I'm afraid so. Look, Hamo, you're still not very strong. Maybe you should try to go back to sleep."

Now that he thought about it, Hamo could barely keep his eyes open. He wondered if there would ever be a time in his life again when he felt normal, and strong, and healthy. At the moment, he doubted it.

Chapter 39

I T HAD BEEN NEARLY A month since they had come home. In that month, Aldrid had seen almost nothing of his older brother. Mother and Stephan took turns nursing him, which meant there was more work than ever for Aldrid. But for once he didn't mind. It was nice having Mother there. Her food was so much better than Stephan's cooking. And he thought it was nice having his brother back, although now that he was here Aldrid was a little nervous.

He did not remember anything about his older brother, and now here he was, a grown man. He wondered what he was like. What if he actually could not stand him? Aldrid could not think of too many people that he truly liked. What if Hamo wasn't one of them? More than anything he was intimidated by him. His entire life he had been told about how heroic and good and brave his brother was, and how not heroic, and not good, and not brave he was. It wasn't a pleasant comparison, especially now that he had an iron band to confirm everyone's worst opinions of him.

The weather had fully turned to spring in that month, and the air smelled sweetly from all the blossoms. Aldrid was in the stable, brushing Casper's muddy brownish gray coat. It was hard to believe how much dirt stuck to the shaggy fur. For at least the tenth time since he started, a slight breeze glided through the barn, filling his mouth and nose with dust.

"Why do you have to have so much dirt on you?" he addressed Casper.

The horse flicked lazily at the flies with his tail and ignored the sound of Aldrid's voice. Aldrid shrugged and kept brushing. He had a fondness for the little half blind horse that did not extend to any other animals on Stephan's farm. Casper had carried him quite tirelessly when he was riding back to the castle with his important news.

"I wonder if you have any idea what an important job you did?"

"I could be wrong, but I'm pretty sure horses don't think like that."

The quiet voice behind him was so unexpected that Aldrid dropped the brush in his hand as he spun around. There, sitting on top of a feed barrel, was Hamo. Aldrid wondered how long he had been sitting there watching him.

"Hamo, you're up!"

"Shhh," Hamo held up his hand to stop Aldrid. "Mother doesn't know I'm out here yet. But I'm really tired of just lying in bed."

"Oh. Should you be out of bed?"

Aldrid bent down to retrieve the fallen brush. He did not know much about sick or injured people, but he thought Hamo still looked awfully white and gaunt.

"I think I'll survive it. Besides, I wanted to talk to you."

"To me?"

"Stephan told me that you're the one I have to thank for saving my life."

"I didn't really do anything much."

"That's not what Stephan said. He said you're the one who shot Forbes. And since Forbes was in the process of trying to kill me, I think that counts as saving my life."

"I guess so. I had no idea it was you, though. I thought you died years ago; we all did. I just saw that man beating someone and it made me mad. I didn't think I'd stopped him in time, either." Aldrid shuddered a little as he thought about that horrible moment when he had pulled his trigger. "I'm glad I did." He wasn't sure what else to say.

"So am I." Hamo smiled a little.

"Did he really try to kill you by leaving you for the wolves and such?"

Aldrid still could not fathom that amount of cruelty. He wished he had not asked the question, though, when he saw the shadow on his brother's face. Hamo was quiet for a long time, looking out the open door of the barn, away from Aldrid.

"Yes. I don't really want to talk about it, though. What about you? How'd you end up here with Stephan? I asked Mother and she wouldn't say, and Stephan just said I should ask you."

It was the one question Aldrid had been hoping his older brother would never think of to ask. He had made up his mind that if he did ask, he would tell him the truth, and that if he never asked, he would just say nothing at all. It was a good compromise in his head. Of course, having the band on his wrist increased the likelihood of Hamo asking, but Aldrid elected to ignore that in his calculations. Now, however, the question was out there and Hamo was watching him waiting for an answer.

"It's a long story." Aldrid looked for a way to stall.

"I'm not exactly in a hurry to go back to bed."

"Well, so I was...uh...I...um." This was no good, Aldrid thought. He might as well just spit it out and hope his brother would not think too badly of him. "I tried to steal from him, actually I stole from a lot of people. But he caught me, and took me to the Magistrate, and I was supposed to work for three years in one of the castle work gangs, but Stephan claimed my service so that I had to go with him." Aldrid had been carefully studying his feet and the ground beneath him as he confessed the story, but when there was no answer from his brother he looked up. For a second, he was taken aback. Hamo was trying very hard not to laugh.

"You tried to steal from Stephan? Didn't you realize that man has been a sergeant for twenty years? He sees behind his back."

"Well, I figured it out," Aldrid said, shamefacedly, and then found himself smiling as well. He liked Hamo, he decided, with relief.

"Why'd you want to steal from him anyway?"

"I had an idea. I thought if I could get enough money, I could buy back the sword Father stole, and then people would stop being angry about it."

"So, you stole to get back something that was stolen?" Hamo looked rightfully perplexed.

"I didn't say it was a good idea, just an idea. It was a long time ago, anyway."

"Oh?"

"Last summer, that was almost a whole year ago." Aldrid felt like it was an eternity ago. He added with an unconscious touch of smugness, "I'm not anything like that anymore."

Once again, Hamo looked like he was trying not to laugh. But his smile disappeared, leaving behind a shadow of sorrow and regret. He'd missed everything. Ten years, ten of the most important years of his life, were just gone. And for what? The war was still going on. Nothing had changed, nothing had been gained by his wasted life. Stolen. That was what it was. Ten years of his life stolen out from underneath him, and there was nothing he could do to get it back.

Outside the barn door and out of sight of both Hamo and Aldrid, Alina stood listening. She had gone in a frantic search for Hamo after realizing he had left his bedroom. In her opinion, he was nowhere near ready to be up and about, although Stephan had told her not to worry about him. Now she listened to the sound of her sons' voices as they drifted out of the barn. She leaned back against the wooden side of the barn, enjoying the sounds of their conversation that she thought she would never get to hear.

It was surprising to hear how different Aldrid was, and how much he had changed in the last year. Here he was telling Hamo about what he had done wrong. Aldrid, who had never confessed to doing anything wrong. She would not have thought it possible. When she had the time, she should remember to thank Stephan for his willingness to take the boy in and help him, Alina thought.

"Found him?" Stephan had come up behind her quietly.

Alina nodded, not wanting to let Hamo and Aldrid know that she had been eavesdropping on them. Stephan listened for a moment as well.

"Sounds like they're getting on well enough," he whispered, a smile spread across his face. "You know, Alina, I think Aldrid might turn out alright after all." He had heard, approvingly, the way Aldrid had told the truth about why he was with Stephan.

"I think he owes a big part of that to you. I must say though, I'm not entirely sure I'm ready to forgive you for taking him all the way into Dorsten with you." She turned toward him, disapproval written all over her face.

Stephan shrugged. "It worked out alright. You know, he's the one who actually saved Hamo's life. I wasn't fast enough, but he was. Thought I was mad at him for it, too."

"I know. It's just, that was so dangerous."

"Couldn't be helped," Stephan said reasonably.

"I suppose not. But if something happened..."

"Nothing happened, Alina. And, I'd say Al's better for the experience. By the way, I've had word from Sir Edwin. He says King Darien would like to meet with Hamo as soon as he is able to."

"Have you any idea what the king has in mind?"

"Not exactly. I know he's wanted to see all of the men we rescued. I imagine he feels as though the country owes some debt to them for what they were put through. He's different than Dival."

"He's a good king," Alina said thoughtfully, remembering her own experience with King Darien's generosity so many years before. "But Hamo won't be ready to travel for a long time. He's still so thin, and weak."

"Oh, I think he's doing alright, all things considered. He's over the worst of it and there's no danger in him traveling. It might be good for him to have something to take his mind off of everything. A lot happened to him over there that I'm sure he'd rather not remember. Besides, Sabina is dying to see her brother."

"What are you saying? That he should go now? He's not strong enough. I won't let him, Stephan. I can't risk losing him again."

"Not right this instant. But soon, yes. Sabina doesn't deserve to be kept waiting all this time. And, no offense, but there's a good chance you'll never think he's up to it." Stephan softened his words with a smile. He knew Alina well enough to know that she would do everything in her power to protect her eldest son from anything and everything in the future. "He'll be alright, Alina. You won't lose him again."

"I suppose you're right. It must be very hard for Sabina to know that he's alive and to not be able to see him. Do you think Aldrid will be alright going into town? You don't think there will be any more trouble for him?"

"People will stare at him, and avoid him, but that can't be helped. Anyone who actually cares about him at all won't care. And as far as the Magistrate is concerned, as long as Al stays with me, he's fine."

"He's not going to know what to do with himself when his three years is up. He's grown so fond of you, you're like a father to him. I'm afraid he won't like coming home very much."

"Hmmm. We'll see," Stephan said. "What do you say to the end of the week? That gives him a few more days to get stronger."

"Alright. I suppose if you think he's able to."

"Then let's leave those two alone for a while and let them get to know each other."

Chapter 40

THE WAGON ROLLED TO A STOP just outside of their home, but Sabina was running toward it before the wheels had come to complete rest. Hers had been perhaps the hardest lot to bear in the last month, for although Stephan had arranged for word to be sent to her of Hamo's return, she had been unable to come.

"Hamo! Hamo! It's really you!" Her voice was nothing more than a squeal of delight. She did not wait for him to climb down from the wagon but climbed up into the bed of it and flung her arms around him. "I thought you were dead. We all did. I can't believe you're really here!"

She tried to brush the tears away from her eyes so that she could get a look at the brother she had not seen in ten years, but it was a futile effort, especially since her arms, wrapped so tightly around him, were quite sensitive to the ridges of scars that crisscrossed his back. She pulled away for a moment. "What have they done to you, those horrid people?"

"Sabina. It's good to see you again," he said, unable to think of anything better to say, but Sabina did not seem to mind.

Hamo had spent the last ten years, and ten of the most formative years of his life, in quiet misery and was not entirely prepared for Sabina's greeting. He suspected Mother's greeting had been similarly emotional, but he was too sick and delirious to know. Stephan and Aldrid had been more reserved, quieter in their welcome, a fact he had very much appreciated.

"Get down and come inside. I've supper all ready, and oh, Hamo, I'm so happy to see you again!"

Sabina slid down from the wagon with Aldrid close behind her. She had forgotten to greet him at all, although, given the circumstances, Aldrid could forgive her the oversight.

Once down, he turned to give Hamo a hand. Hamo's wounds had mostly healed, but Stephan had said there was damage done to the muscles in his back that would probably never heal, and that made it difficult for Hamo to climb up or down anything.

"Thank you," Hamo said, smiling briefly at Aldrid.

He still could not quite get used to the fact that his little brother had grown so much since he had left. It dawned on him that he had only been a little older than Aldrid was now when he went off to the war. He was almost relieved that Aldrid had a handicap that would prevent him from ever being recruited to fight. The war had stolen everything from him, and given nothing but pain, torment, and haunting nightmares in return. He did not want that for his little brother, or for anyone else for that matter.

When Stephan had first said the King wished to have an audience with him, Hamo had been extremely reluctant. Now that he knew how Dival had kept his survival a secret from his own family, he thought less of him than before. It was not until Stephan explained that Dival had died and left the throne to his son Darien, that Hamo had relented. It helped that Stephan also mentioned what King Darien had done for Mother.

Sabina had put all her culinary skills into her preparation of this homecoming supper, and the result was delicious. Hamo smiled a little at the thought. Everything was delicious to him right now, as a result of nine years of meager rations that were barely able to keep him alive. Such an abundance of food would have been a wild daydream in Dorsten, and now here it was, piled up on the table before him.

He remembered the first night he and Drogo had gone up the mountain, how ravenously he had eaten, not even bothering to use a utensil. He still had to fight down the urge to eat in the same manner now that he was safe and well fed. Mother would be appalled if she knew what a thin thread of self-control held him back from snatching the food and gorging himself shamelessly.

Aldrid was helping clear the table when Sabina noticed the band on his wrist. She knew from Mother that Stephan refused to let them put it on him.

"Al, when did that happen?" she asked quietly, being sympathetic enough to not draw everyone's attention to it.

Aldrid briefly explained the situation he and Stephan had found themselves in with Hamo worsening by the hour and information that had to reach Sir Edwin and the King before it was too late.

"I told Stephan I would ride ahead and give them the message, that way he could slow down and keep Hamo alive. We didn't think he'd make it if we kept pushing as hard as we were," Aldrid answered as quietly as Sabina had first spoken, but Hamo caught the conversation.

He first noticed the band when he and Aldrid were talking in the barn, but Stephan had never told him that part of the story of his rescue. Now his eyes caught sight of it again in the firelight, and it brought back such an awful memory of being chained up and helpless that he shut his eyes to block it out.

"Al, are you ready to go?" Stephan asked.

"Go where?" Alina looked up, confused.

"He still has to stay with me, especially now that he's on the Magistrate's bad side."

"Oh." Alina could not quite keep the disappointment out of her voice. She had assumed he would be allowed to stay the night at home.

"It's alright, Mother. It's just for the night, you know," Aldrid said. "We'll be back in the morning."

Hamo stood by the doorway and watched as Aldrid went out and climbed up in the wagon. Stephan went to follow him, but Hamo put his hand on his arm to stop him.

"Did he really get that thing put on because of me?"

"Sort of. We were losing you, trying to make as much time as we could each day. You were just too weak and sick and hurt to keep moving at that pace. He knew that, and he also knew how important it was that our army was warned in time. I explained what could happen to him if he rode back ahead of me to give them the warning, but he insisted on doing it. Said it was the right thing to do, and it really was our only chance."

"And it's permanent?"

"I'm afraid so. Only a King's Pardon can have it removed, and last I checked kings don't bother pardoning petty thieves."

"I see. Well, goodnight." Hamo looked distant and a little troubled.

"He knew what he was risking, Hamo. He chose to do it anyway. We'll be by to get you in the morning."

Hamo nodded and stood in the doorway, watching until they had disappeared around a corner.

Morning found him pushing away an unreasonable anxiety as they approached the castle. It didn't help that the last time he'd seen the place was when he was riding at Father's side to war. Upon arriving, an elderly man ushered him into the throne room.

Hamo had never been in the throne room before, and the few minutes he had to himself in there were interesting. His eyes traveled over the heavy tapestries. He noted that the disastrous winter campaign he had taken part in had not yet found its place in this display of the war. Apparently, it didn't deserve a spot in the gallery of history. It must have been easy for Dival to sit in here and think up epic battles and glorious victories, surrounded by such a tidy version of the actual conflict, Hamo thought. Since he never bothered to participate, he could keep the war so clean, so neat, and so gallant in his mind.

A voice from close behind him caused Hamo to jump back startled. He wished he could control his reaction better, but years of Forbes' abuse had trained his mind to meet everything with fear. Even now, though he could clearly see the man in front of him was not Forbes or anyone trying to harm him, his heart was still racing, his palms cold and clammy with sweat. And he instinctively backed up flat against the wall.

"I'm sorry. I had not meant to startle you," the man, some ten or twelve years older than Hamo, said, smiling easily. He took a step back and Hamo let his breath out.

"It's fine. I just didn't hear you coming up behind me, that's all."

"They are interesting to look at, aren't they?" The man pointed to the tapestries.

"Yes. Although, they're not exactly accurate."

"Not at all. That's the beauty of art, though, I suppose. Artists do tend to take liberties with their work. I find there's something lacking in each of them, something missing."

"Blood. Fear, pain, death, suffering. They missed the rotting corpses and the mangled wounded. I guess those things don't translate to art very well," Hamo said with a touch of bitterness.

"No, I don't think those things fit in very well at all." The man stared at him, an odd look on his face. "You've been in the war then?"

"Yes, a long time ago."

"And what brings you here now?"

"I was told the king wanted to see me."

"Ah. I see. I have someone I was to meet here as well. Someone who has only recently returned to our kingdom having been gone for nine years."

Hamo heard the words but took a second to discern their meaning. As realization dawned on him, his face underwent a series of expressions from surprise to consternation.

"Your Majesty, I had no idea...," he fumbled with the words, wondering if he should bow, or if it was already too late for that.

"Of course, you didn't. I didn't tell you. I must confess I find it much easier to talk to people when they are not aware of who I am. But I am wrong to keep you standing so long. I can see you have not fully recovered. Please, come sit."

Hamo gingerly lowered himself into the chair King Darien had indicated. Getting up or down was difficult and painful, but he was glad the king had noticed he could not stand much longer. His strength was still almost nonexistent. At this point, he was not sure he would ever get it back.

"How are you recovering? Some of the other men have told me what happened to you," Darien asked.

"I'm getting better." Hamo was still confused by the very unassuming manner of this new king. He had grown up under King Dival, and this was something entirely new for him.

"Good. I've told Stephan that if you needed anything further, that our own doctor was available."

"Thank you, but I think I'll be alright."

"You know, you and the others are considered great heroes around here."

"Why?" Hamo looked up, genuinely confused. "All we did was survive."

"Sometimes, surviving is enough. And it's the hardest thing to do. To keep living, without hope, without a life. That is a very brave thing to do."

"Thank you," Hamo said quietly. "There were a lot who didn't, though."

"Yes, I've been told that too. Unfortunately, there is little we can do for the dead, but mourn them. There is, however, something that can be done for the living, the survivors. Considering the sacrifice you made for your country, I think we owe something to you. I understand you are technically still well within the age of conscription should we go to war again, thanks to my father's lowering of the age for that particular campaign, but I think ten years of your life is more than enough to have given to this. Should we engage the Dorstenians again, you are exempt from any service. I understand how difficult it must be for you to adjust to life again back here. Do you have any plans for your future?"

Hamo's head was spinning with how fast the conversation was going. He had spent so many years without any real conversation and could not quite wrap his head around the flow of words. "I hadn't really thought much about it yet. I've only just in the last week or so been able to be up and about."

"I understand. Is there anything I could do to help you? A position you might be interested in or anything? You certainly don't have to think of anything right now, but I want you to know we are more than willing to help in any way we can."

"Thank you," Hamo repeated. "I will be sure to let you know if there is anything."

"Good." King Darien rose to leave and Hamo began to follow his lead.

"There is one thing, Your Majesty. Although, I'm not sure it's really what you had in mind." Hamo was not sure how the king would take his request, but after his conversation with Stephan, he had to at least try.

"Ah! And what might that be?"

"My brother, I want him pardoned."

"A King's Pardon? For what?"

Hamo briefly explained what he knew of Aldrid's sentence, and of the reason he now wore an iron cuff.

"He saved my life, and the lives of a lot of our soldiers by his choice. I don't think he deserves to be punished for it."

"I agree. You know, I think I would enjoy writing that pardon," the king said, smiling broadly. "Geoffrey, summon the Magistrate, if you please." He addressed the elderly man who had escorted Hamo in and had been waiting patiently near the doorway since then. Then he turned back to Hamo. "These things must be properly witnessed, you know. If you don't mind waiting around another half hour or so, you can take the pardon to him today and have his band removed."

The Magistrate came bustling into the room a few minutes later, rather out of breath with his haste, and with the distance he had to walk. As Aldrid had noted earlier, he was on the heavier side of weight, and was not used to moving anywhere very far or fast.

"Sire, you sent for me?" He bowed low, almost as much to catch his breath as to do obeisance to the king.

King Darien hid a slight smile as he watched the man. "Christoff, how good of you to come. I'm going to need you to witness a pardon I'm issuing today."

"A King's Pardon? I'm not sure I understand, Sire. I've heard no mention of a petition for such a thing."

"The petition came directly to me." King Darien glanced at Hamo as he spoke. "I've decided, under the circumstances, that it would be best to grant this pardon without delay. If you would be so good as to draw up the necessary papers here, I'll sign them right away."

"And who might you be pardoning, Sire?" The Magistrate did not recognize the slightly built young man sitting at the same table as King Darien, but suspected he had something to do with it. Now that he had noticed him, though, it did occur to the Magistrate that there was something distantly familiar about the young man's face. Was he the one the King wanted pardoned? The Magistrate could not remember sentencing this particular young man, and he usually remembered that sort of thing.

"Aldrid Serbon."

"Sire, he's a petty thief, hardly worth your notice. It would be most irregular for you to issue a pardon for someone like him." The Magistrate was bewildered. A King's Pardon was not taken or given lightly and was typically only reserved for knights or nobility that had fallen on the wrong side of the law, but who were powerful enough or influential enough that the king would want to overlook their crime.

"It is. Most irregular," King Darien cheerfully agreed. "Now draw up those papers, please."

"You do know who his father is, don't you? You remember what his father did." The Magistrate was prepared to say more but was cut off.

"What his father did?" It was the young man speaking this time. "What did he do?"

The young man must be a stranger to the country, the Magistrate thought.

"Why, he stole the King's sword."

"Yes, he did. He also spent more than twenty years serving this country and keeping you safe. Twenty years of fighting to protect you, and the king, and everything else about this country. Or perhaps you forgot that part?"

The Magistrate shifted uncomfortably. The longer the stranger had spoken the more familiar he seemed.

"But his crime..."

"His crime. How is it that everyone can remember the one bad thing a person did and forget all the good? Besides, how does his one crime affect Aldrid's sentence or pardon? I was not aware that children were held accountable for their parents, because if that's the case, you would find me guilty as well."

King Darien leaned back in his chair, watching the exchange with evident amusement. He struggled to suppress outright laughter as he watched Hamo's last words register across the Magistrate's face.

"You're not... you can't be... Are you his son? The one who died?"

"I am. Although, I think it's clear I didn't die." Hamo leaned back in his chair, suddenly afraid of how much he'd dared to say.

The Magistrate turned back to the king. Now he understood who this stranger reminded him of. It was like looking at the younger version of Maurus.

"You do mean a complete pardon? A removal of his band and everything?" The Magistrate tried one more time.

"Yes, that is what a King's Pardon is." King Darien caught Hamo's eye and grinned.

Half an hour later, Hamo stepped into the courtyard, a sealed parchment held tightly in one hand. His eyes quickly scanned the yard, searching for Stephan and Aldrid who had brought him here.

He spotted Stephan first, standing with a couple of the castle garrison officers, talking, but Aldrid was not with him. Hamo frowned for a moment, until he located his little brother, sitting on a hard stone bench some distance from Stephan. As Hamo approached him, he noticed his eyes were shut, and he appeared to be dozing in the late morning sun.

The sight of Aldrid asleep made Hamo realize just how worn he was from his conversation with King Darien. It occurred to him that this was in fact the longest he had been up since he had been rescued.

"Hey, Al." He shook his brother's shoulder gently until Aldrid opened his eyes.

"You're done?" Aldrid sat up, rubbing his eyes a little.

"I have something for you."

"For me? What do you have for me?"

Hamo held the sealed paper out toward him. Aldrid took it and stared at it for a moment.

"What is it?"

"Well, why don't you open it up and see what it is?" Hamo said.

Aldrid shrugged and broke the seal, unfolding the paper. He read it once. Then he read it again, and then again, a third time. He shook his head and perused the words yet again.

"What is this? Is it real?"

"It's a King's Pardon, and it is absolutely real, and not even an hour old. He just signed it for me a few minutes ago."

"I don't understand. Why would he give me this? He doesn't even know who I am."

"I asked him for it. You saved my life, Al, it was the least I could do in return. Now, why don't we go see that blacksmith, and have this thing off?" He tapped the band on Aldrid's arm.

"Really? I can get it off?" Aldrid was on his feet, his dark eyes bright with excitement.

"Come on."

Hamo led the way to the smithy in the far corner of the courtyard. The blacksmith was in between jobs and looked up curiously as the two approached him. Hamo took in the furnace, and workbench with a practiced eye. His years working for Drogo had developed him into an incredibly experienced ironworker. As he stepped into the heat of the forge though, he recoiled, as his mind went back to Dorsten and the years there. Shaking his head in an attempt to rid himself of the memories, he turned to Aldrid.

"Al, I don't think I can sit in here with you. I'll go get Stephan and then wait outside for you." The heat made him feel sick. Aldrid looked up at him curiously but nodded his understanding. "Just give him the paper and he'll take it off."

He watched Aldrid slip inside then turned to find Stephan again. He was still talking to the two garrison officers. Hamo started toward the group, then hesitated. Nine years of being a slave made it difficult to just walk up to people and start a conversation with them. In his head, he knew that no one here was going to try to hurt him but being near people still bothered him. I'll turn into a hermit at this rate, Hamo thought grimly.

"There you are! I take it you're done in there. Where'd Al get off to?" Stephan noticed him standing awkwardly in the middle of the courtyard.

"In there." Hamo pointed toward the blacksmith's shop.

"Hamo? So, they really did find you over there! We all thought Stephan was making up stories."

The man sounded familiar, but Hamo kept his head down in the old familiar habit so he did not get a close look at the man's face. For nine years, he'd done everything in his power to avoid being noticed. Now to be called out and spoken to made everyone turn and look at him, and Hamo could feel his breath quickening and had the uncomfortable desire to crawl under a rock.

"No, he wasn't just telling stories," Hamo mumbled his reply without looking up, then moved away from the group to sit down.

"What's Aldrid doing in there?" Stephan brought his attention back.

"King Darien said I could ask him for anything, so I asked him for a pardon for Aldrid. He's getting the band off now." He shut his eyes. "Can we go home when he's done?"

"Sure. Are you alright, though?" Stephan was concerned.

"I'm fine, just really tired. I think it might have been too much for today." And I need to get away from all these people, he thought but kept to himself.

"I think so. Why don't you try to get some sleep here now? I'm sure they can find a bed for you somewhere."

Hamo did not protest. He really just wanted to lay down for a while. It was so frustrating to have so little strength or energy. He should have been in the prime of his life and here he could barely stay up for a few hours.

"You can use my rooms." It was the familiar man again.

"Thanks, Edwin. Tell Al, when he comes out, that's where we're at."

Sir Edwin, that's who that is, Hamo thought. He had not seen him more than a handful of times when he had been a soldier.

When Aldrid came into the room more than an hour later, Hamo was fast asleep.

"Look!" Aldrid held his arm up proudly for Stephan to see. "It's gone. I won't ever have to wear it again."

"Hamo told me that's what he asked King Darien for. He felt bad that you only got it put on because you were trying to help him." Stephan smiled at Aldrid's excited face. "You know a King's Pardon means you won't have to come work for me anymore either."

"Oh." Aldrid was taken aback by the thought. "You're not mad about that, are you? I don't mind working for you, not anymore."

"No, I'm not mad about it. Besides, you may still have the chance to work for me yet."

"How? I mean, if you wanted me to, I'd come and work for you. But then Mother would be sad, and I don't want that either." Aldrid's face was stricken.

"Why don't you sit here with your brother for a while. I've a few things I want to go take care of."

Chapter 41

Leaving the castle behind him, Stephan made his way to the small cottage on the outskirts of town. Alina must have been watching for him because the door opened before he had a chance to knock.

"Where are they?" she asked as he stepped inside alone. "Is Hamo alright?"

"He's fine. He was resting when I left him."

"I knew this would be too much for him."

"Alina, he's fine." Stephan shook his head, smiling. "You know, he's not a little boy anymore."

"I know. But he was when he left, and I can't help it if I worry about him. You would worry too if he were your son."

"I would," Stephan conceded with a shrug and moved to sit down.

Alina did the same. "Why did you leave them behind, anyway? He could have come home to rest."

"I wanted to talk to you."

"To me?"

"You know, he asked King Darien for a pardon for Al."

"Oh?"

Stephan nodded. "King gave it to him, too. Al won't have to go with me anymore."

"He's going to miss you," Alina said with a rueful smile. "He looks up to you so much. He's hardly the same boy anymore."

"I'll miss him too. It gets a bit lonely and quiet out on the farm when I'm all by myself."

Alina took up her sewing as they lapsed into silence for a few minutes. Stephan leaned back in his chair and then leaned forward again, resting his elbows on his knees. After a moment, Alina looked up at him curiously.

"So, what is it you wanted to talk to me about?"

"You know, I've been thinking."

Alina waited for Stephan to go on, but he seemed to have forgotten that he was speaking.

"Well?"

"Well, you know, I have a lot of space out at the farm. And Al really fit in well. He did a good job." Stephan paused again and Alina shot him a quizzical look. "Like I said, sometimes it gets a bit lonely. I've never really minded. But I was thinking it would be awfully nice to settle down for good and I've gotten used to having Al there."

"What are you trying to say, Stephan?"

Stephan frowned and leaned back again. "I'm trying to say that I think it's time for me to get married."

"Married? What does that have to do with Al?"

"It has everything to do with Al, because if you say yes, then he comes with me."

"If I say yes?"

"I know it wouldn't be the same as you and Maurus had, and I wouldn't expect that, but I think we could make it work. We've known each other for years and care for each other in some way or another. What do you say, Alina?"

Alina let her sewing rest idle in her lap as she stared at it.

"I don't know, Stephan," she started, still avoiding his gaze. "It would be good for Al. He'll not know what to do with himself without you around."

"It'd be good for you to, Alina. You're lonely here. You've been lonely for years. If you want to just think about it for a while, I understand."

Stephan started to his feet, but Alina's hand on his arm stopped him.

"I don't need to think about it for a while," she said. "I already know."

"And?"

"Yes. You're right. Ever since Maurus... disappeared and died, I've been lonely. But you have always been a very good friend, and you've been a father to my son. So, yes," Alina smiled softly. "I say yes."

Stephan's eyes widened briefly in surprise before his face split in a wide smile.

"Really? Because, honestly, I wasn't sure."

"Really. If I wasn't sure I wouldn't have said."

Stephan slapped his hand on his knee and leaned back comfortably in his chair. Alina picked her sewing up then set it down again.

"We'll have to tell the children."

"Al's really the only one who's still a child."

Alina looked like she wanted to argue the fact but conceded with a nod. Setting aside her sewing once and for all, she stared out the front window.

"It should be a small wedding," she said, thinking aloud. "It's not like we have many friends, anyway. And I'm not sure how Sabina will feel about moving away from Bren. She's quite settled here with her work."

For the rest of the afternoon, Alina's work lay forgotten as she and Stephan talked and planned. It wasn't until late afternoon that Stephan finally rose and started for the door.

"Well, I suppose I should go see if their ready to come home."

Chapter 42

HAMO SLEPT FOR MOST OF the afternoon, leaving Aldrid to himself and his very confused thoughts. The prospect of leaving Stephan's and going home was not as exciting as he thought it would be when he'd first received his sentence. He almost laughed when he thought about how homesick he was that first night and how he cried himself to sleep.

Now, he realized that he not only cared what Stephan thought of him, but that he had grown very attached to the man. He was the father he had never had the chance to have. And the thought of losing him was now as terrible to contemplate as the thought of going with him had been a year ago.

Maybe Mother would let him go visit often, or work for him in the summer or some arrangement like that. Stephan could still teach him things like how to hunt, and how to take care of and train the horses.

No matter how he puzzled over it, Aldrid could not come up with a good solution for his dilemma. He was going to miss Stephan, and that was it. He was glad when Hamo finally woke up again and he had someone to talk to.

"How long did I sleep?" Hamo asked as he sat up.

"A few hours. Stephan said he had to take care of some things and then he would be back. But I don't know how long he's going to be gone."

"Did you get it off?"

"Yes, see!" Aldrid could not hide his happiness as he held out his now free wrist for his brother's inspection. The mark from where it had burnt him was still there, to be sure, but he had lived his whole life with those. "Thank you for asking King Darien for the pardon. You didn't have to, you know. You could have asked him for something for yourself. I would have been alright."

"Al, I have everything I want. I'm home and I'm alive, a month ago I wouldn't have thought either of those things were possible. Maybe someday I'll want more than that, but for now that's more than enough. Besides, I couldn't have people thinking badly of you when you had saved my life."

"What are you going to do now that you're getting better?" Aldrid was not sure he should have asked when he saw the look on Hamo's face.

"I have no idea. The only thing I'm really good at, I don't care to do ever again. Just getting close to the smithy made me sick. I'll figure something out, I suppose. Maybe I'll be like Stephan and get a little farm far away from everyone else, and just live there quietly."

"His farm is really nice. I wouldn't mind having one like that, only I think the animals stink and I don't really like them, except for Casper."

"Then I'd be better at it than you. I actually like the smell of them, and I like horses."

Aldrid wrinkled his nose up. "How can anyone actually like them? They are mean and stubborn and always looking for a chance to get out of work."

"Sounds like someone I used to know," Stephan's voice caused both Aldrid and Hamo to turn to the door.

"I'm not like that anymore though!" Aldrid defended himself. "Am I?"

"Hmmm...I don't know. I might have to think about that. In the meantime, I have something I want you to think about," Stephan said.

"What?"

"Your Mother and I are going to get married."

Aldrid's initial shock over Stephan's announcement dissipated quickly when he realized what that meant for him. He would not have to leave Mother or Stephan, and that was a wonderful thing.

Hamo was a little more reserved about it. Of the three children, he was the only one who had a very clear memory of Father, even though that memory had been slightly tarnished by the stories he had been told, both by Lord Bayner and by his own people. In the end, however, even he came around to liking the idea. Stephan was an easy person for him to like, and he knew what he had become to Aldrid. It was not fair, he thought, to deprive Aldrid of the one man he could look up to in life. Besides, he owed Stephan his life, and more than that. For it was Stephan who pointed him in the direction of his future.

Hamo hated the idea of living in town where he was treated with an overwhelming awe by his fellow countrymen. Just his brief venture to the castle had shown him he did not fit in. He could not get rid of the habit of cringing when someone got too close, or moved too suddenly around him, or constantly looking over his shoulder.

What he longed for most, as he had told Aldrid, was peace and quiet. He enjoyed the tranquility of Stephan's farm, the green countryside, the clean air that still held a hint of saltiness from the sea. It was the sort of place one could heal in. But even on Stephan's farm, he found himself uneasy with the amount of interaction that was expected of him. It was no one's fault, really. Everyone was so happy to have him home again, and he shared their happiness, but the attention was overwhelming for someone who had spent nine years trying to make himself as small and insignificant as possible. He managed best with Aldrid and Stephan. Aldrid, because his brother was the quickest one to get used to him and his ways. He could sit with Aldrid for hours doing something, and Al did not expect him to keep a conversation going. Stephan was easy to get along with because Stephan never asked him questions about what had happened to him, and he was also content to spend long periods of time without talking at all. Sabina and Mother were not, and so Hamo gravitated more and more to the barn and the outdoors.

Here he discovered that there was something he was good at, aside from iron work which he now found abhorrent. Because he was quieter, and generally moved slower than Aldrid, he turned out to be better with Stephan's horses. As his strength came back bit by bit, he found he was able to help Stephan, and that was satisfying.

It came about one night, several months after they had all settled into Stephan's house. Hamo was up, unable to sleep again because of nightmares, and had decided to sit outside where he could not disturb anyone. He hated the fact that he still had the nightmares. He had hoped they would just go away now that he was safe. He was safe. He knew that. But his mind refused to completely accept it. He was sitting with his back against the side of the house now, when he heard someone come up beside him. Even after all this time, it made him start and set his heart to racing.

"Did I wake you up? I'm sorry." He turned to see Stephan sitting down next to him.

"I heard you come out here and thought you might like some company. This where you normally come?"

"I guess so. It's nice to be able to leave the house any time I like. I guess I like reminding myself of that."

"You know, I saw Sir Edwin the other day.'

"Oh?"

"Yes. He asked how you were getting on. If you were able to get around yet. I told him you've become a big help for me with the horses. Al's good at a lot of things, but he doesn't, and probably never will, have the patience to train a war horse. You're good at it, though."

"Really? But I don't do that much. You're the one who does the real work."

"No, you do plenty. You could do more too if you wanted. But I bet you're not wanting to spend the rest of your life living here in my house."

"No, I'm not. I just don't know what I'm going to do. You know, all the people I used to know have either moved on, gotten married and such, or died in the war. And I can't even figure out what I'm going to do with myself."

"You could always ask the king for some position," Stephan smiled as he made the suggestion, knowing full well how Hamo felt about it.

"No, goodness, no. I can't stand being in town. Everyone looks at me like I'm some sort of hero, or a ghost. I'm not sure which one is worse."

"On the other hand, you do have other options."

"Such as?"

"Well, as I was saying, I saw Sir Edwin the other day, and he made me an offer. Rather he made you an offer. He has a nice little cabin in the woods between his estate and my farm. And he is more than willing to let you have it. He also mentioned that if you ever desired to use your skills as an ironworker, he could always use a blacksmith. On the other hand, you could also still work for me, if you prefer that."

Hamo was silent for a moment, contemplating the offer. The idea of solitude had its appeal. It was a step back to normal, maybe the only step he would ever be able to make. And he did enjoy working with Stephan and the horses.

"I think I'd like that."

"I thought you might. It's not far from here, perhaps tomorrow we can go see Edwin about it. And who knows, one of these days you might meet some girl you want to marry. Then you'll have a nice place to start.

"That's not going to happen, Stephan."

"You never know."

"I think I do, actually."

Epilogue

HAMO'S HORSE WAS PLODDING along down the well-worn path through the woods. It was early evening, and Hamo had just finished up at Stephan's. He was glad he had made the move to this secluded little corner of the forest. It was so peaceful, so quiet. And it reminded him only of the good times in his life, the days he had gone hunting with Father, even his wood cutting trips with Drogo. The trees felt protective, the animals welcoming. It was the closest he could come to being happy again.

It was a little lonely, he admitted, and as he had watched everyone going on about their lives, it was difficult to quell the bitterness he felt at having lost so much of his own. He was not old by any means, but he felt like he was. Sabina was going to be married next spring, and although he was very happy for her, he had watched her and her soon to be husband with a bit of envy at how normal their lives were.

As he rounded the bend, his horse's head came up and the animal let out a sharp whinny.

"What is it, then?" Hamo patted the horse's neck, while looking ahead to where his cabin sat. At first glance there did not seem to be anything amiss.

It was not until he got closer that he heard a banging sound and a distinctly female voice calling out. He gave vent to a small sigh of annoyance. The reason he lived out here was because he didn't want to be around a lot of people. His family he could manage, and an occasional visit to Sir Edwin, but otherwise he avoided most people. It was too difficult to fit back in after being a slave for nine years. He just felt awkward and out of place. And he never knew when some awful memory would be triggered and he would find himself, heart pounding, stomach churning, hands sweating.

"Hello! Hello! Is anyone here?" The voice sounded desperate, although Hamo could not see any immediate danger.

He kicked his horse into a canter and covered the short distance. Whoever it was had apparently left the house and was searching the small barn behind it. He swung down from his horse.

"Can I help you?" he called out.

"Oh my! There is someone here! I thought this place was abandoned, or something." The young woman who came out of the barn looked to be on the verge of crying.

"It's not." He wished he did not sound so wary and suspicious every time he spoke to a stranger. It always made conversations difficult. "Can I help you with something?"

"Oh, I hope so. You see, I was out riding, and I lost my horse. It was sort of my fault, actually. I was startled, and I may have screamed a little and my horse just bolted and left me behind. And now I have no idea where I am, or where my horse is, or how I'm going to get back home. I've been wandering around for ages, hours, I think, and this is the first place I've run into. And I've been so scared, I thought I'd be stuck out in the forest all night, and I'm absolutely terrified of wolves. I am so glad someone actually lives here. You can help me, can't you?" When she finally stopped talking, Hamo got the sense that it was only because she had to catch her breath.

Hamo shrugged. "I guess I can try to find your horse. There are only a couple hours left before dark, though."

"Thank you so much. I don't know what I would have done if you hadn't shown up. I suppose I would have been stranded out here all alone." She seemed to shudder at the thought.

"Look, why don't you go inside and rest while I try to find your horse." Hamo was already ready to go back to his solitude. Her voice was spinning circles in his head.

"I couldn't let you do that. It's my horse after all, and it's my fault I lost him. I'll come with you," she said.

Hamo raised his eyebrows. He started to protest.

"No, don't tell me I can't. I feel awful about all of this and I'm coming with you. Besides, I don't know you. What if you decide to get my horse and take off with him? I don't know that I can trust you. No, I've decided, I'm coming with you."

Hamo shrugged again. He was not one to argue very often, and if she really felt like traipsing through the woods, who was he to stop her.

"Fine. Where did you come from?"

"What do you mean, where did I come from? I just got through telling you that I've been lost. I have no idea."

"I meant what direction did you come from to my cabin?"

"Oh. Over there, I suppose. Why in the world would you want to know that, though?"

"It might make a good starting point to look for your horse."

Hamo held the reins of his own mount and led off in the direction she had pointed. Now that his quiet evening was spoiled, the least he could do was get this over with as quickly as possible.

"Wait! Wait for me!" She came running up behind him, nearly upsetting his own horse. "By the way, my name's Edith." She glanced expectantly over at him.

"Hamo. I'm Hamo."

"Hmm. I've never met anyone with that name before. So, do you live out here all by yourself? Are you some sort of hermit or something? Don't you like people? I don't know what I would do if I wasn't around people. I'd have way too much time to think. I would be so incredibly lonely living all by myself. Are you lonely out here, ever?"

"You talk a lot."

"That's rude of you to say!"

"I didn't mean...," Hamo hesitated to go on. He had meant it exactly how she had taken it, but now she was mad, and he wasn't really sure why. "Look, if we're going to track a horse down, I think it might be better to be a little more quiet, alright?"

"I see." Although the look on her face stated plainly that she did not see, she was still mad.

They had not gone very far before Hamo picked up the tracks of a running horse. He knelt down to examine them. They were fresh still, so most likely from Edith's horse. Edith, to his chagrin, had maintained a whispered chatter. She asked a lot of questions, most of which she never gave time for him to answer. Hamo remembered why he wanted to move away from town, and from people. He had spent so many years in the quiet of Drogo's smelter, and at the moment he was wishing for that sort of quiet again. Several times he had made the offer to take her back to his cabin to wait, but she felt duty bound to help search for her own mount.

"How do you know those tracks are from my horse? Don't they look the same as any other horse's tracks? What if they lead us in the wrong direction? My horse could be wandering around anywhere, and we could be following the wrong one."

"Do you have a better idea?" He stood up as he spoke.

"Me? No. I just wasn't sure if there was some trick to it or something."

Hamo nodded and kept moving. For more than an hour, they wandered around, Hamo carefully, and quietly studying the ground, and Edith keeping up her whispered attempts at conversation.

Hamo glanced at the western horizon where the sun was just touching the earth. It would be dark soon.

"We're going to have to give up on the horse. Where do you live?"

"I'm staying at Uncle Edwin's."

"Why didn't you tell me that in the first place? We've gone circles around Edwin's place, and your horse has probably already found his way back there." Hamo could not keep his exasperation out of his voice.

"Well, I didn't know it mattered. How was I supposed to know that I should tell you where I was staying?"

"Never mind. Let's just get back there before the sun goes down completely."

By the tight look on her face, he guessed she was upset about something again. He hadn't said anything to make her mad, he thought.

"So, what brings you to Edwin's?" he ventured after a few moments of terse silence.

"He's my uncle, like I said. I take turns staying with different relatives ever since..." her voice trailed off a little sadly.

"Since?"

"Since Father died ten years ago in the war. Mother passed away shortly afterwards. I think it was just too hard for her to keep living without him. So ever since then, I just travel around to whatever relative is willing to have me. Right now, it's Uncle Edwin."

"I'm sorry."

By the time Sir Edwin's manor came into view, the forest was already dark. Sir Edwin himself was just coming out of the house as they approached.

"Edith, I was just getting worried about you. Where have you been all this time? Hamo? What are you doing here?" He noticed the young man as he was speaking.

"Bringing her back. She lost her horse in the woods, and I'm pretty sure it ran back here."

"Most likely. Edith, I told you not to go out riding by yourself. Perhaps now you'll be more inclined to listen to your old Uncle," he smiled as he spoke.

Edith opened her mouth to recount the horrors of her day when Edwin held up a hand to stop her.

"I'm quite sure it was a terrifying experience for you, my dear. But it is late, and I'm ready for supper, so perhaps you could save your story until we've eaten. You'll join us, Hamo?"

"No, thank you. I'll just head back."

"Nonsense. You've spent your evening helping my niece, the least I can do is provide you supper. Come inside."

Reluctantly, Hamo tied the reins of his own mount to a hitching post near the door and followed Sir Edwin inside. He really just wanted to get back home. Sir Edwin was a pleasant enough person, but he had a way of always bringing up Hamo's past years as a slave and making a hero out of him for it. It drove Hamo crazy. It was the one part of his life he wished he could blot out entirely.

When, more than an hour later, he managed to extricate himself from Sir Edwin and his niece, who still had not stopped asking questions, he was thankful for the way the quiet forest closed in around him. It was comforting, that silence. Still, he had to admit, there was something enjoyable about the evening.

Meanwhile in the North...

The great hall of Chief Gundar was cloaked in icy silence. Seated on his elevated throne, Chief Gundar, ruler of Aruuk, waited for the messenger who'd been announced only a few minutes before. An impatient drumming of his fingers on the arm of the chair was the only outward sign of his temper.

When the doors swung open and a slave entered, leading the messenger behind them, Chief Gundar leaned forward in his chair.

"Well, what news?"

The man dropped to his knees, lowering his head so that his face was hidden from Chief Gundar's gaze.

"There's been no word. And our scouts have seen no sign of them."

Chief Gundar sat back, drawing in a deep breath, his mouth pinched up in a scowl.

"No sign of them?"

"None, Chief."

"If those slaves don't reach us, then we have no arrangement with Lord Bayner," Chief Gundar spoke quietly to himself. "No matter, though. I have no real desire to fight his war for him."

"Do you wish for us to keep a lookout still for their arrival?"

"Of course not. They're not coming. Perhaps Dorsten has decided it no longer needs our aid."

Chief Gundar dismissed the man with a wave of his hand. For some minutes he sat alone in the great hall, his fingers stroking the short beard growing on his chin.

Lord Bayner had promised him slaves – twenty-three to be exact. Although he wasn't desperate for them, the fact that Lord Bayner failed to deliver on his promise irked Chief Gundar. Lord Bayner thought a good deal too much of himself if he thought he could slight the Chief of Aruuk without consequence.

324

The slight clearing of a throat roused Chief Gundar from his own thoughts and he looked up to see an older woman standing in the open doorway. The midwife. Instantly, Chief Gundar's attention belonged to her, although he was careful not to show it.

"I do hope you have a very good reason for disturbing me."

"I do, Chief Gundar. I have come to announce the birth of a son."

"A son?" That was always welcome news. "Whose?"

"Denise. She has given you a son, Chief Gundar."

"Has she? I suppose that I should go and see this son of mine." Gundar rose and crossed the hall. The midwife followed discreetly behind him as he made his way through the hallways to his favorite wife's rooms.

Lying on a bed, a baby cradled against her, Denise looked up at his entrance. Her young, pretty face was pale with exhaustion but when he approached, she held the baby up for him to see.

"Your son, Chief," she said. "What will you call him?"

Chief Gundar stared down at the red, wrinkled newborn face. He thought for a moment.

"Sasha. He'll be called Sasha."

Other titles by S. T. Hobbs

The Divalian Chronicles –

Prequel ~ The Thief and the Slave

Book 1 ~ The Traitor's Alliance

Book 2 ~ The Last Chief

Book 3 ~ The Courier's Apprentice

And coming soon...

Book 4 ~ The King's Successor